Omni and the Blazed Boy

by

BJ & Sheri Ver Burg

Omni and the Blazed Boy

by Benjamin & Sheri Ver Burg

Cardinal font by StarDigitalCreations, used with permission
Illustrations by Sheri Ver Burg
Cover Design by Sheri Ver Burg and Olan Kalapo
Edited by Soul Sonshine LLC

Paperback ISBN: 978-1-960982-38-4
© 2025 by Benjamin & Sheri Ver Burg

Published by Soul Sonshine, LLC
Springtown, TX 76082 USA

Dedication

To our dear sons —
We love each of you, with all our hearts. Today's world is bursting with stories and tales, but is filled with more darkness and sorrow than hope. We pray you enjoy this story as we tailored it for each of you. May it teach you to trust, love, grow and conquer the life you have ahead, and for generations to come.

To our friends and family —
The encouragement and support you have given has been nothing short of amazing. Your love encouraged us to persevere through hard times and kept us motivated and dedicated to a mission bigger than ourselves. We thank you all and can't wait to see what may come of our dream.

Chapter One

Havenshire

"Myles!"

His name echoed sharply through the open window.

"Coming, Ms. Helen," Myles responded with drooping shoulders.

On the brink of his teenage years, Myles emerged from the cornfield rows and jogged up the rustic porch of the orphanage. He paused long enough to pull off his worn, mud-caked boots, the best he'd been able to find from the donation pile.

He raked his fingers through his brown hair, dislodging bits of stalks and leaves. Hopping into the kitchen in his stocking feet, he called out, "Here, Ms. Helen."

She glared at him with chilling disapproval as she dried a plate.

Ms. Helen was an elderly woman, old enough to be his great-grandmother he often thought— an idea she would fervently disagree with. Her thin frame possessed a stamina that would rival that of a young man. Her stern voice kept Myles at attention, "Where are your boots?"

"They were muddy, so I left them on the porch."

Her eyebrows furrowed, "Were you in Mr. Binford's cornfields again?"

"He said he doesn't mind as long as we don't damage the crops. We were being careful."

"You mean you let them *all* play in the cornfield, as well?"

"But we always play in the cornfield."

"Not after a watering day. The fields are a muddy mess." She glanced at the boy's pant legs, speckled with dried brown clay, and pressed two fingers to her temple. "Call in all the children and clean off their boots. Your chores can wait."

"Everyone's? Why do I have to clean them all?"

She seized another plate to dry, "Why did you let them play in the mud?"

"Can't I just..." but her eyes pierced through his words, and he could see there was no way of proceeding triumphantly.

"You are twelve years old, and the oldest. I will always expect more from *you*. Now, please direct them all inside and have them change for tonight."

"Yes, ma'am," he yielded, respecting her position as usual, albeit sometimes begrudgingly.

Myles stepped out and called for the other children. Two emerged from the cornfields. First Holly, holding the hand of young Marguerite. Holly, just a couple of years younger than Myles, had taken on a big sister role for little Marguerite since she came as a toddler two summers past.

Myles called louder for the others to come out, and the stragglers began to emerge. Three boys— Franklin, the second oldest boy, his pudgy face half-painted purple from the honeyberries he had found; James, the most athletic yet ironically the laziest of the group; and little Pete, his left side caked in mud, most likely from an afternoon nap in the cornfields.

They joined Myles on the porch and began to untie their soiled footwear. As Marguerite kicked off her tiny boots, she hugged Myles around the knees, peering up with a smile that could melt solid steel.

"Thanks, big bwotha."

His dimples deepened at the heartwarming gesture. Myles always had a soft spot for the younger children at the orphanage.

Feeling empowered, Myles instructed, "All right, head upstairs and get changed for the festival."

The children responded with haste. A flurry of sock-clad footsteps rumbled up the stairs, splitting at the top to their gender-segregated rooms.

Myles glanced at the twelve mud-caked boots lying on the porch and sighed. He sat down with his feet dangling off, picking between the worn treads. The mud was dried-on and tough to dislodge. Despite the heat of summer's end, Mr. Binford's farm seemed to always have a pleasant lingering chill.

Finishing his task, Myles journeyed back to the kitchen. As he entered, he saw that the dishes were dry, the floors were mopped, every nook and cranny was dusted, and even the windows sparkled.

To this day, Myles could never fathom how Ms. Helen accomplished so much in so little time. He was convinced she must have secret work-elves hidden beneath the house, who helped her in exchange for food and shelter.

Ms. Helen directed Myles, "Head upstairs and get yourself ready as well." As Myles lunged up the steps, her voice called from below, "And make sure the others are getting ready and not just creating a ruckus."

Myles swung open the door to the boys' bedroom. He was immediately welcomed with a wallop in the face by a damp pillow. Franklin, James, and Pete were in the midst of their bi-weekly pillow fight. The added excitement for the night's events had given them a little too much pent-up energy.

Myles shook off the shock of the impact and brushed his cheek with his fingertips, examining what he hoped was just mud from the pillow, as Pete was still half plastered in it. Every pillow in the room was now several shades closer to dirt.

Myles' nose flared with anger, which quickly softened into a playful sense of revenge. He snatched the pillow from the floor, dove to Pete's nearby bed, and grabbed another pillow with his left hand.

Seeing this, the three boys immediately united to attack the older intruder. Franklin aimed straight for Myles' head, swinging with enthusiastic energy. Myles parried with his left pillow and swung an uppercut to Franklin's chin with his right, knocking him backward.

Next, James, aiming for the top of Myles' head, swung his pillow like a hammer while flying midair from his perch on top of the dresser. Myles quickly pivoted on one foot, causing James's pillow to miss. Once James had landed, there was no time to react as Myles' pillow conked him on the back of the head.

Lastly, Pete, the silent assassin, jumped off the bed from behind. He repeatedly whaled on Myles' head with the smaller pillow in his hand. Myles reached behind and grabbed the boy by his collar. He bent forward, pulling Pete directly over his head. Pete landed squarely on James, back-to-back, pushing James flat against the floor with a loud, "Oof."

Myles stood tall, victorious and avenged, that is until quick clicking footsteps echoed up the staircase. All four boys froze. Ms. Helen swung open the door to find the room in shambles, with mud smeared more consistently than a pigsty. They dared not say anything. Her eyes blazed with a fierce intensity, capable of igniting a flame. With flared nostrils, she then spoke, calmer than any of them expected, "Get cleaned up, organize this room, and I will see you all downstairs. We will talk about this..." she circled the room with her finger, "*fiasco*, later."

The boys did as they were told. A small sink next to the door was their makeshift wash station. They took turns rinsing off the smeared mud, then hastily pulled out clean clothes and changed.

Myles wiped the remaining mud off the compass he wore around his neck. As he pulled out a fresh shirt from his dresser, James lunged toward him with a mischievous grin, raising his hand. He aimed to slap the birthmark on Myles' chest, an obnoxious ritual.

Anticipating this usual prank, Myles secured the hanging compass and nimbly rotated his hips. James missed, stumbling a few steps.

Myles clutched James by the arm, "Stop messing around. We're in enough trouble as it is. Put your socks on."

James rolled his eyes, "Yeah, yeah, I know."

They organized the room, placing items back to their proper places. Myles realigned his display of books on his dresser, stories about knights, fantasy novels with dragons and goblins, and science books about animals, adorned beside wooden puzzles and games to keep the children entertained. He straightened the toy swords, fishing rods, and baseball bat that leaned against the furniture.

Ms. Helen's barking voice resonated, "Come downstairs and put your boots back on. Mr. Swanson will be back soon to take us to town."

Pattering feet echoed as the children frantically exited from their rooms and descended the stairs. Myles and Franklin were a bit more hesitant, still mindful of their recent debacle. James and Pete seemed to live a blissful life of naivety.

They all slipped their boots back on, feeling the damp leather against their feet, but spirits remaining undampened.

At the sound of squeaking brakes, the children stampeded down the porch and catapulted into Mr. Swanson's truck bed, perching on bales of hay. Ms. Helen sat in the cab. Myles, the last to mount, leapt into the bed, squeezing in next to Franklin.

Franklin nudged Myles, "Ready for the festival?"

"Yeah, I think so. Let's make it a night to remember... or at least one Ms. Helen will forget."

After a short and dusty ride, they turned onto the town's only paved road and approached Main Street. Their eyes widened.

"Whoa..." gasped Marguerite, at the sight of lights strung from building to building in the town center. Booths lined the street and courtyard with colorful banners. What was often a dim, dull little town was now vibrant, filled with a rainbow of lights and the sounds of lighthearted music.

Their eyes were all drawn to one singular point in the middle of the courtyard where an ice sculpture stood, as tall as a grown man. The lights reflected through the ice, sparkling like jewels.

Marguerite inhaled as she took in the splendor, "What is it?"

"A dragon, I think," Myles squinted to make out the details. "I think it's the biggest one he's done yet."

Marguerite adorably tilted her head, "Who?"

"Mr. Binford," answered Myles. "He always carves an ice sculpture, but I've never seen one this tall."

James stood up in the back of the truck shouting, "I bet I can touch it first!" He prepared to fling himself from the vehicle.

"Not so fast," Ms. Helen's voice cut his eagerness, as she climbed out of the truck, patting down her tousled skirt. Her pointing finger and sharp eyes commanded their attention like a conductor. "Stay in groups, don't cause a commotion, and meet back here at eight o'clock sharp. Also," she paused to soften her tone, "have fun, children. Myles, stay with Marguerite."

Myles gulped, "Yes, ma'am."

He grasped Marguerite's hand as the children ran towards the towering pillar of ice. In their pursuit, Myles noticed Mrs. Swanson carrying a basket of flowers to put the finishing touches on the decorations. She stumbled, causing the basket's contents to spill.

Myles turned back towards Holly, "Stay with Marguerite. I'll be right back." He jogged over to help Mrs. Swanson, gathering the scattered flowers.

"Oh, bless you, Myles."

"Not a problem. It's the least I can do since Mr. Swanson drove us here tonight."

When the basket was full once again, Mrs. Swanson stood up and called out as she walked on. "Thank you again, Myles, you are such a sweet boy."

With a nod of acknowledgment, Mrs. Swanson continued on her way.

Myles spotted a few stray daffodils lying on the ground and quickly scooped them up. He hurriedly tucked the flowers into his right pocket.

As Myles rejoined his fellow orphans standing at the ice sculpture, he could feel the cold mist cascading down from the frozen beast, as if the ice dragon were exhaling a chilled snort. The sculpture gleamed, its intricate scales and fierce expression captivated their imaginations. Looking around, he noticed they were the only audience members admiring the display with their eyes, as the gathered crowds took photographs and videos with their cellular devices.

Franklin leaned closer to venture a lick of the icy figure.

"Watch out!" a man's voice bellowed from behind the children, startling them all. They jumped and snapped around, wide-eyed. It was Allen Binford, the farmer, with a mischievous glint in his eyes as he enjoyed their reactions a little too much.

"Best be careful around this one," he pointed up at the sculpture, with a playful tone. "I haven't had time to break this dragon in yet. She could reach down and nip you... or freeze you with her icy flame."

Marguerite's face was overcome with worry as she glanced back at the sculpture. Allen let out a boisterous laugh, "It's okay little one, she's really just a large lap dog... a lazy and entitled one, at that."

Most of the children giggled nervously, then swiftly shifted their attention to the pie baking contest and ran off to the booths in front of the café. Myles remained by Mr. Binford for a moment, intrigued by the sculpture.

Allen dropped his gaze down to the still-growing boy, "Myles Briggs," he greeted. He brushed away the loose strands of dirty blonde hair that escaped his haphazard ponytail. He smiled warmly, stretching his well-trimmed beard up to his ears. Regardless of the weather, Allen could always be found in his signature long-sleeve flannel shirt tucked into his jeans. Neither the heat nor the cold ever seemed to faze him.

"You've been getting taller every time I see you."

"Uhm, thank you, Mr. Binford."

"Are you going to help again during the Harvest this year?" He squeezed Myles by the arm, "You'll need to keep up the work to build up those muscles."

"Yes, please... I mean, I'd like to, if that's alright."

The conversation paused. Myles admired Allen greatly, even looked up to him, but there was always a lingering sense of intimidation.

"Well," Myles finally spoke, "I had better keep watch of Marguerite." He darted off to catch up with the others.

Helen stealthily approached Allen from behind. They both watched as Myles ran off into the throng of the festival.

"He isn't ready just yet, you know."

Allen practically leapt out of his boots, "Blazing gaffers, woman," he said, hand clutching his chest. "You gave me a proper scare right there."

"My apologies," her face elongated with snooty sarcasm, "is my physical presence that unwarranted?"

She continued to observe Myles, "Maybe another year will serve him best."

Allen cleared his throat, "He's maturing nicely though."

"In stature, you mean. I'm more worried about his emotional intelligence."

A smirk played on Allen's lips, "I find trial by flames works best for that."

Helen's air of disapproval did not change Allen's expression as they both stood at the edge of the festivities, just outside the circle of the brightly shining lights.

Chapter Two

The Festival

"Step on up, sample the best, and see who wins the contest." The town baker called out over the bustling crowd as Myles hurried to catch up to the other children. He sniffed the air as the enticing aroma of freshly baked pies wafted by, beckoning onlookers.

Aiming toward the booths, Franklin shoved his way through the crowd. The rest of the children followed in his wake. He glanced up at the booth worker. "I would like to try each one, please," Franklin told him. "I have to try them all to make sure I know which one to vote for."

Holly smacked his shoulder, "There are dozens of pies here. They have to make sure there's enough for everyone."

Undeterred, Franklin replied, "I'll have small slices."

As Myles, Pete, and the girls perused the festival, they took note of the various activities and attractions, deliberating which challenge to tackle first.

Pete eagerly tugged on Holly's arm. "I wanna go win some prizes." Marguerite echoed Pete's excitement.

"Okay," Holly acknowledged. "Franklin, James, you two stick together and come find us when you're done. We're heading over to the game booths."

Myles couldn't help but notice they were about the only children not viewing the jamboree through an electronic device. Ms. Helen had banished any electronic entertainment from the orphanage, but Franklin and James would not let her forget that they disagreed with her rule. "This is not an entertainment-based orphanage," she would tell them whenever they brought it up.

Pete and the girls decided on their first game booth and stood for a moment, watching. Then Pete excitedly picked up the ball on the stand in front of him. The man behind the booth started to explain the game, but before he could complete one sentence, Pete had already thrown his first ball and knocked down two of the three bottles needed for a prize. With two more attempts, Pete was surprisingly victorious. He beamed with pride, as if he had just slain a dragon.

"Name your prize, son," the booth organizer said as he motioned to the selection dangling above. Most of the prizes handed out at the festival were cheap plastic toys, inflatable weapons or animals, and pointless trinkets, all right up Pete's alley.

Pete pointed up, "That one, the compass." He pointed to a wooden compass hanging on the booth's beam by a string.

"It's yours," said the man handing it to Pete. Pete immediately turned to show Myles who had just walked up.

"Look," he displayed gleefully, "now I have a compass just like yours."

"Wow, Pete, that's great." Myles unbuttoned his top shirt button and pulled out the compass that hung around his neck. The boys compared. Although Myles' was obviously more uniquely crafted with decorative metal inserts and fine carved wood, Pete didn't mind in the slightest.

Pete was thrilled, "When we play tomorrow, we can follow my compass on our adventures."

"Sure, sounds good," Myles said. Pete's grin grew wider than his head.

Myles pointed Pete back toward the booths. Pete was off like a shot, his energy contagious as he bound from booth to booth with the enthusiasm of a squirrel searching for buried treasure.

Myles watched Pete ping pong from a distance, then he felt a tug on his shirt. It was little Marguerite.

"Hey, what's up?"

She pointed to another booth where a few dolls hung from the beam as prizes. She asked, "Do you think we could win that doll?"

Myles gave her an encouraging smile and narrowed his eyes, "We won't know until we try."

As they neared the booth, Holly leaned over to Myles, "Don't get her hopes up. You know how sad she gets when she's disappointed."

But Myles waved Holly off. "It's fine."

Mr. Porter, the booth organizer, welcomed them. "Toss the ball into the tilted basket. If the ball stays in without bouncing out, you win a prize." He gave Myles three balls.

As Myles stepped up to the edge of the booth to attempt his first throw a patronizing tone bellowed from behind, "Aw, is wittle Briggs going to be able to throw the wittle ball into the wittle basket?" This was followed by three boys snickering as if to justify their lack of concern for anyone else's emotions.

The voice belonged to Rodney Hilton and his two friends—or lackeys—as Myles referred to them, Paul and Don.

Myles, now a bit flustered, attempted to ignore the gallery as he took his first throw. As the ball was about to leave his hand, Rodney yelled out, "Heads up."

It didn't appear to affect Myles. However, his first throw just bounced off the rim and fell. The three boys chuckled as they too approached the booth.

"Give me some of those balls," Rodney practically demanded from Mr. Porter.

"Sure, Rodney."

Myles leaned in to attempt his second toss. Just as Myles' body tensed, Rodney pushed on the back of Myles' knee with his boot, collapsing his leg. The unsuspecting boy's knee dropped almost to the ground before he caught himself. The ball left his hand and fell well short.

"Hey now, Rodney," exclaimed Mr. Porter, "let's make this as fair as possible for everyone."

"Oh, sorry Mr. Porter," Rodney's tone dripped with insincere innocence. "We were just playing around like kids our age do, you know."

Mr. Porter picked up the ball and gave it back to Myles, "That second throw didn't count."

Rodney stepped up confidently, "Let me show you how it's done." He arched his first throw, but it lightly bounced out of the basket and fell to the ground. Myles couldn't help but smirk.

Rodney, trying to pretend it never happened, tossed his second throw. The ball hit the brim of the basket and gently dropped to the bottom. Paul and Don both celebrated as if they had accomplished some great feat by simply watching and videoing Rodney.

Rodney boasted, "That wasn't hard."

Myles turned back to the basket in front of him, trying to ignore Rodney and his cheering squad. He lifted the ball and released it. It landed gently in the basket, mirroring Rodney's previous toss. Both Holly and Marguerite jumped up with quiet excitement as the ball settled.

But Rodney belittled, "It's easier when you have someone showing you how to do it."

"Great toss, Myles," said Mr. Porter.

Myles pointed up to the blonde rag doll with a blue sewn-on dress, "I think we would like that one. Right, Marguerite?"

"Yep," Marguerite replied blissfully. But Rodney immediately butted in, "Hold up. I believe I made the first shot. It just so happens, that was the doll I was gonna choose for my little sister."

Myles knew this was a bold-faced lie, but saying that at this moment benefited no one. Mr. Porter turned to Myles, "Rodney is right. Whether he won thirty minutes or thirty seconds before you, he would get to choose first."

Mr. Porter got down the rag doll with the blue dress and handed it to Rodney. Myles glanced at Marguerite as her bottom lip extended outward, tracking the doll with her blurred eyes.

"Is there another one you'd like, little lady?" Mr. Porter asked Marguerite. She rubbed her eye while looking up at the other dolls. She pointed to another fairly similar one with brown hair and a purple dress.

Marguerite took the doll graciously, holding it in front of her for a few seconds to look it over. She then placed it under her arm as they turned to walk away. Myles glanced back at Rodney and his friends, who were insolently playing with the blue-dressed doll and laughing.

Myles squatted down low, "Marguerite, can I see that doll for a second?"

"Mm-hmm," she nodded.

Myles took the doll from her, "I'll be right back." He jogged over and caught up to Rodney and the others.

"Hey Rodney," he called.

Rodney turned and sneered, "What do you want Briggs, more throwing lessons?" Paul and Don chuckled.

"Listen, I don't care if you guys don't like me, but can Marguerite have that doll? It's her favorite color, and she's super disappointed. Could we trade?" Myles knew what the answer would most likely be but figured it would be worth the attempt.

Rodney held up the prize, "What, this doll?"

Then Paul joined in, questioning Rodney facetiously, "I thought you said I could have the doll for my niece. The dress would match her little newborn eyes." Paul grabbed the doll's legs.

"I told you, it's for *my* sister," Rodney taunted, holding on tightly to the doll's head.

"Give it to me," Paul said, as he pulled on the doll.

"No, I won it," Rodney yanked back.

Myles watched in dismay as the doll's head ripped off, torn from its body. Rodney's callous reaction only added insult to injury, as he dropped the damaged figure to the ground.

Rodney threw his hands up, "Oh well."

Myles stooped down to retrieve the two halves from the ground. He brushed off the bits of mud that clung to it, but the damage was done.

Rodney and his cohorts turned away, chuckling delightedly. Anger bubbled up in Myles' chest. He clenched his fists, struggling to contain his emotions.

He snapped at Rodney, "Some big man you are, all you've done is make a little girl cry."

Rodney paused and turned, surprised by the outburst. Maintaining his bravado, Rodney replied, "Maybe I should make *you* cry instead."

Seeing that he was outnumbered and feeling a little threatened, Myles spotted a decent-sized stick amidst the brush. He plunged the damaged doll into his pocket and seized the stick, swiftly breaking off the adjoining twigs to fashion a makeshift weapon.

Rodney scoffed at this attempt, but surprisingly went along with it. He waltzed over to the brushy area. Not feeling threatened in the least, he spent more time scavenging. Eventually, he found a stick that was a little longer and thicker at the base. He inspected it, satisfied with his choice.

"A duel then," Rodney jested.

Rodney glanced over at Don and Paul as if seeking their approval as they lifted their phones to record. Myles couldn't help but notice their grinning faces, seemingly eager to support anything Rodney did. They never seemed to have an original thought between them.

Rodney smiled, "This should get some likes."

Rodney dropped his shoulders and adopted a menacing demeanor. He lifted the stick above his head with both hands and swung with as much force as he could muster. Myles barely had time to react; but he managed to raise his own stick just in time to intercept the blow. The angle, however, allowed Rodney's stick to slide down and strike Myles on the knuckle. With a quick jump to the left, Myles tried to evade Rodney's reach.

Rodney pivoted, raising his branch once more, and swung at an angle this time. Myles managed to duck beneath the swing, creating an opportunity for a swift thrust into Rodney's stomach. The blow seemed to hurt Rodney, who took a couple of steps back, clenching his abdomen. Confusion and surprise flashed in his eyes, fueling a growing anger.

Paul and Don stood to the side with their mouths hanging open. Myles suspected they were still calculating the numerical advantage they had over him but was grateful they chose not to involve themselves.

Rodney launched a second hammering swing aimed at Myles' head again. Anticipating this, Myles leapt as close to Rodney's body as possible. The unexpected move caught Rodney off-guard, causing his swing to lose momentum as he stepped back.

Myles took advantage of the distraction. He maneuvered around Rodney and delivered a swinging kick to the back of Rodney's knee, causing it to buckle. Myles placed a hand on Rodney's shoulder, guiding him down to one knee. Then Myles positioned his stick between Rodney's neck and shoulder, as if to say, "It's over."

Rodney, not feeling like this was a game anymore, angrily thrust his elbow back against Myles, "Get off."

Myles staggered backward. He watched as Rodney stood up with renewed vigor.

Then, like a thunderclap in the night, a voice demanded attention, "Myles Theodore Briggs!"

Rodney paused. Myles froze, his skin instantly grew five shades paler. It was Ms. Helen.

She looked furious, her eyebrows clenching cavernous wrinkles. Visible veins popped out of her forehead. She stood taller than ever, her hands planted firmly on her hips. Holly and Marguerite hid timidly behind her.

Myles gulped, speechless. He couldn't think of a good excuse, nor would it matter. The shock of hearing Ms. Helen's voice had punctured Rodney's temper like a pin to a balloon. Concerned that he might be in trouble too, Rodney tried to weasel his way out, "Come on, Ms. H, we were just playing around."

Without breaking her stone-like glare at Myles, Ms. Helen calmly spoke, "I think you had best be leaving now Rodney."

Knowing this meant no consequences for him and a world of trouble for Myles, Rodney responded happily, "Yes, ma'am." He and the others walked off on their merry way, leaving Myles as motionless as the sculpted ice dragon.

Ms. Helen stepped up to Myles and firmly whispered, "You will stay by my side for the rest of tonight, and we shall discuss *this* at home, as well." Her words seemed to freeze his very soul.

Ms. Helen let out a deep breath, her frustration melting away in an instant, "Now," she asked, "where is Pete?"

Worry crossed his face. Myles had completely forgotten about Pete. His gaze scanned down at the row of booths. Sensing his distress, Holly pointed, "He's over there."

Pete was walking—no, gliding— with both arms filled with chintzy prizes. He was overloaded with stuffed animals, inflatable and plastic swords, a popgun made from wood, and even a silly hat that he proudly donned on his head. His smile was so wide that each end disappeared under the earflaps of his new crown.

Eager to show off his new treasures, Pete carelessly slid between a pair of men. In his haste, he brushed up against one of their legs, causing the majority of his newfound wealth to spill. The colorful prizes scattered.

"Hey," the taller man barked in a raspy voice. Pete scrambled to pick up his items. The raspy-voiced man scoffed, "For a small town, there sure are plenty of younglings."

Myles did not recognize the two men, and judging by her expression, neither did Ms. Helen. With a determined strut, she walked over to Pete. Both men just stood there, their eyes fixed on Pete as he frantically gathered his riches.

Helen bent down and helped Pete collect the last few remaining prizes, handing them to Myles, who followed closely. She lifted Pete up off his knees, then looked up at the two men, "I apologize. Kids are not very aware of their surroundings at this age."

But the men shrugged it off, "It's fine, lady."

Ms. Helen put on what Myles could tell was a forced smile, "I don't believe I've seen you two here before." Her voice was polite, but there was a hint of caution. She pressed Pete slowly behind her, keeping a protective hand on his shoulder as she addressed the men.

Are you new to the town?" she asked.

One of the men, who clearly hadn't thought of an answer for this question, turned to answer, "Ah, yes. We's...ah, happened's to be's passing through, when's we's... ah, saw's the lights and's festivities."

He scanned the surrounding festival, then turned back to continue, "We's are simply curious travelers who's wanted to come's and share's in the fun's of the night's." His eyes darted around before settling back on Ms. Helen.

By now, Myles got a good look at both of the men. The taller man, who remained silent when Helen questioned, stroked his long beard that fell in the middle of his long dark trench coat. He swiveled his gaze around the festival with narrowed eyes, his ponytail poking out of the back of his brimmed hat. His coat fell to a pair of snakeskin boots.

The shorter finicky man, with the unusual speech patterns, rubbed his bald scalp while thinking of answers for Ms. Helen. Then he smoothed out what was left of his eyebrows, which appeared curled and singed. He jostled his long coat around, padding down his pockets. Myles could see a fragment of a tattoo peeking from beneath his collar.

The silent bearded man locked eyes with Myles, his expression indicating a struggle to remember something. Just then, a loud clanging sound pulled everyone's attention. Rodney had thrown a pie at Don, causing it to smear across Don's face. When the pie tin flew past, it collided with a metal pole.

After padding several more pockets, the bald man finally pulled out a pocket watch to examine it. However, before he could, the bearded man snatched it and stared at it while the shorter man stood on his tiptoes to catch a glimpse.

During this bizarre interaction, Ms. Helen herded the children and instructed them to run off and find the others. "I'll meet you back at Mr. Swanson's truck," she said.

Holly, Pete, and Marguerite headed off to find James and Franklin. Myles turned and followed, keeping an ear behind him. He could still hear Ms. Helen, "Oh, those orphan boys," she gestured towards Rodney and his following, "always causing a ruckus. Well, anyway, welcome to Havenshire. I hope you get to enjoy some of our celebrations here. I must go and get the children back to their parents before it gets too late."

The men continued to watch Rodney, Don, and Paul fumble around as Ms. Helen followed Myles and the children. Myles thought he must've misheard the conversation, "That was weird," Myles muttered to himself. *Why did Ms. Helen call Rodney and the others 'orphans'?* However, given his day's track record, he thought it best not to bother Ms. Helen with any questions.

They tracked down Franklin and James. Franklin was finishing up the pies and desserts. James was lurking behind other kids, glimpsing over their shoulders to see the latest social media videos on their phones. Franklin wiped his mouth with his sleeve, painted with every shade of berry.

Ms. Helen directed them all to where the cars were parked. Mr. Swanson was waiting by the truck. The children scrambled into the back. Mr. Swanson started the engine, and they slowly pulled out onto the main road.

Myles handed the doll with the purple dress to Marguerite. This cheered her up to almost her normal contentment. She stared at the doll, still longing for the one she wanted.

"We'll be home soon," Myles told Marguerite as she snuggled under his arm. But Myles was distracted, he couldn't help but wonder who those two men were and why Ms. Helen seemed so flustered around them.

Chapter Three

Vortex

As they drove down the main road back towards the orphanage, Holly noticed glowing lights on the horizon.

"What's that?" she pointed. "Over there, in Mr. Binford's field."

"It's a fire," exclaimed James, standing up while holding onto the back of the truck's cab.

"Sit down," Holly said firmly as she pulled his arm, dropping him back down. Everyone was staring at the radiant glow in the distant field.

"I wonder what happened," Myles muttered.

"Maybe he had a bad field that was infested with something," Franklin suggested.

"Yes, but Mr. Binford was at the festival," Holly stated. "He wouldn't have someone burn his field while he wasn't there to supervise."

"Good point. At least it's not close to our house," Franklin replied.

When they pulled up to the orphanage, the older boys hopped out of the back of the truck, then helped the younger children down. Ms. Helen and Mr. Swanson emerged from the cab in the middle of a conversation about the fire themselves.

"I still have the campsite set up near the forest's edge if you're interested," Mr. Swanson offered.

Ms. Helen gave an appreciative nod, "That should work rather nicely. And you wouldn't mind being out there with them?"

"Not at all," said Mr. Swanson. "And tomorrow morning, I can have them help the Missus clean up from the festival."

"Then it's settled," replied Ms. Helen. "Children, by now I'm sure you've seen the fire over in Mr. Binford's field. Just to be safe, I will have you stay at Mr. Swanson's farm for the night. Now, everyone, please head inside, pack some extra clothes, blankets, and pillows."

The boys and girls had stayed over at Mr. Swanson's farm before, but those visits were for leisurely camping excursions, not emergency situations. As they started up the steps of the porch, James walked ahead to the front door.

He froze for a second when he noticed the front door was ajar. Myles and Holly saw it, too. James brushed off his feeling of unease, and gently pushed the door open out of curiosity.

The house was in shambles. James flipped the light switch, and the few remaining lights flickered on. Bits of wood and shattered glass were strewn about. The bookshelf and cabinets were broken and lying on the floor. The children halted at the door. Myles slowly pushed past James. Then Ms. Helen cut between the children and stepped in behind Myles. She stared at the destruction around her, noticing muddy footprints scattered about.

"Children, outside now, with Mr. Swanson," Ms. Helen commanded. The children turned around and jogged back down the steps. But Myles stayed inside the house, perfectly still.

"Myles, go get Mr. Swanson," Ms. Helen asked, placing her hand on his shoulder. Myles turned and saw the seriousness in her eyes, then followed the other children.

"What's going on?" Mr. Swanson asked as he rolled out of his truck again.

Myles called out from behind the others, "Mr. Swanson, it looks like someone broke into the house. Ms. Helen wants you inside."

Mr. Swanson trotted up the steps and into the open door.

The children waited outside behind the truck. They listened for any sounds of commotion from inside. Young Marguerite hugged Myles' leg.

After a short while, Mr. Swanson and Ms. Helen emerged from the home.

"What happened?" the children wanted to know.

"We don't know," said Ms. Helen with a deep sigh. "It appears someone broke into the house, probably looking for something of value. It's okay, they're gone now. It doesn't appear that anything is missing."

James piped up, "An orphanage is a dumb place to look for valuables."

Ms. Helen calmly responded, "Some people find themselves in desperate times and don't make decisions that you and I would deem logical. Others can be engulfed by greed. But regardless, the house is safe. Everyone, keep your boots on, go upstairs, and gather what you need for tonight? Mr. Swanson's campsite will suffice for a night or two."

As the children started walking, Ms. Helen grabbed Myles by the arm, "Not you, Myles," she said firmly. Myles looked at her, confused.

"We need to get this house back in order. I cannot do it all by myself." Myles didn't believe this to be true in the least. "And due to recent events, that will go unmentioned, I believe you owe me some manual labor."

Myles knew it would be a lot of work, but seeing as this seemed like an easy way out of other consequences, he quickly agreed to the proposal.

James and Franklin were the first two children to step back into the house. Their hearts sank as they looked around and saw the destruction. Next in was Holly with Marguerite clinging to the back of her skirt. Pete came in last wide eyed and holding his wooden sword at the ready.

After they stepped over the broken bits of furniture, they headed up the stairs. The doors were open to both bedrooms. The dresser drawers had been taken out and thrown to the floor. Their clothes were strewn about the rooms. Their beds and mattresses were overturned.

It took them a few minutes to locate their belongings amidst the mess. The boys collected everything they needed. Holly grabbed two sacks: one for herself and one for Marguerite, who was almost too small to carry her own. Ms. Helen herded them all back outside to Mr. Swanson's truck. They threw their belongings into the back and climbed in for what they hoped would be the last ride of the night.

With everyone now in the truck, Ms. Helen gave a stern message, "I want everyone on their best behavior for Mr. Swanson. Do as he asks and help him and Mrs. Swanson in the morning with their chores. I will be by tomorrow to bring you back home."

Mr. Swanson hopped back into the driver's seat, "Any specific time you want me to bring them back if I don't hear from you?" he asked Ms. Helen.

"No," she replied, "I'll give you a call tomorrow when I know how long this cleanup will take."

"Okay then, good luck with the restorations. I'll see if I can rustle up some of the local carpenters to help with the broken furniture," Mr. Swanson said as he started pulling away. Ms. Helen called out to the kids, "Be good, children. Try to rest."

"See you all tomorrow," added Myles. As the truck headed further down the road, Myles turned and looked at Ms. Helen. She was staring at the house, not out of despair or sadness, but with a look of trepidation.

"Ms. Helen?" Myles spoke up, "I'm really sorry about what happened today... you know... with the mud, and then with Rodney..."

Ms. Helen turned away from the house and looked at Myles, "I know you are."

Myles broke eye contact and looked down at Ms. Helen's boots, "It's just that Rodney and the others were being so cruel to Marguerite. I kind of lost my temper."

Ms. Helen extended her hand towards him and lifted his chin, "What do I always tell you?"

Myles sighed. Ms. Helen began reciting, "The storms are short... the valley is wide, the mountain is tall, destiny inside..." Myles reluctantly responded, as he had hundreds of times before, with a casual eye roll, "...during your darkest of hours, in the light you shall hide."

"Now, do you believe your decisions were of the light or of the dark?" Ms. Helen asked Myles.

"I gave in to my anger..." Myles answered wishing the conversation would veer back to the house.

"That's right. Now, let's forget about that for now. Head inside, and let's get to work."

Ms. Helen rounded up some flashlights and lamps to shine more light on the cleanup job ahead of them. Myles headed upstairs to begin work on the bedrooms. He picked up drawers and placed them back in the dressers. The upstairs furnishings weren't quite as broken as the downstairs. After setting up the furniture and putting the mattresses back, Myles started sifting through the clothes to return them to their drawers.

Myles started with the boys' room, but completed the task in much less time than he thought it would take. He then walked across the landing to the girls' bedroom and repeated the process.

As he began the task of folding all their clothes and placing them back in the drawers, he picked up one of Marguerite's shirts. Holly's sewing kit fell out onto the floor. He picked up the kit, and his eyes lit up with an idea. He reached into his pocket and pulled out the ripped doll with the blue dress. Myles had seen Ms. Helen mend some of their clothing by sewing before. *How hard could it be?* he thought.

Myles walked over to the windowsill, sat down, and began sifting through the sewing kit to find the necessary supplies. He carefully pushed the stuffing back into the doll, repositioned its head, and began sewing it back to the body.

On the second pass through the fabric, "Ouch," he exclaimed, accidentally pricking his finger. He sucked on his fingertip, but despite the pain, he persevered until the doll's head was securely attached. It wasn't the neatest sewing job, but as he examined the doll he spoke to it, "We all have scars, but I think Marguerite will still like you."

He placed the doll on the windowsill and smiled, then turned around to continue his work. He caught a whiff of the air, *Smoke?* he wondered. He quickly looked out of the window, scanning the horizon. The fire at Allen Binford's farm seemed to be dying down, and the smoke was blowing in the opposite direction, so that couldn't be the source.

As his gaze drew nearer, he noticed an eerie glow illuminating the ground around the orphanage. He could hear the murmur of voices passing by the window. One voice sounded much deeper than Ms. Helen's.

"Is someone here?" Myles wondered aloud. As he descended the stairs, the smoke smell grew stronger. He leapt off the third step, landing on the floor and quickly scanned the living room in shock. Sporadic flames had ignited around the room. Fire danced up the curtains, spreading onto the walls and crawling across the rug.

At first, Myles didn't seem to notice the smoke, but as the flames continued to consume the only home he had known, the smoke thickened, making it harder for Myles to see and breathe.

Myles heard the deep unrecognizable voice again and looked up over the flames through the open front door. He saw Ms. Helen standing just outside on the porch, her back to Myles with her hands held out. Myles called out through the crackle of the flames, "Ms. Helen!"

Helen snapped her neck around, "Myles, run!" she yelled, without yielding her stance. She then swiped her hand toward the front door as if to slap the air itself. The door slammed shut so vigorously that even the flames bowed to the wind for just a moment. As the flames roared back with even more intensity, the smoke became unbearable.

Myles quickly ran to the back door, fumbling with the deadbolt lock, trying not to breathe in the smoke. Coughing and blinded with stinging tears, Myles finally managed to release the deadbolt and push his way out the back door. Stumbling out on his hands and knees, he coughed, trying to clear his lungs. He crawled off the back porch, then turned around to see flames erupting from the downstairs windows, and dark smoke billowing from his bedroom windowsill. Havenshire Orphanage, his home, was burning.

While stunned by emotion, a dark figure emerged from around the far corner of the house.

"Hey kid, get over here," the deep voice demanded. Every instinct in Myles' body screamed, "Run." The man's pace quickened with each step. Myles turned away and bolted for the fields.

"Hey," the man yelled again, "get back here." Myles pushed his way through the stalks in Mr. Binford's cornfield. The muddy ground squelched with every frantic step. He desperately trudged forward. Myles could hear the cracking of the corn stalks as the man pursued. He prayed the thick, muddy soil would slow down a fully grown man.

"Get back here kid!" the man's voice boomed through the stalks. Panic surged through the boy as he made his way through the cornfields. When Myles lifted his heavy boot off the ground to take another step, it felt like a whip had ensnared his leg. He fell down face-first in the mud.

Myles flipped around to see what had grabbed him. Cornstalks had coiled themselves around his leg, constricting him like a snake. He frantically tried to pull his leg free, but the cornstalks wouldn't budge. Spotting a jagged rock, he grabbed it and hacked at the stalks until the vine was severed.

He jumped to his feet and kept running. The rows of corn seemed endless—a labyrinth under the pale moonlight. A rustle in the stalks to his left sent a jolt of terror through him. He forced himself to focus, pushing forward with a renewed burst of desperate energy.

After a frantic sprint, Myles hunkered down. He fought to silence his gasps, straining his ears into the oppressive silence. Then, a sound, a rustling punctuated by the swishing of mud-caked boots.

"Where'd that brat get off to?" the man mumbled, his voice closer now. Myles' heartbeat like a drum in his chest. He glanced down, seeing the jagged rock still clutched in his hand, and that gave him an idea. He launched the rock with all his might. It glided through the night air without a sound, then smashed through the stalks in the distance. A tense silence followed, broken only by the frantic rasp of his own breath.

The man rustled through the stalks away from Myles. Seizing the opportunity, Myles began his final sprint to the edge of the field. He could see the warm lights coming from Allen Binford's porch like a beacon in the darkness. But just before reaching the field's edge, a rough hand clamped down on his shirt. He was yanked back and slammed into the mud.

"Stay down," a low, familiar voice rasped. Myles froze, heart hammering against his ribs. He squinted upwards to see Allen Binford crouched over him, with his hand firmly pressing Myles to the ground. The man pursuing Myles stepped out of the cornfield and into the clearing by the house. Straining through the stalks, Myles could barely make out a long, dark coat...and a flash of snakeskin boots. *The bearded man from the festival*, Myles realized.

"Don't move," Allen whispered with urgency.

The pursuing man turned slowly, his gaze sweeping the fields like a predator searching for prey. While the man's back was turned, Allen stealthily crept out of the stalks, keeping his distance.

"Can I help you?" Allen questioned, acting as if he were unaware of the evening's prior events. The man whirled around, "Who are you?" he barked.

"This is my farm, and you are trespassing on my land," Allen stated.

The man sneered, "This doesn't concern you. Go back to your little house, farmer, if you know what's good for you."

"Well, I would say whatever happens on my land concerns me greatly," Allen retorted.

Myles flipped to his belly. He could see little more than the shuffling dance of feet through the stalks.

"I warned you, farmer," the man growled.

Through a gap, Myles witnessed something that defied his understanding. An unnatural green light, like a sickly swamp fire, pulsed from the man's direction. The man dropped to one knee pushing the light into the ground. His long overgrown beard illuminated, hovering a few inches above his boot.

Still laying in the icy mud, Myles felt a cold slither underneath him. Myles was sure it was a snake but dared not make a sound.

Then, still behaving like a clueless farmer, Allen exclaimed, "What on earth?!"

Thick, snake-like roots erupted from the ground, coiling around Allen's boots. Allen yanked and twisted, "What is this?" He tried to free himself.

The man, a cruel smile twisting his lips, approached the struggling farmer. "Where's the boy?" he demanded, his voice dripping with malice. Myles' mind raced. He had to do something, but revealing himself could put them both in even greater danger.

"What boy? Who are you talking about?" Allen questioned while bent over, playing at the roots and feigning desperation.

The man loomed over Allen. Myles' heart pounded in his chest, his mind a whirlwind of panic. He had to do something, but his brain refused to form a plan. Suddenly, the green light appeared again, flickering like a flame. The light illuminated Allen's face, revealing a playful smirk, despite his predicament.

"Well," the man growled, "if you don't know what boy I'm talking about, I guess I have no use for you."

Myles watched, as Allen met the man's threat head-on. Allen simply replied, "I guess not."

With a sudden flash of pale blue light, accompanied by a swift chilling gust, the roots binding Allen shattered in an instant. The ground beneath them was instantaneously frozen, slick with ice. Allen whipped his head upward, colliding with the man's chin. As Allen stood straight up, he lifted his knee, kicking the man square in the chest, sending him sliding backwards. He fell with such force, Myles could hear the crack of the ice as the man's head landed.

The man lay on his back, not moving, icicles expanding around his arms and legs, freezing the man to the ground in shackles of ice.

Myles shot up to his feet and emerged from the corn, his mind reeling in disbelief. "Wha...What just happened?" he stammered, his voice hoarse as he gawked at the figure semi-frozen to the ground.

Allen's hand clamped onto Myles' shoulder and spun him around to meet his eyes. "Are you okay?"

Myles managed to speak, "I... I think so."

Allen looked down at Myles' chest and could see the mud-clumped compass still around his neck. Myles looked back at the man on the ground again, "Is he...?" his voice trailed off.

"No," answered Allen, "he's just out *cold*," he said, with a short chuckle. "Myles, we have to go."

"Go? Go where?" Myles paused and remembered, "The house... it's on fire. We need to go back. Ms. Helen, she's..."

"She'll be fine," Allen interjected, "She's a tough old goat. Hard as nails, that one. But we can't stay here."

Allen wasted no time. He jogged to his porch, snatched a backpack. As he sprinted down the slope toward his truck, he called to Myles, "Quick, get in. I'll explain everything later, I promise, but there's no time." Myles, transfixed on the frozen man lying on the ground, saw a green glow pulse from behind the ice. The flickering light was growing brighter then writhed free of its icy prison.

"Come on!" Allen yelled. Myles tore his gaze and scrambled backwards, his steps quickening into a desperate sprint towards the truck. Myles jumped in and slammed the door shut. Allen fishtailed the truck in a spray of dust as he peeled off down the road.

Myles glanced up, and a gasp escaped his lips. Large tree branches were descending from the trees on either side of the road, forming a tangled wall that threatened to block their escape.

"Hang on," Allen bellowed, a manic glint of delight in his eyes.

As they approached the wooden barricade, Myles caught another blinding glimpse of the flashing blue light again. The truck collided with the branches. The shattering impact rang out, as if they'd slammed through a giant mirror. A glittering rain exploded inwards — hundreds of icy shards, sharp and unforgiving, peppered Myles and Allen through the open windows.

Confused, Myles noticed the little fragments were ice. In a fleeting glimpse, he saw the shattered remains of the branchy barricade as the truck hurtled down the dirt road, leaving a trail of glistening ice in its wake.

Myles glanced back once more. The view of the man chasing them, Allen's home, and everything he once knew, were vanishing quickly. Myles plopped back down in his seat and remembered to breathe.

"Where are we going?" Myles' voice trembled slightly.

"Bicon Lake, just down the road," stated Allen.

"Why there?"

"To go see an old friend," Allen answered with a grin.

Again, Myles spiraled into deep worry. "The house, Ms. Helen, the others..." he cried out.

"They will be fine. In case of an emergency, I told Ms. Helen to use my house as a new orphanage."

Surprised Allen had an answer for his concerns, Myles asked "But, what about you?"

"Havenshire was never my real home," Allen admitted. "There's more to this story, Myles, but there's no time to explain now."

Myles didn't know what to make of everything, but he didn't have much time to ponder. Allen turned off the main road towards the entrance to the old docks. He parked the truck, grabbed his backpack, and jumped out.

"Let's go, kid," he called out as he waved for Myles to follow. Allen walked down the dock and uncovered an aluminum fishing boat. Myles stumbled out of the truck and started down the dock toward the boat with a knot of unease in his stomach.

"Well," Allen reached out his hand from the boat, "all aboard?" Myles grabbed Allen's hand. The murky depths seemed to deepen the pit in his stomach. He looked back at the dark tree line, sensing that everything was about to change, whether he wanted it to, or not.

Myles stepped down into the boat as it rocked back and forth. With Myles at the front, Allen pulled the starter and the boat sputtered to life. As they gained momentum, the air and water were tranquil.

Myles had never been on a boat. He was amazed at how the little boat could cut through the water so smoothly; he felt as if they were gliding. He forgot his anxiousness for a brief moment until, "Get down!" The shout ripped Myles back to reality. A volley of projectiles whistled overhead.

Myles barely had time to register Allen's shove before his head was forced down again. Allen hunched over Myles, shielding the boy. He grunted with exertion as he steered the boat in a sharp turn, dodging another volley of missiles. A third wave shot overhead seconds after. One of the projectiles pierced the boat's hull inches from Myles. He examined the wedged object. It was made of wood, like a wooden missile.

"This guy doesn't give up, does he?" Allen complained. "Don't worry, we're almost there."

"Where?" Myles frantically questioned.

Another flock of wooden spikes whizzed past. As the last one sailed harmlessly over the boat, Allen ripped open his right sleeve and held his fist up high, brandishing his forearm. Myles caught a glimpse of an intricate tattoo.

Allen only stood for a few seconds. One hand on the motor controls, the other lifted up. He surveyed the water, like he was waiting for someone to signal back. Then relief washed over his face.

"Okay," Allen said, dropping back down. He grabbed rope from his backpack and hastily started tying Myles and himself to the boat.

Not knowing what was going to happen next terrified Myles. He wished he was back at the orphanage awaiting some grave consequence from Ms. Helen, even the dreaded chore of scrubbing the endless grime off the kitchen floor. At least there, the dangers were familiar.

"Get ready!" Allen commanded, his voice tight with a mix of fear and excitement. He looked more crazed than Myles had ever seen before, his eyes gleaming with a wild energy.

Myles fought down a wave of nausea as he inched towards the front of the boat. He peeked over the bow to see what they were heading toward. Lit by the moonlight, Myles saw a dark hole swirling slowly at the center of the lake. As the boat glided toward it through the water, Myles could make out a dark vortex swirling downward. They were heading right for it.

"Oh no... no..." Myles moaned, as he shook his head in disbelief. He grasped the ropes around his waist and realized his fate was tied to the boat. Myles peered over the edge of the boat one more time, this time gazing down into the waters below. Sporadic lights flashed, like an underwater lightning storm. The random flashes momentarily illuminated a colossal dark shape beneath them. The large mass swam below them, circling the swirling vortex.

Myles spun around, "What is that?" he squeaked out, terrified, "Down there, under the boat?"

"That," Allen paused and smiled, "is our way back."

Back to where? Myles thought, with no time to ask.

The colossal shape below let out a sound that echoed through the water, a low, mournful wail. The hull of the boat had just reached the outer edge of the vortex. It picked up speed as it was sucked forward by the current. The bow tipped downward into a sickening descent that stole Myles' breath. The ropes that bound him, once a symbol of his helplessness, now seemed like a lifeline.

As they dropped, Myles felt the downward plunge hit his stomach. He could not hold back; he screamed and gripped the cold metal boat for dear life. The pressure of the rotating water intensified with each passing second, pushing them deeper. The waters were now a raging torrent, a relentless hand shoving the boat down a steep, watery incline. The boat jarred, continually splashing them as they endlessly spun around the whirlpool.

"Here we gooo!" Allen yelled, his voice a shriek lost in the roar of the water. He clung to the boat like a bucking bronco, a thrill seeker riding a nightmare. Myles strained to hold on. The boat tilted precariously as they neared the bottom of the cone-shaped hole. Myles prayed the end was near and forced his eyes to stay open.

Two colossal shadows, triangular and monstrous, burst out of the water on either side of them. The gaping jaws were lined with razor-sharp teeth. The boat lurched violently as the sharp, dagger-like teeth scraped the boat's hull. Then, in a violent snap, Myles' moonlit world was devoured in an instant by darkness.

Chapter Four

The Inner World

Darkness swallowed them whole. The stench of rotten fish filled Myles' nostrils, a revolting reminder of their predicament. It felt like time had halted. The ropes binding Myles tightened painfully. They were tossed around, tumbling in the suffocating abyss. A deafening grumble echoed from the unknown depths surrounding them.

Gravity felt like it had ceased to exist. The wet splashing of the vortex had disappeared; however, a heavier, slimier liquid replaced it.

Allen's voice called out, "Just a little longer," strained, but strangely cheerful.

Then, within the endless darkness above, faint periwinkle lines of light sparkled into existence. Myles fixated on the glowing cracks, his only reference point.

In an instant, the cracks widened, creating a large, jagged opening above. Myles saw a familiar sight; a moon, but not the moon he remembered. This one glowed with a bluish-purple light.

Then, they were heaved violently, tossed as if caught in the grip of a giant's hand. The boat was flung through the opening and hurled through the air, traveling sideways. Below, Myles caught a glimpse of shallow water before the boat splashed down with a bone-jarring thud. It skipped forward, righting itself with a series of thumps, finally grinding to a halt on a slick murky beach.

Myles didn't move. His white knuckles were still fused to the boat's hull, as he realized he was not dead and miraculously, not hurt.

In contrast, Allen sat up with a grunt and a chuckle, "Rougher than I remembered."

A large glob of slime clung to his cheek. With a look of disgust, Allen casually swiped it away, flinging it out of the beached boat. Allen began untying the slippery slime covered knots from around Myles, "I guess she didn't like the metallic taste."

Myles mustered up the courage to sit up. He could see a lake behind Allen. The waves shimmered as they rippled. Each rippled edge sparkled like the jewel in Ms. Helen's favorite necklace.

But the tranquil scene was shattered in an instant. A gigantic fin arose and resubmerged causing waves of white froth. But before the waves reached the shoreline, a large scaly tail whipped out of the water, then smacked the surface and disappeared again.

Myles shot to his feet and pointed a shaking finger, "What was that?" He scrambled back, clamoring out of the boat.

"That? That was the Gatekeeper," Allen muttered, shoving the slimy rope into his bag. His voice held a hint of annoyance, "Most Gatekeepers just let you walk on through, but she always swallows you up and spits you out," he shuddered. "I have always hated water passages."

Myles stood motionless, still staring at the lake hoping to catch a glimpse of the creature. *Was it a giant fish, or some kind of sea serpent?* he thought to himself. As he watched the water begin to still, his gaze widened away from the lake, drifting upwards. His mouth fell open.

The sky wasn't the familiar blanket of speckled black he knew. He stared up at the purple tinged moon. Well, he thought of it as a moon in his head, but it was more like an illuminated stone, three times larger than the moon he remembered. The surface looked like a giant crystallized geode.

The stars in the sky were also different. They sparkled more than he had ever seen, twinkling like tiny distant fireworks with a medley of colors. For a moment, he forgot the terror of the Gatekeeper, his fear replaced by a sense of awe.

The trees and bushes surrounding the lake were kissed by the moon's brilliance. The sights were so different from anything he'd ever seen before, he thought, *That's it; I'm dreaming,* as his mind tried to make sense of it.

Gawking in wonder, Myles took another step backward, taking in the enormous night sky, but then he stopped. A chilled breath exhaled past the nape of his neck with a forceful snort. It felt like a raging bull had snuck up behind him. Frozen, Myles glanced down. Allen was still on one knee in front of him, organizing his bag.

Fearing what could be lurking behind him, Myles slowly curled his shoulders as his chin sank. His over-the-shoulder peek was met by two enormous yellow eyes staring back at him. They framed the head of a colossal lizard, its glare piercing his soul. Its head was lowered in a predatory crouch.

A primal scream tore from Myles' throat as he launched himself away, landing hard on his back and elbows. Scrambling, he propelled himself away from the monstrous lizard. Its massive head, a nightmare fusion of reptilian poise, loomed closer, the yellow eyes tracking the boy.

Allen glanced up and saw Myles scrambling. He looked over at the scaly beast and straightened up, his gaze locking with the reptile. A low growl rumbled in its throat. Then, with a speed that belied its size, the beast lunged. Myles flinched, bracing for impact, but the attack wasn't aimed at him.

The monstrous lizard slammed into Allen, its massive, clawed foot pinning him to the ground. Allen desperately grasped at the creature's ankle, his fingers struggling to find grip.

"Mr. Binford!" Myles cried out, but he could do nothing. The beast lowered its head down toward Allen. Myles watched in horror as the beast opened its gaping jaw, revealing rows of razor-sharp teeth dripping with a viscous drool. Its long tongue fell out, licking up Allen's exposed neck, seemingly tasting its next meal.

"No..." Allen roared in a surprising boisterous laugh, "you daft lizard." His face was laced with amusement and covered in drool.

Allen met the lizard's eyes again, "There you are, old girl," he said ecstatically. "You waited for me after all."

He reached out, his hands surprisingly steady, and grasped the beast by its massive cheekbones. To Myles' utter astonishment, he pulled the creature's head in as they rubbed foreheads. The colossal lizard, its fearsome demeanor dissolving, responded by thumping its tail. The beast's attention shifted, sniffing vigorously at the mud caked backpack beside Allen.

"I brought you something," Allen remarked.

The giant lizard hopped off his chest and paced in a circle. Allen groaned to his feet and reached into his backpack. He pulled out a well-wrapped package. The creature's head bobbed in anticipation, a rumbling growl escaping its throat.

He peeled away the waxy paper to reveal a large raw steak. The lizard grinned, if a giant reptile could be said to grin. It crouched low, tail held high. Then in a surprisingly nimble move for its size, lunged as Allen tossed the meat. It snatched the steak while landing on its back. The meat was ripped to shreds and devoured in mere seconds.

Allen laughed, "She always did like the taste of outer-beef."

Myles stayed sprawled in the mud, elbows propping him up, not knowing what to think. Allen casually approached the lizard, who rolled back upright. He reached out and scratched under its scaly chin. They nuzzled their foreheads together again, the picture of a bizarre reunion.

Allen's attention fell back to the still-cowering boy, "Myles, I would like to introduce you to Beira, my dragon."

"Your... dragon?!" Myles squealed back, almost completing a year's worth of puberty in one sentence.

Allen chuckled, "Well, technically she's a frost drake, a special type of dragon. Aren't you, girl?" Allen asked while holding her face like a little puppy.

Myles stumbled to his feet, his knees weak, "You have a... a dragon?"

Allen, still beaming from seeing his old friend, explained, "Beira is my Nexus. She is my bonded dragon." Beira let out a big disapproving snort.

Allen yielded, "Okay, I am her bonded human," he said, appeasing the beast. Beira lifted her head as if proud Allen submitted to her will.

"Is it... safe?" Myles asked.

"Yes, quite safe, I assure you," Allen answered, "Beira and I have known each other for a long time."

Bewildered, Myles studied the scaled beast before him. Easily as tall as Allen when standing, she lumbered on all fours, each foot tipped with wickedly curved claws that gleamed in the moonlight. Her body was a canvas of armored scales, each one shimmering like a shard of crystal. The scales flowed down her back in a ridge that continued along her powerful tail.

"Where are her wings?" It was about the only question Myles could think to ask based on his knowledge of dragons.

Allen answered, as if to defend her honor, "Not all dragons have wings. There are many types of dragons that live here, all of them different sizes and having different attributes. For example, Beira here is my queen of winter. Her name means just that."

Myles was still unsure when he would be awakened from this bizarre dream.

Allen plucked a leaf from the muck. "Here, let me show you."

He held the leaf out by the stem placing his palm flat directly below it. A light blue flame burst to life, engulfing the leaf, but the leaf did not burn. The leaf fell into his open hand. The flames extinguished as quickly as they arose.

Myles examined it. Crystals had formed all around the leaf, encasing it in ice. Myles reached out and took the cold, hard leaf. It was frozen solid.

Myles' heart pounded in his chest as a question rose swiftly to his lips, "You have— magic?"

But Allen just scoffed, "Noooo. Although, I guess most people from the outside world would call it that at first glance. I am one of the few who has been blessed with a Nexus connection. My ability, which you just witnessed, is the result of my connection with Beira. I'm able to borrow and share her flame... her attribute."

While Myles was processing, Allen continued. "All dragons are connected through an energy called *Ruach*."

"Roo-awck?" Myles repeated. He rattled his brain, trying to recall if he had ever heard such a word. *It sounds like some kind of ancient language or something*, Myles thought.

Allen continued, "Think of the Ruach like the atmosphere, or air around you. It is the pure essence of life around all living things, all creation. It is in all of us and flows through everything—you, me, the water, the earth, and even the plants and animals. Most dragons are able to draw from their connection to Ruach, granting them their flames. Some abilities are elemental in nature, like Beira's ice, and some are more... exuberant."

Beira snorted disagreeably again, but Allen ignored her outburst. "This ability can be shared through a Nexus connection between a person and a dragon."

As if on cue, Beira inhaled and lunged her head forward, opening her jaw. Vivid blue flames erupted, causing Myles to jump back unexpectedly. The compressed flames expanded outward as they reached further, engulfing a nearby log in a blue inferno. As the flames sputtered out, Myles could see the log and its surroundings had completely frozen over with a coating of ice.

Allen rolled up his still-unbuttoned sleeve again to reveal the symbol on his forearm. Myles looked closely at the marking. The image resembled ice crystals surrounded by intricate lines, swirling around like an icy wind.

Myles had never noticed any markings on Allen's body before. He always wondered why Mr. Binford wore long sleeves on hot summer days, but assumed it was a personal choice, much like how Ms. Helen would never wear a skirt shorter than the heels of her boots.

Allen touched the marking on his arm, "This symbol reads, 'Beira.' When I enseared with Beira's egg a long time ago, I was able to read the symbol you see here and say her name. That is when our Nexus connection was made. Now I can share in my dragon's attribute, or flame, if you will."

Myles became increasingly curious and asked, "Can I..." he searched for the right words, "engage...with her?" That wasn't it, but he did not care. A real dragon, or at least something very much like one, stood before him. It was terrifying yet exhilarating.

Allen glanced over at Beira, who gave a subtle nod.

Myles approached slowly, his hand outstretched towards her broad head. With caution, he placed his fingertips on the bridge of her nose. As he continued forward, his palm made contact with her tough yet malleable scales. Moving alongside her body, his touch met large scaly armor and smooth, horn-like spikes near the back of her neck. Beira glared at Myles then leaned into his touch, as if to signify acceptance.

"Hey there, girl," he whispered in awestruck wonder. "She is beautiful."

"That she is," Allen boasted.

Beira turned her massive head towards Myles. He gulped, a nervous laugh escaped as the colossal lizard lumbered closer. She lowered her head, giving him a thorough sniffing. Suddenly, she recoiled, her enormous head snapping back with a nostril dramatically flared.

With a mighty snort and a vigorous shake of her head, Beira unleashed a ferocious sneeze. She repeated the process, a comical display of reptilian frustration. Finally, she glared at Myles' pocket. Myles reached in and pulled out a crumpled object.

Allen inspected, "Huh, daffodils?"

"Yes, they were left over from the festival," Myles confessed.

Allen laughed at his companion, "We don't have any such flowers here. Seems the smell doesn't agree with her." Beira scowled at the flower in Myles' hand. She grunted through flared nostrils and turned away.

Myles stammered an apology, "I'm... sorry." He was on the verge of tossing the flower away, but before he could, the tranquil lake churned violently once again. The water rippled and frothed as it did before.

Allen's frantic whisper cut through the air. "This way, quickly," he barked, already a blur as he sprinted across the slick mud towards the hard dirt path. Myles and Beira scurried after.

Once on the hard-packed road, Allen turned and led them into the bushes, "Get down low."

Myles obeyed instantly, all three made their way deeper into the foliage. Beira, mirroring a well-trained dog, lowered her head to rest between her paws.

A monstrous head erupted from the lake, moonlight sparkling off the showering splash. It was a prehistoric leviathan, straight from one of Myles' dinosaur books. The sea monster whipped its head with its cavernous jaws open. It threw a projectile from its mouth, a smaller vessel, eerily similar to their own, rocketing towards the shoreline. The boat cartwheeled through the air, landing with a sickening splash that spilled out two figures onto the beach. The monstrous head dipped back under, leaving only watchful eyes gleaming under the surface.

Myles leaned closer to Allen, "Is the Gatekeeper a dragon too?"

But Allen's sharp "shush" cut through Myles' excitement.

Two figures emerged from the shallows, thoroughly soaked. One, clad in snakeskin boots with a long beard, the other bald and shrouded in a dark cloak.

"The two men from the festival," Myles mouthed. A low growl rumbled in Beira's throat.

Allen reached out and gently patted her head, "Steady on, girl."

Standing on the murky beach, the bald one yelled out with frustration, "Sees, I told yous they'd be's long gone."

"Only because you took your sweet time catching up and nicking that boat," the bearded man shot back.

The bald man scanned the bank. "Looks, tracks. Headed north, towards Porkuss."

"This job is getting to be more trouble than it's worth," the bearded man complained.

"Who was that frost-guy whos beat yous?"

"He didn't beat me, Mordred."

"Yeah, whatevers, let's go finds this kid so's we's can be's done with this already," said the bald man, who Myles now assumed to be Mordred.

The bearded man gnashed his teeth, "Fine... but the iceman is mine."

"You's can have him; I'll's snatch the kid."

With that, the two figures disappeared into the moonlit woods as they followed the trail leading away from the lake.

Myles, Allen, and Beira waited for what felt like an eternity.

Finally, Allen gave a barely audible command, "Let's move."

They slowly followed Allen as he melted deeper into the tangled undergrowth. They emerged onto a narrow, overgrown trail, a far cry from the well-worn path to the town. Thorny shrubs snagged at their clothes as they followed Allen in single file.

Myles couldn't help but strain over his current predicament, "Dragons don't exist," he repeated like a mantra. But a glance back shattered the illusion. Beira, colossal and undeniable, followed close behind. A silent exchange passed between them—a flicker of amusement in her reptilian gaze.

They marched on through the leaves as Myles tried to put away the fear of being bitten from behind.

Myles' head was swimming with questions, but before he got the courage to ask, they emerged from the oppressive undergrowth. The narrow trail gave way to a small clearing.

"Here we are," said Allen, pleased with himself.

In the center of the clearing stood an old log cabin, its weathered frame a testament to years of neglect. Allen strode up to the cabin, his boots crunching on the carpet of fallen leaves.

Allen rummaged through the depths of his backpack. "Just a moment... It's in here somewhere. Ahh, here it is." He withdrew a metallic object. It was a curious contraption, six flawless ringed hexagons, making a perfect flower in form.

Myles could see a similar shape adorned the large hexagonal door. Without a word, Allen fit the metallic object into the slot and the device. A metallic click echoed, followed by a grinding groan as the door cracked open.

A wave of dusty air billowed out from below the door. Allen retrieved the metal key and peered into the cabin's dark interior. "Alright, you two. Come on in."

It was a cozy, single-room cabin with a large fireplace. Its hearth dominated one wall. A wooden table stood in the center. Assorted pots and pans hung from the exposed beams, glinting like neglected trophies. A few tools lay scattered near a corner, and a pair of chairs sat patiently beside the table.

Allen ran his fingers over the table which wore a coat of dust, evidence of the cabin's disuse. He knelt beside the fireplace, gathering the stacked logs and kindling. He took a lighter out of his backpack and lit a welcoming blaze. Beira, who had squeezed her shoulders through the doorway with surprising grace, watched the fire-making display with a hint of amusement. A low scoff rumbled from her throat.

"Well, it's not like you're a fire dragon," Allen retorted. "She doesn't like any technology that makes my life easier," he said, turning back to nurture the infant flames.

Not knowing what to do with himself, Myles sat down on one of the chairs at the table. His head spun with questions as he watched the dancing flames mature. As light and warmth began to fill the cabin, Myles looked towards the mantle, finding a large painting. It portrayed a group of people and a few dragons standing behind.

Allen walked over to the table and sat adjacent to Myles. Beira paced, trying to find herself a comfortable space on the floor. She wacked the door almost closed with her tail.

Allen sighed, sinking further into his chair, and looked at Myles, "How are you doing, Myles?"

Myles blinked up from the flames, "I... I don't know." Myles paused for a moment. "Mr. Binford, where...? Is this a different world? And... who are those men?" Myles started sounding more anxious. "And why do they want me?"

Allen's brows furrowed in concern. A weary sound escaped his lips that spoke of burdens best left unspoken, "Well, first things first, you can stop calling me Mr. Binford. Just call me Allen. Now, let's start with the *where* problem. Myles, what were you taught about the center of the earth?"

Myles looked more confused than before. "Well, you have the earth's crust... then the mantle, and then the outer and inner cores." Myles always enjoyed his science books and classes in school. He found a sense of pleasure being able to answer the teacher's questions.

Allen took a big breath, looking up at the gently illuminated ceiling, "You see Myles, the earth isn't just filled with rock and magma as they teach you in school." A baffled look overwhelmed Myles' features.

Allen's face showed a spark of inspiration, "Oh, I know..." he grabbed his backpack and pulled out a large grapefruit. He cut the fruit in even halves. He found a rather large, dull spoon, hanging on the wall, and hollowed out the inside. He put all the meat from the fruit on a plate and placed it down on the floor to get it out of the way. He held the grapefruit husk up in front of him, putting the two hollowed halves together to make a whole sphere.

"This is the earth as you know it. You have all the countries and lands on the outside of the earth's crust. However, if you were to dig directly down far enough into the earth, you would find where we are now." Allen split open the two halves, "Here on the other side of the earth's crust. This inner-world, if you will, is called Escalia."

Myles shook his head with disbelief, "That doesn't make any sense. We are walking on the inside of the earth's crust? How did we even get here?"

"Well, we passed through a water gateway, didn't we? Did you already forget the stench of our slobbery friend?" Myles took a quick sniff of his shoulder and recoiled.

"In this world," Allen continued, "there are certain low points in the topography that make the two worlds touch at a single point. There are several dozens of these locations around the globe, in fact. These points are called gateways; locations where a person only has to travel a short distance to trek between the two sides. I was able to show my marking to the Gatekeeper. That's why she *so graciously* carried us here," Allen explained with a hint of sarcasm.

"What is a Gatekeeper?" Myles asked.

"The Gatekeepers are there to keep outsiders away and will only grant a select few passage."

"So, you are saying we are inside the earth right now?"

Allen leaned back in his chair, "Yes."

But the conversation was interrupted by a rhythmic scraping sound. Allen glanced down to find the grapefruit meat had vanished. Beira was using her long tongue to lap up the remaining juices.

"You reptilian hippo," Allen sputtered, snatching the plate from the floor. Beira raised her head back up still licking her lips. "That was *my* food. I already gave you the steak."

She regarded Allen with an expression that could only be described as shameless. A low rumble emanated from her throat, showing she had no regrets.

Myles began to ask, "Mr. Allen..."

"Just Allen," Allen interrupted.

"Sorry. But who were those men? And why are they chasing me?" Myles asked, troubled.

"Ah, cutting right to the *root* of the problem," Allen said, proud of his untimely pun.

The moment was shattered again, however, by the unmistakable sound of a snout burrowing into the depths of his flopped open pack. With a groan, Allen sprang from his chair again, rescuing the bag from Beira's intrusive exploration.

"What?" he questioned the gluttonous dragon. "Have you not eaten since the last time I was here?"

He rummaged through the pack's contents, extracting a large beet and bit off its long root. Returning to the table, he tossed the beet towards Beira for her to eat. Her head dipped to the side, causing the airborne vegetable to thud harmlessly on the floor behind her. It sat there, unwanted by everyone in the room. Allen stared at the dragon; his eyes narrowed.

Beira, for her part, met his gaze with an indifferent expression.

 He directed his attention back to Myles. "Anyway, from what I can tell, those two men were mercenaries. Hired hands employed to find you."

"But why me?" What would they want with me?" Myles demanded a clear answer.

Allen appeared more serious now. "Myles, you are not from the outer world. You were born here in Escalia. I was the one who took you to the outside world." Myles sat stunned.

Allen paused to think of what to say next, "A while ago, our fold...or group... well, it was disbanded. I came here to this cabin now and again in my travels. One night, years later, Beira heard something outside. She woke me up, and when we looked, there you were. On this very cabin's porch, with a letter from your father, who..."

"You know my father?!" Myles couldn't get the words out fast enough. He shot up from his chair, the strangeness of the cabin was forgotten and replaced by a desperate yearning. All these years, he'd been told his parents died tragically, shortly after his birth.

"Do you know my mother too?" he pressed. "Are... are they here? Can we find them?" Allen held up his hands in a pacifying gesture, urging Myles to quell his excitement.

"Myles, sit down," Allen said gently, his voice firm yet calming. "Let me explain..." Allen slowly nodded. "Yes, I knew your father. But it had been many years since I had seen him before you showed up. The only thing you had with you besides the blanket you were wrapped in, was your compass, and..." Allen rummaged through his pack, "this letter from your father."

Allen produced a small cylinder. He flipped open the top, revealing a rolled piece of parchment, its edges wrinkled with age. He extended it towards Myles.

Myles' hands, damp with nervous sweat, reached out to accept the offered document. He unfurled the paper with trembling fingers. A jumble of emotions warred within him. Taking a deep breath, he began to read aloud, his voice barely a whisper above the crackling flames.

Dear Algernod,

Hello again, old friend. This is our child, Mylo. Our beloved son.

My soul is heavy with grief while having to write this letter and face the reality of what comes next. I'm sorry for encumbering you, my friend. There is no one else Indra and I trust more with the burden of protecting Mylo's future, our future, than you. Please, care for our child with your life, take him far away and let no one know where you are. We will come for him when it is safe.

If my worst fears come true, please be sure to guide him to his birthright. I leave with you his passage, and this compass. It is our hope these items will guide him back to us someday. I wish there was more time to explain. Please teach him as you did me.

"The storm is short, the valley is wide, the mountain is tall, destiny inside. During his darkest of hours, in the light he shall hide."

~ Haldor

Mylo,

If you ever read this, please know you are more precious to us than life itself. My heart aches for you, and for what this means for our family, but I know you will be safe. Please wait for us, hold us in your heart as you will always be in ours. Even now, we are forever so proud of you, our beloved son.

With all of our love,

~ Your father and mother, Haldor and Indra Bridger

Chapter Five

Civilization

Myles was dumbfounded. A single tear dropped to the letter, accidentally smearing a bit of the ink next to another similar dried stain.

"If my parents are still alive, why did they not come for me?" Myles looked up from the letter. "My parents, where are they now? Are they...?" but he couldn't finish.

Allen tried to answer with the warmest hope he could muster, "I don't know, Myles. But I will find out. Mark my words." Allen took back the letter, carefully rolled the parchment and tucked it back into its protective sleeve.

"So...my name is Mylo?" Myles asked.

Allen nodded, "Mylo is the name your parents gave you. I had to improvise a little. Best to keep going by Myles for now though, I'd say."

Allen handed the letter back to Myles knowing he would treasure it, "I think this best stays in your care."

Allen attempted to redirect the room's mood, "But for now, let's try to get you some rest. You have been through quite the ordeal tonight." The sudden shift pulled Myles back from his contemplative spiral.

"Alright, let's see here," Allen muttered.

He delved back into his pack, emerging with two packed peanut butter and jam sandwiches. He placed one on the table before Myles, "Eat up, your body needs something in it after all that."

An ominous slurp sounded from the corner of the room. Myles could feel Beira's large yellow eyes burning into his skull.

Myles took a bite to be polite, but his emotional state made it hard to eat. Across the room, Beira stretched her long neck, sniffing in Myles' direction.

A sharp snap from Allen's fingers sent Beira's head whipping back. Her gaze darted between the boy's sandwich and Allen. Allen, eyebrows raised, met her stare. Admitting defeat, he tore his own, tossing half to Beira. The dragon snatched it midair, a satisfied snort rumbling from her throat.

Myles watched as Allen transformed a dusty cloth into a hammock strung between wall hooks. Two blankets, retrieved from a creaking cupboard, completed the makeshift bed.

"I know you still have many questions. We'll be able to talk more tomorrow in length, but for now, you need to get some rest. I will be back around first light, I think. I need to go and gather a couple things. But you will be safe here tonight."

"Can't I come with you?" asked Myles.

"Not yet, get some rest. It must be well past midnight by now."

Allen took the remaining sandwich from Myles, placed it on the table, and escorted him to the low hanging hammock. It dipped slightly, but the blankets offered surprising comfort. Myles burrowed in, the swaying motion and crackling fire lulling him towards sleep surprisingly quickly.

Allen pried up one of the floorboards. "Again, I'll be back in just a few hours. You should be plenty safe inside this cabin."

He reached into his bag and pulled out the hexagon shaped key once more, placing it into a hole in the floor. A metallic click echoed through the cabin, followed by Allen lifting a trap door. Myles watched in surprise as Beira was able to squeeze her body down into the space below. Allen took a few steps downward and grabbed the open trap door.

He offered a reassuring smile, "We'll be back before you know it." With that, he descended into the hidden chamber, pulling the trap door shut behind him with a heavy thud.

Several hours passed. The fire smoldered out into a couple glowing coals. Not knowing he was asleep, Myles turned over to try to find a more comfortable position. He shifted, but the hammock betrayed him, flipping him onto the unforgiving floorboards. A jolt of pain chased away the remnants of sleep and left him blinking owlishly on the floor.

Allen and Beira were still gone. He got to his feet and approached the closed trapdoor. He pulled on the handle.

Locked, he thought, *I figured.* The sleep he'd had now brought clarity. *It must be a tunnel that leads somewhere, not just a basement.*

He glanced towards the window. Moonlight still bathed the outside world, but a dim orange glow pulsed from the adjacent window. Stretching his back, he raised his arms high, and a putrid odor assaulted his nostrils. The repulsive, fishy reek of the Gatekeeper's saliva seemed to have intensified.

Despite the smell, his stomach rumbled. Glancing at the table, he spotted the remnants of his sandwich. He reached for it, but clumsily knocked it off the table, landing peanut butter side down.

"Ugh... of course," Myles scoffed as he knelt to pick it up.

Half the jam and peanut butter clung to the floor. There was a smattering of dust now stuck to the bread, but Myles managed to finish the few remaining bites, dust and all. He heard a sudden rustling from the weeds outside.

They're back, Myles thought. He hurried over to the window, but he could not see them. The clearing revealed nothing but swaying weeds, a large stone, and the looming silhouettes of trees. As he continued to watch, the large boulder began to lumber. Myles could now see that this was no rock. *It's a dragon, I think...*

Unlike Beira's sleek form, this dragon was a creature of brute strength. Its back, a vast dome, was plated with armor-like stone, each individual scale seemingly chiseled from the earth itself. The neck, short and powerful, connected seamlessly to the massive head held low to the ground. Its tail, finishing in a boney club.

The dragon lifted its head, nostrils flaring as it sniffed the air. Twin tusks curved down from its powerful jaw. This was no graceful predator, but a walking fortress.

It's searching for something, Myles thought.

The dragon kept meandering forward until it bopped its nose on a large stump. It shook off the impact in frustration.

Maybe it's a nocturnal dragon that mostly uses smell to navigate, he thought.

The dragon sniffed his way to the edge of the cabin, following around the outer wall.

As the dragon lumbered around the building, it disappeared from view. Myles darted to the opposite window waiting for the dragon to reappear. But instead, a slow creaking sound arose behind him.

The dragon had nudged the front door ajar with one of its tusks. Myles realized the door wasn't latched. He'd assumed it was closed and locked after seeing Beira slap it with her tail.

With one more swipe of the dragon's tusk, the door swung wide open. Myles spun around to face the intruder. The hexagon shaped door was just wide enough for the creature to crawl through.

The dragon stood squarely in the cabin's only exit. Myles was fixed in place. It appeared the dragon didn't see him, or if it did, paid no attention. He stealthily tiptoed backwards, towards the furthest corner. His only hope was to lure the dragon in further, then sneak around the creature to the open door.

The dragon, oblivious, continued slowly walking forward, sniffing the stale air. It lumbered towards the table and chairs in the middle of the room. Myles saw his opening and stepped ever so lightly towards the direction of the door, hugging the wall.

At that moment, the dragon slammed its thick head into the table and chairs, sending them sliding into a tangled barricade, blocking Myles' escape route.

Myles questioned whether the dragon deliberately ensnared him, but the dragon paid Myles no mind. The creature slurped up the peanut butter remnants from the floor.

Myles' desperate glance around the room revealed jumping over the shifted table was his only option. But before he could move, the dragon's head snapped towards him, nostrils flaring.

Instinct took over. Myles stumbled backwards, one foot stepping onto a rickety bench against the wall, the other precariously balanced on a stack of buckets.

Myles strained to press himself flatter against the rough wood of the windowsill. He glanced downwards, meeting the gaze of the dragon directly. Two enormous eyes, clouded and milky white from the reflected moonlight, stared back.

The beast's relentless sniffing continued. Myles feared the dragon would snap at him at any moment. Its breath washed over him in waves, just like Beira the day before.

In a flash of inspiration, Myles fumbled in his pocket and retrieved the one remaining smashed daffodil. He stretched his arm down, the flower clutched in his sweaty palm. He could almost reach the dragon's massive snout. As Myles strained, disaster struck.

The precarious stack of buckets toppled over causing Myles to tumble forward. He dropped down towards the dragon. His outstretched hand was swallowed up as it slipped directly into one of the dragon's nostrils. A strangled yelp tore from his throat as both he and the dragon recoiled violently. He inspected his hand, now covered in a thick slime, but the flower was gone.

The dragon's enormous snout wrinkled in disgust. Myles knew what was coming next. The dragon sneezed an expulsion of snot and mucus. Its entire body convulsed, turning its back on him as its hammering tail sent a clatter of tools tumbling from the walls. The dragon staggered wildly as it braced for the next sneeze.

With a surge of adrenaline, Myles sprang onto the table. The dragon let out another forceful sneeze. This time its tail swung low, shattering the legs of the table. The tabletop buckled. Myles fell with it, sending him crashing to the floor in a heap. The air pressed from his lungs as he landed hard on his stomach. Myles lunged toward the open door, staying low to the ground.

The sound of another mighty sneeze roared in the cabin. The club-like tail swung over Myles' head with a deafening whoosh, a near miss that sent a jolt of terror through him. He leapt through the open door just a few feet away.

Myles scrambled around the corner of the cabin and stopped. The forest stretched out before him, an unknown labyrinth cloaked in darkness. He turned back towards the cabin. His eyes darted around, searching for escape. Knowing the dragon could emerge at any moment, he found a thick vine crawling up the side of the structure and started climbing. His fingers scrambled at the rough bark. He kicked his legs against the wall, propelling himself upwards. With a final burst of strength, he hauled himself over the edge of the roof, collapsing onto his back, the sounds of the dragon's frustrated sneezes echoing from within.

Moments later, the dragon meandered out of the front door, monstrous sneezes still erupting as it thrust its tail. The poor allergic creature retreated leaving a trail of destruction as it burrowed its way back through the tree line and out of sight.

Myles stared at the sky above, half was now lit up in a beautiful golden yellow as it started overcoming the darkness. In the direction of the light, Myles could see the line of sunshine light up the landscape off in the distance, but he could see no sun. The sunlight slowly moved its way closer. When he looked up, he could still only see the moon, directly above, floating in a bifurcated sea of yellow and purple.

The chirping of birds drifted up from the unseen trees. Surveying the horizon, he could see the Gatekeeper's lake and the dirt path leading away to a small town. The mountains loomed majestically, farmlands met a desert's edge, and a distant town boasted tall buildings. In the opposite direction, a sliver of blue sea peeked through trees.

Myles observed the first rays of warm sunlight touch the cabin. He glanced down, his shadow was directly beneath him. A natural impulse drew his gaze skyward again. The brilliance of the newly arrived sun blinded him, a sliver of its light bleeding into the space previously occupied by the moon. There, in a celestial dance, hung the waning moon, a reluctant companion to the birthing sun.

Through the broken window, he heard a frantic voice, "Myles? Myles!"

Allen burst from the cabin, followed by Beira's snout pressed to the ground, sniffing.

"I'm up here," Myles answered, relieved.

Allen spun around, spotting him on the rooftop. "Thank goodness." A sigh of relief escaped his lips. "What happened? Are you okay?"

"I'm fine. A giant stone-like dragon barged in the front door looking for food. The door wasn't latched."

Allen whipped his eyes toward Beira who pretended to be occupied by a particularly interesting patch of grass.

Allen let out another sigh, "Well I'm glad you're alright. Is it gone now?"

"Yes, it went that way," Myles pointed off into the forest. Allen could see the trail of destruction left in its wake. "Hang on," Myles said, "I'll be right down."

He descended the vines to the ground. When he came around the corner of the cabin, he noticed Allen had changed his attire. Allen no longer wore his usual blue jeans and flannel shirt. He was now clad in a black, V-necked top that was tied with a loose string, baring more chest hair than Myles cared to see. Overlaying the shirt was a reptilian-skinned vest, a leather belt, dark pants, and boots with more straps than a horse's satchel. This was all covered by a large brown hooded cloak, accompanied by several large pouches around the back of his waist.

As Myles approached, he couldn't help but smell an aroma of delectable baked goods. Beira could obviously smell it too, as she hovered around Allen's bag.

"I got you something." Allen produced a pair of honey glazed pastries, nestled beside two hard-boiled eggs. Myles stared, his mouth watering.

"Here, eat up, kid," Allen said, swatting Beira away from his breakfast with a tap on the nose. "Finish up your breakfast and we'll get you cleaned."

Myles began devouring the pastries, much like Beira and her beef.

Allen, pastry in hand, lured Beira around the back of the cabin. They arrived at a curious contraption that vaguely resembled a teepee. A meshed sphere crowned the upper half, surrounded by panels of glass.

"Alright girl, you know what to do," Allen gestured.

Beira lifted her head and released her brilliant blue flames up at the mesh ball. Ice began forming on the mesh crafting a sphere of snowy ice. Myles, with his mouth slightly open, assumed he would never be bored of seeing Beira's flames. Allen pulled out a hanging curtain.

Myles looked confused while almost choking on an egg.

"It's a shower," Allen said as if this was an obvious fact. "Mind you, it will probably be the coldest shower you've ever had. But it'll toughen you up—and get rid of that fishy smell."

Sunbeams radiated off the glass, melting the snowy ball. The melted water started dripping until the drips became a proper trickle.

"Better get in there," Allen prodded, a hint of amusement in his voice. Clearly, Allen himself had enjoyed a cleansing ritual while they were apart, but Myles doubted it involved a bracing ice bath.

Myles approached the contraption, pulled the curtain shut, and began shedding his grimy clothes.

Before hopping under the trickling water, Myles asked, "So... what's the plan today?" Myles reached out a tentative hand to touch the water but recoiled. The water felt inhumanly cold. "Are we going to try and find my parents?"

"Afraid not, kid," answered Allen. "I will go out and search for your parents. You have a different path ahead."

Myles mustered up his courage and thrust his body under the falling water. "What? Why?" he squeaked.

Allen chuckled, "The water stings a bit, doesn't it?"

"I'm coming with you," Myles demanded. "We are finding my parents together." He tried hard to hide his chattering teeth.

"No kid. Don't you remember what your parents' letter said? I, Algernod—and don't you dare to ever call me that—am supposed to guide you to your birthright."

Myles tried to recall the letter, but he was too distracted by his body's convulsions.

"Oh yeah, what did that mean?" he stammered, his teeth still chattering uncontrollably.

Allen tossed a towel over the curtain, which landed squarely on Myles' head.

Allen then hung some fresh clothing over the curtain rod, "When you're dried off, put these on."

There was a pause in the conversation while Myles frantically dried himself for warmth. Then Allen spoke very clearly, "Myles, you were born with the blaze... a marking, there on your chest."

Myles dropped his gaze, "My birthmark?" There, on his right collarbone, nestled the dark brown mark, shaped very plainly like a potato.

"That's no birthmark... that's your blaze, or *burn* as some call it. You were born with the right to make a Nexus connection. Just like me, with Beira. And that mark on your chest proves it."

Myles, half-dressed, finished clasping the belt and threw the curtains open, wide-eyed, "I will be connected to a dragon?"

Allen walked up to him, "You will. And all because of that blaze on your chest." He slapped the mark on Myles' collarbone. The pain was amplified by the cold, causing Myles to gasp, but he bit back a yelp, determined not to give Allen the satisfaction.

Allen, however, saw straight through this facade and smirked, "I thought we had another year before your Ruach started radiating, but you can't argue with destiny. Wish you'd given me a little warning first, though. Your timing is terrible."

"My Ruach?" Myles questioned. "I have Ruach too?"

"Well, of course," Allen boasted. "You were born in this world, after all. In the outer world, you were hidden when you were young. But now that you are of age, your blazed body is radiating Ruach. My guess is that's how those other two found you.

"In this world, everything has Ruach flowing through it, so you are well hidden, but in the outer world, you burn like a flame in the dead of night. It would be even easier to track you if you bled, too. It's like the Ruach oozes out of your body."

Myles thought hard, "My finger... I pricked my finger. Just before the bearded man chased me, I pricked my finger while sewing a doll for Marguerite."

"That would do it. No wonder they found you."

Myles' disposition suddenly changed. "What about the others?" he asked. "What about Ms. Helen and the other children?"

"That old crone?" Allen blustered. "They are all fine. I feel bad for the poor soul who had to face off with hellish Helen. What was his name? Mordred... I think?" Allen laughed.

"What do you mean? Was Ms. Helen attacked, like me?"

"Well, I wouldn't say 'attacked,' maybe more 'bothered.' To be honest, I was surprised when both of those men came back through the gateway. She must be getting soft in her old age."

"I don't understand."

"Helen is a Nexus wielder too, kid," Allen explained. "A powerful one at that, at least when she was younger."

"Ms. Helen has a dragon? And... and powers?" Myles asked in disbelief.

"She did ensear with an egg, same as me, but dragons don't stay with their humans. Even Beira left for a while, didn't you girl?"

Beira sprawled luxuriously in a patch of warm sunlight and pushed out an apathetic snort.

"Anyways, Helen was the one who trained me, when I was just a pup."

"Ms. Helen trained you?" inquired Myles.

"That she did," Allen answered, "and she was even more abrasive back then. So you got nothing to worry about. I'm positive Helen got the fire under control. And hey... worse case, she is using my house as the orphanage now. Seeing as how we aren't going back anytime soon."

Allen caught a glimpse of Myles' expression, the swirling despair and loss.

"Tell you what," Allen attempted to cheer the boy up, "let's solve this little mystery of ours and get those hoodlums off your back, then let's go back out there together and visit."

Myles picked his chin up, "Yeah, that would be great."

As Myles finished dressing, he finally examined his ensemble. It was similar to Allen's, with a mix of unconventional patterns and materials. Allen completed the outfit for him with a black-rimmed, double-pointed wool hat and a pair of leather boots.

"How do I look?" Myles asked.

"Unrecognizable," Allen said, pleased with himself.

Allen locked the cabin door with his hexagon key. Beira, who was still bathing in the sunlight, jolted awake at the sound. Ears perked, tail thumping, she turned towards Allen, expecting a treat. However, her excited demeanor quickly faded as she realized it was time to head out.

"Let's get moving, we have a long way to go," Allen charged.

"Where are we going?" asked Myles.

Allen secured his bags on Beira with ropes, "Caldarian City. To get you signed up for your Nexus training."

"Now?" asked Myles. "But I don't know anything about Ruach... or dragons. I'm not ready for that."

"Exactly. That's why they call it training." Allen climbed onto Beira's back, like a workhorse. "It would have been easier if we had more time, but you had to go and awaken just before the academy year started."

"Academy? Is that the birthright my father wrote about?"

"As close as I could figure. You were born with a blaze marking, so you were born with the birthright of a Nexus."

"Does everyone in this world have a marking?"

"No... not in the slightest. Even in this world, being born a blazed is a very rare gifting. Very few are given this honor," Allen said, as he outstretched his hand towards Myles.

The bewildered boy grasped Allen's hand, as Allen pulled him up onto Beira behind him. Two little clicks from Allen's mouth and off Beira started to trot.

As they rode through the woods, traversing trees and shrubs, Myles continued to ponder what type of dragon he might bond with as he adjusted between Beira's painfully pointy spikes. After what felt like hours of riding, they stopped for water by a crystal-clear creek.

Myles seized the opportunity, "Mr. Allen, I haven't seen the sun move at all."

"And you won't," Allen casually answered, downing a canteen of water. "The sun is always at the center of the sky; it doesn't move like in the outerworld."

"Never?" inquired Myles.

"Our sun is located in the middle of the earth, much like the earth's core you were taught about."

"But that's where the moon was last night?" Myles questioned.

Allen searched for the words, "Think of the sun like a yolk..." he picked a smooth pebble from the ground, "and the moon is the egg's shell."

He then cupped his hand around the pebble, floating it around the stone. "There is a massive hole in one end of the shell which allows the sunlight to pour outward. The shell rotates around the sun."

He turned his cupped hand around the pebble, half the time showing the pebble to Myles, half the time blocking the pebble from sight. "As the shell's hole rotates around the sun, it shines the sunlight in different places. This gives us our days and nights."

After this rudimentary explanation, they mounted Beira again with moans and groans, to press on.

Typically, Myles had good bearings, but with a sun that never rises or sets, he quickly realized he had no idea which direction they were heading. He reached inside his shirt and opened his father's compass.

To his surprise, the compass seemed to be working. The needle spun freely, settling on a fixed point behind them.

"My compass works," expressed Myles.

"Well of course it does," stated Allen, "it is from this world after all."

A newfound respect for the instrument bloomed in Myles' mind. *Compasses must be important to this world,* he thought, clutching the device tighter.

Their journey was punctuated by frequent rest stops. They found streams of running water to refill their canisters and refresh their bodies. Myles was able to glimpse all sorts of wildlife—many types of birds and lizards, squirrels rummaging for food, a skunk, and even a small herd of deer.

One particular creature captivated Myles more than the others. It was a brown hare, not unlike the rabbits he knew from the farm, but sporting a pair of miniature antlers on its head. Unfortunately, Beira's imposing presence spooked the creature, sending it darting back into the safety of a hollowed-out tree.

Despite the plethora of creatures and lush plant life Myles encountered during their journey, the pace remained brisk, falling short of his desire to explore.

Exhausted after a day's hard ride, they emerged from the dense forest into a clear valley. The sight that greeted them was a breathtaking panorama. A patchwork of cultivated fields lay before them, a sign of civilization amidst the wild. To their right, however, the landscape took a dramatic turn. A desolate desert, dotted with abandoned buildings and windmills and dried up streams, stretching towards the horizon.

In the distance, Myles could start to make out what seemed like a colossal wall, nestled at the foot of steep mountains.

The closer they drew, the more the rural landscape gave way to the organized sprawl of civilization. Scattered farms and open fields yielded to a denser concentration of houses and buildings. Allen nudged Beira into a leisurely stroll. Children shrieked with laughter, chasing each other through the streets. Adults bustled about, engrossed in their daily routines.

The town materialized before them, a web of buildings that ended at a colossal iron gate. Fortified walls, seemingly endless, snaked away on either side.

Four guards stood vigilant at the gate, clad in a uniform of dark tunics with plated armor rippling across their torsos. Their armadillo-like helmets gleamed obscuring their faces. One guard, distinguished by gold accents on his tunic and helmet, stood apart from the others. Allen dismounted Beira, helped Myles down, and approached.

Good morning, sirs," Allen greeted with a respectful nod. "We seek passage to the Feylux Academy."

Silence stretched between them. The guards scrutinized Allen. Their gazes lingered on the large scaled beast before them. Finally, the lead guard spoke.

"Where hails your party from?" he questioned, his gaze flickering between Allen and the dragon.

"A small farming community outside of Porkuss," Allen replied calmly.

The guardsman cocked his head, "Never heard of a galliant hailing from Porkuss before." he questioned.

But Allen just laughed, "No... no galliant here. Not all of us are gifted enough to pass the trials. I was just lucky enough to be born blazed, but live a humble life. However, I do have another for training." Allen elbowed back, hitting Myles in the arm.

"Hello sir," Myles nervously bursted.

Allen instructed, "Go ahead son, show them your blaze."

"Oh," Myles said as he wrestled his collar down to bear his birthmark. The guard glanced at his marking and then approached curiously. He reached out his gloved hand, and rubbed Myles's birthmark with his finger as if he expected it to rub off. Seemingly satisfied, he nodded his head to his fellow men in arms and gestured for Allen and Myles to pass.

Then he turned back to Allen, "The dragon stays."

"Is there a problem?" asked Allen.

"Only dragons approved by the parliament and members of a fold are allowed to enter at this time."

Not wanting to argue or raise suspicion, Allen walked over to Beira's head and told her to wait at the edge of the woods. "When you smell my scent approaching, come find me," he whispered. Allen softly tapped her on the neck. She turned back the way they came.

Myles was sad to see her go. She was the first dragon he had ever known and gotten to enjoy learning about. The guard gestured again for Myles and Allen to proceed. The road became paved with cobblestones and mortar. Myles' destiny seemed to solidify before him, as they entered through the town gates.

Chapter Six

Rumors and Rumbles

A gasping "whoa" escaped Myles' lips as he followed Allen down the bustling cobbled road.

Buildings rose on either side. Sturdy structures of stone and timber prevailed. Signs hung proudly above each doorway—blacksmiths, leather and scale workers, taverns, bakeries, and delis. Other shops with more unique banners piqued Myles' curiosity — Ebenezer Stones, Crafting Materials, and Potion Supplies. There was a sign for The First Dragon's Breath Cafe, followed shortly down the road by The Original Dragon's Breath Cafe.

Some signs seemed ordinary while others were lit by flaming letters. Lanterns were strung between buildings, powered by flaming stones. A network of rope lines crisscrossed overhead, ferrying goods in a silent ballet, connected to gears and levers.

"Did we travel into the past?" Myles asked. "Like a different timeline?"

Amused, Allen dismissed Myles' inquiry. "No, nothing like that. Escalia just doesn't have the same technologies your world has grown so dependent on. We have found... other means, of cultivating and using energy. I would guesstimate we are about a couple hundred years, or so, behind the outer world's development."

Myles lagged behind Allen, spinning in a clumsy circle to take it all in, until someone plowed into him. Myles found himself slumped on the cobblestones, with a skinny boy sprawled over him. The boy, who couldn't have been older than Myles, nervously scrambled to his feet.

The boy turned to look behind him, flicking his blonde wispy hair out of his eyes, revealing a wide-eyed look of concern. His clothes mirrored Myles' attire, but more worn and patched.

Just then, three figures rounded the corner. Two other boys, the smaller being the apparent leader, and a bouncy-haired girl glided up to them. Their ages seemed comparable.

"Aw, did poor little Hick fall?" the smaller boy called out with a sneer.

The fallen boy shot back, "I'm fine, Xander," as he inched back toward the group.

Xander and his two companions apathetically snickered. Xander, even amongst his taller companions, held himself with an air of unearned superiority. His brown hair was meticulously combed, each strand in place as if sculpted by Ms. Helen herself.

His clothes were pristine, tailored to fit him perfectly, adorned with more buttons and frills than a fancy quilt. Big, wide eyes dominated his smallish face, giving him a perpetually surprised expression.

His companions were similarly garbed. The girl stepped forward, her fiery red hair cascading down her back in long pigtails. She wore a dress that exploded with ruffles.

"Did the poor farm boy find a friend to cling to?" She shifted her attention to Myles. "At least this one didn't roll in the dirt after buying commoner's apparel." Her round face, accented by a cute button nose, tilted upwards, mirroring Xander's self-importance.

Instinctively Myles stood tall, "No one told me the circus was in town today. When is your performance? I can't wait to see it so I can throw fruit from the stands." The boy beside Myles shrunk into his collar.

"How dare you," Xander said accusatorially. "I do not believe I have witnessed your presence in the Chiliagon before, dear ill-mannered boy, but you shall learn that proper respect must be shown when nobility walks in your midst."

"The way I see it, respect should go both ways," Myles replied. But before Myles could square up with the small-statured oppressor, Allen stepped in front, pushing Myles back.

"I do apologize, my young masters. This is my nephew. He is from the outer reaches of the countryside. He has never seen, much less interacted with such statured nobility. Please pardon his embarrassing attempts at taunting, as I know his ignorance has fallen on gracious and forgiving aristocrats," Allen half bowed.

"If I weren't such an upstanding peer of the realm, I would see him flogged; however, seeing as he is being piloted by a respectable gentleman, I will let you divvy up his punishment and education. Though I tell you, be swift." The boy lifted his nose high enough to touch the clouds.

"Indeed, my poor nephew has always been a slow one. But rest assured, I will brand the lesson on him like a blaze."

"Boys like these being blessed with a blaze? Ha..." Xander forced an outward laugh, "that would cause the death of the kingdom," he said as the three chuckled.

Xander, the girl, and the other boy turned away and waved Allen off. Allen watched them until they were out of sight.

"What is wrong with you?" Allen spun around grabbing Myles' shirt. "You know nothing about this place, yet you stick your nose where you have no business." Allen's frustration scared both Myles and the boy next to him. "You need to keep a low profile. Remember why we are here."

Myles tried to defend his position, "But they were being..."

Allen cut him off, "I know what they were, but it had nothing to do with you."

"I'm sorry," Myles yielded, "I'll be more careful, I promise." Allen loosened his grip and sighed.

The boy next to them mustered his bravery, "Th... thank you. I know you shouldn't have tried to help me but thank you. I have never seen anyone step up to those three like that before."

Allen regained his compassion, "Are you okay, son?" he asked the boy.

"Oh yes, I'm used to it. It happens a lot. I tend to..." he paused, "annoy people."

"Still, that doesn't make it right," said Myles, reaching out his hand. "I'm Myles, it's nice to meet you."

"Oh... uh, my name is Hickalik," he said, shaking the offered hand.

"It's nice to meet you, Hickalik," nodded Allen.

Hickalik hesitantly asked, "Would it be alright if I could follow you two for a bit? Just until I know the others are a ways away."

"Sure kid," Allen answered as he turned and started walking further into town.

Myles and Hickalik walked side by side behind Allen. Myles was excited about the opportunity to strike up a conversation with a person from another world, "Did you grow up here in the city?"

"Oh no, I mean, I grew up in the kingdom's region, but I am from a small farming community. We come to the town to sell crops and get supplies."

"Is that why you are here today?"

"Well... uh... you see..." Hickalik struggled to find the words.

"It's okay, you don't have to tell me."

Myles' gazed darted around and settled on a distant landmark, "What are those?" he asked, pointing toward three towering structures on the other side of the city, in front of the mountain cliffs.

"The towers?" Hickalik asked with a hint of surprise. "Those are the three towers of Feylux Academy." Hickalik answered almost proudly. "They are the newer towers built a couple decades ago, designed by a famous stone craftsman who was commissioned to rebuild the academy. Pretty neat, though, huh?"

"Yeah, they look huge," Myles looked on in amazement.

Hickalik continued on, "Well, the academy is world-renowned. It's kind of the heart of Caldarian City. Most businesses here are centered around supporting the blazed and galliants, or at least taking advantage of their fame."

"I heard my uncle say that word earlier. What is a galliant?"

Hickalik was shocked, "A galliant. Really? You don't know?

Myles felt silly now for asking.

Thankfully, Hickalik did not mind filling in the gaps as a hint of glee sparked in his eyes. "Galliants are the heroes and protectors of our land. They're the ones blessed with a Nexus dragon. They complete quests that are too dangerous for normal people and solve mysteries too hard for local authorities."

Hickalik's enthusiasm was infectious, leading Myles to want to know more, "Are they like the military?"

"No, not at all. There are local police and kingdom soldiers of course, but the galliants work outside those authorities. They work in one of the region's folds and are overseen by the Parliament of Dragons.

"What's a fold? I heard about those too," Myles found himself drawn deeper.

Hickalik, now beaming, "folds?! Folds are amazing. You can only become a galliant if you're accepted into one of the six folds. Each one is vastly different from the others."

Before Myles could ask another question, Allen halted in the middle of the roadway. Hickalik and Myles both bumped into Allen's backside. They peered around Allen and saw a gathering of people obstructing the road ahead.

Allen turned back to the boys, "I'll find out what's going on." He pushed his way through the crowd, snaking between shoulders. Myles and Hickalik followed, barely squeezing behind Allen.

They arrived at the front of the gathering, only to be stopped cold. Their eyes fell downward. A line of flickering gray flames snaked across the ground, cutting off a circle around the front steps of a building. The building looked important with large columns, ornate architecture, and large diamond shaped doors. The citizens stood behind the flame line. On the steps were two men addressing the townsfolk.

A man yelled from the anxious crowd, "What about their blazes?"

This was followed by a lady who cried out, "How do we protect the children?"

The man on the steps, donned in a pristine white uniform adorned with gold and red metals, cleared his throat, "As I said, we are doing everything in our power to locate the persons responsible for these disappearances. We have been fortunate to have the children returned thus far. However, we cannot assume this will continue to be the case."

A disgruntled voice ripped through the crowd, demanding an answer, "And what about the stolen blazes?" The uniformed man stiffened, his expression hardening as he stared in the direction of the outburst. An unsettling silence descended upon the gathering, frightening the naysayer into submission.

The authoritative man continued, "Once the perpetrators are apprehended, we will do whatever it takes to restore the children's blazes. As your Chief Officer, I will be joining this investigation personally. We will find the person or persons responsible and bring them before you." The chief's weighted words quelled the crowd's anxiety.

But one nearby man was not so easily muzzled, "That's all fine and dandy, Chief Gorthin, but empty valor and words protect no one. These are our children's lives and futures at stake, the future of many promising galliants to be." The man pointed behind himself at the academy towers, "We have the kingdom's finest within our walls, yet these atrocities persist." The man stepped over the gray flames to interject his thoughts further. As he did, the gray flames whooshed around the man's ankle, chaining his foot to the ground. The man struggled to free his shackled appendage.

The chief addressed the man, "Mr. Thorn, I can assure you, we are looking into all possibilities. Now, would you graciously step back behind the line?" The chief gently waved his hand toward the ground, and the flames retracted from the man's ankle. Mr. Thorn stepped away, thankful to regain his leg.

"Now, Feylux Academy has offered to contribute some of their most proficient pedagogues, masters of their own powerful and unique flames, to help investigate. Also, the parliament has seen fit to assign one of their safety advisors to assist and evaluate the city's safety measures."

Myles leaned in toward Hickalik and asked, "What's a *ped-a-gog*?

"The academy professors. Most are past galliants who have retired."

Chief Gorthin turned and presented a man, simple and thin in appearance, wearing a high-collared suit standing in the building's shadow behind him. The man stepped forward casually, appreciating the attention of the gathered onlookers.

"Hello, Caldarian City. I am the safety advisor for the Parliament of Dragons." He gestured a pitiful bow. "The name's Getz, Tiberius Getz," he announced, licking his bucked tooth. "This investigation will come to a conclusion soon enough, I'm sure."

A voice, sharp with skepticism, cut through to challenge his words, "How can you be sure?"

Mr. Getz glared, "Because, good sir..." he grimaced, "as I said, I am Mr. Getz. And I get... what I want."

He continued, quickly regaining his composure and ignoring the interruption, "I will cooperate with the pedagogues, or your decorated chief, or whomever they so choose..." Then he muttered, "Not that it will change anything. To be honest, I don't see what the big fuss is about. All the children are returned. No one was harmed in the end."

Grumbles arose from the crowd like a disgruntled chorus, faces contorted in anger.

"For now though, I own this investigation. And I pray you all remember that at its conclusion." The man turned away and settled back underneath the roof's shade.

Sensing the mood souring rapidly, Chief Gorthin stepped back in, "Yes, well... thank you, Advisor," while under his breath, he muttered a barely audible, "for nothing."

He attempted to regain some semblance of control. "In the meantime, please go home and wait for news on the matter. If anyone has any information about these incidents, please contact us immediately."

With a curt wave of his hand, the line of gray flames flickered out. The chief and the advisor retreated back into the building behind. The crowd dispersed with a lingering sense of unease and unanswered questions. Conversations, laced with worry and suspicion, chattered through the air.

Allen was the first to speak out loud, "That's news."

"What is?" Myles asked.

"Well, seems the townsfolk don't have the same faith in the academy or the parliament as I remember. Things have changed a bit since I'd last stepped foot in this city. Nevermind that, it changes nothing. We need to find a place to stay for the night."

Hickalik spoke up bashfully, "I should be heading out too. Thank you, though... for helping me earlier. And for letting me tag along for a bit." He started walking off, but called back to Myles and Allen, "Hope to see you again soon." And with that, Myles' new and only friend in this world disappeared into the still jostling crowd.

Allen led Myles through more cobbled pathways until eventually they came to The Fold's Fortune Inn, its name proudly displayed on a carved wooden sign. Allen, ever the pragmatist, made a direct line for the bookkeeper at the front desk. The innkeeper was explaining no vacancies were available due to the time of year. This did not faze Allen, as he started to haggle and bargain with the receptionist.

An older man came to speak with Allen from a backroom. He scooted in front of the inn's logbooks, shuffling the worker out of his way, and erased some of the writing on the ledger. The little man then filled in the now blank space and gestured for Allen to follow him down the corridor.

"Myles, let's go." Allen called back.

The old man ushered Allen and Myles towards a peculiar elevator tucked away in a corner of the lobby. A whirring of gears and a rhythmic groan filled the air as the elevator lurched into motion. At the top, the old man, his face twinkling with amusement, handed Allen a golden key, "Only the best for our blessed."

Allen thanked the old man as he descended back down, then looked at the golden key: "Room 508."

They located their room and stepped inside. Myles' jaw dropped, "This is bigger than the entire orphanage."

Rich, linen drapes framed the windows, and gold accents shimmered on everything from furniture to rugs. Each piece boasted intricate dragon carvings. Towering windows offered an immaculate view of the city, with the three central towers dominating the cityscape.

"Get comfy," Allen told him. "I'll take the bed. You can have the sofa for the night."

The sky darkened orange, then purple. Myles busied himself with arranging the pillows on the plush sofa. Allen had retreated to the bathroom for a cleansing soak.

After taking turns bathing and gorging themselves on a decadent buffet, compliments of the Inn, Myles and Allen called it a night. The couch was the most comfortable thing Myles had ever felt. Allen snapped his fingers and the lights in the room faded out. As Myles laid in the dark, he revisited what he learned during the day's events.

"Mr. Binford..." he started to ask.

"Just Allen," Allen slapped back.

"Sorry... but, am I going to become a galliant?"

Allen sighed from the darkness on the other side of the room, "That is entirely up to you, kid. But be warned, the life of a galliant can be difficult and very lonely. It is not for everyone... nor should it be."

Chapter Seven

Registration and Regulation

A thunderous roar shattered the tranquility of sleep, shaking the building. The chandelier chimes sang while they shook. Myles launched himself off the couch. His panicked state was interrupted by Allen's boisterous laugh, standing at the window, "The old boy's still got it," he boasted.

Myles walked up behind Allen to join him at the window. He looked up at the yellow morning, where blimps hovered overhead. Just then, a large shadow swooped by the window, causing Myles to instinctively flinch.

The building shook again, but Allen didn't move a muscle. He looked on with pride. It was a large dark dragon, with outstretched wings and two hind legs. With a final beat of its mighty wings, the dragon landed atop the tallest of the three central towers.

Allen pointed. "That is Zalaph. The Nexus dragon to the provost of the academy, Rhetta Prudencia."

"It's huge," Myles breathed.

"He is indeed, at least twice as big as Beira, and a crafty one in battle too."

A series of colored fireballs shot upward from the academy grounds, exploding in a majesty of colored flames in the morning sky.

"Well, kid, are you ready to start your training?" Allen asked, watching the revelries.

Myles answered with unease, "I guess so."

"You guess?" Allen questioned back, humored, "We are going to have to work on that confidence a bit more. But I get it, until two days ago you didn't even know about this world... or dragons."

They packed their bags and ate what leftovers they could from the night's feast. As they left their room and walked down the corridor, Myles heard an obtuse voice from behind, "Who let filth like you into this establishment?"

Myles whipped around to find Xander emerging from another room, accompanied by a snobbish looking couple. The man, impeccably dressed in a maroon suit and sporting a neatly trimmed beard, glared at Myles with disdain. The woman, slender and elegant with auburn hair in an elaborate updo, mirrored his icy demeanor. She had a pointy chin and high cheekbones too, equivalent to Xander's.

"Mother, father, this is the insufferable young boy I told you about," Xander explained. The man looked down at Myles while holding his chin elevated, "Seems this establishment has no standards anymore."

"Why are you here?" Xander asked Myles, now more curious than condescending.

Allen interjected, "Same reason as you lot, I presume."

"Don't be absurd. You shall presume nothing," the father denounced, "The House of Bane has always produced some of the kingdom's most prestigious. We are here to indoctrinate our son into our illustrious ranks, not just to watch the festivities from the sidelines."

Allen seemed to like the confrontation: " It seems our reasons are one and the same. This here is my ah... nephew, Myles Briggs. We were just on our way to register him for the academy."

"Him?" Xander questioned. "The friend of the farmer boy?" Xander and his parents chuckled. "Is he even burned, or did you simply rub some dirt on his skin?"

Wanting to do anything to upset Xander, Myles pulled his collar down, revealing his birthmark. But to Myles' surprise, the threesome let out a roaring laugh.

"Is that painted on?" they jested, "That is much too dark to be a blaze." After seeing this, Xander pulled his collar over his shoulder, exposing a lighter brown splotch. Xander's father quickly slapped Xander on the side of the arm with his cane.

"Put that away," he hissed, now serious again, "You have nothing to prove to these simpletons. Besides, I doubt that blaze is even real. No Nexus will be made with a muddy stain like that."

Then the father turned his attention to Allen, inquisitively, "What house do you hail from?" he inquired.

"That question will have to wait for another day, my Lord," Allen replied in sarcastic reverence, "We wouldn't want to be late for registration day. I would hate for the House of Bane to lose face for such a trivial reason."

"Indeed," the father agreed begrudgingly, "this is a waste of our time. Come Xander." The father said as they turned away towards the elevators.

Myles questioned Allen, "Why did you antagonize them? I thought you told me to keep a low profile."

"That was before I knew you'd be going to training with that runt. No sense in keeping the secret now since we're headed to the same place. Also, yesterday's lesson was for you, not me. I am allowed to be as condescending as I'd like." Allen dropped to one knee and met the boy's eyes, "Once you start training, you're on your own. I will not be there to protect you."

"You mean you're leaving me? Today?"

"Parents and guardians don't stay with their children when they go to Feylux," Allen answered. "And as we've spoken about before, I have my own tasks to accomplish. You'll be fine. And I will try to write soon with news of my exploits."

Outside, the air thrummed with electric excitement, a palpable buzz for the approaching registration day. Merchants touted their wares as families hurried their children. High above, the colossal dragon, Zalaph, made another majestic sweep across the sky. Children, wide-eyed with awe, pointed and gasped at the magnificent creature.

Cobblestone crunched beneath their feet as they navigated the bustling streets, eventually emerging into a large clearing. The heart of this plaza was dominated by a magnificent tree. The tree's trunk had grown in a way that mirrored a dragon's body, with its willowing branches reaching out like wings to the sky. A wide path, bisecting the courtyard, led to a tunnel directly beneath the tree's colossal form.

Allen steered Myles straight for the center. A long line of participants snaked to a booth. Myles spotted Xander a few contenders ahead, standing confidently beside his haughty-looking parents.

Allen's hand rested reassuringly on Myles' shoulder, "Now remember Myles, you are here to go through training. The academy will supply everything you need. I went ahead and sent in some money to your account if you find a need."

"Thank you," Myles said, surprised.

"Whilst at the Academy, obey the rules and keep a low profile. Getting mixed up in someone else's drama will not benefit us in the slightest."

Myles nodded, then looked ahead. Left of the path, stood a series of twelve elevated seats. A man, regal in a flowing purple robe adorned with an insignia on the left side of his chest, rose to his feet.

"Who is that?" Myles whispered, nudging Allen.

The man's air of authority was undeniable, "Ah, that's Sylas Dragoon," Allen explained. "He is the chancellor of the Parliament of Dragons. All twelve of those seated there make up the parliament, you see. High-ranking nobility."

"The group that oversees the folds?" Myles inquired, remembering what Hickalik told him.

"Yes, now hush."

Chancellor Dragoon held up a crystal-gray stone to his lips. The stone amplified his voice across the entire courtyard.

"Citizens of Caldarian City, thank you for joining us once again on this memorable occasion. These young men and women you see before you today signify the future and hope for our prosperous kingdom. Let us all welcome them with enthusiasm, anticipating their bravery and perseverance to come. And, for those of you who are walking the path set before you, our hearts are filled with hope and gratitude. We pray that the flames will forever burn bright in your hearts. Now, without further ado, let us welcome our new recruits."

The crowd boomed with cheering amongst the falling petals, as a young woman confidently strode down the central path.

"Hailing from the House of Gunther..." an announcer's voice rang out, "Aberdeen Gunther."

Myles shifted, craning his neck for a better view. *That's the girl from yesterday with Xander.* But gone were the frilly clothes. Today, she sported a flowing robe emblazoned with her family crest.

Aberdeen, the very picture of elegance, acknowledged the cheering throng with gracious waves and practiced smiles. As she neared the chancellor's seat, Sylas Dragoon himself rose to greet her. A brief exchange of words followed. With a final, confident nod towards the chancellor, Aberdeen continued her walk, disappearing beneath the colossal tree.

"Hailing from the House of Lobtail... Bach Lobtail."

The crowd continued to applaud, though less energetically than they did for Aberdeen. Myles recognized this boy as well; the taller, quiet boy from yesterday, who shadowed Xander.

Then, "From the House of Bane..." The announcer paused for dramatic effect, "Xander Bane."

The people bellowed with even more vigor, I guessed the Banes are a big deal, Myles thought.

Xander slowly strode down the path, waving dismissively at the crowds as if he must appease the people. Myles looked on but was distracted by a young boy being dragged out of the booth and carried away by two of the onsite guards.

"It's real," the boy exclaimed. "My blaze is real! What are you doing?" The guard paid no attention to this and continued to drag him away.

Some of the nearby applicants mocked. "Some commoners will do anything to steal glory for themselves," one boy chuckled. Panic clenched Myles, as he pulled his collar down to inspect his dark birthmark again.

Name after name was announced as participants paraded down the path. Myles was next to step into the registration booth. He swung open the entry curtain and stepped inside and then stopped still.

The boy who was in front of Myles in line now faced Myles. He had his trousers pulled down, exposing his posterior to the evaluator at the table. He made eye contact with Myles and immediately turned red. He quickly pulled his pants back up to his waist and cinched his belt as respectfully as he could.

"Oh... ah, sorry." Myles panicked nervously.

The boy hastily tucked his shirt back into his pants. "Blessed, like myself, do not get to choose where they are blazed," the boy explained.

"I wasn't judging," Myles said nervously. The boy finished pressing his clothes and finessing his shoulder length hair. He regained the rest of his composure before stepping back out of the booth.

"From the House of Lemont, Sigurd Lemont," the announcer declared.

It was now Myles' turn to step up to the registration table. A tiny elderly woman sat in a raised chair. "Name and house?" she asked with her head down, pen hovering over the legal documents.

"Myles... from the House of Briggs."

She shakily glanced up at him, perplexed. She looked over at Allen.

"He's a distant nephew, from a more common region," Allen explained.

The worker looked unsure through her bifocals, but continued, "Your blaze?"

Myles pulled down his collar. She squinted as she leaned forward to investigate, elongating her stub of a neck. She stretched toward Myles, licked her thumb and rubbed the marking.

The lady reclined back to her chair looking puzzled, "Signal the tower," she grumbled to one of the men standing behind her.

"Is there a problem?" asked Allen.

"No... just confirming Mr. Briggs' acceptance to the academy," she explained.

Allen tried to reason. "I assure you, it's quite real."

She gestured to the exit drape that led to the courtyard path, "Would you both please proceed for me?"

They stepped out of the booth and onto the courtyard. All eyes were fixed on them. This time, there was no announcement, no roar from the crowds. Myles could hear the faint whispers on the wind. He took one step forward to continue, but Allen grabbed his shoulder, halting him in place.

In a flash, they were cast into darkness. A swirling vortex of wind almost knocked Myles off his feet. The large gray dragon, Zalaph, had plunged down and landed just in front of them. The chatter of the crowd died into an awestruck silence.

An eagle-shaped head crowned his powerful neck, its surface adorned with menacing spikes and elaborate frills that trailed down his spine. Scales, shimmering in hues of dark silver and gray seemed to absorb the remaining sunlight, casting a massive inky shadow.

The dragon's eye fixated on Myles, seeing the half uncovered dark blaze, from under his shirt. It outstretched its neck while producing a low, clicking hiss. It lifted its chin and took a large inhaling sniff of Myles' hair, then pulled back and cocked its head curiously, looking as surprised as a threatening lizard could.

Zalaph turned to Allen, who raised his eyebrows gently and gave a subtle nod. The beast looked back at Myles. They locked eyes. Zalaph's eyes were pitch black, with long slender white pupils. Then the dragon's body relaxed. It casually walked to the side of the path and sat down.

Sounding flustered this time, the announcer's voice rang out once more, "Hailing from the House of Briggs... Myles Briggs."

A few questionable claps came from the crowd. Allen grabbed Myles by the shoulder and turned the boy to face him.

"This is the path your parents set before you. Do not doubt yourself... your heart, or who you are. Have courage in every decision you make. You will be well cared for here. Be proud of this. I know your parents and I both are."

And with that, Allen turned him around to face his future. He gave Myles a good smack on the back, jolting his body forward. He walked hesitantly at first but picked up speed as he continued. Zalaph whooshed back up into the air behind Myles, flapping his wings to soar back to his perch. After watching the dragon, the crowd returned its gaze to Myles. Some clapping started to grow a little.

A few people from the crowd even called out, "Good luck, Myles," and, "Way to go, kid."

Myles walked until he reached Chancellor Dragoon. The chancellor stood up out of his chair and outstretched his hand. Appreciative of this gesture, Myles took the outstretched hand and shook.

The chancellor was an older gentleman with a kind face. He had a longer shaped beard that continued down from his chin, but always kept its shape, like the white wool of a sheep. His robe was made of fine glistening materials with an emblem on the left side of his chest, showing twelve dragons biting each other's tail in a circle, with six stars in the center.

The chancellor used his other hand to prop himself up with a beautiful golden cane. The handle was shaped like a dragon holding a fiery red orb in its jaw. He showed a proud face, "We will all be watching you, Mr. Briggs. I look forward to seeing what you are capable of." He then pointed down the remaining path to the tree.

Myles glanced back at Allen one last time, who gave a trusting nod. Myles reciprocated a less confident nod back, then resumed towards the illustrious tree and walked through. On the other side of the tunnel were all the other participants in a clearing, waiting in front of a flaming gate.

"Myles?" A voice questioned from behind.

Myles turned, "Hickalik," he burst out, ecstatic to see his friend.

"I didn't know you were burned, too?" Hickalik questioned, relieved to see a friendly face.

"That's why Mr. Allen... my uncle... brought me to this city. But what about you? You didn't say anything about it either."

"Sorry," Hickalik apologized. "I tried to keep it hidden. I always thought the other boys and girls in town would mock me if I showed them. But that's great that you are here. Would it be alright if I tagged along with you?"

"Only if you can teach me about everything I don't know," Myles said jokingly.

Hickalik's demeanor shriveled, "Oh, I can do that... I guess."

"I was kidding," Myles urged. "You don't have to teach me anything," he explained, trying to correct his mistaken humor. "You are the only person I know here as well."

Hickalik perked back up, "Oh, really? Sorry, I'm used to others using me, then just ignoring me."

"That's terrible."

"It's okay, I don't really wanna be friends with them either. Being commonly born makes it hard for me to find others to befriend in the capital."

"Poppycock," came a voice beside them, "A person's status should come from the labor of their efforts, not their place of birth."

It was the boy from the registration booth earlier, "I plan to earn my status in life, and not just accept my family's reputation as my own."

"You were in front of me in the line, weren't you?" Myles asked.

A blush crept to his face, "Y-yes, that's right," he stammered, eager to move on. He reached his hand out to Hickalik, "Sigurd Lemont, the honor is mine."

Hickalik was untrusting of his respectful attitude and grasped Sigurd's hand hesitantly, "Hickalik... Hickalik Milbred."

"The pleasure is mine." Sigurd turned to Myles to reach out again, "And you are?"

They shook hands. "Myles Briggs. So, are you from a noble house too?" Myles asked curiously.

"In a way, yes," Sigurd answered, trying to sound humble.

"And, in a way... not in the slightest," Xander, who had overheard, walked up with Bach and Aberdeen in tow. "He is a noble by riches only, not by power or rank."

"Ahh yes... Xander. I heard you were enrolling this year," Sigurd addressed the verbal intruder.

Aberdeen stood with her hands folded together, "You may have wealth, but your blood is still impoverished. You do not have Ruach-rich blood coursing through your veins." Although her words were piercing, she made them sound sweet.

"Pish posh, blood has nothing to do with power or success," countered Sigurd. "Just look at these two fine gentlemen," he threw his arms over Myles and Hickalik.

Xander cackled, "I believe your statement is counterintuitive."

"Thank you," answered Sigurd, not understanding this to be an insult.

Xander rolled his eyes, "The doof, the farmer boy, and the boy with the dark smudge. Your true colors will be publicized soon enough." He looked back to Sigurd, "I look forward to proving you lot wrong this year... not that it will take that long."

Before any of them could argue further, "Look out!"

A black ball of fire was plummeting down. As they looked up, it was too late. The flames impacted, swirling with a whirlwind of black winds. The blackness expanded outward encasing them from all sides.

Myles opened his eyes to find them surrounded in a dome of swirling black flames. He looked at his hands, to his surprise, he could see clearly in the absence of light. He scanned the darkness and could see the other children as well. No one was hurt by the flames, or the impact. But the group was all they could see. Blackness had engulfed their surroundings, the ground, the sky, everything.

A hole swirled open on one side of the black room, and the outside daylight poured in. A lone figure stood in the opening, a stark silhouette. As their eyes adjusted, the children made out the form of an older woman, tall and imposing. Her wide-brimmed hat curled downwards like a fantastical seashell. A long, shimmering robe flowed down her form, its color morphing in the light. In her hand, she grasped a dark wooden staff with sharp, fang-like teeth inlaid into the wood. Myles immediately had a flashback of Ms. Helen.

"My dear hatchlings," she spoke softer than they anticipated, "you have been incubating for far long enough. Today marks the day you will emerge from your shells and evolve into something greater. I am Rhetta Prudencia, the current interim provost to the Feylux Academy. You may already know my partner, Zalaph of the shadow."

As if on cue, a loud roar rang out through the darkness.

"Do not fear him; you are now kin to his eyes. He will only see to protect and watch over you. I expect remarkable things from you all. Some come from established lineage, while others will fight to prove their worth more than most. Nevertheless, you all stand here as equals at this moment, having accomplished nothing and having everything to gain."

The provost slowly flicked a few of her fingers. Two smaller archways expanded open on either side. To her right stood a man. His golden-brown hair, meticulously groomed and short, framed a face dominated by a black eye patch that shrouded his right eye. A fitted robe adorned with intricate gold stitching was draped over his broad shoulders. He held his head high, a cleft chin jutted out. But Myles' attention was immediately drawn to the absence of his right hand.

Completing this trio was a woman who stood on the other side of the provost, dwarfing everyone. She mirrored the man's attire, clad in a white robe embroidered with the same gold thread. Unlike her companion, however, her arms were bare, revealing incredible musculature beneath. Her dark hair, tightly braided on either side of her head, flowed into a thick ponytail that swung down her back. Every line of her body spoke of raw power, a force of nature contained within a human form.

"Let me introduce you to your tower wardens, Gareth Petroff and Matilda Managol. Should you have any pressing matters, these will be your associated advocates. Ladies, please follow Warden Managol, and gentlemen, you shall be escorted to the Tower of Wisdom by Warden Petroff."

With that, the darkness burned away, revealing the daylight once again. In front of them perched Zalaph on the top of the institute's gates. He glided down beside the provost. She climbed onto his back as the beast assisted her with his wing.

She faced the children one last time, this time seeing Myles in the crowd. "Welcome all, to your destiny." Zalaph leapt up in a flurry of dust and flew her toward the center tower.

"Alright, little ones, let's get a move on," commanded the towering warden. She and Warden Petroff led them through the dissolving flames of the gate as the children soaked in the spectacle.

The sight that greeted them was nothing short of breathtaking. Three colossal towers, each seemingly scraping the heavens. Their bases converged into a massive stone building. An ornate bridge, a ribbon of intricately carved stone, led away from the building, spanning a wide, sparkling river.

The academy grounds sprawled before them. Lush green fields stretched out, dotted with what appeared to be training grounds, some enclosed with domed cages. Patches of woodlands provided a tranquil contrast, while smaller buildings and huts hinted at the vast infrastructure. Myles' gaze spun, glimpsing the walls that encircled the academy grounds.

"Come on Myles," Hickalik said, pulling at his arm. "Let's go. I've waited my whole life to see this."

Chapter Eight

Welcome to Feylux

The new students trailed their newly appointed wardens up the ramped bridge. They came to a large, thick wooden door. Warden Petroff placed his hand inside an etched circle on the door. With a loud creak, the doors groaned open of their own accord.

The children gasped as the doors revealed a grand foyer. Towering stone pillars were paired with dark wooden archways and trusses. Large hovering chandeliers glistened with flowing flames burning within. The stained-glass windows, awash in vibrant colors, depicted heroic battles and mythical creatures.

"Ladies, follow me," directed Warden Managol. "Boys, head that way," she said, pointing in the opposite direction. Behind their wardens, the children marveled at the displays lining the corridors—depictions of illuminated spears, hammers, swords, and bows and arrows. Glass display boxes contained the hilts and handles of weapons.

One extensive display, which was particularly captivating, showcased an entire ecosystem encased within a translucent wall. Lush greenery thrived, miniature waterfalls cascaded, and creatures unlike anything Myles had ever encountered roamed within—even a creature he could only describe as a horned fish-frog.

"Those are dangerous to touch," Hickalik informed. "They secrete a toxic slime that is absorbed through the skin. They say it will make you hallucinate for days. They call them poisonous pufkins."

The creature sneered and lunged at the glass, making Myles flinch, then feel silly. Reaching the hallway's end, the students saw rows of stone pedestals, one for each student, topped with a soft, sandy surface.

"Place your right hand on the top of a pedestal," Warden Petroff instructed.

Once the last hand was placed, the fine sand started to tremble and bubble. A shrill scream came from the front of the line. Xander's hand was pulled into the sand up to his elbow. As the other boys looked down the row they too were pulled in just as swiftly.

They felt movement around their buried hands, pressure, like a snake slithering between their fingers. Some of the boys squirmed, desperately trying to pull their arms free. Upon release, Xander fell backward. All hands were freed. Their ring fingers were now adorned with a strange metal hexagonal ring topped with three divots.

"What is the meaning of this?" protested Xander as he scrambled back to his feet. "Some kind of practical joke? I did not concede to having my appendages bound to wear such gaudy jewelry."

"This is how all students are granted access," Warden Petroff calmly informed. "Do you wish to withdraw your enrollment, Mr. Bane?"

"Of course not," Xander answered, trying to regain his composure. "A little warning would have been nice, that's all."

One boy smiled while pointing at the warden's missing hand, "Did one of the pedestals forget to release your hand?" He scanned the room, expecting to see appreciation for his humor, but no one dared.

"Gavin Dafton, I believe," Petroff addressed. "Please step forward so we can test your theory."

Gavin cautiously stepped forward. Petroff gently placed his hand behind Gavin's head and dropped his chin to look Gavin in the eyes, "A pedestal did not take my hand. I have the utmost faith in the institution's safeguards for all their students." He pulled Gavin's head in closer and whispered in his ear, "Hold your breath."

Petroff thrust Gavin's face into the sand, burying his head like an ostrich. Gavin tried to free himself with muffled grunts and a flailing body.

Disregarding the distraction, Warden Petroff went on to explain, "These rings are your keys to the academy. They will grant you entry to any place you are allowed as first years, including your sleeping quarters."

Gavin's legs kicked faster. Ignoring this, Petroff continued, "These rings have been endowed with your individual schedules. There are three indents on the top of the ring. If you have somewhere to be and are not close enough to travel to the location within the allotted time, the rings will start to warm. This will be your reminder... to move. Hold your ring up in line with the hallways. When all three indents are lit aglow, the ring is pointing in the right direction. Simply follow the ring to where you are supposed to be."

Gavin's head popped out of the sand, gasping for air. A new fan-dangled ring was pierced through his earlobe.

Petroff casually returned his attention to Gavin, "It suits you... like a cattle tag," he remarked.

This time snickers were heard from the group as Gavin tried to take the ring off his ear.

"Sir?" asked a taller boy in the back.

"Mr. Hughes," Petroff acknowledged.

 "What will happen if we don't follow our schedule?"

"Then you will see how hot the ring can get," Petroff foreboded.

He turned and placed his own black ring in the center of the knob, and it clicked to the door like a magnet. Petroff pushed open the heavy door with a groan of aged wood, "Three to a room. I don't much care with whom you choose to partner."

Myles craned his neck, taking in the space. Unlike the grandeur of the foyer, this room held a more utilitarian feel. Arched doorways led off in various directions, hinting at the individual sleeping quarters beyond, as well as bathrooms, study rooms, and game rooms.

The boys scattered like rats. Some inspected the firmness of the beds; others surveyed the window views.

Witnessing Xander head left, Myles and Hickalik instinctively went right. The beds were being claimed with haste. The second room they peeked into still advertised two available beds. They entered to find Sigurd testing his pillows and mattress by the closest bed.

"Hello again," Sigurd greeted. "You are more than welcome to bunk with me if you'd like," he offered, "but I have been told I snore a little since I broke my nose a few years back."

"That won't bother me," Myles said, shaking his head. "I grew up with one of the loudest snorers you have ever heard," he said, thinking semi-fondly of Franklin.

"And I have slept with actual pigs," Hickalik confessed, making them all chuckle.

"I don't think I'm that bad," said Sigurd. Myles and Hickalik approached their beds.

"Place your ring on the headboard," Sigurd instructed.

Hickalik pressed his ring against the wooden headboard. Orange flames scorched from his ring across the headboard, spelling out "Hickalik Milbred." The boys were mesmerized by the scorching flames.

"Do yours," Hickalik said excitedly. Myles approached the bed near the window and placed his ring on the wood. Flames burrowed across the headboard once again. Myles stood still, not knowing what to say.

"Mylo Bridger?" Sigurd read aloud.

"Yes, sorry. I just go by Myles, though," Myles deflected. "Would you mind if I used your extra pillows? I like to sleep propped up," Myles asked Hickalik.

"Sure, here," Hickalik handed a couple of pillows to Myles, who used them to cover most of the seared name.

Warden Petroff's loud, commanding voice echoed from the common room: "If you all have found your accommodations, gather for instructions... now."

Petroff waited for the last of the stragglers to join. "You are now free to explore the grounds until the feast," Petroff announced as the group chattered excitedly.

"With many exceptions," he continued. "You are not to go outside. You are not to go up any towers. You are not to go into the basements. You are not to go near the ladies' dormitories. You are not to go anywhere your rings do not grant you access."

Xander rolled his eyes, "Is there anywhere we are allowed to go?" he asked in a patronizing tone.

"Yes, Mr. Bane. You are allowed to go anywhere I did not just mention."

He addressed the group again, "Inside your dresser drawers you will find your uniforms. Change your attire and we shall see you in the refectory. Are there any further questions?"

Myles raised his hand sheepishly, "What's a refectory?" he asked.

"The great hall... where we eat our meals." Warden Petroff simplified. The warden glanced around the room one more time with narrowed, untrusting eyes, then turned and exited.

Immediately, every boy darted to unveil their uniforms and change. The uniforms were made of dull gray satin material, with black pants and boots. The embroidered designs were silver with a hexagon over the left breast. But the uniforms were oversized, much too long and too wide.

"What is this?" called out Gavin from the common room as the boys all emerged in oversized uniforms, sleeves dangling over their hands. "We look like children wearing our father's clothes," he said, still messing with his new ear piercing.

Xander's friend Bach was trying his best to adjust the clothing to find a better fit. While doing so, his ring brushed the inside of the hexagon-shaped insignia. His uniform burst into a green fire, engulfing him in flames. He let out a whimpering scream but then noticed the flames did not burn.

The other boys watched in amazement as the clothes burned shorter, smaller. The pant legs and sleeves crept backward to a perfect length. The waistline shrank to fit, and the boots shrank to his appropriate foot size.

Xander was next to place his ring inside the empty crest as if trying to prove he knew what to do all along. Again, the uniform burst into a dull green flame, shrinking to his perfect petite size. Gavin looked to his roommate, Gordon Hughes, standing next to him, who was much taller. Gavin slapped Gordon's crest. Yet again, the flames engulfed, but this time, shrinking the clothes far shorter and tighter than appropriate for someone of Gordon's size. The group laughed at the ridiculous sight.

"You are all such children," Xander belittled. He led Bach as they exited the room with their noses turned up.

Gordon placed his ring over his crest to correct the shortened uniform, but nothing happened. He pressed his hand against his chest again, still nothing.

"I guess it's not one size fits all," Gavin teased. Gordon then smacked Gavin's chest, igniting him and shrinking the uniform, although still obscenely long for Gavin's smaller stature. As Gavin and Gordon hastily undressed to switch uniforms, the rest of the boys ignited their ensembles one by one to reveal perfectly fitting outfits.

Excitement crackled as the new students burst into a flurry of exploration. Sigurd decided to join with Myles and Hickalik. Their first stop was a large, sunlit billiards room. Next, the library beckoned with its floor-to-ceiling bookshelves on every wall, pillar, and column. They discovered gymnasiums, a verdant greenhouse, and numerous locked doors their rings did not open. They explored until a warm tingle was felt on their fingers.

"It must be time for the welcome feast," Hickalik recalled.

They lifted their rings in line with the hallway, but nothing happened. As they turned around, the indents on the ring lit up with all three divots.

"This way," Myles led, following his ring.

The trio passed through two semi-spherical doors into the vast room. The great hall was capped with a translucent dome ceiling, revealing the purple-tinged dusk outside.

Hickalik yanked Myles toward the first-year section. An amoeba-shaped table awaited, extending out in peninsulas around the room. Their centers boasted a network of rotating belts conveying plates and bowls of cuisine for selection. The boys sat down together. Myles watched a parade of food on display—turkey legs, pasta, bread, steaks, vegetables, glazed hams—even pancakes and waffles.

As Myles watched, his focus shifted to a girl sitting adjacent to him, staring directly at him. Her fingers were interlaced over her lips, elbows on the table, eyes squinting with curiosity.

"What's it going to be, newbie?" she questioned.

Myles didn't understand, "Excuse me?"

"I said, what's it going to be, newbie? First decision you will make at the academy; don't mess it up." She continued to glare across the table as the food swayed between them.

Myles frantically scanned the approaching menu. Hickalik and Sigurd were no help as they were busy making their selections. Myles looked back, but the girl's gaze did not falter. Without thinking, he reached for the first item he could reach with both hands, but the plate stuck to the conveyor. It nearly took Myles with it as the plate continued down the belt.

Noticing his friend nearly kidnapped by a dinner plate, Hickalik instructed with his mouth full, "Your ring... Use your ring."

Myles looked at his right hand and his newly procured ring. He reached out for another plate, this time not gripping as tightly. The plate was stuck firm, but when his ring made contact, it dislodged from the conveyor.

"Pancake balls and eggs for the new awkward kid," the girl announced. "I approve of the genre, but I'm a waffle girl myself." She picked up a giant waffle, covered it in peanut butter and slathered it in syrup.

"Kamara Kingsley," she introduced. "It's fun seeing uncomfortable people squirm. That cringe-worthy performance will get me through the rest of the night," she said, showing no empathy.

"Myles. A pleasure to meet you?" He replied, not meaning for this to sound like a question.

Myles now noticed that she was a pretty girl with a soft face, a darker complexion, brown eyes flecked with gold, and hazel-highlighted hair. She glanced at Hickalik and Sigurd, "Why were you three almost late? Not much for rule-following, I see."

Hickalik heard the question. He forced too large of a bite, nearly choking, then fumbled a few words, "You see, we huh... were exploring... I mean, looking..."

But before he could fit the rest of his foot into his mouth, Kamara interrupted, "I actually don't care." She took another unnecessarily large bite of her dripping waffle, "I am happy to say you two might be the most socially inept pair of barely passable humans here."

Hickalik and Myles felt sad for a moment, not living up to her standards. She continued, "That settles it. We will be friends for the remainder of this academic prison sentence. Your sheer awkwardness alone will give me entertainment for months."

"We aren't awkward," Hickalik protested.

Kamara smirked a little and gave a tiny nod, "The fact that you believe that makes this so much sweeter. You two are going to need my help, for sure, if you want to survive this place."

Hickalik, being shyer in nature, and Myles, feeling lost in his newly bestowed double life, both looked at each other and said, "We accept."

"What are we accepting?" Sigurd chimed in while patting the corners of his mouth with his tucked-in napkin.

"We made a friend?" Hickalik answered, also not meaning to sound questioning.

"Excuse me, gentle-boys, I must use the ladies' lavatory," Kamara said as she stood up.

As she walked away, Sigurd leaned closer to the other two. "Best be careful around that one, gents."

"Why's that?" Myles asked.

"She's not as lady-like as you might think. I heard a couple of boys were out playing wibbly in the town courtyard a few weeks ago, but they wouldn't let her play. She baited a couple snuffels to the fields. Needless to say, the boys got sprayed good. They reeked for a week straight. Couldn't even sleep in their own homes, the smell was so bad. The city officials are still trying to eradicate the snuffel infestation. The fields were closed off to everyone. She's an awful one, that one."

"She doesn't seem that bad," Myles defended, "I'd say those boys had it coming." Confusion settled on Myles, "What's a snuffel?"

Hickalik took this question, "A snuffel is a large slug-like animal. They burrow underground. And when they reach their destination, they come up to the surface and spray their pheromones in every direction. It helps them defend against predators and attract other snuffels at the same time." Then Hickalik stood up, "I need to use the facilities as well. Be right back."

Myles pondered for a moment then asked Sigurd, "But how did she attract the snuffels in the first place?" Myles asked.

Sigurd thought on this for a moment. "I have no idea," Sigurd said, realizing he did not have an answer for this.

Two strong knocks rang out across the room as Provost Prudencia struck the floor with her staff. The room fell almost fearfully silent as the audience turned. She and the other faculty stood on a raised platform, along with the tower wardens.

"Welcome, one and all, to another year. May your Nexus be strong and true. I am pleased to see so many returning faces and so many new ones bursting with potential."

"I know this will be a year of achievement as your hard work will see you excel beyond your own limitations. But first, a special thanks to the Landsbury estate this year for donating all the necessary student literature. Their generosity will help support your ever-burning futures." The hall filled with the thunder of clapping, with a couple of thank you's thrown out.

Xander's annoyed voice piped up from somewhere behind. "And the peasants cheer," he disparagingly narrated. "I was unaware the Landsburys had any capital left to lose," he mocked.

"Good on the Landsburys," Sigurd applauded approvingly, "keeping up with charity during rough times. A top-notch display." Hickalik clapped as well, returning to his seat next to Myles.

Provost Prudencia held up her hand to quiet the hall, "This was not a cheap investment to make in your future, and I'm sure you each will have the opportunity to thank the Landsbury house in time. You shall find your books assigned to you in your dormitories upon your return. Do not let this generous gesture go to waste."

"To our returning third-years: good luck on your sponsored year. Work hard, and do not disappoint your respective endorsers. For those of you who have free training privileges on the grounds, the forest training arenas will be off-limits for the time being."

A couple of disappointed moans were heard from the far corner of the room.

"To our returning second-years: hone the use of your attributes and show your unique skills this year in your trials. Demonstrate your potential, then surpass it."

"And finally, to our newest recruits, be ever watchful. Learn from those who have come before you and succeeded. Not all of you will remain in the short time to come."

Myles felt the provost was staring straight at him. "Choose bravery over fear, and wisdom over luck, but above all else, guard your heart, for everything you do flows from it."

"Lastly, also for the first years," she continued, "due to weather patterns and current geological events, the Harvest has been moved up and will occur in one month's time. Unite your mind and heart as one, and ready yourself, so you might be chosen."

"And with that, we will officially kick off the beginning of this year's academics. Welcome to Feylux Academy." The provost gave one last clap of her staff. Fireballs were sent into the night sky, bursting into every color outside the translucent ceiling.

"Oo, wow," Kamara sarcastically commented, "colorful fireballs, how original."

"When did she get back?" whispered Hickalik.

Myles shrugged.

After finishing only half the food on his plate, Myles placed the plate back on the conveyor belt. Almost immediately, the plate was struck by a wet-whipping object, and it disappeared in an instant. The first years jumped, except for Kamara.

"Up there," pointed Hickalik. Atop the side pillars stood amphibious gargoyles. They were the same color as the walls and pillars, so most of the first-years immediately mistook them for statues. Their chameleon-like eyes could look in any direction. They had a large bulging throat that grew larger as they consumed the dirty dinner plates. Anytime a student placed discarded food on the conveyors, a long tongue whipped from their mouths, stuck to the plate, and reeled in the grimy dishes.

"They're bulrogs," exclaimed Hickalik. "I've never seen one in person. They can camouflage themselves in any environment, their tongues can lash out at 100 meters per second, and they secrete acidic saliva that can dissolve its prey, bones and all."

As the painted night sky died down and more dinner plates were snatched by the bulrogs, the students started to head back towards their dormitories.

"We had best get back to our rooms, too," Hickalik advised. "Classes start tomorrow, and we should probably get a head start on our reading."

The boys said goodnight to Kamara, who didn't pay much attention to their politeness, then they went back towards the dormitories.

As the boys started walking down the corridor, Myles stopped. He had stepped into a large puddle. Looking around, he found a hole shattered in one of the large glass ecosystems.

"I don't remember seeing that before," commented Sigurd.

"The broken glass could hurt the animals," said Hickalik. He reached his hand into the glass case and started picking some of the larger shards of glass out of the plants.

Just then, a high-pitched scream from down the hall pierced the air.

"There's a lady in trouble," announced Sigurd. He stood heroically, ready to jump to action. But it was not a lady. It was Xander's friend, Bach.

He barreled down the hallway, howling nonsense. "The hand hole! The hand hole! Watch, just watch. They grabbed me." He continued to bellow while running past. A hunched woman was chasing him. She was older and had uncapped hair. Her long brown coat had many tears and rips, fastened to her thin frame with a utility belt filled with various tools. She carried a large net strapped to her back.

"The pufkins are out again," she grunted as she chased after Bach, who was still screaming.

"Who was that?" asked Myles.

"That was Ms. Blumpkin," answered Hickalik. "She takes care of all the animals and beasts on the grounds. She's not on the faculty, but she is an expert in zoology. I have two of her published books at home. Although, she looked a little more civilized in her author illustration."

"Did she say the pufkins were out again?" asked Sigurd.

"You don't think he touched one, do you?" inquired Myles.

Hickalik answered, "That would explain the outburst and why Ms. Blumkin is involved."

"Poor fella," said Sigurd.

When the three boys returned to their sleeping quarters, Sigurd stopped after entering the room, "Do you two smell something burning?"

Myles ripped the pillows off his headboard. The headboard was seared from one end to the other with branch-like burns leading out from one corner. All that remained legible were the letters "M. Y. L."

"This is unacceptable," protested Sigurd. "I will demand that you get a new headboard immediately."

Myles stopped him, "No, no, please. It's fine. It was probably just a malfunction with the headboard's design," he said, not knowing how the headboard necessarily worked.

"But what if it combusts again?" Sigurd asserted.

"What happened, happened. I really don't mind," Myles hoped Sigurd would drop the topic. "Besides, I think it looks kinda neat. The smell is almost gone anyways."

Sigurd seemed to be calming down, "You're a little different, Myles. But I respect that."

In preparation for their first day of class, they focused on their new academic books piled high on the dressers. They scrutinized the literature. Myles was staggered by the intricacy of each book. There was a book on herpetology covered with hard scales, like the ones he felt on Beira. At the center was a reptilian-looking eye.

Myles dropped the book on the floor with a thud. Sigurd and Hickalik whipped around.

"It blinked," Myles stated, not looking away. They waited for several seconds, but nothing happened.

"Myles, you're being paranoid," Sigurd insisted with a light chuckle.

Myles decided to open the book and face the eye down on the bed. The book was filled with information about different types of dragons and large reptile creatures. It had categories based on color, size, type, and abilities.

He placed the herpetology book on his nightstand and selected the next largest book, "Ebenezer Artistry, Imbuing Ruach for All." Its cover had a large clear stone in the middle and was lined with gold embossing. He placed the Ebenezer artistry book over the herpetology book to hide the eerily watching eye.

The three boys tried to read at least the first chapter of each book. But the adrenaline of the first day was wearing off. One by one, they fell asleep while reading in their beds, ill-prepared for tomorrow's lessons.

Chapter Nine

School of Ruach

A sliver of sunlight filtered through stained glass. Myles thought he'd slept in until noon based on the direction of the sunlight.

Hickalik and Sigurd began to rustle as well. Myles gave a big stretch. "Ouch," he recoiled. He had a sharp pain on his finger. The others felt it, too. Their rings were warming up. Their eyes widened as bedding was thrown into the air. All three scrambled out of bed. They had slept in.

"Books," remembered Hickalik. They shoved their books into the academy bags and raced out of the dormitories. Conveniently, they'd fallen asleep still wearing their uniforms. When they came to a four-way intersection in the halls, their rings pointed them in different directions.

Myles followed his ring straight and left his friends behind to follow their own paths. The hallways were filled with chaotic first years. Students ran back and forth, following their outstretched hands. Some crashed into decorations or pillars and others crashed into each other. Second-years were posted up in prime observing locations to enjoy the first-day festivities.

Sliding into the classroom with hair disheveled and out of breath, Myles felt awkward. At the front stood a shorter gentleman, his fiery red hair also short but not maintained. Bifocals perched precariously on his nose, magnifying his green eyes.

"Sorry, sir," Myles addressed the pedagogue at the head of the class. "It won't happen again."

"Ah yes... I thought we were one short," he said with a funny lisp while straightening his bowtie. "First-day jitters, I hope. Have a seat, Mister...?"

"Myles, sir," Myles informed.

"First name?" asked the pedagogue.

"Yes, Myles, sir," Myles answered again.

"Myles Myles?" asked the now confused pedagogue.

"No sir, sorry sir, Briggs sir."

"First name?" the pedagogue asked again.

"Sorry, first name Myles, last name Briggs, sir," corrected Myles, now more nervous than when he arrived.

"Well, Mr. Briggs, you can have a seat wherever there is a seat left."

Myles scanned the room. As he walked up to the last desk, he saw Kamara sitting at the desk next to it. She had a satisfied smirk across her laid-back face. As Myles sat beside her, she mouthed a sincere "thank you" for the performance.

"Is this seat taken?" Myles asked.

"It was," answered Kamara as she looked back at a boy in the back corner, "but I think I made him cry." The boy's eyes scoured the room for anything to look at besides Kamara.

Myles placed his heavy bag on his desk. The classroom's décor truly hit him as he glanced around. Lining the walls were a series of glass cages, each a menagerie of slithering reptiles and amphibious creatures. Their forms, an array of scales, warts, and bulging eyes, filled him with fascination and unease.

Above, suspended from the ceiling like chandeliers, were the skeletal remains of terrifying creatures.

The man muttered to himself, flipping through his notes, "Where were we? Ah, yes. For those of you who weren't here for the first three times, I am Pedagogue Emmet Alistair, and I will be instructing your Herpetology course, that being the study of dragons and all reptilian creatures. Now, let us open our texts to chapter one."

Myles pulled out his scale-covered textbook, opening it as quickly as possible so as not to make eye contact.

Pedagogue Alistair lisped his way through several different known breeds of dragons: wyverns, wyrms, amphipteres, coatyls, hydras, drakes, orcs, feydragons, and basilisks. He lectured on the different variations in scale colors, types of tails, differing horns, varying wing types, and even patterns found on their eggs.

"Remember," added Alistair, "your dragons could have any of these combinations. And it will be up to you to care for this hatchling once it arrives." Just then, a loud bell chimed twice.

"It is time for your second course. Please read through chapter two and study some of the recorded dragon types listed in the back of your books."

Kamara glanced over at Myles, "See you around, Briggs." The first-years stood awkwardly in the corridor outside class, staring at their knuckles. Then, all at once, their rings lit aglow. They scattered like bees from a hive, running around with their arms outstretched.

At his second morning class, botany and horticulture, Myles was pleased to see Hickalik once again. Lush greenery filled the space. Potted plants lined every windowsill, while others hung from planters adorning the walls and ceiling.

Myles found Pedagogue Greenwald teaching this class. Her pondering gaze seemed to look for an escape from her own classroom.

Compared to the passion Professor Alistair had poured into their morning dragon lecture, Greenwald's herbalism class felt like wading through mud. The students were called on to identify the necessary herbs to craft an ointment for a burn.

When a student asked Greenwald how to identify the correct ingredients, her response was a withering snap, "Did you not read your text?" A theatrical sigh punctuated her words, followed by a dramatic roll of her eyes.

"Hickalik, was it?" she singled him out. "Teach them how to make the ointment." Hickalik stiffened up as his name came off her lips. "Well, did you read it?" she asked.

"Yes Ma'am." He started searching around the room. He verbally reiterated everything he was doing, "Some vitalis root, a little crystalmint herb, and tranquil larkspur for the pain." His hands shook from his nervousness, his voice kept cracking as he instructed his classmates. His jitters caused him to drop his pestle twice while grinding the herbs in the mortar. Eventually he finished his task and sat back down.

Xander and his companions sat in the back row, "Great, now he can make his own burn ointment when his dragon cooks him alive."

"Quiet down," Greenwald cracked. "Everyone get that?" No student dared say no.

She continued, "Hickalik, see me after class about your lesson. Now, open your books and study plant identifications until the bell rings."

They did as instructed, and soon enough, the bell rang three times. The students lingered again in the corridor, then scattered to the corners of the building.

Myles' next course was Ruach Fundamentals with Warden Petroff. Petroff conducted a strict class setting. He did not allow any horseplay or comments. He even used his pointing stick to smack Gordon and Gavin in the back of the head for whispering. Never once did he ask the class to open their textbook. However, he did cover the six base Ruach giftings: fire, earth, water, verdure, air, and arcane. Myles' attention wandered. He continually found himself fantasizing about which Ruach attribute his dragon would wield.

Before he knew it, the bell rang four times. He buzzed his way through the halls to Pedagogue Muddle's Escalian history. The classroom was magnificent. The floor, a dark platform, floated near the bottom of an encapsulating sphere of a room, bigger than a house. The sphere slowly rotated, giving a glimpse of an entire world map, the whole inner world around them. Lines and borders were lit aglow, like neon lights, by tiny lines of flames. However, Pedagogue Muddle was not as impactful. He was a chubby man with a long-curled mustache and a monocle over his left eye. He casually scanned the rotating room, then often paused as if he'd gotten lost in his own head.

Myles was joined by all his new friends for this course, which made him feel more at ease. Xander was also there, on the other side of the room. Muddle started his lesson by explaining how the six folds came to be. He spoke in a monotone voice and veered off-topic several times with odd ramblings. He paced while speaking and accidentally knocked items off his desk or sometimes ran into a chair. Underwhelmed, Xander had fallen fast asleep.

Myles, however, was quite excited to see a demonstration of Pedagogue Muddle's flames. Half asleep and slumped in his chair, Xander was suddenly surrounded by a burst of colorful translucent flames that spread out in every direction, gliding through the air. The flames traveled through solid objects with no resistance. One even flew directly through Xander's head, waking him up with a jolt. This gave Myles and his friends a good chuckle. The sight was beautiful to behold, especially in the dimly lit room.

"They call it phantom-flame," whispered Kamara, "Spooky, huh?"

"I think it's beautiful," commented Myles.

After five chimes rang out, the group found themselves back in the great hall. The conveyors whizzed by with a decadent selection once again, and the bulrogs slurped up the leftovers. The boys realized this was the first meal they'd had all day, and they stuffed themselves. Gavin and Gordon gobbled up every plate of sweets they could get their hands on; however, this did not bode well for them.

After lunch, Myles joined Gavin and Gordon outdoors for Field Exercise Training Aptitude, or FETA, with Warden Managol. She was ruthless. The children had to sprint endlessly, do line touches, push-ups and sit-ups, lunges, and even calisthenics with little to no breaks. Gavin and Gordon were both bent over with their heads in the bushes, regurgitating their sweet tooths.

Myles regretted every bite he ate, but not as much as Xander and Bach. Bach tried to support his friend, but every time Xander had another dry heave, Bach lost more of his lunch.

As the day neared the end of their scheduled courses and students reached their next destination, Myles found himself standing in an empty corridor. His ring stopped glowing, and there was no burning sensation.

He kept walking down the hallways and found his ring repeatedly guiding him right back. He called out a hopeful "Hello" in each direction, but nobody answered. Luckily, Warden Managol walked by in a perpendicular hall.

"Warden Managol," Myles shouted.

Her head popped back into view, "Briggs?" she redirected toward the lost boy. "I was just on my way to get my second lunch. What are you doing out of class?"

"I'm not sure where to go. My ring seems to be malfunctioning or something. It keeps leading me here."

"That's hogwash. Let me see that," she grabbed Myles' wrist and yanked him around back and forth like a ragdoll as they walked up and down the hallway.

"Huh, seems to be malfunctioning or something," she concluded. Myles was not impressed.

"Here, I probably shouldn't be doing this, but I trust you kid." She took her black ring and tapped it on Myles' ring three times. His ring unhinged and she took Myles' ring off his finger to look at it closer. "Make sure you go see the Masoner after your schedule and get it looked at," she told him as she returned the unclipped ring.

"I will. Thank you," he said, "But how will I know where to go for my last two classes?"

"Oh yeah... first-year, first day," she laughed at herself. "Well, what courses have you been to so far?"

Myles started listing the day, "I had Herpetology..."

"Uh-huh, lizard stuff..." She started counting with her fingers.

"Then Botany and Horticulture, Ruach Fundamentals, Escalian History," he continued slowly.

"Okay. Plants, flames, and globe room," she continued counting.

"Then I went to your training after lunch, and that's it," Myles finished.

"Alrighty, that means you have either normal school stuff or stone making. This way."

She led Myles down a couple more corners and up two flights of stairs. Warden Managol threw open a door, slamming it on the stone wall behind. The crash was so abrupt the whole classroom jumped and stared.

"Hey Humphkins, are you missing one?" bellowed the warden.

A little lady in perfectly pressed clothes held her tiny hand to her large forehead in frustration. "We have been over this, Warden Managol, it's Humphrey... Pedagogue Humphrey," she said in a sweet yet perturbed tone. Humphrey glanced up. "What does his ring say?" she asked.

"It's busted," Warden Managol answered.

Pedagogue Humphrey looked down, exhaling as she shuffled papers on her desk. "Let me see... Ah yes. Briggs, is it?" she asked.

Myles nodded, "Yes, ma'am."

"Perfect. Worked out after all," said Warden Managol. She gave Myles a hard pat on the back, knocking him further into the room as he stumbled. And with that, Warden Managol slammed the doors shut again making Pedagogue Humphrey wince.

"Take a seat, Mr. Briggs," she instructed, seeming vexed in her high-pitched breathy voice.

The only seat available just happened to be in front of Kamara. Wondering who her victim was, Myles slowly meandered over and sat down.

Kamara leaned forward and whispered in his ear from behind, "I am just so happy."

Myles dropped his head in shame and opened his textbook. He'd missed the introductions and half the lesson at this point. Based on the textbook, it seems this class was Core Coursework: basic math, science, and writing. Even more surprising, the curriculum seemed to be a couple of years behind Myles' education in the outer world. The bell rang seven times.

"Hey Kamara, would you happen to know where the 'stone making' course is? I don't have a working ring at the moment."

She answered with a sigh, "Yeah, come on, I will show you to your *stone making class*. That's where I'm headed anyways." She led him straight past the waiting mob in the corridor, all still looking at their rings for guidance. Kamara and Myles were joined once again by Hickalik and Sigurd and Xander's dreadful threesome.

"Good afternoon. I am Pedagogue Zilberstein, instructor for Ebenezer Artistry." She was a slender woman with black hair, tightly slicked back into a braided ponytail. Her harsh accent made her hard to understand.

"We will start these first few weeks by talking about the theories behind making ebenezers; however, after you have your Nexus attribute, you will learn to craft your own."

As she continued addressing the class and lecturing about the theories behind ebenezer stones, Myles leaned over to Hickalik, "What's an ebenezer?"

Hickalik looked a little surprised, "They are stones or crystals infused with an attribute flame."

After hearing Pedagogue Zilberstein's lecture about ebenezers and learning they could be purchased in most markets for day-to-day use, Myles felt silly for asking.

After classes, Kamara and Sigurd returned to their rooms for some rest. They all made plans to meet for some extra studying before dinner. Myles then told Hickalik about his ring malfunctioning.

"How strange," remarked Hickalik, "I've never heard of a Ruach-enriched device malfunctioning."

They found Pedagogue Muddle standing stooped in the hall.

"Excuse me, Pedagogue Muddle, could you point me in the right direction for the Masoner?" asked Myles.

"Oh, by golly, the mason worker," he repeated as he swayed back and forth in a circle. He appeared to be trying to remember the way. "The rings, yes, oh the rings. Tell the ring, and the path will sing." Off he strutted back in the direction he came from.

Myles and Hickalik were perplexed. "What on earth did he mean by that?" Myles asked.

But Hickalik was repeating the pedagogue's words, "Tell the ring... and the path will sing." He lifted his ring to his mouth and asked, "Can you lead me to the Masoner?" Hickalik spun around, testing the ring, but nothing happened.

Myles stopped him, "Don't ask it... tell it."

Hickalik's eyes widened, "Lead me to the Masoner."

Two indents lit up on top of the ring. Hickalik turned his body until all three were lit, and the boys were off. They raced down the corridor, following the ring.

They found themselves facing a long corridor dimly lit by lantern's light. All the other hallways and rooms had generous windows and skylights to help brighten the areas, but this hallway seemed to stretch on and on into darkness.

"Come on, let's go," Myles insisted.

"I... I don't like dark places," informed Hickalik. "They creep me out."

"It will be fine, Hickalik. I'll be next to you the whole time."

Hickalik mustered his courage and sheepishly followed. As they strolled down the lengthy corridor, the lanterns seemed to get spaced further apart, dimming their surroundings. They reached the end, which opened to a large industrial stone room. There was a furnace on one side providing a soft dim light.

"Hello?" Myles called out. They heard a metal clink as something dropped to the floor on the darker side.

"What you want?" a raspy voice answered.

Myles peered into the darkness with narrowed eyes. "Sorry to bother you. I was told by Warden Managol to come see the Masoner about my ring."

The voice started grumbling, "Fix the ring, fix the wall, fix the doors, fix the plumbing. All they want me to do is fix, fix, fix."

A short skinny man lumbered out of the darkness and stood hunched over. He had no hair on his pale-skinned head. His nose was large and crooked, and his eyes were extremely dilated, like obsidian stones. His face drooped to a long red beard that just dusted the floor.

"Are you the Masoner?" Myles asked.

"Of course, that is me. The one everyone forgets until they need me," he griped again.

"You're a Dindrole, aren't you?" asked Hickalik, surprised, coming out from behind Myles.

"And so what if I am?" The man snapped back. Hickalik retreated.

"Sorry. We've just never met a Dindrole." Myles explained, not knowing what a Dindrole was himself.

The short man scowled. Myles pulled his ring out of his pocket and held it up to the man's sight line, "I was sent here. My ring is malfunctioning."

"Malfunctioning?" The man snatched the ring from Myles with a large, muscular hand. He quickly put a loupe magnifying glass to his eye. He then sniffed the ring and licked it. Then he spit on the floor.

"These things don't malfunction," he said, turning around and scrambling through his toolboxes.

Myles whispered to Hickalik, "What's a Dindrole?"

"They're a clan of people who lived for centuries mining underground Ruach-enriched materials and gems. They normally never come above ground. I had no idea they had one working here."

"They are humans?" Myles asked curiously.

"Yes, but the long exposures underground started to change them over the generations."

The hunched man sounded more passionate now: "These are Ruach-infused artifacts. I cannot fix them if somcone else creates them. What was given from the tower can only be corrected by its architect."

"Well, where can I find him?" asked Myles.

"We don't speak of him here," He snarled again, breaking eye contact.

"What's your name?" asked Myles.

"My name?" the man questioned back, "You care to know my name?"

"Well, of course, sir. You are the one helping us, after all."

"I have worked here since the academy's second fabrication. I have been called many names in this place. But never 'sir...' and never by my name, at least not by the students. My name is Gruburg. Gruburg Orlik."

"It's nice to meet you, Mr. Orlik," Myles said, trying to win over his favor with politeness.

"No," he barked, perturbed. "Orlik is my father's name. Just Gruburg."

"I appreciate you helping me with my ring, Gruburg."

Gruburg twitched with a quick side smile, then turned downcast. He looked at the ring on his workbench once more.

He then instructed Myles, "Go to the pillar in the corner of the room. Get a new ring. I will examine this specimen." Myles did as he was told. He placed his hand on the sand on top of the pillar, and just as before, his hand was sucked inward, and a new ring was placed on his finger.

"Thank you, Gruburg," Myles said while they started to exit.

As they left the room, they could hear Gruburg talking to himself as he clanked tools together, "Sirs and 'thank you's? Ask my name? They were nice, but don't trust... can't trust."

Chapter Ten

The Harvest

The days started blurring together. Myles was mentally and emotionally fatigued. Each new day seemed like a continuation of the previous one. He would hasten to meet Pedagogue Alistair, eager to start with his favorite subject. Occasionally, Kamara would prod him in class, making him jump awkwardly and inadvertently interrupt Alistair's lectures. She would set traps at the students' desks, ensuring chaos when they sat down. Sometimes, a small ebenezer stone would deliver an electric shock, tearing through their pants, or even setting them on fire. Most of the classroom laughed, while Kamara simply looked pleased.

Then it was off to Pedagogue Greenwald's class on botany and horticulture, where an unlucky student would be selected for the day's lesson. Some students performed admirably, while others were less fortunate. One such student was Hendrick Hubble. His sleeping potion was so poorly concocted that he spent a week napping in the infirmary. Hickalik was singled out more frequently than most by Greenwald, likely because he was the most competent.

"Performance punishment," Myles called it, recalling Ms. Helen.

Petroff was relentless in his Ruach classes. At the mere sound of a chuckle or laugh, he would turn around sharply as if he had been disrespected by the unruly hoodlums he knew them to be.

When you make..." he corrected his thought, "*if* you make a Nexus connection, you must know your attribute's limitations." Petroff used ebenezer stones to demonstrate types of Ruach attributes and their uses, showing bursts of flames from every attribute, something Myles thoroughly enjoyed, although with little understanding.

Escalian history class seemed hit and miss, depending on the day. Some days, Pedagogue Muddle was able to focus on the lesson. He taught wonderful historical stories about the kingdom, the folds, and ancient civilizations who believed in the first dragon. Other days he seemed lost in the clouds as his mind wandered from topic to topic, wandering to Ruach powers and mythical relics as he played with his mustache. Occasionally, he would show off his translucent flames of every hue, using them to wake up a snoozing participant.

Myles, and plenty of others, learned quickly to rise early, eat a good breakfast, and then a light, healthy lunch. Rain or shine, Warden Managol's field exercise lessons would not let up. She seemed to enjoy picking on the weak or disinterested students. Myles noticed those with a higher social standing tended to struggle with her physical training regimens.

"This is senseless," Xander criticized while keeled over. "My dragon and noble bloodline will make me strong, not this carnal pageantry." But Managol just ignored the heaving boy, and sometimes pushed the class harder because of him.

After this, with arms and legs like limp noodles, Myles would repeatedly find himself in an empty corridor. No matter how many times he exchanged his ring with Gruburg, the new ring would still lead him back to the same dead-end hallway. Eventually, Gruburg provided Myles with a fake ring so he could go about his day without burning his finger off. Gruburg grew excited when Myles stopped by, but quickly retreated back to the safety of his solitude.

Myles, now more familiar with the hallways, could navigate to his classes without the use of a working ring. In fact, after about a week, all the first-year students could find their classes without assistance.

Not growing up in this world, Ebenezer Artistry felt too convoluted for Myles. Everything, from the shape or thickness of the outer shell to how the stone was imbued with a person's flames, seemed to go over his head by leaps and bounds.

Gavin and Gordon seemed to be in the same boat, although this didn't give Myles much comfort. Kamara did not bother paying attention most days, yet when called upon was an expert on the topic.

In the evening, the boys would frequent the common areas with Kamara, despite Sigurd's weariness of her lack of ladylike qualities. One evening, after a long day of studies, Myles finally found the courage to ask Hickalik and Sigurd a question.

"I have been hearing a lot of students talk about the Harvest coming up soon. What exactly is the Harvest?" Myles hesitantly asked.

"You mean you don't know?" questioned Sigurd, "This whole time you haven't known? It's only a week away."

This question did not phase Hickalik though. "The Harvest is when we are sent into the Caldera."

"What's the Caldera?" Myles queried.

"The Caldera is the huge crater behind the school, the biggest in the world. The mountains behind are just the outer walls of the crater. It's a place where dragons go to nest and lay their eggs."

Myles grew concerned, "We go in there with nesting dragons? Like, wild dragons?" he asked, thinking about his encounter in the cabin.

Sigurd laughed, "The dragons don't stay there. They nest and lay their eggs, yes, but then they leave. They return once a year to check on their kin. Dragon eggs can take decades to hatch if a Nexus with a human is not made. Sometimes, a dragon will return to lay more eggs before the first litter has even hatched."

"I thought it was some kind of farming or botany class field trip," Myles confessed. Both Hickalik and Sigurd couldn't help but laugh.

"It's called the Egg Harvest," Hickalik explained. "It's the time of year when the eggs have been incubating the longest before the dragons return to check on their nests. We need to get in and out before the dragons return."

As Sigurd and Hickalik turned in for the night, Myles lay awake, consumed by anxiety about his upcoming adventure. Aside from the wardens' classes, for obvious reasons, Myles dedicated all his time to studying his herpetology literature.

After dinner, Hickalik, Sigurd, and Myles congregated in the library. They studied herpetology books closely, reading up on different types of dragons and what climates their eggs could be found in. A few types of dragons were even listed in the herpetology texts with locations inside the Caldera.

"It's great that we know which environment to start looking in, and all, but if we don't know where each climate is located, we could be searching for days," Hickalik pointed out.

Sigurd suggested, "We could always head to the highest peak near us, to get a vantage point and find different areas."

As if on cue, a large old parchment slammed on the table between them. It was Kamara. As she lifted her hand off the parchment, in front of them, the boys saw a great map showing the various regions of the Caldera.

Astonished, Hickalik asked, "Where did you find this? I searched everywhere in the geology and topography sections."

"In the history section," Kamara showed them an old-looking book titled An Eastern Land: From Cratered to Cultured.

"I never would have thought to look there," said Hickalik. The boys all leaned in closely to scrutinize the map.

"It's the only copy in the library," she said, sounding bored with herself. They continued to cross-examine their herpetology books and the new information found on the map until an obnoxiously slow and overconfident voice rang out behind them.

"Look, Xander. They are trying to plan their hunts." It was Bach, accompanied by Aberdeen and Xander.

"Ahh, yes. I always forget the simpletons must undergo such dribble for their meager rewards." Myles ignored the approaching circus the best he could, still heeding Allen's words.

But Kamara engaged, "Better than an inbred reptilian-brood-cow."

Xander tried to laugh this comment off. Aberdeen added with her sweet innocent-sounding voice, "Selective breeding has always produced the finest of Nexus connections and abilities. However, it is nice that there are means of procuring dragons elsewhere for those less fortunate."

"Indeed, fair maiden," agreed Sigurd.

Kamara looked at Sigurd. "You know she's talking about you too, right!"

Myles couldn't help his curiosity. "Are you saying you already have dragon eggs?"

"Of course," Xander boasted. "Do you think we would leave our legacy up to chance? The academy has offered us the opportunity to participate in the Harvest if we wish. But I believe our arrangement will prove much more beneficial than scavenging for eggs in the dirt."

"Where is it?" asked Hickalik, hoping to see an egg up close.

"Not here, of course. It is safe at home in the family vaults. I will have it delivered when appropriate."

"You mean when the others are dragging their eggs out of the mud?" Bach snickered.

"Have fun planning your little adventure," Xander belittled. "Maybe you can find a dragon that can help you be less impoverished. Or for you, Briggs, maybe you can find a mud dragon to match that dirty stain on your chest." The three of them turned away, proud of their display.

"What's wrong with a mud dragon?" asked Hickalik, confused. Myles shrugged.

"Isn't she lovely?" Sigurd asked while still watching Aberdeen walk away. "She's just so... ladylike."

Kamara rolled her eyes, "Yeah, as ladylike as a hog in a dress."

"How uncouth. You take that back," Sigurd demanded.

Kamara ignored Sigurd's disapproval, "You boys have fun with your map. I'm turning in for the night. I'll see you again soon enough." She left the library as the boys drew copies of the map.

As they all studied daily and spent more time together, questioning strategies and probabilities, time flew by, and the day finally came. The Harvest was upon them.

Their rings did not lead them to class. Luckily, Hickalik noticed before Myles left the dormitory since he was wearing a non-working ring. The rings led all the first years to a large auditorium.

Prudencia faced the onlooking assembly, "Today... is a momentous day in your journeys. But before you venture forth to claim your connections, I implore you to think hard about who you want to be in this world. What your heart says about you will be reflected in your Nexus partner. As water reflects the face, so one's life reflects the heart. The dragon that chooses you is choosing your heart."

"Now then, please direct your attention to Warden Petroff as he covers some of the event's safety procedures."

The stoic man stepped forward, arms behind his back. "Each of you will be equipped with a bag of food rations and camping gear. You have three days to make it back to the drop site." The auditorium was filled with mumbles.

"Three whole days?" questioned Myles.

"Yes, it is usually five," Hickalik whispered, surprised by the lack of time.

Petroff did not continue until the murmurs subsided. "Due to the weather patterns, the dragon's return is estimated to be nearing. We can only guarantee your safety for three days. And by safety, I mean from dragons. Keep in mind that other creatures hunt in the Caldera as well. If you find yourself in need of assistance or in danger, all you need to do is shatter a flare-ebenezer. Once the stone breaks, the flame will be sent straight into the air. Our spotters on the towers atop the Caldera walls will pinpoint your location, and you will be swiftly rescued. If you are rescued and are able and willing to continue, you will have to restart at the drop point."

"Drop point?" whispered Myles.

"We are dropped off by a ferry," Hickalik softly answered.

Petroff continued, "Each of your bags will also be equipped with an assortment of ebenezer stones. Use them... sparingly. Lastly, you will select any tools from the implement room you wish for your journey. I am sure each of you thinks you have a plan for your success; however, don't put all your eggs in that basket. When you find your egg and ensear, bring your egg to the drop point and wait. If you find no egg and cannot ensear, return by noon on the third day. Questions...?" he asked as if he wanted none.

A studious girl in the second row named Phillis Schnep fixed her glasses and raised her hand, "Pedagogue Petroff, how will we be able to find our way back?"

"Follow your rings," Petroff answered begrudgingly.

Myles' eyes grew wider, as he looked down at his fake ring but then remembered he, Sigurd, and Hickalik had plans to travel together.

As Warden Petroff exited the center stage, Pedagogue Zilberstein stepped forward to address the students. "We have given several ebenezers for your use. All ebenezers supplied are rupture stones. Simply break the outer-crystal to activate the Ruach within. Fire-stones will release the fire within and burn outward. Lightning-stones quickly gather static electricity in the atmosphere and send lightning bolts. Be warned, do not be in the area when it strikes. The invisibility-stone will turn you invisible if you need to go unnoticed by a creature or escape its gaze. Lastly, the wind-stone. The wind-stone will send a powerful upper gust of wind almost instantaneously. Any questions?"

Myles had all sorts of questions but dared not ask.

Zilberstein walked off the stage without waiting.

Prudencia walked back to center stage. "If you haven't already, decide in your mind what kind of person you wish to be. For some of you, power will be granted, a power that can help others or a power that can corrupt one's heart. How this gift develops will reflect your true self. I wish for all of you a strong Nexus... and a pure heart." And with that, Prudencia turned and thumped her way out of the room with her staff.

The double doors groaned open. The implementation room was a vast chamber overflowing with tools. Tables strained under pickaxes, climbing gear, and thick ropes. Walls displayed breathing tubes for deep dives, grappling hooks, and even curious boots with empty stone inlays.

"Only choose what you think you will need," exclaimed Petroff. "These items can be extremely heavy when you are exhausted, and some of you will be walking for days," he added grimly.

Sigurd whispered, "I'm starting to think Warden Petroff doesn't want students to return."

Myles inspected a hardy pair of boots.

"The empty inlay on the bottom of the boots was for an ebenezer stone," Hickalik explained, knowing Myles was aiming for a fire dragon. "With the ice-stone inserted, you should be able to walk on hot ground in the lava region for a short time."

Once all selections were made, Warden Petroff called out, "Head to the top of this tower. I will see you all there."

Down the hall a short way was the start of a spiraling staircase. Myles, fueled by a potent mix of excitement and nerves, shoved Sigurd and Hickalik playfully, propelling them towards the stairs. Laughter erupted as they all surged forward.

Sigurd and Hickalik gave chase up the ever-winding stairs. Every few floors, bridges connected the Tower of Power to its neighboring towers, offering glimpses of distant hallways and the bustling activity below. But the boys' focus remained fixed on the top. Time seemed to warp; the adrenaline-fueled climb turned into a slog. Packs weighed heavier with every step, and their breaths came in ragged gasps. After what felt like an entire class with Warden Managol, they made it to the top on their hands and knees.

"Impressive," a voice mocked.

There stood Kamara. She looked around, taking in a deep breath in the altitude's fresh air, as if to prove her lungs could still function. The whole class was there. The last of the class stepped off a hexagonal lift, onto the roof. That is when Myles looked up and gasped for even more air. He saw the ferry that would usher them to the Caldera.

Beside the imposing peak of the Tower of Power, rested a magnificent vessel. It bore a striking resemblance to the colonial ships Myles read about in school. A wooden behemoth with billowing sails stretched taut on either side was docked midair. Yet, this wasn't your ordinary ship.

Above the hull, enormous blimp-like structures floated, tethered to the vessel by a complex web of ropes and cables. This wasn't a ship designed for the calm waters of a harbor; it was built to conquer the skies.

"That's the ferry?" Myles wheezed.

Sigurd answered as he tried to hide the pain from his cramping side, "Indeed."

The class traversed a rather rickety wooden bridge despite the wind. One by one they crossed. As the last student boarded, the bridge was swiftly booted off the tower by Petroff and was retracted.

The students looked up to the ship's helm. There, an imposing figure stood, sending a tremor of nervous anticipation through the students. A salty breeze whipped his long, unkempt hair around his face, momentarily obscuring his features. When the wind died down, they were met with a grizzled expression. Deep wrinkles carved a map around his squinted eyes, eyes that seemed perpetually narrowed either from the relentless sun or a lifetime of scrutinizing the horizon. Half his lower lip drooped permanently downwards, forming a slight hole in his mouth he used to spit through.

The man reached for a lever next to him, "Hitch your rumps," The man snarled.

Not knowing what he meant, half the class was knocked over as the vessel lunged forward. Just then the cabin door swung open below the man. Out came Pedagogue Alistair, who also did not seem to appreciate the abrupt start.

"I say... my dear Captain Nordic, let's be a little more conscientious about our passengers."

The captain spouted back, "Down in the doldrums, then three sheets to the wind with a chock-a-block. There be tweaks when castoff bells ring."

"You never even rang the bell," responded Alistair spouting his frustration.

"Cat's tongue gets bit hardest when it yawns," Captain Nordic yapped back.

Myles leaned over to Hickalik, "Did you get any of that?" he asked. Hickalik shook his head worriedly.

Giving up, Alistair waved the captain off as he turned to face the students, "Welcome children, to the Harvest. We have now cast off on our adventure. We will climb above the caldera's mountain peaks, then down to the plateau in the center. From there, you will be able to choose your own paths; both literally and figuratively."

He lifted a finger, "Oh that's right."

He reached next to him to open the lid to a wooden crate. "These are your egg satchels." He pulled out a round leather satchel with a soft cage woven into the sides and bottom. "They should make carrying your eggs back much easier, and safer for your dragons as well."

"Great, another thing to carry," Xander complained from the back.

"Xander?" asked Sigurd, "What's he doing here? I thought he already had an egg waiting for him?"

Myles happened to be towards the front of the crowd, nearest Alistair. Alistair held out the satchel towards Myles, "Here son, take one."

Myles quickly grabbed the bag, shoved his face inside, and hurled his previous meal directly into the bag. The class grimaced.

Sigurd sympathized, "Poor chap," as Hickalik patted Myles' back from a long arm's reach.

Kamara's lip tugged upward, "Exquisite..."

Captain Nordic yelled down to them, "Be no chunder slinging upon worthy cutters."

Myles moved to the side of the ship as the rest of the classmates received their satchels.

The ship continued cutting back and forth, weaving its way up the mountain side. Myles was forced to jaunt from side to side to tilt his head over the ship's gunwale. The air became cold, and the wind cut through their uniforms. They eventually pushed through the clouds. There were white kissed peaks jutting through the plain of clouds now below.

"I have no strength," Myles whizzed with his mouth gaping. "My body... feels heavy."

"I imagine it's because we are so high up," Hickalik ventured. "The closer you are to the sun, the more it pushes you down. That's why no one has ever been able to fly much higher than this."

"Correct," Sigurd interjected. "We have tried to go higher in our family's dirigible, but we were just pushed away. I am astounded we made it this high. Hats off to the captain."

Myles tried to look back at them from the edge's grip, "What's a... dirigible?" He managed to blubber out.

"An airship, you silly goose." Sigurd answered. "You are on one right now." That reminder was all it took for Myles to fling his head back over the side.

The captain yelled again, "Peak pulse swayed; downcast whaler been droppin' tail gales."

Myles slowly turned his head with narrowed eyes to see the captain on his perch, "What now?"

But before the others could try to answer, the captain pulled another lever and the bow dipped downward sharply. Everyone's stomachs, including what was left of Myles', were instantaneously thrust into their throats. The crazed captain started galloping in place while laughing, overjoyed by the feeling.

The captain pointed his hand forward as if he was holding a sword, "Narrow tempus peaks, hilts up."

The ship gained speed as it flew down into the clouds below. Everyone was holding on for dear life. Captain Nordic pulled another lever and the ship leveled again, coming to a tranquil coast. The students regained their courage and eventually released the ship's rails.

"Crazy old kook," Xander said, showing his disapproval while fixing his hair.

"Look," called out Florky Bunson, as everyone rushed the taffrails. They were surrounded on all sides by distant mountains cascading down toward diverse landscapes. On one side, lava flowed down to a black and steaming surface. This dark topography was adjacent to sandy brown deserts. On the other side of the vessel towered snowy mountains with rivers feeding down to a vast lake.

As the children gawked, the airship made its way to the top of a large, lifted plateau in the center of the crater. The landing was surprisingly gentle as the ship's hull rested down. Professor Alistair extended the departing bridge, then turned to the children with his arms outstretched, "Welcome to the Caldera." And for Myles, not a moment too soon.

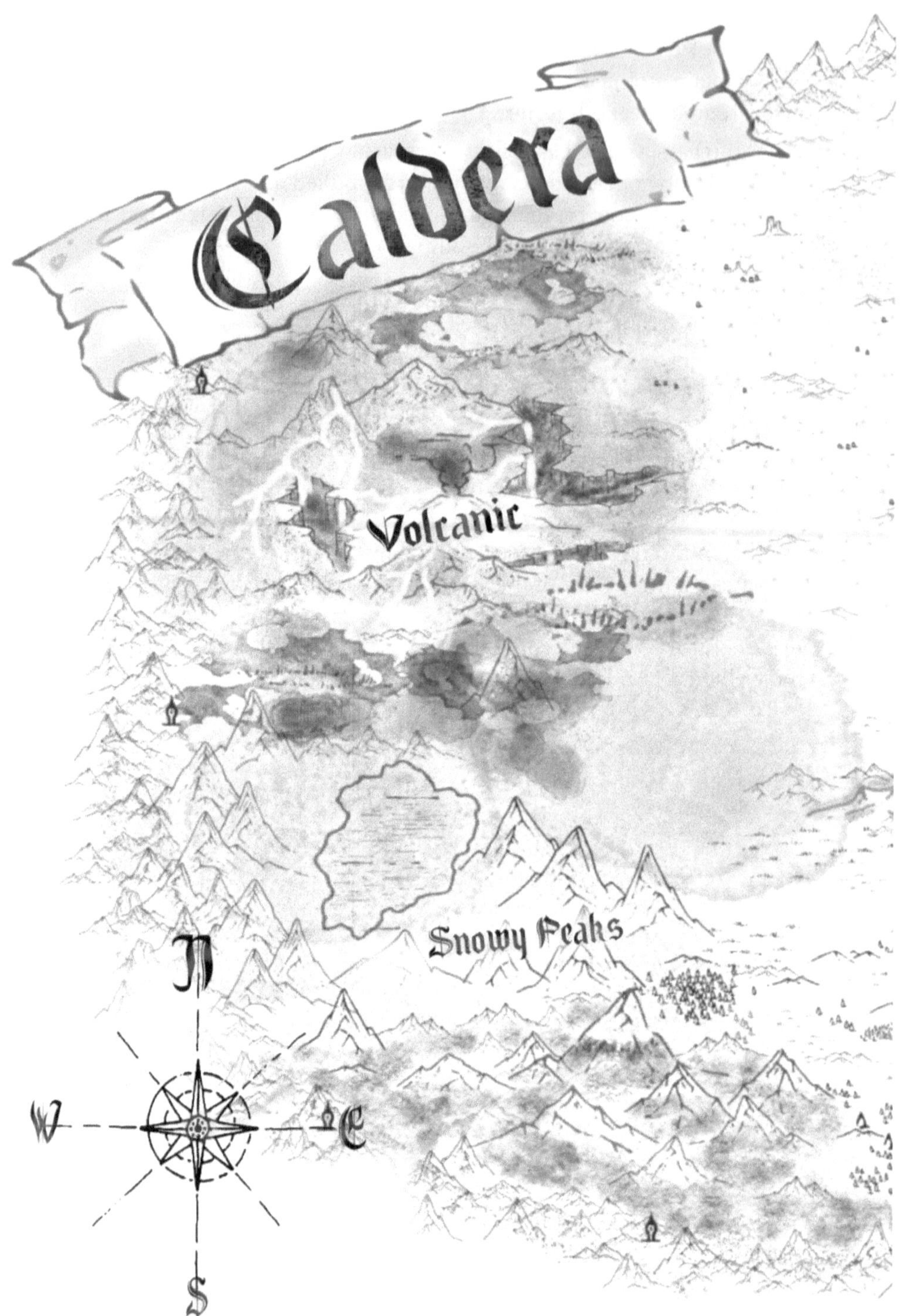
Caldera
Volcanic
Snowy Peaks
N
W
E
S

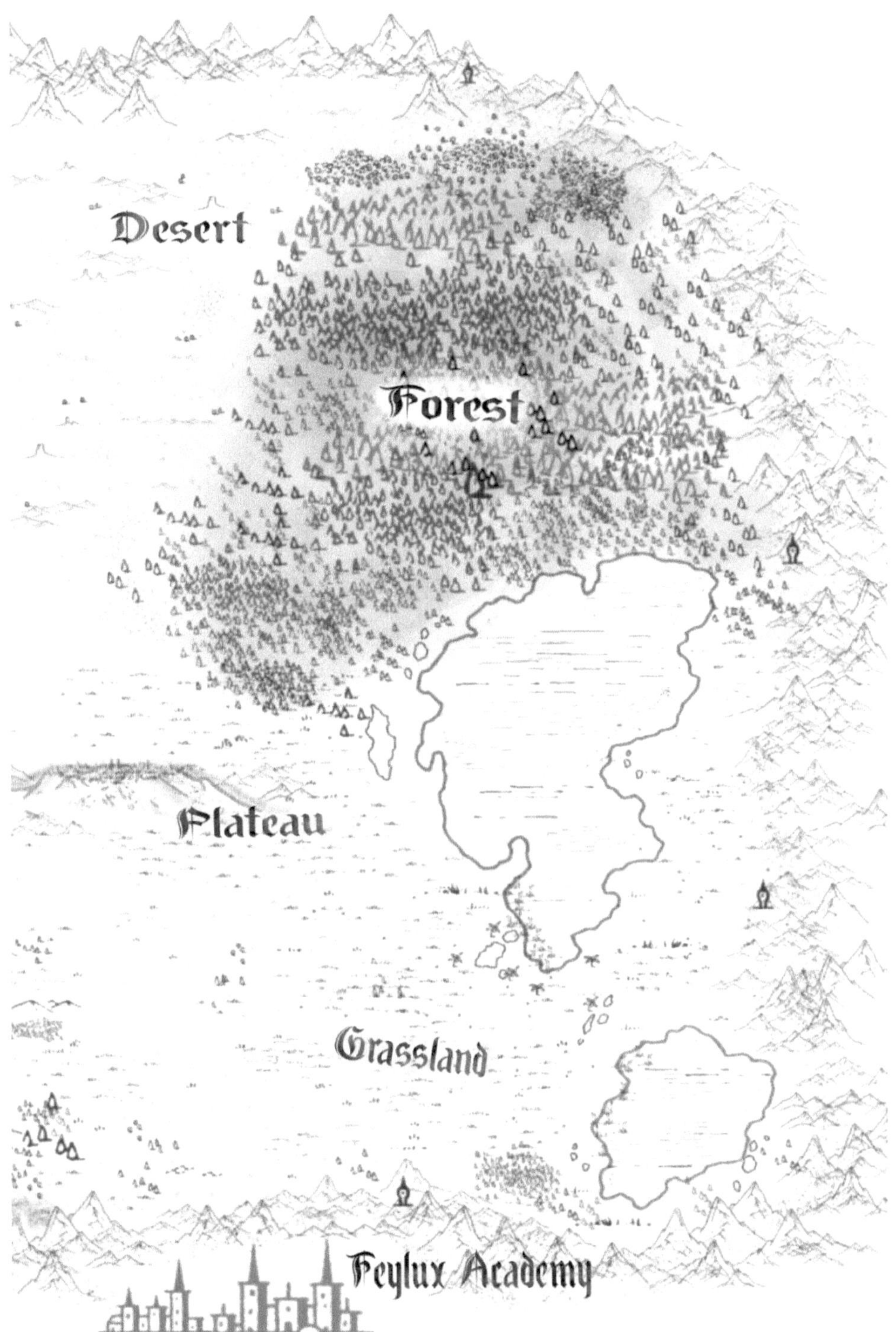
Desert
Forest
Plateau
Grassland
Feylux Academy

Chapter Eleven

Sticks and Stones

One by one, they shuffled down the rickety wooden ramp, backpacks and tools slung over their shoulders. Myles, stomach still churning from the turbulent flight, nearly tumbled off the ramp.

They found themselves on a vast, flat-topped plateau nestled amidst a towering ring of mountains. The ground was a patchwork of dusty earth and knee-high grass. The oppressive weight of the cloudy sky pressed down upon them, blotting out any hope of sunshine.

Standing on the edge of the ship, Pedagogue Alistair spoke to the group, "Remember children, you have three days to meet back here for the return rendezvous. Although these lands should be mostly uninhabited, keep your ebenezers close and use your flares if you feel you are in any danger. We have rarely lost anyone during these hunts."

"Rarely?" inquired Myles.

His question went unanswered; however, Gordon raised his hand high—not that he needed to as he towered over the others, "But Pedagogue, why are we not being escorted by the faculty if it can be so dangerous?"

"This is your journey, your futures to fashion, not ours. We will not meddle in your destinies. Search hard with your eyes, ears, and hearts. The more you can think like the dragons while in their environment, the more attuned you are with that attribute. The harsher the environment, the stronger the dragon must be to survive. Follow your instincts. Let your dragons guide you to them."

And with that, the airship started rising upward. "Good luck, students," he yelled as he flew upward, out of sight.

"Trust your instincts?" balked Xander. "What a load of rubbish."

"Why are you and Aberdeen even here Xander?" asked Myles. "You already told us you have an egg waiting for you at home."

"Well, I wouldn't miss the chance to see the great Caldera. Even for nobility, this is a once-in-a-lifetime experience," Xander stated, with a haughty hint of sarcasm. "Who knows? We could even find an egg here that would suit us better."

Aberdeen added in her fake caring tone, "Not to mention, our dear friend, Bach, does not have quite the established roots as our illustrious houses. We are present to encourage our friend in his tribulations."

Just then Gavin called out from a distance on the plateau, "I found a nest." Most of the class dashed over. As they arrived, Gavin placed his hand upon the largest of three eggs. The nest was made of dried mud and weeds mixed together.

"I... I can feel a tingle," Gavin verbalized to his observing classmates. Then Gavin started to sink. The soil below him turned to mud. Before they knew it, the mud had sucked him in up to his knees. He tried pulling his feet out, but the suction of the mucky bog held firm.

"Ah...Help?" he said nervously. Gordon reached his long arms over and tried to pull Gavin out, but Gordon just got stuck himself. The mud sucked Gordon also down to his knees, and Gavin was now down to his waist and panicking quite cowardly now.

Hickalik advised, "Hold still so you don't sink further."

"Easy for you to say, you're not drowning in sludge!"

"Fair point," commented Kamara, who was way too calm for the situation.

"Here," said Myles, grabbing Hickalik's rope off his backpack. Myles tied a lasso on the end of the rope, just like Allen taught him during years of helping on the farm. Myles swung the rope and threw it around Gavin's head and raised arm.

"Impressive," complimented Kamara.

Gavin shoved the rope around his waist and Gordon grabbed on to it as well. It took half the class to pull them out.

"Leave it to commoners to touch the first egg they see," said Xander as he meandered past the group.

"Not to mention get stuck in filth," cackled Bach.

 Omni and the Blazed Boy

"He found more eggs than the infamous Xander," Kamara surprisingly defended.

"Dear undesirable Kamara, quality over quantity. Although, I am sure you would settle for any, at this point. The seventh daughter may require seven attempts," Xander mocked. "Second time's the charm, aye Kamara?"

Xander laughed maniacally as the three turned to take their leave. "Good luck finding your eggs. Between the four of you, I am sure one of you will ensear with something," said Xander in parting.

Hickalik narrowed his eyes, "I don't trust them."

"Don't worry your pretty little noggin," said Kamara while rubbing Hickalik's head, messing his hair.

"What did they mean by 'second times the charm'?" Myles asked curiously. Kamara let out a reluctant sigh, "I was enrolled last year," she confessed nonchalantly.

"You were?" asked Sigurd. "What happened?"

"I couldn't find an egg that would ensear," she stated.

"Did you touch any eggs?" asked Hickalik.

"Yes, dozens," she exhaled, "Now, if you don't mind, I will be off on a stroll."

"A stroll? By yourself? Why not stay with us?" asked Myles. "We are heading north."

"I know," she said.

"How do you know?"

"Every boy heads north. That is where the lava, desert, and forest lands connect."

Myles asked, "Kamara, what attribute are you looking for?"

"Whichever I happen to find. Now, do not get killed out there, gents." She turned and started walking away, south.

Sigurd had his fists clenched, "I am sorry. I know we had a plan, but no matter how unladylike she may act, I cannot let a lady wander on her own in such dangerous lands."

"Okay..." Myles said, not knowing what to say back.

Sigurd raised his hand and yelled out, "Kamara, I will escort you."

As he ran off to catch up, her steps quickened when she heard this, but Sigurd left a determined cloud of dust in his pursuit.

"Well, Hick, it looks like it's just us," said Myles.

The rest of the students descended the slopes of the plateau in various directions. Kamara had been correct; Myles and Hickalik indeed headed north, alongside a few other groups of boys. However, as the day wore on, the groups became increasingly distant.

They hiked for the better part of the day, every once in a while checking the map they had copied from the library. Their packs were becoming heavy and their bellies hungry. The clouds above started to drizzle, then turned into a downpour.

"We need to find shelter," said Hickalik who, much like a dog, did not like getting wet. They climbed up a small hill.

"Down there," Myles pointed.

On the other side of the hill was a cave opening formed under the base of some trees just before the forest started. Thick roots framed the cave's mouth in the side of a dry embankment.

"Let's go," agreed Hickalik, who would do anything to get out of the rain. As they ran, they saw a flare rocket up, west of their position.

"Should we help?" asked Myles. They paused for a moment watching... listening. "Let's see if we can help," but as they turned to head west, a shadow raced overhead, cutting through the rain. Then they saw the silhouette of a dragon lifting a person up, heading back towards the plateau in the center of the Caldera.

"That must have been the rescue," said Hickalik, pulling Myles along as he ran. They ran down the muddy slope and ducked into the cave. Glad to be out of the rain, they explored the cave's entrance a little ways in.

"Do you think it's safe?" asked Myles.

"It's dry," said Hickalik. Myles tried to focus his eyes to see further into the darkness.

Hickalik stood still. "Do you feel that?"

"What? Do you sense an egg?" Myles asked excitedly, but Hickalik shushed him, still listening.

They could hear a low rumble. Myles could feel it too. They looked toward the cave's entrance. Water was now flowing by and starting to pour in. The water rose quickly—too quickly—in fact, for them to go back outside.

"It's a flash flood," exclaimed Myles.

The muddy water gushed in violently, pushing logs and rolling boulders.

"Run!" shouted Myles.

The boys jetted into the cave. Hickalik reached into his backpack and pulled out the fire-stone. The stone emitted a faint glow on their path. As they sprinted, jumping over logs and rocks on the cave floor, they could hear the thrashing of debris growing closer behind them.

Myles pointed ahead as they struggled to outrun the rapids, "What's that?"

There, in the middle of the cave floor, was a wide gap where the ground had collapsed into a sinkhole, dropping into a dark void below. Glancing further, they could see the cave continuing on the other side.

"We can't jump that," huffed Hickalik.

Myles reached into his bag and pulled out a stone, "What is this?"

"Flare-stone," Hickalik answered. Myles reached for another, "This one?"

"Lightning," Hickalik gasped. Debris from the cave was rattling off the walls and ceiling from the force of the pursuing torrent. Myles ruffled around in his bag for another stone.

"We aren't going to make it," cried Hickalik.

Myles pulled out another stone, "Jump!"

They put all their remaining strength into one last leap over the gap. As they jumped, Myles threw the stone on the ground, cracking it in pieces as they lifted off. Gray flames erupted around them as a strong gust blew the boys upward. Their arms flailed like windmills as the gust blew them over the gap. Their backpacks thudded against the cave ceiling followed by stout belly flops on the cave floor, knocking the wind out of their lungs as they skidded to a halt.

Gasping for air, Myles grimaced, "We made it."

They looked behind them. The flood of rushing water was flowing down into the deep hole. They swayed back to their feet.

Relieved, Hickalik asked, "How did you know that was the air-stone?"

Still breathing deeply, Myles answered, "I didn't know. I thought it was ice."

Hickalik looked dumbfounded, "Ice? Why ice?"

"I thought I could freeze the water to hold it back."

They turned again to look at the gushing currents. They said nothing more on the matter. The boys turned to the unknown darkness ahead.

Myles, noticing Hickalik's growing unease said, "Well, onward and hopefully upward?" They slowly ventured on for what felt like hours and came to a fork. Hickalik decided to create an arrow on the ground out of some nearby driftwood to mark the direction they came from.

"What's that for?' asked Myles.

"In case we somehow double back to this point. That way we know which way we already went and the direction we came from. I read about it in my Galliant's Guide to Survival book."

Then they came to another fork. They decided to go right. Hickalik made another arrow. This path led them to a collapsed dead end.

"Do you hear that?" Myles asked.

Hickalik froze, "Another flood?"

"No, that clicking noise," Myles said. They both stood still, but they heard no sounds.

"Never mind, it's probably the water dripping down from those cone things on the ceiling," Myles dismissed.

"Stalactites," remarked Hickalik.

"Bless you," excused Myles.

"No...Stalactites. And those ones on the ground are stalagmites." Hickalik gestured to the cones forming on the floor pointing up.

"What I wouldn't give for some stalag-lights," Myles chuckled in the dim glow, but Hickalik was not amused.

As they returned to the previous fork, the wood used for the arrow had been pushed up against the walls.

Myles looked around confused, "What happened to your arrow?"

"I don't know," answered Hickalik, even more perplexed.

"Which way was it pointing?" asked Myles.

Hickalik looked for their footprints by the stone's glow, but there were none. The ground was evenly scratched with hatching-like patterns.

"This was the way we came, right?" asked Hickalik, doubting himself. Myles' stomach made such a grumble, it made Hickalik jump.

"Let's camp here tonight," recommended Myles.

"Here? Inside the cave?" Hickalik whimpered.

"We can rest, make a fire for warmth, and eat some rations."

They built up the wood in the center of the forked intersection, and Hickalik pressed the fire-stone against the wood, which ignited well. They sat with their backpacks on, leaning against the walls and eating what Myles thought must be lizard-jerky by the scaly texture.

Hickalik looked down and saw a brown stick. The stick wiggled closer. It was a large centipede.

In an astonishing feat of acrobatics, Hickalik jumped straight to his feet. "It's a centipede," he screeched as he kicked the bug away with a whimper. Myles just watched with amusement. It was hard not to laugh.

"I... I do not like bugs," Hickalik said shamefully.

"That's obvious," said Myles, "Look, it's gone now, anyway." The centipede had squirmed its way out of the fire's light.

Myles volunteered to take first-watch so Hickalik could hopefully get some sleep. It was later than either boy knew, and before long, they both were asleep, held upright by their backpacks.

When Myles woke, the flames were down to a flicker. He realized he had fallen asleep. Shame gnawed at his conscience. He snapped to his feet hoping Hickalik didn't notice, but Hickalik was still slumbering peacefully.

The silence, once comforting, was marred by the return of the clicking sound. This time, it was louder, echoing ominously. The vast chamber amplified the noise, making its origin impossible to discern.

"Hickalik," Myles whispered with emphasis. He kicked Hickalik's foot. Hickalik jolted awake. When he realized where he was, he popped to his feet as well.

"Do you hear it?" asked Myles.

Hickalik strained his ears. "Yeah, I can."

Hickalik grabbed his fire-stone and held it up to one of the cave forks. They heard the noise, but could not see anything, nor tell where it was coming from.

They turned back-to-back as they rotated around, hoping to get a glimpse. Myles picked up a stick from the fire, using it as a torch.

Hickalik started to whimper again, "I don't like bugs," he sniveled.

"Don't worry about the centipedes," said Myles, "I'll shoo them off."

"It's.. no, not... cen... cenep...p...pedes," he stuttered.

Myles turned around to calm Hickalik but noticed Hickalik looking at the cave ceiling. Myles lifted his makeshift torch. There crouched three scorpions, roughly the same size as them, walking on the ceiling. The biggest one was just above poor petrified Hickalik, clicking more vigorously now.

Myles pulled Hickalik away, "Run!"

They sprinted down one of the caves. As Hickalik turned, running by sheer instinct, he let out a low building scream, "I don't like bugs!" he cried.

Myles would have told him to stop screaming, but it seemed to help spur Hickalik on as he gained momentum. The scorpions gave chase, continuing the clicking noises as they scurried behind. The cave forked again. Hickalik was about to run to the right, but Myles pulled him left at the last second.

The boys were running out of steam, and the scorpions were closing in. This amplified Hickalik's panicked state. He reached into his bag and started throwing every ebenezer stone he could find. A flaming flare bounced around the cave. A bright flash and booming crack shook the cave walls as a lightning bolt struck the smallest scorpion. It instantly laid on its back with its legs curled smoldering.

This did not deter the other scorpions, however. Hickalik continued to throw stones. A stone shattered and light blue flames erupted forth. The ground and walls around the pursuers became encased in ice, making the scorpions fall off the walls. They slipped and slid, trying to find traction, while they gave Myles and Hickalik a much-needed gap. But the scorpions quickly regained their footing. Hickalik threw another stone, and this one sent gray flames and a rush of air that lifted the scorpions to the ceiling and back down again.

"That brought them closer!" shouted Myles.

In desperation, Hickalik threw his remaining two stones. A massive fireball erupted, filling the cave behind them with exploding flames, which propelled the boys forward with a burst of heat, causing them to fall on their faces. The explosion echoed down the cavern, then the air fell silent. They both turned quickly, expecting to find the creatures ready to strike. However, the scorpions had vanished. A few nearby pieces of debris still supported a few small flames from the blast.

Shaken, Hickalik reached into Myles' backpack and retrieved another fire-stone for more light.

"You did it," Myles praised.

"I did? I did do it," Hickalik realized. "Take that you ugly bugs."

The boys walked up to the explosion site to investigate. Hickalik stopped smiling as he constricted his eyebrows, "Where are the bodies?" he asked.

"Disintegrated, I guess."

Hickalik accidentally kicked a shard of crystal on the ground from one of the stones. He reached down and picked it up, holding the glowing fire-stone closer to examine it.

"This is the casing for an invisibility-stone," he said aloud. Myles and Hickalik locked eyes. From the darkness behind came a quickened, clicking noise, approaching fast. The boys took off again as Hickalik's screeching fired up once more.

"You turned them invisible?!" yelled Myles.

"I was trying to kill them!" he yelled back.

"Now what?" asked Myles. Hickalik reached into Myles' backpack and threw more stones. Again, the cave walls froze behind them. Then a loud crack boomed with a bright strike of lightning.

"Did it work? Did you get one?" asked Myles.

"I don't know! They're invisible!" Hickalik whimpered back.

Hickalik threw another stone. A flare bounced around the cave once more, but the clicking persisted. They ran into an adjoining underground creek. The current was fast, but it was shallow enough for them to continue running downstream.

"Look ahead," pointed Myles. They could see another fork in the cave. The right side looked dark. The water flowed left, down to what sounded like a waterfall.

"The water, follow the water," Myles shouted.

As they approached the fork, Hickalik shouted, "I see light." He pointed to the right, but it was too late. Myles' momentum took him left and Hickalik went right. Myles tried to stop but was taken over the top of an underground waterfall.

He flipped over in the air and landed below with a splash. He was able to fight up through the water, gasping for air. He hoisted himself out of the water and lay on his side, using what little strength he had to breathe. Now in total darkness, Myles was soaked and cold.

"Hickalik," he cried out. "Hickalik," he yelled out again.

"Hickalik..." this time recoiling as he started to blubber. Tears formed in the corners of his eyes. He could hear nothing but the sound of rushing water. He was alone in the damp blackness. His mind drifted away. He thought of the home he left behind, the warm fires Ms. Helen made, and the other children jumping off the walls until she banished them outside.

"I wish I never came here," Myles sniveled to himself. "I had hope, but now I will just die in a cave... alone. I just wanted to meet my parents... and feel their hugs. I wanted to hear them say they loved me. And that... they were proud of me. I wanted someone to love me unconditionally and never give up on me."

Myles wept.

He remained on the cold rocky floor, which drained the warmth from his body. Shivering, his spirit was broken. A single pebble rolled to a stop in front of him. He lifted his head, straining to hear any further movement.

Suddenly, there was a whoosh of cloth as a rough sack was thrown over his head. Panic surged through him. He grabbed onto the sack and rolled to his knees. He blindly lashed out, his arm connecting with something furry.

One hand frantically fumbled with the sack, trying to tear it free. He spun around, kicking out like a wild horse, hoping to ward off the animal. Something jumped onto his backpack pulling hard on the head covering. His backpack straps were severed and removed.

Sharp claws dug into his shoulder blades. He lurched forward, trying to dislodge the unseen creature clinging to his back. Another set of claws raked his ankles, pulling his legs out from under him. He slammed face-first onto the hard ground. Before he could recover, his wrists were seized and yanked outwards.

There were so many of them. He could not move. Every limb was pulled taut, his body contorted and bound. He struggled, twisting and turning, but it was futile. Ropes, rough against his skin, bound his wrists together. Then, his legs were pulled tight and secured. Three, no, four figures now weighed him down, pinning him to the ground.

He could feel them rummaging through his pockets. They unfastened his satchel. He could hear them frantically searching through his backpack.

A spark of hope flickered through his mind—*Maybe they just want my stuff*, he thought. Soft hands reached for his neck. A strangled cry escaped his lips. "No," he rasped, "not my compass." But his plea fell on deaf ears.

The compass was yanked from his neck. Now that the fight was over, Myles thought he could hear them muttering.

"Wub, lubnub, wubble lubb," he heard a creature mumble.

"Wub bub, nubbub," another answered. They were talking.

"Hello," Myles tried to speak to them, "I'm Myles. Can you understand me? Could you untie me please? I don't mean you any harm. You can keep all the stuff; I just need that compass. Please?"

Two paws grabbed the knot by his hand.

"Thank you," Myles said, but then the paws pulled the knots tighter.

Tightly bound, Myles was carried deeper into the caves by many small furry hands. Although terrifying, the journey took so long that Myles found himself asleep at one point.

After a long trek, he heard a deeper-voiced creature speak as he was set upright, "Nubble, wub ubb," it demanded. The head covering was ripped off. Myles blinked and stared, then blinked again trying to shake off what he thought was a hallucination.

Ordinary Beginnings

"Pandas? Red pandas?" The words escaped his lips in an unbelieving gasp.

He cast his gaze around, taking in the extraordinary scene that unfolded before him. He wasn't in a cave anymore, not exactly. He stood rigid, still tied with ropes, on a wooden platform that jutted out into a vast, cavernous space, a deep rift under ground level.

But the most astonishing sight wasn't the cavern itself. It was the inhabitants. Red pandas, hundreds, swarmed the cavern floor. They were clothed. Some sported fine leather garments, others wore comfortable tunics of cotton or wool. A few even wore hooded cloaks, their distinctive pointed ears peeking through cleverly cut holes.

Myles craned his neck upwards. The cavern wasn't entirely enclosed. Lush green canopies peeked through a wide opening high above, bathing the space in a cascade of dappled sunlight. Gigantic, ancient roots spiraled downwards like the arms of a slumbering giant, their twisting forms filling the cavernous space.

Nestled amongst the roots were huts with windows carved into their woody flesh. Intricate stairs, ramps, and even slides, all meticulously crafted from the wood, provided access between these elevated dwellings. The winding paths through the village were carved from the very roots themselves. Remembering the sun never moved in this world, Myles noticed all the village pathways were constructed in the cracks of light pouring down through the rift above.

In front of Myles, a crackling fire cast flickering shadows on the cavern wall. An older red panda sat on the other side, perched on a comfortably large rock. Wisps of gray fur intermingled with his fiery coat. He raised his paws to gather the attention of the others.

The elder panda spoke, his voice surprisingly deep and gravelly for such a small creature, "Nubble lubb, wub bub. Lubble wub gubb."

Myles had no idea what was said, but this panda seemed to speak authoritatively to the others, and Myles assumed he was their chief. The chief cut a distinguished figure in a green tunic and leather belt with a white cloak draped over his back. Feathers perched between his perked ears cast a shadow over his brow, adding an air of wisdom.

"I mean you no harm," Myles pleaded, praying he was understood. We were lost in the cave, and the scorpions were…" But the pandas erupted with loud squeaks as they jumped and growled, showing their teeth.

They sound like angry little otters, Myles thought, thinking they were the cutest things he had ever seen.

"You hate the scorpions too?" Myles asked. Again, an uproar of high-pitched chatter erupted.

"I just came here in search of a dragon egg. I did not mean to…" he was interrupted again.

"Lubble nub, wobble bub," the chief sternly pointed at Myles with his whole paw.

Two of the pandas approached, barely as tall as his waist. They sniffed Myles, lifted his pant legs to look at his ankles, lifted his shirt and sniffed his skin. Myles squirmed at their tickling whiskers. One climbed up his body and pulled down his collar, exposing his burn marking.

The chief jumped back, raising both hands in shock, catching himself with his tail. The chief paused momentarily, then spoke to the others, "Nullubb nul bub bub."

The pandas untied Myles. The ropes dropped to the floor. Myles was then forced to take a warm bath. They washed his clothes and fed him delicious fruits he had never seen before. They laid him down on a large, soft bed. Myles could tell the sun was fading above. The pandas climbed to the root-rafters above and fell asleep. Their little furry tails and paws dangled downward as they breathed deeply through their black leathery noses. Myles felt strangely safe amongst the furry village as his exhaustion took over.

Disoriented by a night of unfamiliar surroundings, Myles shot upright. His abrupt movement shattered the peaceful morning. A discord of startled squeaks filled the air as the furry creatures plummeted ungracefully from the network of branches; one landed with a soft thud on Myles' head.

After a breakfast of more delectable unknown fruits, Myles was escorted around the village, through the winding pathways. Eventually, they halted at a large hut.

Unlike any other hut in the village, this hut stood bathed fully in the warm glow of sunlight. Its walls were ornately sculpted with intricate designs supported by gigantic roots serving as its frame. A massive open archway curved around the entrance.

With surprising efficiency, the villagers bustled about, producing a hodgepodge of what could only be described as armor. Made from a combination of leather and what appeared to be vegetable husks, it lacked the quality that characterized the rest of their clothing. Myles was uncomfortably encased from head to toe. Even his hands were encased in awkward leather mitts. He couldn't help but feel rather preposterous.

"Is this really necessary?" he asked, but he didn't know if he wasn't understood or just not listened to.

After dawning a coconut helmet to complete the ensemble, the chief invited Myles away from the majestic hut ahead to a smaller hut on the left. Inside, he was greeted by four pandas, each appearing even older than the chief. No other villager followed Myles into the hut. The four elders scrutinized Myles, reading his eyes, then sniffed him and knocked on his coconut.

They argued for a time, then repeated their examinations. Myles, still not understanding a word, could only watch as an elder ascended a winding staircase. He returned shortly, carrying an object carefully concealed beneath a worn tarp. As the elder approached, he removed the tarp, revealing a sight that caused Myles' heartbeat to quicken.

There, nestled in the elder's paws, was an exotic red egg. Deep scarlet hues swirled across its smooth surface.

This is it, Myles thought, my dragon egg.

The elder panda extended the egg, gifting it to Myles. He cradled his hands underneath to lift it from the elder's paws. Myles' eyes widened, his heartbeat hammering a frantic rhythm as his hands began to tingle.

"Ouch," he recoiled.

The egg burnt his hands. An elder panda quickly threw a pail of water at Myles. Nearly all the water hit Myles in the face and drenched his armor. He pressed his hands on his now soaked garments to cool them.

"Wubb nubb ala shub," another one exclaimed, cutting the others off loudly as it pivoted toward the back stairwell and returned with an egg. This egg was lavender-gray with more vertical lines splotching the shell.

Myles, still feeling the tingling burn from the last egg, gave a testing tap to the top of the egg, but nothing happened. The elder did not seem amused, hoisting the egg towards Myles forcefully.

"Nub wubble," he commanded.

Myles slowly placed all his fingertips on the sides of the egg and waited. A breeze began to whirl around them, lifting leaves off the ground. The breeze intensified to a swift gust, blowing his feet out from under him, crashing Myles to the floor where his feet stood.

Myles grunted and shook off the impact, "Okay, I get the armor now."

Scrambling to his feet, another egg was offered—this time it was a crystal blue egg with blotted dots. Myles mustered the courage to press his hands on the shell. His hands were instantly encased in ice. The panda pulled the frozen hands to the floor. A large wooden mallet was waywardly swung, smashing his stinging hands free, now numb and bruised. Myles was starting to lose faith in his new furry friends' wisdom.

That day was a brutal initiation for Myles. Fireballs scorched, electricity crackled, thorns raked. Each presented egg pushed him to his limit. He endured frigid blasts, searing heat, sand blasting in his eyes, even being oxygen-deprived for a minute. Whenever there was a flash from a fireball or bolt of lightning, you could hear other pandas still gathered outside the hut oohing and aahing at the spectacle.

An elder brought out another egg, but Myles raised his hands in surrender.

"I can't, no more," he shook. "It's not going to work. I...I'm not special."

But the elder panda stood firm, shaking the egg in the defeated boy's face, "Nub wobble, nub wobble."

Myles quarreled in his head, "You've all been so kind to me, but I can't." He inhaled deeply and looked at their innocent eyes. "One more," he grimaced.

As he grabbed the last egg with shaking hands, a shockwave ripped through the hut. The force hurled Myles through the doorway, and he landed with a bone-jarring thud on the wooden pathway outside. The chief and the gathered villagers scattered around him.

The world tilted as Myles pushed himself onto his knees. His ears throbbed, and a persistent ringing drowned out the discord of voices around him. His inadequate armor hung in tatters. The coconut helmet lay forgotten somewhere in the wreckage.

The villagers buzzed with frantic discussion, their accusatory glances flitting between him and the bewildered elders who emerged from the hut, fur ruffled and voices raised in heated dispute. Gestures flew, all pointing towards Myles, but Myles was beyond caring. The exhaustion that gnawed at him overshadowed the chaos. All he could do was let the world fade away as he struggled not to collapse.

All of a sudden, the ringing in his ears went silent. The dizziness grew into tunnel vision as the pandas' chatter faded. His aching body numbed to nothingness. He turned, taking a couple steps without any conscious thought. A warm, inviting light spilled from the grand ornate hut. His feet seemed to have a mind of their own, carrying him in a slow, unsteady bearing towards the rounded archway, leaving the discordance of the arguing mammals behind.

Drawn by compulsion, Myles stumbled into the large hut. Its walls were adorned with a tapestry of detailed pictographs. Sunlight streamed through the open ceiling, casting a warm beam upon the center of the room. There sat a wooden nest lined with vibrant green leaves. Nestled inside lay a single, solitary egg. Unlike the others, this egg wasn't adorned with vibrant hues or swirling patterns. It was dull white, unassuming, and ordinary. Yet, to Myles, it pulsed with a captivating glow.

Just as he was about to lurch closer, two figures jumped in front of him. Armored red pandas, their expressions grim, blocked his path.

"Lubble nub wullub," they demanded, pulling Myles out of his dream state. In their paws, they held burning green flames.

"Ruach?" Myles questioned.

But the two pandas did not warn Myles again. They each spun a ball of green flame off their paws which set the wooden archway ablaze. Branches grew quickly off the archway and tightly whipped around Myles' arms. They pulled him down to his knees, securing him tightly. Myles could not help but gaze at the egg basking in the light.

Then a burning sensation boiled on his chest. It felt like a smoldering cattle brand was being pressed to his skin. He cried out, still immobilized by the wooden restraints. He pulled at the roots but could not break their grip. He was at his limit, about to pass out, when the pain mercifully subsided. He took a big gasp of air, trying to recover. The roots released their grip, and the guards recalled their flames.

Myles put his hands on his chest. His tattered shirt was warm; his skin was hot. He pulled his collar down. His birthmark had changed, morphed into something different. It was a much lighter color. The shape showed three winding curved threads swirling through each other, interwoven to a center point.

Never seeing this symbol before, Myles instinctively read, "Omni."

A wave of stunned silence washed over the pandas, then erupted into ecstatic wonder. They crowded Myles, petting his arms and body while sniffing him.

They chanted, "Lub nub, lub blub," repeatedly.

But when the chief raised his paw, they went silent once more. He gestured to the plain egg in the center of the room. The crowd divided, giving Myles a clear path to the nest.

The pandas lay down their cloaks, coats, and large leaves on the path. The chief rotated his wrist as flames of vibrant purple swirled on his paws. The egg arose from its nest and slowly floated toward Myles. It stopped and floated just in front of him.

"Omni," Myles said again, this time to the egg. He placed his hands under the egg. It gradually descended into his care. There was no explosion, electric shock, or burning sensation, just a warm, peaceful embrace.

"I... found my dragon," Myles said audibly, coming to terms with what just transpired. He glanced toward the jovial red pandas, who were now petting and touching him again.

His chest was still smoldering with pain, but he didn't care. "This is unreal. A dragon chose me." From the wooden pathway, a small red panda, nimble and quick, scurried through the furry mob, returning Myles's stolen satchel, surprisingly clean and mended. Myles carefully placed the egg inside the satchel and placed it over his shoulder.

He was then paraded through the village, this time with much more enthusiasm. Red pandas were lined up down the pathways. They all wanted to touch him and pet at him as he walked by. They rang bells and played tambouring-like instruments. Some of the leading pandas used their green flames to bloom flowers on the surrounding roots. Pandas hung out windows tossing pedals and grains out on the path.

He was presented with a great feast of yet more fruit and a panda party filled with dancing, jumping, and hanging from vines and branches. Myles dazzled the pandas with some rudimentary magic tricks he did for the children back home. The tricks only ever impressed Marguerite, but the pandas were elated.

Throughout the evening, Myles reached down to touch his egg, a reminder of his selection. The revelries continued into the night with adorable squeaks and Myles' laughter. The squeaks were replaced by peaceful slumber. Pandas sprawled on platforms, curled in roots, or hung precariously from vines. The chief himself snored softly, his head where his legs should be, his tail draped over his throne-like chair.

Myles felt safe amongst the roots, and welcomed. The thought of leaving the next day made him sad, but he needed to get back. He needed to care for Omni now. As he laid there amidst the heavy-nose breathing, he worried about Hickalik, Sigurd and Kamara... Allen, and his parents. His thoughts stirred him to sleep eventually.

The next morning, he found himself back in the soft bed once more. Omni's egg was with him as the pandas fell from their perches yet again. He was greeted by yet another sweet and ripened breakfast, which his stomach was beginning to disagree with. He was herded back to the chief's hut, where he was presented with his stolen belongings as if they were a gift from the pandas.

"How thoughtful," he said sarcastically.

The cut straps of his backpack were sturdily sewn back together. Myles was most relieved to see his father's compass returned, but before Myles could grab the compass, it was snatched by a swiping paw. The chief stared at the instrument and sniffed it all around. He then sprouted a lot of gibberish words that Myles wished he could understand. The chief touched Myles's hand and pointed to his fake academy ring as he gave the compass back to Myles.

Myles thanked the chief and the village, awkwardly giving a bow for some reason. He turned and was led out of the hut. The two guards from before guided him up a very windy open staircase.

At the top, the red pandas used their green flames to open a wall of roots like a wooden curtain. Myles ventured out and found himself at the base of an enormous tree amongst thick vegetation, happy to have solid ground under his feet again. He turned to face the two red pandas to bid them farewell.

"Thank you for everything," Myles waved.

One panda gave a bow, mimicking Myles' performance. The other swatted the bowing panda's ear. This started a fluffy fight as the roots closed on his newly found friends.

Myles spun around, taking in the lush green forest surrounding him. He carried his backpack, compass, and egg-filled satchel. The egg felt warm to the touch as he placed his palm on its shell. The air was fresh, with hints of mint. Then, he realized he did not know which direction to go. He searched his backpack, but Hickalik had used all his stones in the caves.

A forceful thud struck Myles' shoulder. He jumped and looked around but saw nothing. Reaching up, he felt a slimy residue on his shoulder. Another thud sounded in the bushes beside him, followed by another behind him. He crept closer and knelt, moving a fern branch out of the way. There on the ground was a giant yellow slug, the size of a small, obese snake.

"Banana slugs?" Myles said curiously.

A fireball erupted high above the treetops, pulling Myles' attention upward.

"Was that for me?" he wondered aloud, then grimaced as another slug plummeted from above. Before he could dwell on it, a darting shadow swooped over the canopy, snatching something from the large tree.

Then, the sky above began to darken, an expanding mass blotting out the sunlight. Myles squinted, as a realization dawned, the explosion above caused a pulsating mass of falling banana slugs, raining down towards him.

The falling slugs dislodged more of their brethren, a cascading avalanche of slimy yellow from the branches above.

A frantic dash through the undergrowth sent adrenaline coursing through Myles' veins. He weaved through the forest floor, leaping over fallen logs and ducking under tangled undergrowth. The air drummed with the sickening splat of molluscan bodies hitting the ground.

A flicker of white caught his eye amidst the chaos. A rabbit. A rabbit with a magnificent set of antlers. He thought he was seeing things but had no time to think as the slimy barrage persisted.

Continuing further, he saw the same rabbit he passed earlier sitting again in front of him, watching. This time the rabbit turned, hopped twice, then paused, as if it wanted Myles to follow. The rabbit took off, gracefully dodging and weaving through the forest foliage.

With no plan of his own, Myles followed the creature's lead. The rabbit, a beacon of white, darted through the forest with an uncanny agility. Miraculously, both the rabbit and Myles remained unscathed. The rabbit kept running, seemingly quickening its pace. Myles tried his best to keep up, but the nimble creature quickly disappeared amongst the vegetation.

Myles bent over, clutching his cramping ribs and gasping for air. He continued walking and soon came to a clearing. In the distance, he could see the plateau.

"I have to make it by noon," he told himself. He realized he was back in the dried riverbed he and Hickalik had traversed before entering the caves.

"I hope Hickalik is alright," he said worryingly.

Time being a factor now, he hiked up steep ridges and climbed several nearly vertical cliffs. Fortunately, the cliffs were neither too tall nor too difficult.

A forming shape in the cloud cover caught his eye—the airship emerged, returning to the plateau.

"I need to hurry," he said aloud.

He reached the top of his next climb and found himself on a wide outcrop. Glancing up at the next highest ledge, he saw Xander standing on the edge.

"Hah, the dirt-stained commoner. How quaint. What are you doing down there you buffoon, trying to get eaten?"

Myles scanned his surroundings and spotted a large plated egg under an overhanging rock. A low snarl came from the shadows, but Myles saw nothing else. The egg began to unravel as bits of fur emerged and transformed into a large wolf-like creature. Its back and tail were covered in armored scales. Myles' frantic search for a weapon yielded nothing. In a desperate attempt at defense, he ripped off a boot and held it behind his head, ready to strike. The wolf's head hung low, its teeth bared, and its tail tucked.

An annoying laugh came from above, "You certainly are helpless, Briggs,"disparaged Xander."Here, a token of my prestigious grace."

He tossed a stone down to Myles from above, but Myles didn't dare take his focus from the circling predator. The stone fell to the ground in front of Myles, and shattered.

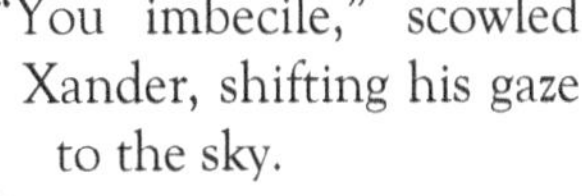

"You imbecile," scowled Xander, shifting his gaze to the sky.

Myles didn't understand until it was too late. A blinding flash of light split the sky, a bolt of lightning arched down just in front of the monstrous wolf. The thunder cracked, a deafening roar that sent a shockwave through Myles, shoving him backwards. His foot, already precariously close to the ledge's edge, lost its footing with the sudden shift. The ledge crumbled.

Myles tumbled down through the air, his body twisting and turning in a sickening ballet. Below, the ground rushed up to meet him. He needed something to break his descent, but the unforgiving space between him and the earth offered nothing but air.

"That's it," Myles reached into his bag and threw his last remaining ebenezer stone downward seconds before impact. The stone shattered, and gray flames whooshed, sending a geyser of air upward, slowing Myles to a float just above the ground. He was even lifted back up higher than he was anticipating. He waved his arms, then fell back down, landing hard. But the blast of air had dislodged the egg from his satchel. He opened his eyes to see his egg falling. It dropped to the ground with a devastating crack.

"No," he roared, scrambling towards the fallen egg. "No. No. No... Please be okay. Omni, please." he begged. Myles scooped up the cracked egg and placed it back into his satchel.

A clatter of pebbles fell from above. He glanced up to see the monstrous wolf nimbly descending the cliff face. Myles lurched to his feet. Screaming in protest, his legs propelled him forward in a clumsy sprint. But he knew outrunning the fanged nightmare behind him was a fool's hope.

The frantic dash continued, his eyes darting behind, searching for any sign of the wolf. Suddenly, an object got tangled in his feet, sending him sprawling face-first into the dirt. It was another student's backpack.

Someone must have left it when they were rescued with a flare, he thought.

He hastily dumped the bag. Sure enough, the flare-stone was gone. But he found lightning, flame, ice, and air-stones. With panic pounding in his mind, he quickly weighed his options, "Even if I fight it off, I will be stuck out here. A rescue is my best chance. But no one could see me down here if I used the fire-stone."

He looked down at his one remaining boot. He took it off, "I hope it works."

A glance up confirmed his worst fears. The wolf had reached the bottom of the cliff and was picking up speed. Grasping the flame- and air-stones, Myles placed the fire-stone inside the boot and attached the air-stone in the boot's bottom inlay.

The wolf's growls intensified; it was getting closer. Myles knew he only had one chance. With a silent prayer, he slammed his boot down onto the rocky ground, shattering the air-stone with a satisfying crack. The boot, propelled by the gray burst of compressed air, shot skyward like a rocket. Myles shuffled backward keeping his eyes fixed on his prey.

The wolf was only steps away. Myles could see the whites of its eyes, and the drool dangling from its mouth. He threw his last stone as hard as he could. The stone hit the ground just in front of the wolf. A bolt of lightning boomed once again, striking the wolf who let out a horrendous yelp. Myles glanced at the flying boot, a fireball blazing above. The lightning struck the fire-stone in the boot, causing a fiery explosion. With one fell swoop, Myles was able to send a beacon, and ward off his attacker.

A satisfied huff escaped Myles' lips as the fireball sputtered out, but a glance towards the plateau's peak sent a jolt of despair through him. The airship was already ascending, carrying the students back to the academy without him.

An intensifying low growl arose. Myles turned back in horror, as the wolf slowly lifted itself back to its feet, its fur smoldering.

Now out of ideas, Myles turned and ran. The wolf growled aggressively and gave chase. Myles sprinted but was so exhausted that his pace slowed. He knew it was only a matter of time before the wolf pounced on him. He couldn't press on. He turned to face his attacker. Myles squeezed his eyes shut and covered his face with his arms.

Claws snatched his shoulders as his body was thrust airborne. The wolf's snarls faded quickly, to distant howls. Myles opened his eyes. It was Zalaph. Myles had been snatched by the shadow dragon and was now soaring high above the ground. Both shock and relief came over him, overshadowing his airborne fears.

Zalaph was swift and quickly caught up to the dirigible. Myles could see Hickalik, Sigurd, and Kamara all onboard. Hickalik and Sigurd were cheering Myles on, while Kamara looked semi-pleased.

Myles could hear Captain Nordic on the wind, "Flap yonder black death bat, yee frantic gusts sever aeronautics!"

Zalaph did just that. Myles was quickly flown past the airship and over the peaks. The added gravity from the altitude made his shoulders scream for a short distance. The winds were cold but did not last long as Zalaph dropped hastily to a lower elevation. The three academy towers came into view. Zalaph approached, dropping Myles abruptly on top of the center tower, and at the feet of Provost Prudencia.

Chapter Thirteen

Incubation

On his hands and knees, Myles lifted his gaze to meet Provost Prudencia, her imposing figure clad in her sweeping coat and leaning on her wooden staff.

"Myles Briggs, I presume? Little Allen was never very creative," Prudencia remarked as Myles dusted off his knees and stood up.

"You know who I am?" Myles asked in surprise. "And Allen too?"

"I know all the students that come to Feylux, including those who come under fictitious names," Prudencia replied.

"Did you know my parents?"

"I knew of your parents, as you will come to find, all here do. Your father became much more infamous than he would have liked," she responded cryptically.

Myles felt a flood of questions but held his tongue, recalling Allen's cautious warnings.

She looked down at the cracked egg inside his satchel, "I see your dragon may need your help sooner than most."

Myles pulled out his egg. "It fell when I was being chased by a wolf."

She nodded, "Ah, you met a guzzle, did you? Tenacious creatures. It's no wonder you look the state you do. Although they seem threatening, they are mostly egg hunters. They feed on the nests of larger animals. Most likely, it simply wanted your egg. The fact that you were able to escape with your egg intact is quite commendable."

Myles ran his finger across the shell's fracture, "How do I help him?"

"Well, there was once a rumored spring here on the grounds. The water was fed from the Caldera itself through underground streams. It was said the flow carried natural Ruach from the dragons' nesting grounds and could help mend young hatchlings and their eggs. But unfortunately, rumors are just that. If one did exist, it has probably long dried up."

Myles lost his hope once more. The provost pondered for a moment, "Speak with Pedagogue Greenwald. She may have a remedy to help your newfound friend."

A bell rang from the docking ship. The plank was extended, and the children were allowed to disembark. Hickalik and Sigurd raced to Myles, nearly knocking him over, with Kamara strolling behind.

"You made it," exclaimed Hickalik, excited to see his friend. "I was worried you got captured by the scorpions. I was telling Alistair to send a rescue party, but then we saw Zalaph carrying you away."

"Doesn't look like you took the easy way out," Sigurd said, nodding to Myles' tattered appearance.

Kamara was keen to persecute Myles. "How did you mess this up? It was a simple task. Look for an egg and touch it to ensear." As she said this, she whipped her satchel out from behind and held it open. Inside was a smallish egg, small for a dragon egg anyway. It was perfectly rounded, spattered with gray markings and bright yellow highlights.

Myles gasped, "You got an egg. What's its name?"

"No clue." She turned and pulled down her collar where a sliver of her burn could be seen on her shoulder blade. "I can't see my blaze. I'll check it later in the mirrors."

"Where did you find it?" asked Myles.

"On a snowy mountain peak. After I ditched the loyal lap dog."

"Ditched? Sigurd interjected. "You mean abandoned. I was bravely risking myself for your safety. We were being attacked by a couple of noghogs. I held them at bay with my pickaxe so she could climb a cliff and get away, but when I climbed after her and got to the top, she was gone."

"You told me to escape, so I did."

"Not from me, from the noghogs."

"Same difference." Kamara then continued her story. "After that, I went on a hike upward and just kept climbing. That's where I found this little guy in a nest made of smooth round ice. There were three larger eggs, but I wanted the runt."

"That's great," exclaimed Myles. "I'm so happy for you."

"Don't forget about us," said Sigurd. Both Sigurd and Hickalik opened the tops of their satchels as well. Sigurd showed his egg—dark brown, sprinkled with faded gold. Hickalik's was crystal blue with lines of every shade.

"Wow, that's amazing," Myles exclaimed, "What are their names?"

Sigurd cleared his throat, "I uh... I will also have to find out later."

Kamara smirked, knowing Sigurd's blaze must have an unfortunate placement.

Hickalik stared at his prize with wonder in his eyes. "This is Galacia. I found her up in the tallest tree in the forest."

Sigurd was shocked. "You climbed up that high?"

"The higher I climbed, the higher I felt I had to go," explained Hickalik.

A glint of recollection flickered in Myles' eyes, "But how did you escape those scorpions?"

"Remember when we separated? I told you I saw light. The tunnel ramped up to a clearing in the forest. I still heard the clicking behind me so I just kept running, hoping they were chasing me and not you. But they stopped, I think they didn't like being outside."

Hickalik saw Myles' satchel, "You found one, too? Let's see it."

Myles looked apprehensive as he unveiled his egg.

Sigurd gasped, "What in Escalia happened?" He was nudged in the ribs by a sharp elbow from Kamara.

"Ouch," he glared with disapproval.

Myles explained with an embarrassed tone, "We fell off a cliff. I was able to catch us with an air-stone at the last second, but when the stone blew us upward, it fell out of the bag and landed on the ground."

"That was some quick thinking," Sigurd encouraged Myles, trying to make up for his ignorance. "Without that, you both would have been goners."

"He's right... for once," added Kamara. "You protected it the best you could, better than most could have." She said, surprisingly empathetic.

"Is there anything we can do for it?" asked Hickalik.

"The provost said I should go talk to Pedagogue Greenwald to see if she knows of any remedies that could help."

Hickalik gulped, "You mean go talk to her... outside of class? Like, without witnesses?"

"Come on, Hick. It's to help... Oh, wait." Sigurd paused and looked at Myles again. "What's your dragon's name?"

His eye fell down at his cracked plain egg, "It's Omni," he said with care. "Yeah, it's for Omni. Our new friend."

As they spoke, Xander walked past towards the elevator with Aberdeen and Bach. Bach was carrying his egg. Xander and Aberdeen remained empty handed. Myles looked up at Xander; however, Xander never said a word, nor acknowledged Myles in any way. He simply strolled by statuesque.

Gavin sprung into the circle, uninvited, "Did you guys hear? Florky Bunson didn't return. They are sending out a search party now."

"Florky?" Myles clarified, "Really? I think we saw him heading northwest towards the volcanic region at one point."

"I'll let them know," Gavin hopped off as quickly as he came.

"I wonder what happened. I hope he's okay," worried Hickalik.

"The pedagogues will find him, don't worry," Sigurd faithfully stated. "He'll be back before dinner."

The students were directed to their dormitories to clean up after their expedition. Fresh uniforms awaited them, neatly laid out. They were instructed to dispose of their soiled exploration attire in the nearest disposal bulrog or the dormitory incinerators. Each headboard now featured an additional branch that had sprouted seamlessly from the wood, curling into a perfect perch for their new eggs.

One by one, the students placed their eggs upon the new perches. Hickalik's branches began to grow patches of icy snow amid the emerging pine needles, "It's just like the nest I found her in."

Sigurd's branch sprouted a large mix of packed crystals, quartz, calcites, and even copper.

"It's gorgeous," Myles commented. But before Myles could place his egg, Sigurd spoke up hesitantly to Myles and Hickalik. "Would you two comrades be willing to..." he faltered as a flush of pink filled his cheeks, "assist me?"

"Yeah, of course," answered Myles.

Sigurd searched for the right words, "You see... I am not able to read my dragon's name... since its location is a bit... unorthodox."

Myles and Hickalik glanced at each other, "Yeah..." Myles mustered, "we can help."

Sigurd perked up. He ran over to the dormitory restroom. Hickalik leaned closer to Myles, "Where is his blaze?" he asked, fearing the answer.

"On his... posterior," Myles answered.

"His what?" exclaimed Hickalik in a whisper, hoping he heard wrong.

Sigurd jogged back into the room carrying a mirror from the bathroom wall, "This should do the trick."

He placed the mirror on the floor in front of Myles. Sigurd turned around and dropped his trousers. Both Myles and Hickalik tried to find anything interesting on the ceiling.

"What's it say?" asked Hickalik while staring at the stained-glass windows.

Sigurd stared intensely over his shoulder letting out a sigh of relief, "Gullynn," he spoke. "My dragon's name is Gullynn," he paused with wonder and love for the name.

Sigurd hastily redressed and tightened his belt.

After returning the mirror, Myles placed Omni on his branch, but nothing happened. They all waited and watched in anticipation, but the branch stood still.

"It's fine, I'm sure," encouraged Hickalik. "That probably means it's a wood dragon, since it has no reaction with a wooden nest."

"I did find it in a wooden nest connected to tree roots. There were green leaves interwoven, but those were probably put there by the red pandas."

"The what?" asked Hickalik.

"The red pandas. There was a whole village of them."

Both Sigurd and Hickalik looked puzzled.

"You found a village of red pandas?"

"Yeah. They tied me up at first, but eventually they were quite friendly. They fed me lots of fruit and even introduced me to dozens of eggs. They could use Ruach, too."

"You saw a village of... wubbalubs?"

"I don't know, is that what they're called?"

"They aren't real," explained Hickalik. "Those are just stories parents tell kids when they're young. There are children's books written about them, but I didn't think they were real. Supposedly, they have an amazing connection with Ruach and can control it themselves like dragons. They are known as protectors of dragon eggs."

"I did see them use Ruach flames."

"That's incredible," added Sigurd. "I have never heard of anyone seeing a real wubbalub in person.

Distracted, Myles ran his fingers over the cracked egg once more, "I need to see Pedagogue Greenwald."

Sigurd stood up and moved away from his bed. "I will accompany you."

"Did you want to come too, Hick?" Myles asked.

"No, sorry. I have other things to do. And I don't much like Pedagogue Greenwald."

"Why?" Myles asked, "You seem to be her favorite student... which isn't saying much."

"That's the problem. She is always picking me to do things and expects so much. I would just rather not go, if that's okay."

"Yeah...of course. That's fine. We'll see you at dinner then," Myles said, as he grabbed Omni and left with Sigurd.

Sigurd and Myles found Pedagogue Greenwald's office door closed but could hear the rustling of papers from underneath the thick wooden door. Myles knocked. There was a clunking unlatch, and the door creaked open. They slowly peered inside.

"Pedagogue Greenwald?" Myles called out.

"Yes, yes. I'm here," she answered. She was poring over papers for each of her first-year students.

"Sorry to bother you ma'am, but Provost Prudencia informed me you might be able to help."

"The provost sent you, did she?" She surveyed the two boys and stood tall, looking cross. "Did she also tell you to disgrace this academy and shame yourselves as well?" She gestured to their untucked and lazily buttoned uniforms. The boys quickly scrambled, tucking in their shirt tails.

"Our apologies," Sigurd replied, embarrassed. "I hadn't noticed. We are usually much more attentive than this. It has been an exciting day. But that is just an excuse, there is no acceptable reason, ma'am."

Myles noticed he missed a button on his shirt, making it lopsided. He frantically unbuttoned and rebuttoned. Greenwald leered at the boy. "What's your name, child?"

"Myles Briggs, ma'am. I am in your second class. I sit next to Hickalik, Hickalik Milbred."

"Do you now? And what important task does the provost expect of me, Mr. Briggs?"

Myles presented his egg. Her demeanor instantly changed as she looked at the damaged shell, like a woman swooning over an adorable newborn.

"Oh, the poor little one," she stared at the egg, then scowled at Myles. "There is nothing I can do," she said, as she pushed the egg back onto Myles.

"Oh... I see," said Myles, deflated.

"There is no remedy for a dead hatchling."

"Dead?" questioned Sigurd. "How do you know it's dead?"

Greenwald's voice came stern again, "Once a dragon's egg has been unsealed, the natural Ruach inside that is meant to nurture and feed the dragon leaks out. If this dragon is not dead, it will be soon enough."

"No," Myles uttered, "I can't give up on Omni."

"I am sorry for your loss. But there's nothing that can be done. Now, if you both will excuse me I have lots more paperwork to go through."

The two boys stood in the hallway outside her office, their gaze locked on the cracked egg.

"I'm not giving up," Myles said, determinedly. He started off down the hallway as Sigurd followed. "Where are we going?" he asked.

"To see Gruburg."

"What's a Gruburg?" inquired Sigurd, catching up.

"He's the school masoner," explained Myles. "He keeps up the facility and fixes things for the academy. I think he may know something about what the provost told me."

A few more hallways and a staircase later, the boys found themselves staring down the long dark hallway.

"Spooky," whispered Sigurd.

"Hey," a voice boomed from behind them, making both their hearts hammer against their ribs. Myles almost lost his egg a second time. It was Kamara. She was thoroughly enjoying their reactions.

"What in the outer world is wrong with you?" asked Sigurd, now feeling quite cross.

"What are you two doing here?" she asked.

"We're going to see Gruburg, the masoner," said Myles.

He was expecting another line of questioning, but Kamara simply said, "Ok, let's go." She cut between the boys and started walking down the torch-lit hallway. Myles and Sigurd caught up quickly.

"Gruburg. Gruburg? It's me, Myles."

A grumpy whispering could be heard across the room, "Again, they beckon and taunt my name. Liars or friends, 'tis quite the game." Sigurd seemed hesitant to step foot in the room, but Kamara seemed driven by curiosity.

"You're a Dindrole?" she said with a smile.

"Myles, you bring more to gawk and stare?"

"Oh, no. I would never. These are my friends. This is Kamara and over here is Sigurd." Myles pulled Sigurd forward.

Sigurd hesitantly spoke, "It is nice to make your acquaintance, good sir."

Gruburg questioned but with a happier tone, "Good sir? Now I'm good, he says. Sir and good... you baffle and confuse me with words."

"Myles stepped forward, "Gruburg, I need your help. I found my dragon, but his egg... it's cracked. Do you know where the underground springs are on the academy grounds? The waters that flow from the Caldera? You said before, you have been here since the academy's reconstruction."

Gruburg scoffed, "I know not of any springs and waters under these grounds. Check the old maps." He pointed to the corner of the room.

There was a wooden crate with hundreds of smooth speckled stones. Gruburg picked up a bronzed circular item that looked like a decorative trophy and placed it on the table, dusting it off with a rag. The plume of dust made Sigurd sneeze repeatedly.

Kamara picked up one of the smooth stones, "They're map-stones," she enlightened.

She walked over to Gruburg and placed the stone on the bronze machine. A burst of lights and color came forth around them, depicting a map of the academy grounds, from the perimeter walls to the Caldera's mountains behind. The towers looked different, but the topography was beautifully displayed. However, there was no sign of the rumored streams.

Sigurd stepped back to try to see the whole image, but then his eyes closed and his nose crinkled. He sneezed again, this time tripping backward over some old brass placards.

Myles reached over to help him up, "You okay?"

"Yeah, sorry. Bad allergies," he sniffed.

Myles apologized, "I'm sorry Gru..." but was interrupted.

Gruburg, who had lurched over to Sigurd, hoisted him up off the debris, "Get off you fool," Gruburg commanded.

"I'm sorry," stated Sigurd again. "Here, let us assist, sir."

Gruburg grumbled to himself while picking the placards off the ground, "Sir? You destroy my precious memories, then call me 'sir'?"

As Kamara was lost in the wonder of the map, Sigurd and Myles helped Gruburg reorganize the disturbed mess. Myles picked up a placard, then froze. His face turned pale as he read the sign in his hands.

"What's up, Myles?" Sigurd checked on his immobilized friend.

Myles said nothing. Sigurd came over to investigate and read the sign out loud, "Hereby commissioned by the Parliament of Dragons, in the year 8624, the reconstruction of the Feylux Academy. To blaze a flame in the hearts of future generations. Designed and constructed by Master Architect, Haldor Bridger."

In shock, Myles could barely speak, "That's my father. Haldor Bridger."

The room fell silent. Kamara walked over to read the sign for herself. She was the first to speak, "Myles, your dad, was the Architect of Death?"

Chapter Fourteen

Encompassing Truths

"Architect of Death?" questioned Myles, "What is that?"

Sigurd tried to clarify, "Haldor Bridger, the Architect of Death, is your father?"

"I don't know, what is that?" Myles asked again.

Kamara explained, "Myles, your dad, single-handedly destroyed the kingdom's entire agricultural economy, starving the kingdom for years... and, you know... was an architect to boot, hence the name. The kingdom's farmlands shriveled up overnight. The people were on the brink of starvation. Thousands of farm workers were unemployed for years. And all because your father took the verdure dagger."

Myles looked even more confused, "He took the what?"

Shock flickered in Sigurd's eyes, "The verdure dagger. You don't know? It was a totem... or artifact found in the middle of the farmlands by the house that controlled the farms. It was said to emit strong Ruach into the farmlands, helping the lands prosper, which in return, helped the kingdom thrive. I thought everyone knew about the verdure dagger, and yet you are the son of Haldor Bridger?"

"I think I am," Myles answered. "I never knew my parents. I grew up in an orphanage in the outer..." he quickly checked himself. "Outer regions of the kingdom."

"Mate, I'm sorry. This must be quite a blow," Sigurd sympathized.

"Why did he take the dagger?" Myles questioned.

Sigurd sighed, "No one really knows. Your father was a great galliant, truly. He was a rising star amongst his fold. His work with stone and gem attributes was unprecedented. He was even commissioned as the master architect to design and reconstruct the academy towers. Shortly after the towers were completed, people say he went mad, wanting more power. He took the dagger and ran off. No one has seen him since."

"What about my mother, Indra?" asked Myles.

"I don't know much about her to be honest," Kamara answered. "People said Haldor must have kidnapped her when he fled, or he..." but she stopped, not wanting to further upset Myles. The trio were silent as they all searched for the right words.

Gruburg had been waiting to the side, listening intently. His breathing deepened as he locked eyes with Myles. "You..." spit sprayed from his mouth as he pointed his calloused finger at Myles, his eyes watery and red, "You are the son of Haldor. You are his offspring?" Gruburg stepped ominously closer to Myles.

He reached out, grabbing Myles by the shoulders, then embraced him while starting to weep. "Your father... was my only friend," Gruburg wiped his snotty nose on Myles' cloak. "He was the only man to ever treat me as an equal. We built these towers together."

His face shriveled back to its normal state, "Then these *overcooked coals* started spouting blasphemy, saying he doomed the Kingdom."

Gruburg raised his voice higher, "If Haldor took the dagger, then he had a blazed good reason. And that's that!" he preached. Kamara and Sigurd were silent, not wanting to invite Gruburg's wrath on themselves.

Myles processed Gruburg's words, "You think he did it to help or... or to protect someone?"

Well of course he did," said Gruburg, "Haldor hadn't any flicker of darkness in his heart. He was a good man... a kind man. And... and I miss him." Gruburg threw his head over Myles shoulder once again.

"That settles it," said Myles, trying to prop Gruburg back on his own feet, "I'll clear my father's name."

"That is a tall order," interrupted Sigurd. "Even if your dad did what he did to save someone, thousands suffered at his hands. There are few who could forgive him for that."

"Not to mention," Kamara interjected, "there is the little problem of no one seeing your parents for years. The trail is ice cold. Where would we even start?"

"We?" asked Myles.

"Well... yeah. We are all friends, right?" replied Kamara nonchalantly, but to Myles this meant the world.

After patting Gruburg's back for a while and promising they would visit again soon, Myles was finally able to leave. While winding their way back to the dormitories, Myles felt almost giddy, "I can't wait to tell Hickalik."

But Kamara cut through his excitement, "Myles, you know Hickalik grew up on a farm, right?"

"Yeah, why?"

Kamara looked at him with probing eyes, "His family was probably one of the farming families who were hit hard by the famine your dad caused...I mean, was said to have caused. He may not respond well to hearing who your father is."

"I didn't think about that."

Against his better judgment, Myles decided not to speak with Hickalik on the matter, at least for now. Sigurd and Myles bid good night to Kamara and navigated their way back to the boys' dorms.

Hickalik greeted them with a surprisingly chipper disposition. He was holding a small bowl covered by a cloth, his hands covered in bandages.

"What's this?" Myles inquired.

"I did some digging, in the library, and found an old book on dragon eggs. The book was useless mostly; however, I found some old notes scribbled in the back of the book. It was an ointment for eggs... dragon eggs. I foraged around the academy grounds to find the ingredients."

Hickalik unveiled the bowl. It held a thick off-white paste and smelt like a livestock barn on a hot summer day. Sigurd immediately turned away, revolted by the odor.

"Hick, thank you. That's amazing. Pedagogue Greenwald said there was no remedy."

"Well, I'm hoping she is wrong about a lot of things," Hickalik smiled.

Myles held his egg while Hickalik carefully smeared the pasty solution, covering the shell's crack.

Myles thanked Hickalik again with a renewed sense of hope, "I don't know what to say."

"It's alright. I know you would do the same for me and Galacia."

As they settled in for the night with eggs on their perches, Sigurd slept under his sheets to filter out the aroma. Myles was riddled with guilt for not telling Hickalik about his father. After all the talk about the Architect of Death, Myles took his compass off his neck.

"I'm hoping I'm right about you, dad," he whispered. He reached over and placed the compass on the dresser next to his textbooks and hoped sleep would clear his emotions.

The symphony of snores that had lulled the students into sleep was interrupted. Myles awoke first, ungluing his eyelids. A faint noise hummed. He turned his gaze towards his egg, still nestled in its makeshift cradle. A purple glow pulsed about its surface, casting an eerie violet light around the room.

Myles perked up, rubbing his eyes. He was wrong, the glow was emanating, not from the egg itself, but from the wall behind the egg.

Myles shuffled out of bed. An oval-shaped hole had materialized above the dresser, filled with blackness, void of any light. Its edges were lined with swirling violet flames. He reached out to dab the black with his finger, but before he could, a gloved hand swung out of the black void, slapping his hand away.

Myles scrambled back, desperately putting distance between them. Unfazed, the hand snaked downwards, its long fingers scraping the compass off the dresser top.

In a reflex, Myles snatched a pillow from his bed and swung it with all his might. The pillow connected with a resounding thump, sending his compass flying across the room. It slammed against the opposite wall with a final crack, shattering off a piece of its ornate lining.

The hand whipped back into the void. The swirling violet flames dwindled and died out, and the portal shrunk rapidly until it vanished without a trace.

Across the room, Hickalik and Sigurd jolted awake. Sigurd snorted, "What was that ruckus?"

"The hand. The hand... did you see it?" exclaimed Myles.

"Whose hands? Your hands?" asked Hickalik in a dazed fog.

Sigurd stared at both of his hands with heavy eyelids, "I have mine..."

Myles pointed to the corner where the compass lay, "It grabbed my compass."

As if responding to his accusation, the air in the corner shimmered. The purple-rimmed hole ripped open once again, this time from the wall just above the compass laying on the floor.

"There!" shouted Myles.

The boys' eyes snapped open, drawn to the corner where the compass lay. The gloved hand shot out from the void, this time with a frantic urgency. It snatched at the compass, missing it by a hair's breadth. But with a second, desperate lunge, it seized the prize and gripped it tightly.

Myles lunged forward. Reaching out, he grabbed the wrist of the gloved hand just as it began to retreat back into the darkness. The hand pulled and strained but could not shake the determined boy.

With great strength the gloved hand pulled itself back into the void and Myles' hands with it. He was up to his elbows in the deep murky blackness.

"I still have it," Myles heaved, refusing to let go. He planted his feet on the wall, holding his position.

Hickalik sprang to action. But instead of assisting Myles, he grabbed a candlestick off the dresser. He hoisted it high and crashed it down on Myles' ebenezer textbook, shattering the inlaid stone on the cover. Looking frightened and breathing deeply, Hickalik swung two more times, smashing the stones on his and Sigurd's books, as well. The other boys were both perplexed, but Myles couldn't strain much longer.

With a final heave, born of pure desperation, Myles pulled back with all his might. The force of his exertion sent him flying. He slid across the room, his head crashed with a sickening thud on Sigurd's bedpost. In his hand, clenched tightly, was a single black glove. The compass was gone.

"My compass..."

Sigurd blurted out surprisingly useful information, "Portallers are usually short range."

Hickalik grabbed his satchel, "Quick, grab your eggs," not daring to leave them unattended. The boys stuffed their eggs in their satchels and ran out into the dorm common area. They saw no one. The entrance door leading to the corridor was wide open. They darted out the door and scanned the halls.

"This way," led Myles. The three raced down the stretching corridor.

"Out for an evening stroll?" a voice called out to them from the rafters above. Down dropped Kamara. "I didn't take you three for the rule breaking types."

Myles hastily explained, "There's no time, quick..." he sprinted off. "Someone stole my compass."

"Stolen? By whom?" she inquired.

"That's what we're trying to find out."

"Why are you out here at this hour, Kamara?" heaved Sigurd, winded. "A lady shouldn't be breaking curfew and lurking around at night."

Kamara glared back, "I never said I was a lady... especially your variety of pomp and circumstance."

"To the right," Kamara instructed, "I heard a door open a couple minutes ago."

As they approached, the door to the fog-chilled night was also wide open. Without hesitation, they burst through, the cool air a shock against their heated skin.

"There," Sigurd pointed towards a grassy slope in the distance, where a hooded figure sauntered away from the towers, a satchel slung carelessly over its shoulder. The hooded figure continued to walk at a leisurely pace.

It didn't take long to close the distance. Sigurd lunged forward, tackling the suspect at the knees and wrapping his arms around the ankles in a vice grip. Myles vaulted, landing squarely on the back and pinning the person down.

"Gotcha," said Myles.

Yet again, Omni's egg slipped from his satchel and rolled down the person's back, stopping with a clunk at the head. Myles quickly snatched his egg before it could roll down the grassy slope.

"What's going on?" struggled an angry, but familiar voice, "Get off me, you ingrates."

Myles leapt off the body and Sigurd released his death hug.

"Xander?" questioned Myles.

Xander scrambled to his feet, "What is this? How did I get here?" he demanded, whirling around to face the other students. His voice trembled with a mix of anger and confusion, "What have you done to me?"

As he spoke, his satchel began to move. With a choked whimper, he flung the bag away as if it were a venomous snake. He scrambled back, his face contorted in disgust, as a creature emerged from the depths of the satchel.

"It's a pufkin," Sigurd stated.

Hickalik pointed, "That must be one of the escaped pufkins Ms. Blumpkin was searching for."

Xander's eyes filled with rage, his finger stabbed accusingly towards Myles. "You... you poisoned me. What is this? Some kind of revenge? I was trying to help you, you daft fool."

But Myles didn't back down, "Where's my compass, Xander? I don't know how you did it, but give it back."

"What are you talking about? You kidnapped me. And dragged me out here for dragons know what reason."

"We didn't kidnap you. You were walking out here by yourself," Myles barked back.

"Oh really?" Xander facetiously asked, "And you four magically woke up together to come looking for little old me? Shove off Briggs! You poisoned me with a pufkin, made me hallucinate some weird dream, then dragged me out here."

"Where's my compass?" Myles repeated firmly.

"What compass, Briggs? Why would I want your pathetic excuse for a compass?" Xander started storming off. "Just wait until the provost hears about this. My parents will have your dumb dragon's egg for breakfast." But before Xander could march off, a voice echoed from the haze.

"Hey Dax, I's thought they's said it woulds only be's one kid's tonights. Like's this one's in the crater's."

"Shut it, Mordred," a grimaced voice snapped back, "and I told you not to use my name."

Two figures emerged from the fog. One, completely bald with a head that gleamed like a polished apple, the other, pulling on a long, tangled beard.

Recognition smacked Myles, "The men from the festival."

"Well, what's do's we's do's now?" asked Mordred, itching his neck. But Dax's eyes locked with Myles who was standing defenseless, hugging Omni's egg.

"You," Dax pointed at Myles menacingly, "You're the brat from the farm. Where's your little ice friend? Not here to help you this time? Too scared to try and trick me twice?"

Mordred's eyes widened, "Oh... he's the one's we's were suppose to find's at the orphanage's? The one's who's gave's you's the slips, right?" A visible vein protruded from Dax's forehead. "But, didn't they's say we's were to leave's him alone's now?"

"Shut it, Mordred," Dax grimaced. "No one escapes my hunts."

"Well, except's that's kid's," mocked Mordred, laughing at the expense of his partner.

"What are you depraved scum doing here?" Xander mustered up the courage despite his cracking voice. "This is academy grounds and you both are trespassing," he puffed.

Mordred laughed again, "Oh, are's we's little one's?"

Dax was not so amused, "That's the one we came for, the shrimp with the proper mouth... and the stench of privilege."

"But how's did he's wake's?"

"Who cares. We'll wipe his memories later, or something."

A sense of dread fueling his body, Xander bypassed the observing group, colliding shoulders with Myles, and launched into a full sprint towards the tower door.

"He's mine," gnashed Dax. He sparked a green flame in his hand, and thrust it into the ground. The soil around them began to tremor. Roots sprang up, grabbing Xander by the ankle. He crashed, catching his fall with his face.

Before the boys could act, Kamara drew a stone from her pocket and launched it at the two attackers. It shattered between them, billowing a thick gray smoke cloud as sounds of coughing and gasping were heard.

"Quick, this way," Kamara led, pulling them toward the towers. As Myles ran, holding his egg, he glanced back, witnessing a flicker of light from the smoke. He watched the dark smokestack and saw a faint orange glow from within. The glow flashed brighter, as a ball of fire surged outwards, soaring toward Myles.

A strangled cry of "Look out!" was all Myles could manage before the inferno roared upon him. He pivoted to face the flames, but a misplaced step sent him sprawling. The fireball, a monstrous onslaught of flames, hurtled towards his clutched egg.

The fireball slammed into them, and Myles was thrown back with tremendous force. He landed heavily, a sickening crack echoing as his head slammed against the ground. The world dissolved into blackness; the purple tinged night replaced by the oblivion of unconsciousness.

Chapter Fifteen

The Day of Emergence

Myles stirred groggily, struggling to breach the fog of sleep. He found himself propped against stiff pillows in a narrow bed enclosed by walls of cold stone. Thick timber columns marched upward, supporting a network of ornate skylights that cast a dappled light across the room. Sigurd's silhouette stood out against the luminous squares, his muffled voice breaking through Myles' daze.

"He's awake," Sigurd called.

A flurry of movement followed. Hickalik and Kamara appeared beside him, nearly toppling the flimsy bed in their haste.

"You're awake," Hickalik repeated.

Myles squinted, taking in his surroundings while rubbing his eyes, "Yeah, that's what I heard too."

"You're in the infirmary," Kamara explained, "You took a pretty nasty blow to that thick cranium of yours."

Myles gingerly touched his forehead, wincing at the throbbing pain, "That sounds right." A low whooshing sound seemed to reverberate in his ears.

"How are you feeling?" Hickalik asked.

Myles opened his eyes to a squint, "like my head is underwater."

Kamara was amused, "You couldn't be further from the truth."

Myles managed to pry open his eyes; his vision was blurry. Reaching for a nearby mirror, he caught a glimpse of his reflection. The back of his head was engulfed in a ring of fire. Panic surged, and in a knee-jerk reaction, he tried to extinguish the flames by swatting at them. But before he could, a stinging slap landed on a newly discovered goose egg on his head.

"Stop that, you silly child," a gruff voice scolded him. She was a plump woman, which helped the slap not hurt as badly. She displayed rosy cheeks, even though her temperament was anything but. A starched uniform identified her as infirmary staff.

"What's the matter with ya?" she pointed her plump finger at Myles like a person scolding a dog. "You'd think you'd never seen healing-flames before."

She shooed Sigurd to the side to update Myles' charts. "Now don't you touch my flames again." She grabbed his head and forcibly turned his face away to examine the injury. "Should be good by mornin'," she said, giving him another undeserved slap, this time on the side of his head.

"Ouch," Myles quietly protested.

She ignored his discomfort. "It's a good thing they brought you in when they did. Any longer and you would be as still as that egg of yours for weeks."

Myles widened his eyes when he remembered, "Omni," he gasped, snapping his neck around to look for his dragon, immediately regretting it.

"It's all right," Hickalik said soothingly, lifting Omni up to Myles.

"The stench should've clued him in a little," murmured Kamara.

"Hush," Sigurd retorted, trying to comfort Myles with an awkward smile. "We are glad you are both all right."

Myles thankfully accepted the egg and examined it, "But the fireball," Myles explained, "it hit us; it hit the egg. That's what knocked us backwards. How were we not burned?" Then he stopped to remember, "Wait...the two men? Xander? What happened?"

"Relax, will you?" Kamara tried to calm him down. "Obviously, we are all okay."

"You should've seen it, Myles," Sigurd donned his storytelling voice. "After you got knocked out, quite bravely I might add, Xander was just sniveling on the ground trying to pull himself free from the roots. I rushed to your side, of course, to protect you from those two evil men. What were their names, again? Hordon and Rax? Or something like that..."

"Mordred and Dax," inputted Hickalik, sounding surprisingly impatient.

"That's right," resumed Sigurd. "You were lying on the ground there. Your egg started rolling away again, so I reached out and saved it. But that nasty bearded fellow must have really not liked you for some reason. Roots sprang out of the ground around you and tied you down. I started pulling them off you the best I could, but..."

"But then you were trapped in the roots as well," Kamara interjected.

"Yes, but that doesn't make my efforts any less noble," defended Sigurd. "Anyway, then that Gax guy..."

"Dax," both Kamara and Hickalik corrected.

"Dax, that's what I said. He walked out of the smoke that Kamara set off, walking straight to you. He broke the large spiked end off of a standing root." Sigurd paused for dramatic effect. "He had malice in his eyes as he started to lift the spike up to strike. He wanted you dead. Before he could strike, I leapt over your unconscious body, still protecting you and your egg."

"You were lying on his legs," Kamara corrected again.

"Not much of a human shield, really," added Hickalik.

"More like a human shin-guard," Kamara patronized.

"It was a frantic and chaotic time; we all remember things differently," Sigurd defended again. "Then before that Nax guy..."

"Dax!" they corrected.

"Yeah, yeah, Dax. Before he could strike, Kamara slid a stone under that Dax guy's feet. The stone rang out with the voice of Xander, crying and pleading. Then the smoke cloud lit up again. That Mordrill guy..."

"Mordred," Myles corrected him this time.

"That's what I said. Mordred threw another fireball. This time directly toward the bearded guy. The impact must have blown him thirty paces back."

"Wait..." Myles interrupted, "Why was the stone making the sound of Xander's voice?"

Kamara held out a flat oval-shaped stone, "It's called a resonating-stone. It can record sounds and then repeat the sound's vibrations as many times as you need it to. I knew the two men wanted Xander, so as the 'hero' protected your ankles, I ran to Xander and recorded his sniveling voice while he tried to escape the roots. Then I simply waited for the right moment and slid the stone below Dax. I knew Mordred wanted Xander, so I made him think Xander was where Dax was standing. Mordred couldn't see through the smoke, just hear. Worked like a charm, really."

Sigurd gawked at Kamara, "You are a terrifying enigma."

Kamara looked pleased, "That might be the nicest thing you have ever said to me."

"Then what happened?"

Hickalik took over the story. "Dax jumped to his feet and yelled at Mordred, of course. The smoke-stone cleared, and both men were approaching again. And then..." Hickalik paused, "their shadows stood up behind them and grabbed them both."

"Hang on..." Myles stopped the story again, "Their shadows?"

"Yes," Hickalik acknowledged, enthralled with his own storytelling, "the moonlit shadows of Dax and Mordred, like dark flames, stood up behind them. They were their exact silhouettes but completely black. Their shadows grabbed the two men from behind and restrained them. A terrifying low growl came from the shadows next to the building. It was Zalaph, out on a night patrol, I assume. He used his shadow-flames to turn the men's shadows against them. With a burst of green and orange flames, Dax and Mordred broke their shadowy bonds. But before Zalaph was able to swoop in himself, Dax held a stone to his mouth and called out, 'Zalaph is here.' Then two purple flaming circles appeared on the ground around them."

"Like the one in our room?" exclaimed Myles, excited to make a connection.

"Yeah, but bigger. Dax and Mordred dropped through before Zalaph could capture them. It was wild. After that, Zalaph sniffed you good. Then he picked you up and flew you up to the medical wing roof. We raced after, but found Pedagogue Greenwald patrolling the halls on our way up."

"She was livid to find you guys out past curfew," Kamara said, amused.

"Yeah, that's right," Sigurd grew suspicious. "You weren't there when we got caught. Where did you go?" he asked. "You were with us in the hallways running up, but when Pedagogue Greenwald found us, you were gone."

"I wasn't going to get caught," Kamara replied.

Myles dropped his head as he grasped at his chest where his compass normally hung.

Hickalik spoke up, "Myles, it wasn't Xander. He doesn't even have a flame yet, and he wouldn't want anything from you, even your compass... no offense."

"I know, Hick." Myles wanted it to be Xander, but Hickalik was right. Now they had no leads. "Why would someone want to steal my compass?"

"Didn't you say it was your father's compass?" asked Hickalik.

"Yes, but..." Myles hesitated, realizing Hickalik didn't know who his father was, "...but, it was all I had from him."

"I'm sorry," said Hickalik, not knowing what else to say.

The somber silence was broken by Sigurd once again, "Oh, and guess who they found out there?"

"Who?"

"Forky Blunson," Sigurd said excitedly, "he was in the haze behind the two men."

"Shhh," Hickalik silenced him, "have a little more respect would ya?" He said looking around the room as if trying not to get overheard.

"And it's Florky Bunson you buffoon," Kamara jabbed in.

"Florky?" asked Myles. "That's great news. Is he okay? Where is he?" But the trio was hesitant to speak.

Hickalik cleared his throat nervously, his expression grave, "They... they took his blaze."

"What do you mean?"

"Dax and Mordred. They must have taken his burn somehow, then returned him to the academy last night. After we told the staff what happened, they went out to where we were attacked. They found Florky just standing there. I overheard them saying his blaze is gone... erased. He is still in a sleep-like state now."

Myles felt a wave of concern wash over him, "But what does that mean for Florky? What does he do now, without a blaze, I mean?"

Hickalik shook his head solemnly, "I don't know, Myles. No one's ever seen anything like this happen before," he explained. "Nothing can be done. With no blaze, he is just a normal person."

"But that's not fair," said Myles.

After this, the visiting students were expelled from the infirmary by the uncouth nurse, and Myles was ordered to rest. Eventually he was released from her unwilling care and was sent straight to the dorms for the night before starting his normal class routines the next morning.

The healing-flames had done their job; however, his body felt more tired than when he first woke from his injury. He stepped back into the familiar confines of their dorm room. Sigurd lay sprawled on his bed, emitting a symphony of snores while Hickalik slept, blissfully unaware. Myles' gaze drifted to the corner where the compass was taken, almost wishing to see the iridescent purple glow once more. But the space was empty except for the shattered remains of the compass' inlay.

He bent down to pick up the metal debris. It was more intricate than he'd initially realized. The silver fragments consisted of six perfect hexagonal rings, surprisingly unharmed. These interlocking hexagons hinged freely in any direction yet remained stubbornly attached. He could fold them into a neat stack or manipulate them into an array of configurations.

"Like they're held together by magic," he murmured, a sense of wonder creeping in.

He slid back into bed, Omni's egg perched in his nest, and the metal hexagons nestled comfortably on his finger. A question gnawed at him, "Who would want my father's compass, and why would they go to such lengths to get it?" But exhaustion soon lulled him asleep.

The weeks that followed were a cumbersome dance for the students. Each student was responsible for the care of their egg, as if it were their own offspring. Some students hoisted eggs comparable to the size of pumpkins. Over time, the eggs even started to swell slightly, with the exception of Omni's egg, which stayed the same size and still reeked from Hickalik's remedy.

Xander and Bach frequently congratulated Myles on discovering the elusive "sewage dragon."

Though academy life outwardly resumed a normal rhythm, a subtle tension crackled beneath the surface. Curfews were tightened, and an increased number of night patrols stalked the campus grounds.

Pedagogue Alistair dove deeper into the anatomy of the dragon types seen in present times. A stroke of unexpected fortune arrived in the form of Pedagogue Greenwald's sudden absence. Summoned to heal a sickly dragon in the kingdom, which was a task Myles believed was more suited to Hickalik than the apathetic teacher. However, this made Hickalik seem less on edge for a while.

Since the attack on the school grounds, both wardens seemed to be more demanding than usual in their courses, as well as their tower curfews. Pedagogue Muddle was his normally unpredictable yawning self. He had been assigned to help Florky Bunson recover, utilizing his unique dream flame abilities. Pedagogue Humphrey continued to expect very little from Myles with her passive aggressive comments, regardless of how well Myles performed on every test. Although this made Myles feel quite accomplished, he was continually humbled just after, in Ebenezer Artistry.

The news of the attack rippled through the student body like a pebble tossed into a pond. Disbelief and fear became the prevailing emotions. Some scoffed, dismissing it as a tall tale, while others clung to the coattails of any nearby academy staff member, seeking the comforting illusion of safety.

The one constant for every first-year student was guarding their eggs with their lives. Occasionally a panicked shriek would pierce the hallways as an egg rolled down the hall chased by a frantic first-year. Gordon's egg needed to be extracted from a bulrog after being left on the dining table after dinner. Luckily, both the egg and the bulrog were in good health afterward.

A month—an eternity under the wardens' glares—had passed since the Harvest. Breakfast buzzed with energy, and the air was thick with anticipation.

Suddenly, Hickalik leapt up, "It moved!" he shouted.

Silence slammed the room, followed by the creaks and squeaks of benches and chairs sliding out while a surge of students gathered.

A tremor, then twitches, ran through Hickalik's egg. A gasp rippled through the crowd as a crack, like a lightning bolt, split the shell. A glistening blue claw emerged, met with gasps and murmurs. The crack widened, a scaled tail with an axe-like tip whipped out, narrowly missing Gavin's hand. Finally, a tiny reptilian nose poked through, followed by a magnificent pale blue head. It chirped softly, sniffing toward Hickalik.

"It's a drake," called out a student. Then a second nose poked out of the egg.

"Two dragons?" asked Gavin excitedly.

"It's a Hydra," called out Gordon behind him.

The egg erupted, wings bursting forth like sails catching the morning light. The hatchling wobbled on its hind legs, tail whipping for balance. Tiny front arms reached towards Hickalik.

"She is a dragonette," Hickalik stated in surprise.

"Yeah, with two heads," remarked Kamara from across the table.

Myles furrowed his brows, "Is that normal?" He never considered multiple heads were a possibility.

"Congratulations, young man." Pedagogue Alistair was eagerly peering over the jostling heads. "A fine specimen indeed. Dragonettes are usually one-headed creatures; however, this one seems to be a special case. I did teach you about different variances in class."

Hickalik reached out his hands to pick up his dragon. Before he could, a blue flame was hiccupped from one head's mouth, freezing the conveyor belt in place with icicles of frost.

"Seems we have an ice-attribute as well," Alistair observed.

"Ice?" questioned Hickalik. "But I was searching for a verdure dragon."

"But this is the dragon who chose to accept you, young Mr. Milbred. There is always a reason. Our wants and desires are so often flawed. Release your ambitions, and let your Nexus guide you."

As the pedagogue spoke, the second head reared and spat a lighter blue flame at the conveyor belt. The ice burst into steam, almost instantly, and the conveyer started moving once again.

"How very intriguing..." Alistair studied.

Hickalik seemed confused by this development. He reached out again, the lizard sniffed his hand, then extended its chin over his finger. Hickalik gently scratched the scaly neck as the dragon leaned into the gesture and gave a cooing chirp.

"I think she likes you," commented Myles.

"Well of course she does." Alistair pushed through the crowd, "she chose him after all." Hickalik picked up the hatchling and looked at its two heads, not sure which to make eye contact with.

"It's nice to meet you, Galacia."

A smug voice shattered the reverence. "Hah, knew it."

Xander's egg, which was delivered just after the Harvest, shuddered violently. The shell fractured with a series of sharp cracks. A menacing blackened wyvern, forked tail glinting, rose on unsteady legs. Jagged spikes ran down its back, leading to a horned head. Unlike the others, its wings merged with its front legs, an echo of the legendary Zalaph. The light shown through its thin wing flaps with an iridescent red. Glowing saliva, like molten lava, dripped from its mouth, burning the table below.

The students again wowed at the sight as they gathered to gawk.

Xander spoke up with pride, "This is Voldin, the dragon I will use to forge my future."

"Remember," called out Pedagogue Alistair, "your dragon is your partner, your friend, the one who chose and accepted you. They are not tools to use as you see fit."

Xander paid no mind to the pedagogue's heeds and was simply pleased with himself. Two loud knocks rang out. Provost Prudencia and the rest of the staff gathered at the front of the banquet hall.

"I believe the time has come. Now that your eggs have made a Nexus contact with you, the incubation period has passed. The day of emergence is now here. Please care for your dragons carefully as they hatch into this world. First-year courses will be postponed for the week." A third of the room was filled with cheers, while the staff seemed smug, as if they knew something the students did not.

"This is your chance to bond and gather understanding about how your new partner uses their Ruach abilities, for those abilities will soon be yours to wield." She finished and turned away from the assembly. "Oh…" she remembered, "one more thing. Your accounts will be billed for any irreversible damages your dragon causes."

Hickalik's eyes widened, as he watched the scorching table in front of Xander continue to burn, then glanced back at Galacia with concern.

"Welcome your new friends into this world… and do be patient with them, they are babies after all. Your dragons are not yours to control, but merely to teach and guide." She smiled with amusement, "Good luck."

The atmosphere lit with excitement. Myles chuckled as Kamara kept trying to freeze Sigurd's hand with Galacia's icy breath. But the commotion was soon eclipsed by other spectacles. Different dragons began to emerge, some gently pushing through their eggs, others exploding out, quite literally.

"Look out," a frantic voice shrieked. Before Myles could react, a silver flash erupted above his head, out of his vision. He barely registered the startled shout before something heavy slammed onto his back, followed by a rain of vegetables. A mangled roast turkey fell apart on impact.

"What was that?" Myles questioned.

"Teleportation," enlightened Alistair, "Exhilarating, isn't it?" He seemed more enthusiastic than the students at this point.

A sudden crack shattered the excitement. An egg exploded, showering students with debris. In the smoke's wake, an armored drake stood tall, its body etched with veins that pulsed with a fiery glow.

"Ooh, be careful with this one, Phineas." Alistair warned while helping shy Phineas Felton back to his feet.

"Explosion attribute dragons can be dangerous at first." Alistair kept his gaze fixed on the dragon as he inched closer. "Could it be glycerin based, or perhaps ammonium nitrate… or even just Ruach based expansion?" he speculated. "Nevertheless, I think it best we move him outside for the time being."

Alistair pulled an ebenezer from his pocket. He danced his hand above the hatchling, like a snaking cobra. The hatchling was captivated. Alistair slid the stone on the table below the lizard's head. A green tea light flame lit from the stone. The drake continued to be mesmerized, until it swayed to sleep. He scooped up the slumbering dragon and handed it to Phineas, who wanted nothing more than to hand it off to someone else.

"Perhaps the stone courtyard would be a better place for bonding and study, Mr. Felton." Phineas agreed with a nodding swallow. And carefully rushed out of the hall, reminiscent of a person carrying a bomb.

"That's not a bad idea," spoke Myles, still brushing bits of food off his cloak.

Hickalik nestled Galacia into his satchel with her heads poking out and they headed outside to the lawn under the cloudy overcast day.

"I always thought this day would be a sunny, warm day," said Sigurd.

Kamara sat on the ground holding her still tiny egg in her hand, "That's because you're a hopeless optimist," she replied.

Hickalik let Galacia out on the ground. They kept their distance as she hunted insects, freezing them in place and chewing up their iced exoskeletons. Myles was comparing Galacia's ice-flames to Beira, wondering if the dragons could be related.

"So, what now?" asked Myles.

"What do you mean?" Hickalik asked back.

"Like... do you train Galacia?"

"I think you just guide them and observe their abilities," he explained while chasing after Galacia, who was sliding away on a now frozen patch of the slope.

"Does this mean Hickalik can use his flame attribute now?" Myles asked.

"Not even close," inserted Kamara. "It takes years for a Nexus wielder to use their flames free-hand."

"Then how do we use their flames?

"Next they will have our hilts crafted, I assume," answered Kamara as Hickalik rejoined the group with a dizzy Galacia in hand.

"Our what?" Myles clarified, "Hilts? Like on a sword? Then why haven't they given them to us yet?"

Sigurd seemed amused by Myles, "Well, we need our dragons first, silly," he explained. "We need a part of our dragon to integrate into our hilt."

Myles held Omni closer, "That's horrible."

"No... not like that," Kamara rolled her eyes. "Like a tooth, claw, or first scale shedding. Something that is naturally discarded in their first months."

"Oh," Myles felt foolish, "but why do they need a part of the dragon in the hilt?"

Hickalik explained while they observed Galacia hunt another cricket to eat, "You and I don't know how to wield Ruach yet. But the dragons are born with it flowing into them and is theirs to call upon and release. Although we have a Nexus with our dragons, we do not know how to absorb this Ruach, so we use a piece of our dragon to help train us to both collect and disperse it freely."

"They are basically our Ruach training wheels," added Kamara.

But as she spoke, her egg elongated. "It's time," she said calmly with a warm smile. "Come on out my little companion." As the first crack splintered open, beautiful coral feathers poked out as a wing emerged.

Sigurd laughed, "You got a bird. How did you ensear with a bird?"

But he was quickly silenced as Galacia froze his foot to the ground. A snake-like head with a frilled neck pushed its way through the feathers. It slithered the rest of its long olive colored body out of the egg and fluttered its wings.

Myles gawked, "Wow, the colors are striking," wondering what other colors dragons came in.

"It's a coatyl," Hickalik remarked.

The feathered serpent coiled its way up Kamara's arm, sniffing her with its forked tongue. Kamara softly spoke, "It's nice to meet you, Hanish." Then Hanish coiled back down and perched regally on Kamara's hand, its beady eyes following Galacia's swift movements as she hunted the unsuspecting cricket.

"Looks like he wants to play," Sigurd grunted with a struggle as he chipped away at the ice encasing his foot.

Hanish fixated on a butterfly flitting near a flower. The group leaned in, wondering if he would hunt, but disappointment rippled through them as the butterfly fluttered away. But Hanish remained focused, his beady eyes following its flight. Then, with a whiplash, he lunged forward, jaws agape.

Hanish unleashed a powerful bolt of lightning. The cracking thunder boomed. The ground scorched in a line all the way to the outer wall. The butterfly was nowhere to be seen.

Silence descended, with the exception of their ringing eardrums. The sheer crack would have been enough to give a healthy man a heart attack, but the power of the blast is what scared the boys the most. Kamara hastily scooped up Hanish and hurried back inside, leaving the bewildered boys with no explanation.

"What was that?" cried out Sigurd. "First her dragon tries to kill us, then she leaves without a word?"

"I think she was upset that she almost hurt us," Myles contemplated.

"But we're fine. She has nothing to be ashamed of," urged Sigurd. "What a silly girl."

"That... was... amazing," breathed Hickalik, still in shock.

"It shocked me," joked Myles, receiving acknowledgement from Sigurd.

Hickalik's mouth was still open, "Her dragon... that power. A hatchling should not be able to use that much Ruach. It was comparable to a galliant's ability, or a full-grown dragon."

Myles looked down at his bandaged egg, "I wonder what flame you will have?"

Myles, Sigurd, and Hickalik ventured back inside. The once-organized tranquil halls resembled a disaster zone. Scorched claw marks marred the walls, shards of shattered glass glittered like deadly daggers, and once-sturdy columns were reduced to crumbling piles of sand. Flashes of silver flames burst, as items teleported out of thin air and dropped to the floor.

Then, from the ceiling, Gavin Dafton fell through the floor above, passing through the wooden ceiling, like a ghost. He thudded hard onto the floorboards.

"How'd you do that?" asked Sigurd, looking up at the ceiling.

"Are you okay?" asked Myles, assisting Gavin to his feet. He winced and held his elbow.

"It was my dragon, Draugr. He is awesome... but he keeps running away. He can run through things, like solid objects and stuff. Pedagogue Alistair called it phasing. But every time I catch him, he just passes through my arms and runs off again. He turns and waits for me. It's like he is taunting me. I almost had him again upstairs, but he lit the floor beneath me on fire and I fell right through. I don't get it. Why doesn't he like me? Everyone else's dragons are cuddling up to their partners."

Myles chuckled until Sigurd nudged him, "That's not very helpful, Myles. Poor form."

Myles spoke up, "Gavin, your dragon's not running from you because he doesn't like you, he is playing with you. A little girl at the orphanage did the same all the time. She was just slower and couldn't run through walls."

"Really? You think?" asked Gavin.

Just then an object fell to the floor behind Gavin. There stood a six-legged lizard. Myles thought its appearance was reminiscent of a beefy iguana, but with more spikes and teeth.

"A basilisk, how wick," stated Hickalik.

"There you are, Draugr. You found me." Gavin reached out and picked up the dragon who didn't seem to mind. "Thanks Myles, I think that helps a lot."

Myles smiled, "Of course. If there's one thing I've learned about...." but before Myles could finish, Draugr blew a cone of flames toward the ground. Gavin's face turned to horror, as he once again fell through the floor and out of sight with his dragon. The bronze hued flames vanished.

Hickalik sucked his teeth, "Did they just go into the basement?"

"Warden Petroff told us it was off limits, right?" Sigurd recalled.

"Should we tell someone?" asked Myles, but all three kept silent and didn't want Gavin to get into trouble with Warden Petroff again.

Exhausted from searching for Kamara and entertaining Galacia all evening, the boys finally called it a night. As Myles lay in bed, staring at the ceiling, he realized why the academy staff was so smug, "They knew what was coming," he muttered.

Throughout the night, the dorms echoed with the chaos of students struggling with their hatchlings. Deep, guttural rumbles shook the walls, punctuated by muffled screams and frantic shouts. Sounds of crashing furniture and breaking glass rang out. But for Myles, these were mere background noises compared to their personal climate control courtesy of Galacia.

One head unleashed icy blue flames, engulfing half the room in frost. Just as their bodies adjusted to the bone-chilling cold under their covers, Galacia would rear her other head, vaporizing the ice with a blue burst of steam. The room transformed into a sweatbox, leaving the boys drenched in perspiration. Sleep, under such circumstances, seemed a distant dream.

Chapter Sixteen

Carafe Half Full

As the morning light cascaded in, Myles was sprawled out in the humid room. His body and bed were soaked in sweat. Hickalik was lying on the floor, leaving Galacia curled up on the bed. A faint muffled voice drifted through the humid air.

"Help," Myles heard. He popped up and looked around, half expecting to see a purple flaming oval once again. To his surprise, he saw Sigurd's bedding, replaced with golden sheets.

Myles heard the mutter again, "Sigurd?" he questioned.

"Help," the distorted panicked voice called out again. Myles jumped over to Sigurd's bed, nearly tripping over Hickalik. The lumpy bedding had turned to solid gold. He tried to lift the rigid sheets, but they were perfectly sculpted to the bed, like a hardened mold. Sigurd was encased underneath, trapped.

Hickalik jolted awake. Both Hickalik and Myles tried to lift the sheets with no success. Hickalik raced to his bed and grabbed the snoozing dragon, pointing her at Sigurd.

"Go... flame it," he ordered, but she turned her heads and looked at him, annoyed. "Come on Galacia, before he suffocates in there." He placed her on top of the golden blanket, "Please?" but still no flames.

Aggravated, Hickalik dropped his head to think, but then he saw something. He pounced on the floor, cupping his hands, then stood back up. Inside was a little cricket. Myles knew exactly what Hickalik was doing and grabbed the heavy candlestick off the dresser. Hickalik placed the cricket on the gold blanket. Galacia instantly began hunting. A blue flame emerged from her mouth freezing the cricket and covering the blanket.

Hickalik grabbed Galacia and pulled her out of the way, "Now," he yelled out.

Myles raised the heavy candlestick and hammered down on the frozen gold. The blanket cracked as pieces of gold fragments dispersed around the room.

A deep gasp rang out as Sigurd pushed through the remaining pieces of the golden blanket. He was soaked in sweat too, taking deep breaths. He was finally able to cough out a "thank you."

From under the golden blanket remnants, popped a golden head with wavy slicked-back horns. Its slender body and boney wings crawled out. It had no arms or legs.

"What kind of dragon is that?" wondered Myles.

"It's an amphiptere," answered Hickalik. "They are said to be good luck."

"Good luck for whom?" Sigurd interjected, still coughing. After catching his breath, Sigurd regained his sense of regalness, "Why, hello, my Lady Gullynn."

"So, she can turn things into gold?" asked Myles.

Hickalik shrugged. "That's my guess."

"That's amazing," praised Myles, "You're rich... well richer, I guess."

"Why is that?" asked Sigurd.

"You could turn anything into gold, right?"

"Yeah, he could," Hickalik replied, "but gold is pretty common and not worth all that much."

"Really?" Myles asked, shocked, wishing he had this ability back home.

Despite the extensive repairs overnight, the corridors and building bore fresh scars of the previous day's pandemonium. Breakfast was a chaotic affair. Hatchling dragons filled the great hall with spontaneous flames of every color. Sigurd proudly displayed his golden luck dragon; the near-death experience seemed forgotten.

Kamara was at breakfast, acting her usual self, like nothing happened the day before. Her feathered serpent Hanish perched calmly on her arm. Myles and Hickalik continuously leaned out of his direct line of fire.

The constant sounds of screams and crashing dining plates became a normal symphony. All dragons were now hatched and thriving in the academy walls, all but Omni. Myles surveyed his classmates, and seeds of doubt sprouted in his mind. Xander walked by as Bach followed, carrying a shiny-handled cage. Myles hoped Xander would keep to himself, however unlikely it seemed.

Xander spotted Myles with his egg and stopped in his tracks, "The sewer pup hasn't hatched yet?" he sounded genuinely surprised. "Sounds like a dead dragon."

Kamara jabbed back, "And where is your lava-drooling lizard? Did it run away, or simply melt its own tiny brain?" Xander paid no mind to the insult and gestured to the cage Bach was carrying.

"You caged your dragon?" Hickalik questioned, concerned.

"Of course, I couldn't have him melting everything around me like the rest of you simpletons. The Xander house has always produced strong fire-attributes. I had my father order me a custom molybdenum cage to contain his heat."

Hickalik spoke again, "But your dragon is supposed to be your partner... your friend..."

"Friend?" questioned Xander amused, "It's a beast, a wild animal. I acquire its power regardless of it being in a cage or not. In three months' time, it will go on to live its life. This truly doesn't matter." He raised his chin away from Hickalik and walked off with Bach trailing.

"I wish the dragon would burn all his perfect hair off," Hickalik said, sulking.

With two loud taps of her staff, Provost Prudencia grabbed the room's attention. Even the hatchlings seemed to calm in her presence.

"Good morning to one and all. I hope some of you were able to sleep last night. And for those who did not, the week to come will not prove any easier. I hope you all enjoyed meeting your dragons and learning about your new partners. And for those who are still waiting, the end of something is better than its beginning. Patience is better than pride."

Myles could sense most of the room glancing his way.

"Now we have a few special guests among us on this day. They came to observe, for themselves, the future leaders of the next generation. Today we welcome two fold gaffers back to this institution. Please give an honorable welcome to the Gaffer Leon Nimbus, of the Crescent Sun, and the Gaffer of the Silver Talons, Draven Bane."

Myles choked on a bit of hardboiled egg, and Sigurd smacked his back.

He looked on in horror. Xander's father stood, exuding the same air of haughty entitlement that had marked their encounter at the hotel. Just a table away, Xander himself sported a smug expression that seemed to amplify his father's arrogance.

"As our esteemed guests stay with us for the next few days, please show them every courtesy you already do for our illustrious staff. They are here to observe both your dragons and you. It is an honor to have them roam these halls once again."

For the rest of that day and the next, most of the children avoided the gaffers as best they could. Draven Xander hovered in the halls, silently judging the students and their uncontrollable dragons, while Leon Nimbus loudly encouraged the students with an overly zealous slap to the back.

The third day after the hatching day, Myles found himself alone, seeking solitude amidst the chaos and glee. He sat on a tower overhang outside an open window, looking out over the academy gardens. Clutching his unhatched egg, a tear splashed the top, dripping from his chin.

His fingers twirled the broken compass rings he still had. When he first placed them on his finger, it felt like an instrument of hope, yet now they felt heavier than he could carry.

"Myles?" a voice came from behind. He couldn't find the will to turn around.

"I just want to thank you," the hesitant voice began. It was Florky Bunson.

Myles wiped a tear off his cheek. "I didn't do anything."

"I heard you and your friends found me out there that night and even fought off those two men that had taken me."

Myles shook his head, "No, it was Kamara. She stalled them long enough for Zalaph to get there. She's the one you should thank."

"Oh, okay..." Florky paused while gazing outward.

"You know, I think it's pretty cool that you were picked by a dragon. I know you didn't get to meet him, but at least you know he felt something in you that was worth trusting." Florky glanced down at the students playing with their dragons on the courtyard below.

"I never got the chance to ensear. And now, with no blaze of my own, I guess I will never know. But I am still glad I got to come and see this place. Coming here and being blessed with a burn is a one in a million chance. Especially for a person like me. My family didn't come from a blazed bloodline. Now I am the same as my dad and my brother, and I have realized, there is nothing wrong with that."

Florky stood back up, "I guess what I am getting at is I am sorry for your loss, but I believe there are still better things to come... for both of us."

"Thanks, Florky," Myles replied.

"They are sending me home today. But I wish you the best, Myles. We may not have dragons, but there is still a fire in my heart. And I will still make a name for myself in the world. You can count on it."

Myles wiped his cheek, smiled, and stood to shake his hand goodbye, "I know you will."

After Florky left, Myles went to find Kamara, Hickalik, and Sigurd, who were gathered in the conservatory.

"Hey, Myles. Any movement?" Hickalik asked, hoping for some good news.

"No, nothing." He took a deep breath. "I think it's time for me to go talk to the provost about... leaving."

"No," exclaimed Sigurd. "Give it more time. Omni is just storing up more Ruach than the other dragons. I am sure of it," he said in desperate naivety.

"Stop it, Sigurd," Kamara spoke up. "Myles thought hard on this. No one has the right to deny him his choice. This is hardest on him."

They escorted Myles to the provost's office and knocked on the door. The door forcefully swung open.

"Well good afternoon there, laddies," the boisterous gaffer from the Crescent Sun welcomed them. "Four kiddos, three dragons, and an egg..." he waved his hand in front of his nose. "A rotten egg at that."

Behind him sat Provost Prudencia at her desk with Draven Bane standing at the window.

"That is the smell of peasantry," Draven stated with displeasure.

"Come in," Prudencia waved, "You must forgive the gaffers, they are not known for their... social intellect."

They approached the desk. The words caught in Myles' throat, "I am ready to resign from the academy," he announced.

"Oh?" Prudencia acted surprised. "And why might that be?"

"Well, Omni... my dragon, will not hatch. I cannot continue without a dragon."

"Do you think your dragon has given up on you?" she asked.

"No ma'am, but I believe my dragon is..." he paused as his voice dropped, "dead." It was more difficult to say out loud than he thought.

"And why do you believe this?" she asked again.

"That's what everyone else says. Even Pedagogue Greenwald said there was nothing that could be done when I brought my egg to her, like you suggested."

Prudencia dropped her gaze to the egg, "Yet it seems something has been done."

Hickalik interjected, "I tried to help it."

Myles spoke again, "It's been three days since the other dragons hatched. And my egg has never grown or moved since I found him... since I... cracked his egg." Provost Prudencia slowly paced the room.

"Can this not wait until after our business has concluded?" snapped Draven from the corner.

"These children are our business. They are the future of even your ranks, Gaffer Bane."

Draven scoffed and turned back to the window.

Prudencia refocused her attention on the students, "What is a dragon's egg meant to do?" she asked.

Sigurd answered first, "The egg protects the hatchling while they grow."

"Yes, that is one of the simpler functions."

"Simpler is what he knows best," Kamara couldn't help herself.

Hickalik got excited when he remembered the answer and projected, "Ruach. It holds Ruach inside and collects Ruach from its surroundings to feed to the dragon."

"Very good, Mr. Milbred," she nodded.

"There's a smart lad," the large gaffer complimented.

Prudencia walked over to a large bowl of water in the corner and picked up a glass carafe. "When I place this carafe under the water, what happens?"

"It fills with water," answered Sigurd.

"Simply put, Sigurd," Kamara added, holding back her smile.

Then Prudencia emptied the carafe, "Now, this time I will fill the carafe again, but I will use my hand to block the opening." She did, placing her fingers over the opening before plunging the carafe back under the water. The container slowly filled as water pushed between her fingers.

Hickalik watched intently, "The carafe took longer to fill," then his voice grew more excited, "because the opening was much smaller."

"Indeed," agreed the provost.

"What does that mean?" asked Myles.

"The ointment," shouted Hickalik, "it blocks the Ruach from entering the egg. Omni is just taking longer because of the ointment."

"That is an astute hypothesis, young Milbred. An act of love will never blossom quickly but takes time to mature fully."

Just then, the egg's side bulged. The shock of the movement made Myles jerk, almost dropping the egg again. A line started splintering down the middle of the hardened ointment.

Prudencia smiled, "Seems your carafe is finally filled."

The room fell silent. Even Draven couldn't help but turn to observe as he narrowed his eyes toward the egg. The crack continued around the egg. Myles couldn't believe it. He leaned in closely to watch each crack steadily extend. His heart was pounding, as the earth stood still.

With exploding force, an armored tail whipped out from the egg, cracking Myles right on the nose. Eyes instinctively shut, he was met with instant pain. All he saw was the impact's flash of white, then heard a cooing growl.

Chapter Seventeen

Omni, The Sickly Elden

At long last, Myles had his dragon. He just couldn't see it yet. The intense impact caused his eyes to water. Unbeknownst to Myles, he had held his egg upside-down. The hatchling emerged tail-first, whipping it outward with surprising force. The unexpected impact caused Myles to fumble, and the tiny creature to tumble out of the cracked shell and onto the floor. Blinking rapidly, the blurry image before Myles sharpened.

On the floor lay the cooing hatchling, its scales a delicate interplay of gray and white. Its posture conveyed timidity and weakness as it tilted its head upwards, inquisitively observing Myles.

Myles dropped to his knees to gently reach out and touch the hatchling's face. He felt the prickle of tiny frills retreating down the dragon's neck. Two nubs protruded from the top of its forehead. Tracing his hand down the smooth, scaled neck, he encountered wings folded against its back. The hatchling attempted to stand, then wobbled back into a sitting position.

Myles locked eyes with his new-found friend. One iris shimmered blue, while the other displayed a mesmerizing swirling of black, white, and purple hues. The creature returned the gaze with a spark of curiosity.

Myles addressed the tiny creature, "Hey there, Omni. It's nice to finally meet you."

"It can't be," Draven gasped. "Boy, where did you acquire that egg?" The accusatory tone made Omni scramble into Myles' arms.

"In the Caldera, like everyone else," Myles answered, rising to his feet.

"Yes..." he dismissed, "but where... how?"

"With the red pandas. Or racoons? I wasn't really sure..."

Sigurd stepped forth. "He said there was a whole village of... well... they sounded like the Wubbalubs. You know... the children's stories."

"Do you take me for a fool, child?" the gaffer snapped back at Sigurd, his eyes never wavering.

"It's the truth," defended Myles, "and why does that matter anyways?"

Gaffer Nimbus spoke up in a calmer tone, but still enthralled himself. "Laddie, there are no dragons like that in the world anymore. Your dragon... is reminiscent of the tales of old, when the elden dragons still cared for this world."

"That is a myth," barked Draven, "an old story for old souls."

Confusion fell on Myles. "Is this a bad thing? Is there something wrong with him? Isn't it just some type of variant, like Pedagogue Alistair taught about?"

Prudencia approached, leaning over and cupped her hand under Omni's chin. He cooed and rubbed his head against her hand. "Seems you found a very special dragon indeed. Or that is... a special dragon found you."

Draven, disbelief etched on his face, took a hesitant step forward. His eyes, previously narrowed in envy, now held a spark of wonder. Myles, still wary, allowed Draven to cautiously approach. Just as Draven extended his hand, aiming to gently stroke Omni's chin, Omni lashed out, nipping his finger, and drawing blood.

Draven recoiled with a hiss, sucking on the wound, "Filthy rodent. It's a rat... a bottom feeder, not a dragon... a mistake. Just look at its boney ribs, and weak complexion, this... this thing was never meant to survive. The boy's damaged his egg, and therefore his dragon." With that, he turned toward the door swinging his long coat behind him. Omni lunged his neck out, biting and latching to his coat tails.

"We shall finish our affairs once the room is cleared of filth and this... stupidity." He then attempted to storm out the open door; however, he was hindered by the yank of his coat. He whipped his head around, glaring at Myles holding Omni, and Omni holding the end of his coat.

"Give me that," Draven yanked. Myles, determined to protect his companion, held Omni firmly. The tension ripped through the fabric, leaving a jagged tear. Stumbling backward through the doorway, Draven regained his footing in the hallway. He ran a hand through his hair, a futile attempt to restore his composure. With a final glare at Myles and Omni, he stalked off, his anger barely contained beneath a facade of forced propriety.

Watching the events unfold, Kamara held a blissful expression, "That was masterful."

Hickalik and Sigurd joined Myles, and Gullynn dipped her head in a gesture that resembled a bow before nuzzling affectionately against Omni. Hanish, meanwhile, maintained a cautious distance, his head lowered in a display of curiosity at the pale dragon.

Omni opened his mouth wide. The group collectively leaned back in anticipation of a flame, however, the yawn that followed brought a wave of relief.

"Mr. Briggs," the provost stepped forth calmly, "This dragon is unique, as you could tell by the gaffer's outburst, but that is not what makes it special. What is special about Omni, is that he is your dragon and chose you to ensear with when you touched his egg."

"Oh, I didn't touch his egg," Myles explained. The room ignited a series of puzzled expressions.

"What do you mean you didn't touch his egg?" asked Hickalik.

"I mean, I didn't touch his egg," Myles clarified. "I touched a lot of eggs that day, and most either froze me, or lit me on fire, or just exploded. Omni enseared with me when I saw his egg. I couldn't get any closer. That's when I felt the burning on my blaze."

"Your blaze burned?" asked Sigurd.

Myles replayed the events of that day in his mind, "When my blaze changed, the pain was intense. It burned like I was being branded with a hot iron."

"Well, Omni is pretty hot stuff," Kamara added to no one's amusement but her own.

The large gaffer stood up. "Listen here laddie, you're tellin' us, that you never touched your egg? And, your blaze burned like the dickens when you enseared? That's a mighty tall tale you're swingin' about there. Are you even sure you have the right egg?"

"Gaffer Nimbus," Provost Prudencia quickly interjected. "I am sure Mr. Briggs knows what happened better than you or I, since he was there for the ensearing."

"I know but... I mean, I know dragons pick their partners but this is going a wee bit far don't you think? It was three days late hatching after all."

Provost Prudencia's tone dropped, "That is enough of that talk Gaffer Nimbus, and I will ask you to refrain from speaking on the matter any further in the students' presence."

She turned back to the children and pondered for a moment. "Now, I am very grateful I was able to witness this event with you all, but I must attend to my duties with the gaffers." She gave a wave to Gaffer Nimbus, "Go fetch our fickle noble from the halls so we can complete our business."

"Aye, I'll wrangle the rascal down."

"As for you young Briggs, I would suggest keeping your newly hatched friend close for now. As you saw, he may raise some eyebrows, to say the least."

As Myles stepped through the archway into the hallway, Provost Prudencia called out, "Oh, and Briggs, best to keep your ensearing story to yourself... for the time being." And with a nod, Myles and Omni were off to start their new lives together.

Myles found the daytime easy with Omni. He was an exultant little dragon, like a puppy discovering the world for the first time. He would wrestle the other dragons until he was pinned down. He would fetch almost any item Myles would throw; though, the item would never be returned. Every time Omni would open his mouth, Myles watched eagerly for what flame he could embody, but alas, no flame ever came forth. Omni did however chew on everything; the bedposts, the chairs, one of Sigurd's non-frozen boots, and sometimes even his own tail after chasing it around the room.

The ease of the day could not be said for the night. Galacia's relentless temperature fluctuations persisted. This didn't seem to bother Omni, who thrashed into a new position every five minutes. Myles would awaken to repeated sharp ear nibbles and claw scratches, a thudding tail to the throat, or a wing flapped across his face.

"Oh, look everyone," Xander boasted in the halls, "the freak show is in town. The orphan boy and his sickly dragon with no flame."

Aberdeen would remind him, "It is not polite to emphasize the lack of fortune of those with no affluence." This somehow felt more like an insult than Xander's unimaginative taunting.

Daydreaming, Sigurd watched Aberdeen's locks bounce from afar, "Isn't she just the best?"

"Best at what, exactly?" asked Hickalik.

"You know, being proper and elegant."

"Uh, yeah, I guess," Myles looked on in bewilderment.

Returning to their own room the night before classes were to resume, the boys met with a different challenge: their unkempt lifestyle. Sweating from the humidity, they moved heavy lumps of broken golden items around to dig out their literature. Thanks to Galicia, the room became a chamber of ice soon after, as they bundled up to study.

Myles picked up his "Ruach Fundamentals" textbook, only to find his purposefully hidden Herpetology Encyclopedia staring back with its reptilian eye. A shiver ran down his spine, suddenly making the cold room feel even more frigid.

Omni, perched beside Myles on the bed, took notice of the book. The oversized eye on the cover appeared to widen. Myles leaned away in horror. Its central pupil glowed before the eye snapped its gaze toward the pale dragon. Then, in a display of unexpected animation, the book lurched open, pages flipping rapidly as if caught in a sudden gust of wind.

Across the room, similar chaos unfolded. Sigurd and Hickalik's books, buried under a mountain of dirty laundry and broken golden trinkets, mimicked the movement, flinging debris in all directions. A commotion erupted from the dorms as every textbook seemingly sprang to life. All the books ended up open to the same blank page, following the chapter titled "Categorized Dragon Species."

A tiny flickering flame danced across the empty page, searing words into existence. Hickalik read out loud:

The elden dragon. This dragon species was presumed to be either extinct or simply mythologized. They were believed to be the first dragons before thousands of years of breeding created the dragon types known today.

Full Grown Size: Unknown.

Species Characteristics: Elden dragons stand on four legs. Wings protruding from their backs.

Associated Attributes: Unknown

Regions: Unknown

Ecosystem: Unknown

Distinct features: Antlers

Scale colors: Heather White

Dietary needs: Unknown

Myles petted Omni's head, touching the nubs, "So they aren't horns, they're antlers." He then looked back to Sigurd and Hickalik, whose chins were practically on the floor.

"What?" Myles asked, confused.

"That confirms it," said Hickalik. "Omni is an elden dragon."

"Is that a bad thing?" asked Myles.

Still processing, Hickalik didn't hear the question, "He... I mean, Omni confirms the elden dragons were real. He is the only elden dragon humans have ever seen or recorded.

"That's great," Sigurd added, giving the appearance he understood the gravity of the situation.

"Myles, this challenges everything we think we know about dragons and where they came from. There are religions and cults dedicated to the belief that elden dragons were real... or are real."

At this point they were interrupted by Gavin and Gordon sliding into the archway. "Did you guys see?" Gavin huffed, "The books? The books just came to life and wrote about your dragon, Myles... Your dragon. How wick is that?"

Most all the boys in the dorm gathered in the now crowded archway to peer in at Myles and his elden dragon. They were bombarding Myles with question after question, giving no time to answer.

"Did you know he was an elden dragon? What is an elden? What's his flame? Do you know his attribute?"

Seeing Myles flustered, Sigurd cried out, "Oi, don't you think Myles would have told us if he knew? You've all seen the dragon for yourselves, and none of you knew it was an elder, neither."

"Elden dragon," half the boys barked back at Sigurd.

"That's what I said. Now off with the lot of you." Sigurd waved his arms, motioning the crowd to return to their rooms. "Let the man breathe. He only just learned the same as what you all did. He doesn't know anything else yet. Now off, off with you all."

The drove of curious onlookers shuffled back to their rooms, discussing their fictional knowledge of elden dragons.

"Sorry about that, Myles," Sigurd closed the door and turned back to his friend feeling triumphant. "Some people only think of themselves when big news hits without regard for other people's emotions."

But emotional is not really how Myles felt. He felt something different. For the first time in this world, he felt proud. He sat in bed holding Omni as the lizard playfully and painfully gnawed his arm. He was grateful to be chosen. He knew he didn't earn it, but it was given, none the less.

Across the room, Sigurd let out a groan of exasperation, the biting cold a crisp reminder of his lack of warm non-golden blankets.

Dawn broke, and even Kamara seemed filled with a quiet anticipation to see Omni. The pale hatchling was the talk of the academy. Every twitch of its tail, every yawn, drew a captivated audience. Students Myles had never crossed paths with before, even some from the upper years, found themselves drawn to his corner during meals, eager for a glimpse of the elusive elden dragon.

"Hickalik, you're awfully quiet today," Kamara pointed out, petting Omni like an old friend. "I would have thought you would be babbling on about the mythology of elden dragons, or something of that sort."

Hickalik looked up, eyes wide and glazed over.

"I think the elden news may have fried his brain," laughed Myles.

"What are you laughing at, Briggs?" Xander stood up from the end of the table. "Don't go thinking you're something special now. That stupid book mistook your crossbreed mongrel for a fairytale myth, that's all. You and your oversized albino rat will amount to nothing. My father is already on his way to Gregus Nymph's home to have him strike that page from the book forever."

Hickalik snapped to his feet, staring intensely at Xander.

Xander laughed, "Did I lite a fire under you, little Hick? Seems I hit a nerve."

"Your father was the first one to recognize Omni as an elden," Hickalik defended.

"Was that before or after Briggs told him the egg was given to him by fuzzy little Wubbalubs?"

Hickalik, not fully understanding this as an insult, answered firmly, "Before, I believe." The room hummed with murmurs.

"Elden dragons are real," Hickalik boasted, "my granddad told me so."

"Yes, because I'm sure a lowly farmer is the highest educated among us all on these topics." Xander sounded more somber now, "Look Hick, adults lie. Some for fun, some to try and save the weak from harsh truths. But that dragon... that thing, is not special." He spun around to the onlookers, "The sooner you all realize this, the better. It is a lizard, an off-shapen hybrid that looks like an old legend long dead. It doesn't even have a flame."

He turned back to Hickalik. "The sooner Briggs accepts this truth, the sooner he can leave. Only pain and hardships await him if he continues. Maybe if he had noble blood; strong blood makes stronger kin. The blood of the weak only produces disappointments. Even you have more right to be here than he does."

"That's not true, Xander," Hickalik squeaked back. "Myles is the son of Haldor Bridger."

The temperament of the room shifted. A deafening silence poured over the great hall. Myles' eyes nearly popped out of his skull while Sigurd choked. Sigurd cleared his throat repeatedly, "I didn't tell him that. Did you?"

Myles shook his head. Kamara seemed to delight as the room's tension ever tightened.

Even Xander had a hard time processing what he just heard, "What did you just say?"

"Myles is the son of Haldor Bridger. A former galliant, and one of the youngest prodigies of the flame that this kingdom had ever seen."

Xander's leer glazed away from Hickalik and homed onto Myles like a predator seeing its prey come out of hiding. "Your father... Briggs... You are the offspring of the Architect of Death?" The room was silent. "You're telling me, this orphan boy is the son of the man who brought a decade of ruin and death to the kingdom?"

Myles searched for words, "I don't really know. I mean, I only recently found out my father's name."

Xander ignored Myles' response. "I should have my father arrest you right here and now. The king would hang you out in the Chiliagon stocks for all to flog and pelt."

Myles stood up to meet Xander's eyes, with anger churning to courage, "I don't know why my father did what he did, but I will prove his innocence."

"Innocence?!" Xander answered in kind. "I reckon half the people in this room had someone die due to your father's actions, whether by famine, or war."

"War?" Myles asked, confused.

"Oh, are you going to act oblivious now?" What do you think happens when one of the world's most powerful kingdoms suddenly loses its infrastructure overnight? War happens, Briggs. A war that was fought by starving citizens. Desperate young men and women... trying to find a way to supply for their family. Forced into dire means because of one man's selfish acts."

The room seemed to stretch, darkening with heavy shadows growing forth from the walls. "Enough!" Provost Prudencia's voice rattled the surrounding pillars. Xander jumped back. The room felt like an ever-sprawling purgatory before them.

The provost calmed her demeanor and quietly diminished her shadows, "The transgressions of a father do not pass to his kin. No one should be judged, and especially prosecuted, for the actions of one's forebearers, just as none of you could control the actions of your parents when you were born. Every person is given the choice to determine who they will become through their own actions. I suggest you remember that, Mr. Bane."

Her stern logical words smothered the flames of anger and hatred flashing over the room. But the seeds of doubt were planted, and rumors spread like wildfire on the winds.

Chapter Eighteen

The Aftermath

The untimely shared revelation of his father cast a long shadow over Myles' days. Confined to indoor activities by winter storms, the hallways became a gauntlet of awkward encounters. Fleeting sideways glances and hushed whispers followed him wherever he went. The pride and fame he felt, for so brief a moment before, were twisted into judging stares and avoided lines of sight.

Omni, blissfully oblivious, remained a whirlwind of boundless energy. Myles felt like they were two sides of a magnet: the wonder and mystery of the elden dragon drawing curious onlookers, only to be repelled by the whispers of Myles' tainted house name.

As days blurred into weeks, most students were frantically cramming, desperate to make up for lost time wrestling with their hatchlings. Myles and his friends found themselves in a cozy study room off the main library. Outside the windows, snow floated by as an ornate fireplace crackled warmth into the space.

Kamara reclined in a chair, her boots propped on the table despite Sigurd's repeated, albeit futile, attempts to shoo them off. The playful tugging of Galacia and Gullynn on his pant leg beneath the table went largely unnoticed. Meanwhile, Hickalik, engrossed in a book titled "Ice Dragons, a Warning of a Frozen Heart," glanced up to find Myles staring blankly at him.

"What's up, Myles?" he asked, snapping Myles out of his trance.

"Oh, nothing. Sorry," Myles replied. "How's the studying going?"

"Well, I have five more chapters to read, three reports to write, and one test to study for, and a presentation to prepare... so great." he answered with genuine enjoyment.

However, a burning question gnawed at Myles. "Hey, Hickalik, how did you know Haldor was my father?"

Feeling tensions possibly rising, Kamara sat up in her chair and swiveled her eyes between them. Sigurd froze, staring wide-eyed at his book.

"I've known since the first day of school."

Myles asked again, "How?"

"Well, between your age, the fact you grew up as an orphan outside most of society, your ties to Algernon Binford... and then the inscribing of your name on your headboard... 'Mylo Bridger.'"

"Wait... You know about Allen? My uh... uncle?" Myles interjected.

Kamara raised her hands to pause the conversation, "Wait, wait, wait... Your name is Mylo?" she asked, enthralled with the secrets revealed.

"Yes, but I don't go by Mylo, I have been called Myles my whole life. I only found out about my father and my name a couple of days before I came to the academy, in the letter."

"There's a letter, too?" Kamara asked, sounding even more invested.

"Yeah. It's the letter my father wrote for me."

"Haldor is still alive?" interrupted Sigurd this time.

"No... I mean, maybe," Myles tried to explain. "I don't know what happened to him. He wrote the letter years ago while I was still a baby. Allen gave me the letter just before bringing me here." Then Myles turned back to Hickalik. "But how do you know about Allen?"

Hickalik leaned back, "That one took me a little bit. There was a rumor in the market the day we met, about a man with a dragon at the front gates. Dragons have not been permitted in the Chiliagon walls for years now. So, I knew it had to have been a galliant, but someone who hasn't been around in a while. Being that registration day was the next day, I figured they were there to bring forth a new blazed, or wanted to see the new students for themselves maybe. I didn't think much of you and Allen at the time, other than I was thankful for your assistance with Xander and the others. But after seeing you here, I concluded Allen must have been the galliant at the gates."

"But how did you know who he was... his name?"

"Well, he wasn't a current galliant, or else he would have been identified at the gates. Even retired galliants are fairly well-known, so he must have been hidden for years for people to forget his face. I couldn't find him in my Fold Almanac. This led me to believe he was part of... that fold."

"Oh..." said Kamara, surprised, "The Blood Flames."

"That's right," Hickalik agreed. "It took me a while to find a picture of him in the history book. Then I found one of him standing next to a crystal blue drake."

"That's Beira," Myles answered excitedly. "So, Allen was a... Blood Flame? How come I haven't heard of them?"

"There was a major incident that happened years ago. I heard the fold went against the parliament's orders. After that, the parliament voted to disband the fold and they tore down their headquarters."

Kamara added, "That's why there are only six folds now."

Myles was stunned for a minute, then looked up at Hickalik. "How did you figure all that out? And why didn't you tell us?"

Hickalik's neck shrunk down like a turtle retracting into its shell, "Well, I have this habit of finding out people's secrets. I don't mean to, it just happens. My stupid brain just pieces things together. So many people have gotten upset with me for it, I've learned to not share what I see or think."

"Hickalik..." Myles spoke, as Hickalik braced to be scolded, "that's amazing."

Hickalik perked back up, "Really? You're not mad at me?"

"No. It's incredible. You know more about me and Allen than *I* even do."

Sigurd leaned in, "But maybe next time don't blurt it out in front of the whole academy."

"Although I thoroughly enjoyed watching," Kamara admitted.

"Yeah... sorry about that," Hickalik apologized. "Xander has a way of pushing my buttons."

Kamara nodded, "That's his full-time occupation."

"Do me, do me," exclaimed Sigurd, "Do me. What have you learned about me, Hick?"

Stunned by the request, Hickalik scrambled to find something, "I don't know any secrets about you. You are just kind of an open book." To which Kamara let out a roaring laugh.

Myles absorbed it all momentarily, "So, you knew who my father was since the beginning of school?"

"Yeah, I guess so," Hickalik casually answered.

"And you're not mad at me? Or my father?" Myles clarified, a tinge nervous to ask. "I mean, you come from a farming family. Didn't your family suffer because of what my father did? Taking the dagger?"

"It wasn't your fault, though," Hickalik remarked. "Actually, my grandfather was a big fan of the Blood Flames back in the day. He said there had to have been a reason Haldor took the dagger. Once the famine hit, my parents had to go to war just to support me and my grandparents." Hickalik's gaze dropped, "I was still a baby at the time, so I never got to meet them." He looked back up, "But I don't blame you, or your dad really."

Myles felt terrible. "Hick... I am so sorry." The depth of pain his father's actions caused was becoming more tangible. "I still don't know why my father did what he did, but I will find out... someday. If you want to know the truth too, I'm sure I will need someone to help figure out all the clues along the way."

Hickalik perked up, "Of course I will. You guys are the only friends I have ever had."

"Wow, isn't this great?" nodded Sigurd, "Four friends just sharing all their truths and growing their trust?" He slowly cocked his head toward Kamara, eyebrows raised.

"What?" Kamara asked, annoyed.

"Are there any secrets you, Kamara, want to share with the group?"

The boys waited in anticipation.

"Nope," she casually replied.

Myles asked first, "Kamara, the day Hanish hatched... what happened?"

Kamara sighed and rolled her eyes, "It wasn't a big deal or anything. I had..." she paused, "I just never thought that day would come."

"What day?" pushed Sigurd.

"She means the day she got her dragon and her attribute?" Hickalik explained. Kamara shot Hickalik a glance.

He shrugged, "Sorry."

But Kamara was intrigued, "What else do you think you know about me, Hickalik?"

Hickalik started to panic, "Well, umm..." He wasn't sure she was really wanting him to say everything he thought. "I know you are the youngest daughter of Duke Colton Kingsley, the seventh daughter actually."

"Go on..."

"I uh... I read about your dad, and the fact that he was a well-respected and successful galliant. That being said, I know each of your elder sisters were all blazed and attended this school. That's most likely why you know so much about the staff and school grounds. But none of your sisters were ever accepted into a fold to pass on your father's legacy. That's probably why he brought all of you here to try out for a fold sponsorship, but none of your sisters ever passed the trials. Some of them have gone on to use their attributes in successful business ventures, but I suppose that was never quite fulfilling enough for your father."

"Then, when you weren't able to ensear with an egg your first year, your father must have been disappointed yet again. That's why you wanted to be alone when we hunted for our egg during the Harvest, because the shame of not ensearing again would have been devastating. And, when Hanish was hatching and showed such strong attribute potential, you were probably overcome with emotions that you could make your father proud, and that his youngest and last daughter could finally fulfill his dreams."

Myles and Sigurd's faces were rigidly dumbfounded. But Hickalik, still stuck in his own head and not realizing how long he'd been babbling, continued.

"Growing up in a well-off home with so many Ruach users is most likely why you are so knowledgeable and well-versed at using ebenezer stones, and why you have such a stockpile at your disposal. As to why you took your school ring off and wear that fake ring, I would guess it is to hide your presence during your late-night school escapades, so you could not be found or tracked."

Both Myles and Sigurd glanced at her ring. It looked close to a school ring, but the three divots were missing.

"I'm assuming you used your fabricated friendship with Warden Managol to teach her that secret handshake. I noticed the hand shake conveniently makes her tap your rings together three times, unlatching your ring."

Kamara glared from across the table, "Lucky guess."

"Lucky guess?" exclaimed Sigurd in shock. "Which part?"

"Most of it. But in truth, I don't care what my father thinks. I will be selected into a fold for myself, not him."

Sigurd jumped up, "Ouch! She bit me again."

While playing with Sigurd's pant leg under the table, Galacia bit Sigurd's skin this time. He reached down and revealed a small white fang he picked out from his ankle.

"Ooo, another one," said Hickalik excitedly, "It's a bigger one too."

"Yeah," Sigurd complained, "I could feel that."

"I think I will use this one for my hilt instead," said Hickalik, grabbing the tooth and placing it in a little satchel on his hip.

"Hilts?" reiterated Myles, realizing the horrible reality. He had been so preoccupied chasing Omni and studying he had forgotten about the quickly approaching hilt crafting day.

Sigurd questioned, "Myles, don't you have your Hilt ingredient yet? I got a skin Gullynn shed off the other night under the bedding."

Myles nervously glanced at Kamara, "Don't look at me, I have a couple hatchling feathers Hanish shed as well."

Then Myles' worried gaze fell down to Omni. He was rolling around on the floor biting the club of his tail without a care in the world. "I don't have anything," Myles announced anxiously.

"Don't tell me you threw them away?" asked Hickalik, "...teeth, claws, scales, all of it?"

"No, I didn't throw anything away. He never shed anything."

Sigurd said, trying to calm Myles, "You still have a little time. I'm sure Omni will give you something soon. Just as I was sure Omni would hatch one day," he said proudly.

The following day returned a sense of normalcy as the academy reinstated its regular class schedules. Due to the suspension of classes, some students forgot their way, reverting back to following their rings. Yells and winces echoed in the halls as students, rings ablaze, chased their rambunctious dragons down incorrect corridors. Thankfully, most dragons had bridled their impulsive flames by then, a testament to the wisdom of the temporary class suspension during hatching season.

Pedagogue Alistair dissolved into an investigative sleuth of reptilian proportions as he poured over every new dragon in the room. His beady eyes were magnified by his thick glasses as he mumbled about each specimen. Hickalik seemed to be about the only person who could decipher his foreign language.

"Yes... yes... A teal feydragon, subspecies to Anolis sagrei, or maybe cristatellus, two hundred seventy-degree optical oscillation."

The dragon puffed out a colorful bulge on its neck. "Oh yes, a matured dewlap with impressive expansions."

Alistair acknowledged little Maple Blackwood sitting awkwardly next to the scaled interrogation. "And what attribute, I wonder. What flame? What Nexus is shared?" He asked, never giving an opportunity for her to answer, as he poked at his reptilian victim.

Maple was able to get out a quick reply, "His name is Ubique, and he has a..." but before she could complete her sentence, Ubique looked up at the ceiling and let out a smokey silver flame. It burned through the air, bursting on a wooden beam above. As the flames dispersed, there was Ubique, hanging from the beam, leering down at the pedagogue mistrustingly.

Alistair let out a fantastical gasp, "Teleportation? Space manipulation? Or maybe molecular displacement? Stimulating..."

This interaction summed up the majority of the herpetology classes for weeks to come. It seemed the pedagogue's favorite specimen to pester was Omni. He couldn't help but pour over the elden dragon. He would poke and prod, turn his back and jump around to scare, feed varying kinds of plants or meat, to which Omni ate it all with not even a second thought. But no flame, no sign of a shared Nexus to be had, just a content lizard who would never sit still like the other dragons with their partners.

Much to Hickalik's displeasure, Pedagogue Greenwald had returned from her dragon doctoring. However, she returned in even worse spirits, which Myles didn't think possible. Her head was bandaged, much like Myles after the attack that night. An arm, held aloft in a stabilizing sling, flickered with the faint glow of a healing-flame. Her breathing remained measured with a hand to her ribs as she addressed the class.

"Yes..." her voice strained, "as you can observe, I sustained injuries while attending to a particularly brutish ill dragon. He was not a hatchling, to say the least, and this will be the last I speak on that horrid beast, understood?" A wave of silent nods shuffled throughout the classroom.

Most of the botany and horticulture classes after this consisted of healing remedies that she would concoct and apply to her own injuries. Surprisingly, she rarely called on Hickalik anymore. The students assumed this was because she wanted full control over her remedies.

Myles' performance in Warden Petroff's classes continued to be met with harsh criticism. Sigurd harbored a suspicion that Petroff might have had some prior, unpleasant dealings with Myles' father.

"Now," Warden Petroff paced with both arms behind his back, "we have thoroughly beaten the fundamentals of Ruach into those of you with brains enough to cultivate. The utilization of Ruach through ebenezer stones has been demonstrably presented, as have the various methods of condensing and releasing it in flames."

"For safety reasons, our future classes will be held within the colosseum. Your rings will be modified to reflect this change in your schedules. Once your hilts have been assimilated and returned to you," he locked eyes with Myles, "we will start our lessons on Ruach control and release."

This announcement sent a wave of eager anticipation through the student body, the prospect of wielding their newfound abilities for the first time igniting their excitement. Myles, however, remained preoccupied with concerns regarding Omni's flame, his own anxieties dampening any potential joy.

The rest of their classes resumed as if nothing changed. Pedagogue Muddle drifted in and out of sleep as he mumbled topics and lessons intermittently. Humphrey's classes were thankfully still fairly easy for Myles, with the exception of when science and Ruach were mixed as common knowledge.

Not much had changed in ebenezer artistry other than Myles learning the purpose of the class from Hickalik. Apparently, the course was preparing the students to capture their own Ruach flames inside an ebenezer stone for later use, which was quite the revelation for Myles.

But as time passed, hilt crafting approached, and with no offerings from Omni to choose from, Myles had another grim view of his adventure ending early.

"Anything yet?" Kamara asked the night before.

Myles' head dropped to Omni, panting like a dog with his tongue to one side, eyes fixed on the balled-up sock Myles was holding.

Myles lifted his hand and with a grunting throw, "Not yet." Omni gave chase down the hall. "It's a bit worrisome. I mean, Omni hasn't shed anything. He hasn't even grown compared to the others."

They watched Gullynn and Galacia, wrestling on the floor who had matured a bit already. Omni had retrieved the balled-up sock and now sat a good distance away.

"He's the same as I found him. Don't get me wrong. I love him and don't want him to change, but if he doesn't shed something tonight I'm finished."

"That's not true, he is not the same," added Sigurd. "At least he hatched. We just have to take it one step at a time and be patient with the little guy, like we did before with his egg."

Hickalik's eyes nearly bulged out of his head, "That's it. Sigurd, you're a genius."

"I am?" Sigurd asked, confused.

"He is?" added Kamara.

Chapter Nineteen

Unicorns, Rainbows, and Pixie Dust

The long-awaited crafting day arrived, much to Myles' apprehension. He yearned for Omni to produce a suitable offering, but the dragon remained stubbornly attached to all his appendages. Waking with precious little sleep, Myles grasped Omni and his supplies as he headed out the door with Hickalik and Sigurd.

The school day went normally, not that Myles could remember much about it. Following the evening meal, their rings guided them to a preordained gathering point at the base of the Tower of Strength. The first-year students buzzed with nervous excitement, chattering within the passageway about the potential applications of their attributes once their hilts were complete.

"Isn't that a sight?" probed Xander, "What are you doing here, Briggs? You have no need for a hilt. You don't require a hilt to operate nothing, just use your hands for that," he laughed obnoxiously with Bach. Aberdeen covered her mouth while suppressing her chuckles.

The awkward silence that followed was shattered by the abrupt opening of the door. A torrent of icy wind swept in, momentarily obscuring Pedagogue Alistair's figure in the doorway. His coat was half covered in ice and his combover frozen upward. Closing the door, he caught his breath and addressed the students, "Now then. Is everyone present?"

"All here and re-counted twice, sir," answered Phyllis Schnep.

"Good, good," he thanked Ms. Schnep. "Now then, you will all follow me to the forge. It's quite uncomfortable out there. Most dragons not blessed with the attribute of ice tend to hate the cold, so bundle up and keep your dragons warm."

He forcefully reopened the door and began traversing a sloshy path. The students followed into the frigid darkness. Myles and his companions formed the rearguard. The door slammed shut behind them as if it were weary of the cold itself.

Despite the icy wind, which felt akin to a swarm of tiny wasps repeatedly stinging his face, Myles derived a perverse sense of amusement from the situation. He had the distinct pleasure of witnessing Xander lose his footing and fall twice in the snow. Furthermore, Xander sustained a minor burn on his hand when, seeking momentary support, he grasped his dragon's cage that Bach continued to carry.

Omni cautiously extended his head from the backpack and coat, peering over Myles' shoulder. "You don't seem to mind the cold," Myles said. "Are you an ice dragon of some sort?" he asked to no avail.

In the distance, the neighing of horses carried on the wind. But it was too dark to see very far in the snowfall.

Xander almost slipped a third time on a precarious slope. In a desperate attempt to regain his balance, he grasped Aberdeen's hair with a tactless maneuver, a gesture both Aberdeen and Sigurd were very displeased with. Xander's footing dislodged a snowball, which began to roll downhill, gathering both size and momentum. Observing the descent of the snowball, Omni extracted himself from beneath Myles' coat and pursued the rolling object.

"Omni, wait," cried Myles, but the gusting frost obscured his voice. Omni continued his descent, hopping in and out of the fresh powder. Myles pursued. Hickalik and Kamara followed. Sigurd, however, remained preoccupied with his conversation with Aberdeen, oblivious to the others vanishing behind.

As the slope eased into a canvas white clearing, Omni caught up to the slowing ball and pounced. The snowball crumbled under Omni's predatory bite. The proud reptile turned his gaze back towards Myles, chewing snow like a cow chewing its cud.

Myles and Kamara caught up to Omni with Hickalik trailing a ways behind in the snow. As Myles reached down to retrieve Omni, Hickalik let out a terrifying squeal as he abruptly leapt away and fell into the snow. A formidable black stallion materialized, effectively obstructing Hickalik's path towards the others. Its eyes emanated a palpable aura of aggression. A jagged black horn protruded from its head, while its form was further accentuated by a pair of immense, black, feathered wings.

"It's one of the unicorns," shouted Kamara over the wind.

Myles was stunned. He had always heard of unicorns as majestic, beautiful creatures, associated with rainbows and butterflies. This beast looked like it was born out of a nightmare. Its nostrils spurted flames as it pranced around Hickalik, snorting and stomping. Saliva dripped from its mouth while it gnashed its teeth. It jumped up on his hind legs, kicking toward Hickalik below.

Myles yelled, "Hickalik, look out."

Hickalik held out his hands towards the horse-like creature and closed his eyes. With a heavy thud, the unicorn stomped down, just missing Hickalik. It stretched down to his hand and sniffed, then swerved away and exhaled another burst of flames. It stomped again, appearing vexed by Hickalik, but did not harm him. Hickalik slowly peeked from one eye to see if he was still alive. The wild stallion turned away and moved his gaze toward Myles and Kamara.

"Run!" Hickalik shouted. Agreeing wholeheartedly, they turned. Off they shot as fast as they could over the powdered snow. Glancing back, they saw no sign of the black beast in the dark. They could only hear the thumping of its hoofs and heavy breathing giving chase.

"Where do we go?" asked Myles.

"This way," she pulled him left.

Myles held Omni tight against his body as he glanced back again. Fire blew out from the unicorn's nostrils, illuminating its dark face, and a second unicorn now beside it.

"There are two of them now," he yelled at Kamara. "Why are they attacking us?"

"Our rings," she shouted.

"But we don't have real rings."

"Exactly," she roared, annoyed.

Out of the corner of her eye, Kamara caught a fleeting glimpse of a swooping shadow, "Get down." She grabbed Myles and Omni and pulled them down into the snow with her. A unicorn plunged just above their heads, nearly pummeling them with its hoofs.

"They can fly?" asked Myles, shocked, rolling to his back.

Kamara sat up quickly and glared, "What did you think the wings were for?" she answered as sarcastic as ever. They fixed their attention forward while sitting in the snow, now seeing three dark winged figures, approaching slowly, ready to pounce.

Kamara pulled up her sleeve revealing Hanish coiled around her arm tightly. "Time to steal one of your grand ideas. Get ready to run again."

As the three beasts leapt forth toward them, Kamara laid on her back and thrust her dragon toward the dark snowy night.

"Hanish, now," she yelled. Hanish thrust his head high and opened his mouth. An exploding flash of lightning cracked through the air. The unicorns squealed in terror as they turned away shaking their heads to clear the shock.

Kamara and Myles were dazed, their sight blinded by the flash and their ears ringing louder than Hickalik's bug-fearing screeches.

Kamara got to her feet, pulling Myles by the arm while he still clutched Omni. They pushed ahead, not being able to hear if their pursuers were still chasing.

"Up ahead, I see it," Kamara shouted.

They approached a dark walled tree line, stretching high out of sight. With no time to question, they pushed through the first line of shrubs, weaving through the vegetation. The snowfall seemed to lessen due to the trees' canopy.

They turned to face the way they came, scouring for any sign of the stallions. Backing further into the forest, a mound of snow plopped down on them from above. The unicorns broke through the leafy canopy. They gracefully glided down, swerving around trees and branches.

"Why are they chasing us?" asked Myles.

"They are protecting the school and think we're a threat. We don't have our rings," she answered, as they stood back-to-back.

"Duck!" she yelled as a winging hoof nearly bludgeoned her head and nicked Myles' cheek. He held on tight to Omni while the menacing black creatures swirled above.

One of the unicorns, executing a swift downward maneuver, targeted Myles in a direct assault. Faced with this imminent threat, Myles froze. He reflexively tightened his hold on Omni and braced, his eyelids squeezed shut.

A piercing squeal erupted from the horse-like creature. Myles opened his eyes. The unicorn was entangled within a network of branches. The branches around them slithered and struck like snakes from the trees. Another branch lashed out, ensnaring the unicorn with a constricting grip, then another. The higher branches held the other unicorns back. Below, a colossal leaf unfurled, revealing a large surface pulsating with a vibrant array of colors.

"It's a Venus flytrap!" called out Myles.

"More like a horse-trap," commented Kamara.

The equine beast's frantic whinnies echoed through the trees. Omni looked up at Myles, and Myles returned the gaze before refocusing his attention on the captured creature. It was being steadily lowered towards the gaping flower.

Myles clenched his fists and took off toward the flower, "Come on, we have to save it."

"But it was just trying to kill us," Kamara argued.

Myles hoisted Omni back onto his shoulder and into the confines of the backpack. As Myles approached, a thorny vine erupted from the ground.

Myles swerved around a tree trunk, moments before the vine would have struck. The vine coiled around the tree but lacked the necessary length to reach Myles. Having out-maneuvered the vine, he felt confident, until his foot collided with a hollowed log concealed beneath the snow. The momentum of his descent propelled him forward, as he skidded to a halt in the snowdrift.

Compromised, Myles swiftly raised his head, but it was too late, his advantage was lost. The vine unfurled itself from the tree and secured Myles' ankle. Abruptly hoisted into the air, Myles found himself dangling helplessly. The vine moved Myles closer to the open flytrap, joining the flailing unicorn.

"Uhh, Kamara?" Myles called out worryingly, "Little help please... Kamara?"

Myles found himself abruptly dropped back down to the ground, landing on his head. Kamara was able to sever the vine with her pocketknife.

"Ow," Myles rubbed his head, "you could have warned me."

"You're welcome," she replied apathetically, "Now, remind me why we are doing this, again?"

"It's not the unicorn's fault, it was just protecting the academy. It didn't know we're students. It's innocent."

"Oh yes... it innocently tried to kick your head off like a wibbly ball. So, what now? Any more brilliant ideas?"

Myles scanned the snow-covered ground. He bent down and lifted one end of the hollowed out log he tripped over.

"Here," he instructed, "grab the other side." The frantic unicorn was almost within the rainbow-colored flower.

"You've got to be kidding me," Kamara protested. But since she had no good ideas of her own and no ebenezer stones at the moment, she begrudgingly hoisted the other end of the log.

Myles led the charge, "Let's go."

They ran closer, carrying the log as Kamara yelled, "This... Is... Stupid!"

With a coordinated heave, they propelled the log overhead. It landed squarely upon the vibrant feelers on the open flower. They waited with their gazes fixated on the pulsating monstrosity. Finally, the colossal leaf-like jaw snapped shut with a whirling clap.

"It worked," cried Myles.

"Surprisingly," added Kamara.

The desperate whinnying above brought Myles' attention back to the captured beast. "Now we just have to free the unicorn."

Suddenly, with an eruption of whooshing air, the carnivorous plant opened once more. With a display of renewed animation, a series of vines erupted from beneath the snow encircling the flower, lashing out erratically. The vines hoisted up the log, flinging it away.

Kamara watched the rising branches, "I don't think it liked your idea much."

From under the snow, unseen vines secured their ankles. They were abruptly hoisted into the air, finding themselves dangling upside down.

"Not good," cried Myles.

"Oh really?" replied Kamara sarcastically.

The carnivorous plant began pulling them in closer.

"Don't worry," Kamara yelled, "we aren't vegetarians," but if anything, the plant carried them in faster.

"Okay, Plan 'B.' Hanish," Kamara called. Hanish, still wrapped around Kamara's arm, poked his head out of her sleeve. He effortlessly wrapped his way up Kamara's body to her ankle and began biting at the thorny vines.

Omni watched from the hanging backpack. He then climbed up Myles' body, painfully piercing Myles' skin with every step, like a cat climbing his leg. Mimicking Hanish, Omni chewed the vines.

With one more chomp from Hanish, Kamara fell to the snow, just before the plant's gaping chops. She scrambled to her feet, determined to avoid further entanglement.

However, Myles and Omni landed upon her with an unavoidable thud. Dazed, they collectively sat upright, their gazes fixated upon the crazed plant before them. The relentless flower, its fury unabated, unleashed another flurry of thrashing vines in their direction.

Just before their entrapment, a translucent gray flame blew by, crossing the incoming vines and slashing them in two. More slashing flames continued to appear, cutting the vines up like a knife through soft noodles. The relentless flames attacked the main flower, slicing deep cuts with torrents of what felt like wind. The leaf-like mouth thwacked closed to protect itself.

A gruff voice rang out behind them, "Venomous herbals thristin' for chevaline." It was Captain Nordic, with a deep scowl and a sickle of frozen spit dangling from the corner of his drooped lips. He glanced down at the children sitting in the snowdrift, "Banning disciplines for frosted dreams."

"Captain Nordic?" asked Myles, surprised. They turned to see the captain grouchily throwing clear disc-like flames at the remaining branches, making quick work of the ensnaring limbs. Freed, the unicorns fluttered off, out of the trees. Nordic grabbed his back and hunched over, "Aviante rats..." he sniffed upward, "forests be thicken with ill 'tent. Balance quiverin' a dagger's edge." He turned away from the children and started walking off the way he came.

Still coming down off the adrenaline, Myles breathed out a "Th... thank you, sir."

"Brats," he muttered with his back turned, "files in singles, or manure be."

"Oh, yes. Sorry," Kamara swiftly retrieved Hanish and positioned herself behind the captain. With a decisive gesture, she beckoned Myles to follow suit.

As they followed the captain, they could hear the unsettling creaking and moaning emanating from the ancient timbers. Finally, they emerged from the confines of the forest.

The captain then led them on a precarious ascent up an ice-coated hillside. Their destination became apparent as they approached a large, whimsical structure resembling a hut. From its colossal chimneys, plumes of smoke billowed skyward. Intricate metal pipes snaked in and out of the building, radiating a palpable heat that melted the surrounding snow.

Ascending the steps, Captain Nordic then forcefully pushed open the doors with a booming proclamation, "Reptilian whelp, where be allegiances for them learned populus?"

Alistair hurriedly maneuvered himself towards Kamara and Myles, his expression etched with relief. "Oh my. You two are in a sorry state. What transpired? Have you sustained any injuries?" He then assumed a kneeling position and commenced a meticulous examination of Omni and Hanish.

"We're fine..." answered Kamara knowing, quite well, his concerns were not meant for them.

"Myles. Kamara," Hickalik's voice rang out running up. "Are you two okay? What happened?"

"We're fine," Myles informed, "Luckily Captain Nordic found us in the nick of time."

Nordic sniffed, "Keep a gander out ye drove, less be dawns of gray." And with that, he returned to the cold night.

The children were herded towards the counter. Seated behind it was a petite elderly woman, engrossed in paperwork. Her wizened features were accentuated by remarkably long eyebrows. Her pointed ears mirrored the sharpness of her nose. Having meticulously reviewed the documents before her, she punctuated the process with a forceful stamp.

"Approach," she rasped. Kamara stepped up and handed her documents from her bag.

The elderly woman's gaze remained fixed upon the document, "Items for smelting?"

Myles leaned closer to Hickalik, "What is she?"

A surprised look fell on Hickalik, "You've never seen one before?"

"I don't think so. Should I have?"

"She's a pixie; a clerical worker."

"A pixie?" Myles asked, "I thought pixies were little people, with wings, and magical dust and stuff?"

"Well, there is a smell of dust, and they are pretty old, but there's nothing magical about it. And they are small people, but no wings or anything. They are still humans, just shrunken from old age. Pixies handle most of the clerical work for the kingdom."

Hickalik scanned the room, as if not wanting to be overheard, "The story I was told is that a village of women were fed up nagging their husbands to get things done that they promised to do. So, the women all made contracts with the men to hold them accountable, but the men never followed through. One by one the women left the men and started their own village where everything was documented, reviewed, inspected, and completed on time. They became overly dependent on their rules and documentation. Some people say a pixie wouldn't save her own sister without first submitting forms to their council for review and approval— stamped in triplicate. There is always more work to be done, so they don't die, they just continue to do their daily tasks."

Myles pondered, "Where are the men?"

"No one knows. Some say they starved to death; others say they must still be trying to complete their tasks from their signed contracts. My grandpa said one time that they still wander these lands searching for belongings they once put down and can never find again, but his laughter made me think he was just joking."

The tiny lady stamped Kamara's form and belched, "Approach," again.

Myles stepped up. He retrieved his forms from his pack. They were torn and clawed from Omni, who peered over his shoulder with complete innocence. He slowly slid the papers across the desk. The frowning pixie stared at the dilapidated forms through her thin glasses at the end of her nose. Her eyes shifted to Myles, unamused.

She reached behind, pulled out a form from a cabinet, and slapped it down.

"What's this?" asked Myles timidly.

"Form disposal and re-application form."

Myles swiftly completed the disposal form as requested and presented it to the woman. After a thorough review, she stamped it with a decisive thud, searing a seal of approval into the paper. She then offered a new blank application form to Myles, discarding the tattered one into a nearby incinerator.

Myles filled out the necessary information, the same as before, and presented. With a tremor in her hands, she grasped the form and meticulously scanned its contents.

"You didn't provide your dragon type," she stated, sliding the paper back.

"I know but... there was no option for Omni. He is an elden dragon, and that was not on the list of options."

She rolled her eyes over to the wall next to them. It was covered in a rainbow of colored forms. "Yellow forms, labeled, Undocumented dragon type Hilt Application," she instructed.

"Oh, thank you," Myles reached up and grabbed the yellow form. He recorded his information once more. However, after subjecting the form to her gaze, the pixie once again returned it.

"Fill out your flame attribute," she demanded.

"I... I can't."

"What do you mean you can't?"

"He hasn't shown me any flame or attribute. I don't know what he has."

With a heavy sigh, she gestured towards the rainbow wall once more. "The red form is for unknown flame attributes." As Myles reached, leaning over the counter, an involuntary sniff caught a whiff of her dusty aroma.

Her hand then rose in a gesture that halted his movement, "Wait... Yellow is for unknown dragon class; red is for unknown flame attribute. You need an orange form for both unknown registration categories."

Myles held a puzzled expression.

"There is a reason for all of it," she rasped begrudgingly.

After now filling out the orange form, she again returned it with a scowl, "What's your designated hilt class selection?"

"Sorry, but what is a 'hilt class selection' exactly?"

Casting a glance around the room beyond Myles, the woman evidently sought the presence of another adult to offer clarification.

Fortunately, Hickalik intervened. "There are five hilt classes. Basically, the higher the class, the more rare and expensive the materials you get to use, but it is terribly expensive. Only the nobles and social elites can afford that."

"Does the material matter?"

"Oh yes. At least, that's what they say. I read the higher quality items help you gather and hone your attributes faster, which is good, considering we only have until next year before the trials. It can give the wielder quite an early advantage."

Myles looked back at the lady behind the counter, "What's the highest classification?"

"Master class materials," she pointed to the form, "Most all your classmates selected this."

Myles thought for a moment. "I have no money; how do I pay?"

She groaned with impatience, "The charge will be taken from your institutional account." Then Myles remembered Allen saying he deposited money in his school account before leaving.

Attempting not to annoy the lady further, Myles gently asked, "How would one know how much they have in their account?" and after filling out an Account Balance Request Form, he got his answer.

The pixie pulled a file from the cabinet behind her, never needing to glance for her reach, and read his balance.

"Eight hundred seventy-five thousand, four hundred and twenty lagoons."

"And how much is the master class again?"

She spoke with her teeth clenched this time, "One million five hundred thousand farlings."

"And... how much is a farling to a lagoon?"

Myles felt a tap on his shoulder and turned to find Hickalik with his mouth gaped open. "Myles, all you need is one point five lagoons for the master class."

"Oh, that's great. Thanks, I'll do that, then." He turned and marked master class on his application. Once he slid his paper over to the receptionist, she quickly stamped the form, almost searing Myles' hand in the process. Then she yelled out in angst, "Approach" very impatiently to Hickalik, who was last in line. Myles took his approved form and waited for his friend a few steps away.

Hickalik turned in his form. There were no mistakes, but just one question, "Designated hilt class?" she asked, already annoyed.

"Sorry ma'am. I was hoping before I selected, I could turn in this form." He passed another form over the counter. She read out loud, "Monetary Grant for Potential Future Galliants Request Form."

She picked up a larger stamp this time and with a heavy stamp thudding the paper, announced "Declined."

Hickalik's head drooped, "Oh... I thought the grants were still open this year," he said. "I'll just take the basic hilt class." Then Hickalik felt a hand on his shoulder.

Hickalik turned to face Myles, "Hick, let me pitch in. You deserve the master class more than I do. I don't even know if I will have any Nexus flame to wield. But you have Galacia, and she will make you strong, I know it. Let me help."

A tear bubbled up in Hickalik's eye, "Myles, you don't understand. I can't let you. It's too much. I could never repay you."

"No it isn't," Myles replied, "I'll still have like eight hundred seventy three thousand... or something like that. It's fine, really."

"Myles," Hickalik attempted to explain, "one point five million farlings is more than my grandpa's entire farm. That's more money than I will probably ever see. You are probably one of the richest kids at this school. I have never heard of anyone having that much in a school account or any account."

Myles' eyes widened. He had been utterly unaware he possessed such a sum. He had never had money before, except for a couple of dollars here and there from helping farmers back home.

Why did Allen give me so much? he thought to himself. *Was it a mistake? Did he have to pay Allen back?* Myles shook the thoughts from his head for now.

"I don't care," Myles said, stepping past Hickalik. He demanded the pixie take his funds and paid for Hickalik's hilt. And after three more forms, and a notarized co-signing, the boys were on their way to build their hilts.

Hickalik whispered, "Kamara would have loved to witness all that.... with the pixie."

"Don't you ever tell her, or I'll take your hilt back."

They entered a spacious chamber where a handful of students, including Kamara and Sigurd, diligently toiled. Gavin and Gordon were pretend-sword fighting, accidentally knocking over displays, while another pixie scolded them profusely.

The walls served as a majestic display, showcasing a diverse array of metallic components, leather and scaled wrappings, beautifully crafted handles, and gleaming jewels. They approached another pixie, whose demeanor presented a more agreeable contrast to the previous one, although she looked and smelled about the same.

Having secured their approved documents, they received a hilt construction manual and a rolled parchment. The form outlined the necessary components, categorized as either mandatory or optional, for the applicants' selections. The task at hand involved acquiring a tang, grip, shoulder piece, guard, button, pommel, and quillon, among other components; the terminology was mostly foreign to Myles.

Hickalik, however, approached the decision-making process with utmost seriousness. He carefully selected a hilt component from the wall, then pressed the item against the parchment, scorching a mark. As he repeated this action with subsequent selections, the image on the parchment gradually morphed to resemble the hilt of a sword.

"Oh, I get it," said Myles. "So, which items do I get to select from?" he asked the dusty pixie.

"All of them," she replied. "There are no limitations for the master class."

Myles felt like a kid in a candy store. Suddenly, he thought himself an enthusiast of swords. He envisioned elegant rapiers and imposing knightly swords. After much deliberation, he designed and selected his hilt components.

One by one, students brought their finished blueprints to the forges, where they found Pedagogue Alistair. They presented their designs with their collected dragon items. Some used fangs or teeth, others a claw or scales. Myles was the last of the class to present to Alistair. But before he gave up his item, he noticed a large fat animal behind Alistair near the forges.

Too distracted by the bizarre creature, the words just fell out, "What is that?"

"Oh..." Pedagogue Alistair turned, "that is a bulrog. But I guess not the type you are familiar with from the great hall. This bulrog is from a different region. They are much larger, as you can see, and live in desolate lands, they feed on Ruach as a source of nourishment. They digest and break down Ruach enriched materials, such as your dragon items you have collected and have brought today. Once I use my flame to merge your dragon's offering to your hilts, this bulrog will digest the hilts, using a catabolic process to merge your dragon's ability to use Ruach with your hilt materials."

Gavin raised his hand from the back, "So, our hilts are going to be..."

"Digested and defecated. Yes," Alistair answered matter-of-factly. At this news, the students grew uncomfortably silent, with the occasional giggle from Gavin and Gordon.

Alistair looked back to Myles, "And what did your dragon bless you with, young Briggs?"

Myles opened his backpack and slowly pulled out Omni's broken eggshell.

"An eggshell? How interesting, although a bit unorthodox. I don't know if we have ever smelted an eggshell before. Tell me, why the egg?"

"Well sir... Omni never dropped any sort of offering for me to collect," Myles explained. "Also, during the attacks, this egg protected me and Omni."

"How peculiar... Perhaps elden dragons do not shed like other dragons. Perhaps the egg provides protections we have not yet explored. Nevertheless, I have a perfect idea about how to smelt your eggshell into your hilt. Whether functional, well... it is yet to be seen."

Chapter Twenty

Gifts and Gripes

The weeks crept by. Confined by the relentless winter, most scholastic activities were relegated to the indoors. Both the students and their dragons were restless, bouncing off the walls. In Omni's case quite literally. The academy had decked the halls with festive decorations, garlands, red berries, wreaths, and lit candles that never melted or burnt out. The halls filled with the scent of pine. The date of Christmas day, as Myles knew it, had already come and gone with no mention, but the atmosphere of a time he loved to celebrate was all around him.

One afternoon, the first-year students' rings lit up, summoning them to the great hall. Myles had learned to simply follow the crowds when this happened. They all lined up at a long table stretching the room. Each place at the table had a set of shiny tools: chisels, picks, and hammers, neatly displayed. There was a large pine tree in the corner of the room, beautifully arranged with gemstones and ribbons. Hundreds of candles glistened as a larger flame burnt at the top of the tree, thriving at the peak. Under the tree were dozens of round egg-shaped clay orbs.

With two taps of the provost's staff, the room's anxious energy was pulled toward her.

"Dear students, I wish you all a Merry Christmas this day."

Today? Myles thought. *Today is Christmas?*

"Each year we have the students create their own hilts. Each year they receive them on this day. However, those are not gifts, but merely a transaction in which you receive what you paid for. Today is when you receive your first glimpse of a gift much deeper than a superficial handle. The gift of your Nexus connection begins to be realized. It is a gift like no other, a gift that is freely given to those who did not earn, but will receive, nevertheless. You will each find an egg-like coprolite under the tree, marked with your unique blazed symbols. Once you have found yours, you may open it and find your new hilts inside. Now... Merry Christmas and open your gifts."

In a mad dash, the students rushed the tree rolling the orbs around to find their matching marking. They took their hardened orbs back to the table, where they began chiseling away the hard clay-like exterior.

Sigurd struggled to find his marking, since it had been so long since he had seen it well, but eventually was able to locate it by process of elimination. Myles, however, found not a round orb-like item, but a box with his blazed symbol seared onto it. There was a sealed envelope on top. He took his box back to the table.

"Well, that's not fair," said Arica Eclat, staring at the box. "We all have to chisel away for hours while he just has to open a box?" He picked up the envelope, broke the seal, and read out loud.

Dear Mr. Briggs,

We do hope you are doing well this Christmas Day. Your gift almost didn't make the delivery schedule. I was able to smelt your eggshell into the other materials for your hilt, however it seems your hilt was causing the bulrog some indigestion. Luckily, Pedagogue Greenwald was ordered to remedy some approved laxatives to help with the process, however this made your gift a bit more rushed, as you might have conjectured. Sorry for the mess."

Best Regards,

Pedagogue Alistair

Myles put down the letter and opened the box. The putrid smell nearly knocked him unconscious.

"Wait..." said Sigurd, connecting the dots, "does that mean all of these orbs are..."

Most of the room came to the same conclusion. There was a moment of uniform disgust.

"Gross," exclaimed Xander at the other end of the table. "I thought these were some sort of packing or holiday gimmick. This is the creature's actual fecal matter?!" he protested. He picked up his gated dragon, "This is disgusting. Bach, finish this up, wash my property thoroughly, and deliver it to me."

"Umm, yeah. Okay, Xander."

"Mine too," demanded Aberdeen, mortified that she even touched the object. As they both stormed off, Warden Petroff addressed the hall, "I can assure you all, the material is very sterile. You have nothing to fret over, that is all but Mr. Briggs, of course."

Myles was given a long pair of gloves and a bucket filled with water. The other students looked away in disgust, chiseling their spheres while trying to avoid skin contact.

Myles donned his gloves and reached into his box. The consistency of the liquefied substance was one he wished he would never know again. But he was able to feel something hard. He carefully pulled it out and immediately started washing off the object in the bucket. It was the hilt he had created. The handle grip was black. Dark jewels were inlaid down the branched knuckle guard. All the metallic pieces were a dull gray. He held out his new gift by its handle.

"It's perfect," he marveled.

"Everything except the smell," commented Kamara.

"Maybe don't wave it around until you give it a deeper cleaning," Hickalik chuckled.

One by one, each student chiseled their way to the center to find their hilts. There were so many different styles and unique designs. Kamara showed them her double grip design as she split it into two mirrored pieces, each a full hilt in its own right.

Myles was amazed, "I didn't even know that was an option."

Two taps echoed in the hall once more. "Now, be warned. Please do not try to muster up your Nexus ability by brandishing your new hilts before Warden Petroff has the opportunity to train each of you."

But, before the provost could finish, Gavin had pointed his hilt down, tightening all his muscles, shaking his body. A whip-like flame burst out of the hilt and lay on the ground around him.

"I did it." He exclaimed. Then the floor below lit a blaze as both Gavin and Gordon plummeted through the burning floors without a trace.

Provost Prudencia just sighed and rubbed an eyebrow with her finger. "Warden Petroff, would you mind?" she asked.

"For you, my Provost." As he turned to go find the missing students somewhere below.

"As I was saying. Again, please wait before attempting to activate your Nexus through your hilts until Warden Petroff has had the opportunity to properly train you in your studies." Her tone dropped. "Furthermore, hilts are bound to you through your Nexus connection with your dragon. Under no circumstances are you to try to use another's hilt. It is your property alone." Then she lightened up again. "Now, enjoy your gifts, your Nexus training, and Merry Christmas to all of you."

The weeks flew by as their class schedules were increased with a double lesson in Ruach Fundamentals. Now that Myles had a chance to use a Nexus flame, he hung on Warden Petroff's every word in Ruach Fundamentals.

"There are two types of Ruach," Petroff explained, "your Nexus connection allows you control of both types through your hilt. There is your dragon's flame and the natural Ruach that flows through you every day. Your dragon's flame attribute is usually displayed in some form of an elemental gifting, such as fire, water, wind, etcetera. This is usually the principle of their power; however, the much-less-known ability at your disposal is releasing the Ruach that resides inside your body and flows through you every day. This form of Ruach is known as natural Ruach, which is less powerful, but easier to control. This is where we will begin.

Warden Petroff pulled out his hilt, made of a beautiful green bronzed-like metal blooming into blue crystals, "Let me demonstrate."

He thrust with a lunge toward a round stone on the other side of the room. Clear wispy lines like threads glided to the stone from his hilt, connecting to it. He pulled back, straining against the stone's weight. To the students' amazement, the stone started rolling toward them, picking up momentum. He then waved his hilt, disconnecting the thread lines as the pedagogue stopped the rolling stone with his foot. He then spun and whipped his hand out toward another stone, hilt pointing straight out. A ball of the same wispy strands shot out from his hilt colliding with the stone with great force. The boulder bounced away and cracked in half. Heavily breathing through his flared nostrils, Petroff returned his hilt underneath his coat.

"Sir," asked Gordon, "Was that your Nexus attribute?"

Pedagogue Petroff sighed as he pressed his lips in disappointment, "For those of you who need further explanation, this is not my attribute. This is a shared Ruach connection we all have and can now manipulate. It is using your natural Ruach, not your dragon's flame. Once you learn how to control your natural Ruach, you will be able to learn how to call upon your flames through your hilts."

"Think of natural Ruach as an extension of your body. If you desire to whip an object and control where you pull it, think of the hilt as a whip. Extend the Ruach flowing from your body, through your arm, and into the whip. Once you can visualize the cords extending out and feel your hilt, you will be able to manifest strains on command."

"Once you learn to control this ability, your imagination will guide the use of the strains. However, be warned, using natural Ruach is using your own essence, depleting your body's supply. This means you are limited, and will become exhausted if used too much."

"Now, let us begin," Pedagogue Petroff pulled out a marble, placing it on the ground.

For the rest of the extended class period, the students whipped their imaginary whips at the marble. However, the marble never moved and no cords of Ruach were seen. Myles was too busy keeping Omni from attacking the marble.

This process went on for days, until one day, Kamara had stopped trying. She simply stood still. She breathed in deeply and flicked out her hilt, a visible translucent cord was seen, casting out and connecting with the marble. Then, with ease, she pulled her wrist across her body, sending the marble whisking through the air.

The marble hit Xander in the forehead.

"Ahh," Xander exclaimed. "You insolent imp. You did that on purpose." He continued to moan, holding his forehead.

"Hush," Petroff dismissed Xander's performance of pain, pushing him to the side to approach Kamara. "Very well done, Ms. Kingsley. You can move on to the next lesson with Warden Managol," who greeted Kamara with their secret handshake.

Days passed by, with the students' arms numbed from the consistent casting of their hilts. Phineas accidentally threw his hilt a couple times and had to retrieve it in front of the class.

"Pitiful," commented Xander, who was fairing no better.

Then one day, after talking with Kamara some more, Hickalik threw out a thread the whole class could see. To his own amazement, he hooked the marble and pulled it to his feet. Then others started following; Aberdeen Gunther, Phyllis Schnep, and Maple Blackwood were next. One by one the class started showing their promise. Even Gavin, Sigurd, and Bach were able to snatch the marble and move it a little, awarding them the next lesson: all but Myles and Xander.

"Why are you even here, Briggs?" Xander asked. "You don't have a flame. I doubt you even enseared with that pale mutant you call a dragon. Even if you somehow managed to force a flame from that monstrosity, no fold gaffer would ever choose the son of a traitor."

Myles tried his best to ignore the childish taunts as they both continued whipping, flinging, and flailing their hilts at the small marble on the floor.

Pedagogue Petroff kept his arms crossed and watched each of their failed attempts, never faulting. Myles wondered if he ever blinked. Then with a grunting-tired swing, a thin thread was seen, and the marble skipped over closer to Xander.

"Hah," he let out, "I knew it was just a matter of time."

And with that, Pedagogue Petroff waved Xander on to the next lesson.

"Go home Briggs," Xander gloated, "No one wants you here, and no one wants your family to have any part in this kingdom. There is only ruin ahead for you here. Heed my words, Briggs, for they are meant as sympathy." Wearing a smirk of superiority, Xander turned to walk away.

Myles felt furious. On one hand he worried that Xander could be right, that he never truly did ensear with Omni, or Omni had no flame of his own. On the other hand, he wanted to defend his family, defend Omni... defend himself.

As Xander strutted, Myles whipped his hilt, envisioning the hilt coiling around Xander's ankle. He swiftly retracted the hilt, wishing to see his adversary stumble. To his astonishment, Xander's ankle involuntarily jerked backward, causing him to plummet flat on his face.

Myles was stunned, "Did I do that?"

Xander jumped back to his feet and stared at Myles, equally stunned. He looked around but the only other person there was Petroff, which even Xander didn't dare challenge. But Petroff had dropped his arms and glared at Myles. There was no Ruach cord like the others. Myles looked at his hilt, then down at Omni who was now playing with the marble.

Petroff walked up to Myles and grabbed his hand with the hilt still clutched. He examined it for a moment, then pushed it back down to Myles' side. "Seems a righteous anger is the only thing that gets you fired up, Mr. Briggs."

"Proceed," he said begrudgingly.

Over the next few weeks, they attempted to lift objects in the air, pulling and pushing large round boulders, launching waves of Ruach at targets, swinging hilts like hammers and swords. Kamara seemed to be at the head of the class for Ruach control being able to eventually perform all the challenges thus far. But Myles never saw another spark of movement from his hilt again.

The next day, interrupting the daily class schedule, the entire school was summoned by their rings to the great hall. Provost Prudencia addressed the school with a remorseful tone.

"Last night, first year, Maple Blackwood and her dragon, went missing. Her ring was found in the corridors outside the first-year dormitories. What happened to her and where she went is uncertain. At this time, it is assumed she has been taken. If anyone has information that may help Ms. Blackwood, please see your warden immediately."

Quiet chatter mumbled through the great hall. Sigurd leaned in and whispered, "It was one thing to have the first attack outside on school grounds, but to have an abduction from the inside? That's unfathomable."

The provost silenced the room with one tap of her staff, "With the additional deterrent measures already implemented outside, we are now adding security measures inside as well."

Kamara glanced at Myles, "Better not be more unicorns."

"Each dormitory common area will have an academy staff member reside from first moon to first light. Strict curfews will be put in place. Furthermore, the parliament will be sending a security advisor to evaluate the institution's safekeeping procedures. Keep in mind, your safety is always of the utmost importance. We will find Ms. Blackwood and hopefully more answers as to these disappearances. In the meantime, be vigilant. Our greatest assets are the future leaders here in this room. Thank you all, for your cooperation in this matter."

"Institutionalized is apt." Xander scoffed, who wasn't used to living in such close quarters. "Could this place feel any more like a prison?"

Later Myles met up with his friends in the now-supervised auxiliary courts with Omni as usual perched on his shoulder. Gullynn and Galacia were wrestling on the ground as Hanish watched from the comfort of Kamara's lap.

"Can you guys believe Maple was taken?" asked Sigurd.

"More like disappeared…" corrected Kamara, "The provost said they didn't know what happened to her."

"It is safe to assume Dax and Mordred were responsible, though," added Hickalik. "It's pretty brazen of them to do it inside the academy, even with help."

Shock sparked on Sigurd's face, "You think they had help?" he asked. "Like an inside job?"

Kamara rolled her eyes, "Of course, I think most everyone in the school knows there is something going on now."

"Wow," exhaled Sigurd, "I always thought of the academy as one of the safest places to be. And how did they disconnect her ring?"

"That's why it's assumed they had inside help," snapped Kamara. "School rings don't just magically malfunction."

"Well, mine did," added Myles.

"Hah, true. What are the odds?" laughed Sigurd. "Your dad made all the school rings, yet you, his son, are the only one who got a defective one."

Hickalik's attention was grabbed away from watching Galacia and Gullynn, "What if... What if your ring didn't malfunction?"

"What do you mean?" asked Myles. "I was stuck in that hallway every day, even with a replacement ring."

"Exactly. What if your dad meant for you to go to that hallway? What if there was a reason?"

Myles pondered for a moment, "But he made the academy and the rings before I was even born."

"But what if he came back?" Hickalik's eyes glazed over with thought, "What if he came after you were born. What if he left something for you to find? Something important? Something just for you?"

Hickalik realized everyone was staring at him, "Sorry... But we could go look at the location. We have a few more minutes before curfew." They looked at each other. Excitement built as the idea of an investigation materialized in their minds.

They collectively raced toward the west wing corridor.

"Here," directed Myles as he stopped in the middle of the corridor. "This is where my ring led me, I think." They looked around the stone floors, and walls with skylights above.

"What are we looking for?" asked Sigurd.

"If we knew that, we wouldn't have to search," Myles answered.

Kamara faced Myles, "What do you remember from when your rings would lead you here?"

"I don't know." Myles thought for a moment looking around. "I stood right here. But it was afternoon, so the sun was brighter through the skylight, and warmer."

Sigurd pointed to the wall, "There's a sun, on this wall-stone carving thingy."

Hickalik rushed over, nearly pushing Sigurd out of the way. There, on the wall, was a depiction of the valley beneath a mountain range. Above, storm clouds floated below the sun blocking the sunlight, except for one ray of light piercing through, cascading down to a small cave in the middle of the mural.

Myles was drawn in. He ran his fingertips over the grass field and looked up at the mountain range covered in clouds. He slowly started reciting, "The storms are short... the valley is wide... the mountain is tall, destiny inside..." his fingers traced the beam of light down to the cave, "...during your darkest of hours, in the light you shall hide."

Instinctively, he pressed in on the mural's cave opening. A loud clunk sounded. They jumped back. From underneath Sigurd's now golden boot, there was another thudding clunk.

On the ground, in the center of the hall, a part of the floor retracted revealing a familiar shape, at least to Myles. It was the same shape as was on the door of the cabin; six hexagons linked together in a circle.

"Well, that was unexpected," said Sigurd comforting Gullynn, who had jumped up his pant leg.

Kamara bent over, touching the indented shape, "What is it?"

"It's a keyhole," said Myles. "I saw one like this before."

"Do you have the key?"

"No, Allen did."

"Do you think we could pick the lock, you know, like a door lock?" asked Sigurd.

The three boys looked at Kamara. "What? I don't do that. At least not for specialty locks like this."

"What do you think it does?" asked Hickalik.

Myles speculated, "Well... Last time I saw it, it unlocked a door. But there is no door here."

"Bummer," Hickalik said, sounding frustrated as he pounded the pillar, "if only your dad or Allen left you that key."

Myles was surprised Hickalik was so upset on his behalf, "It's okay though. It's really neat just knowing my father was thinking about me. I was kinda hoping he left me something though. The only thing I had from him was taken now that the compass..." Myles paused. A revelation struck him. He hastily grabbed his finger and pulled off the compass inlays he was wearing as a ring.

"Six..." he said, "Six hexagons." He started unfolding the rings until it connected back to itself perfectly.

Sigurd dropped his jaw, pointing. "That's the key."

"Shhh..." Kamara hushed his enthusiasm.

"Why are you hushing me?"

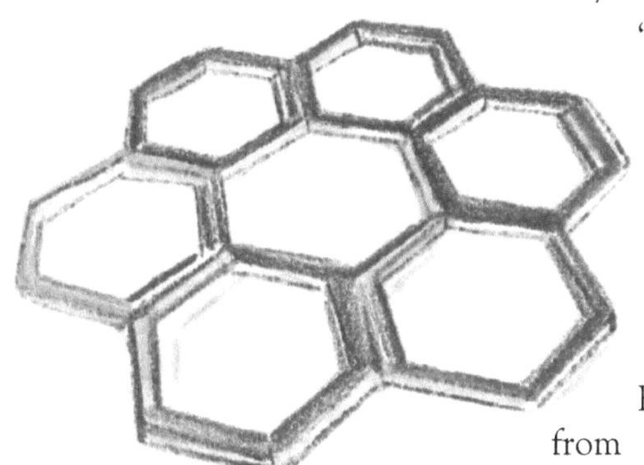

"Well for one, it's so obvious it is the key, boots for brains." Sigurd didn't understand the insult until he saw his boot was frozen to the floor again.

"Galacia..." he said with breathy frustration. He pulled out a metal pick from his pocket that he now carried around with him.

"Secondly, we don't want to attract any attention," Kamara finished.

"Why not?" he asked, picking away at the ice.

"If the school staff sees whatever this is, do you think they will let us continue? Explore inside an unknown door by ourselves? Or let Myles keep whatever his father might have left behind?"

"Kamara's right," agreed Hickalik.

"Good point, I guess," said Sigurd, reluctantly.

Myles bent down and slid the rings into the keyhole. They fit perfectly. He started twisting the stone. Then with a click, and another loud thud. The stones around the keyhole started shifting. Some slid under others, while some lowered into the floor. Hickalik almost fell in, if it wasn't for Myles catching him and pulling him back. One by one the stones started forming the beginnings of a spiral staircase leading downward.

"Who's there?" A voice called out from down the hall. Myles quickly grabbed the ring and turned it back the other way. The stones stopped, and reversed their movements, filling in where they originally were. From around the corner, Warden Managol appeared just as the last stone slid into place.

"Why are you four out here? Curfew should have just started. And what was that clinking I was hearing?"

They froze, no one knew what to say. Even Kamara was caught off guard for a moment.

Then Sigurd spoke up, "Sorry Warden, Hickalik's dragon froze my boot to the floor again. I was picking away at the ice. I guess it did make a weird clinking sound."

No one was more stunned than Kamara at Sigurd's quick thinking.

"We were going to head back," Kamara regained her wits, "But we thought it safest for Sigurd if we stuck together as a group while he freed his boot. We didn't want to leave him alone after curfew. He would be an easy..." she paused, "...well, *easier* target by himself."

Sigurd sent her a quick glare.

"Oh, well that makes sense, I guess," Managol nodded. "But we better get you all back to the dorms before anyone realizes you aren't back in time."

Sigurd continued chipping at his boot.

"Here," Warden Managol grabbed the pick from his hand and with one formidable stab, shattered the ice. His foot was unfrozen, but Sigurd's body was still immobilized out of fear she was going to stab his foot in the process.

After hoisting the pale boy to his feet, Managol escorted the boys to their dorms, transitioning them to the care of Captain Nordic, who was charged with safeguarding the first-year boys' dormitories. Then she left with Kamara toward the Tower of Strength.

The next day, the group discussed the hidden stairs. Each day they attempted to go back, this time with two of them as lookouts, but it was no use. The halls were too busy with traffic to dare open the stairwell during the daytime. Defeated, they sat at dinner as the plates of hot food slowly passed by.

Myles pushed a meatball around his plate, "I wish we could see where it led to. Maybe there is another way to get there."

"Unlikely," added Hickalik, "your dad did a fantastic job hiding and protecting that passageway. I doubt we could just walk in through another door."

Sigurd thought hard, "Well, is it a secret passage to the basement? Students aren't allowed down there for whatever reason."

Myles had a realization, "But we know someone who has been down there."

Hickalik caught on, "That's right. Gavin fell through the first floor into the basement." They searched the room for Gavin, but he wasn't anywhere. Gordon said he had left supper early and was going to head to Pedagogue Humphrey's office for some help with his studies." All four of them turned and looked at the head table where Humphrey sat with the rest of the staff.

"Right..." said Kamara, disbelieving. They hurried toward the staff offices. As they turned the corner, there was Gavin, holding Draugr and pointing the dragon at Pedagogue Humphrey's office door.

"Come on, you," he whispered frustratedly, shaking the poor dragon, who clearly had no intention of helping. Gavin noticed the others and straightened up, turning away from the door.

"Oh, hey there guys," he said, nonchalantly. Have you guys seen Pedagogue Humphrey by any chance?"

Sigurd answered, "Yeah, she's in the great hall still."

"You know, where you just were," stated Kamara.

"Oh, that's right," Gavin started to walk back. "I'll try again later."

"Wait," called out Myles, "Before you go, we need to ask you something."

Curious, Gavin stopped, "Proceed..."

"We were wondering if you could tell us about the basement." Gavin's face drooped, turning pale. "You went down there when Draugr made you pass through the floor, right?"

"Yeah, I was down there, but it was totally not wick." Then Gavin shook off the fearful memory, "But why should I tell you lot? What's in it for me?" he asked.

Myles hesitated.

A mischievous glint grew in Gavin's eye, "Tell ya what, if you all help me get into Humphrey's room so I can peek at the test questions, I'll tell you all about it."

The boys looked troubled by this proposal, but Kamara spoke up, "Or, better yet, we could just tell Pedagogue Humphrey what we saw here." She let out a confident sigh, "It would be four to one, and I am told you may not have the best track record."

"You wouldn't dare," challenged Gavin.

"Why not? Doesn't harm any of us. And even if she doesn't believe us, chances are those test questions will be much more secure after we plant the seeds of doubt in her mind."

Gavin's shoulders drooped, his confidence deflated, "Okay, fine. I'll tell you. It's not somewhere you want to go. It was dark and musty smelling. I fell right on a big root, which hurt bad."

"A root?" asked Myles.

"Yeah, a root. The walls and floors were covered in them. It's like they were growing in through the stone. I didn't really know where to go so I just started walking, some halls were caved in." Gavin's demeanor grew serious, "But there is something down there."

"What do you mean?"

"I don't know, but it didn't like me being there. It stayed in the shadows and made the scariest noise I have ever heard. Some kind of roaring screech. I picked up Draugr and we ran. It chased after us. Luckily, Draugr was just as scared as I was. We ran up to a heavy wooden door and he let out a big blasting fireball, biggest he has ever done. The doors lit ablaze and we jumped through. Then we were outside, near the rear western doors."

"Did you see anything else down there?" Myles asked, "like a spiral staircase leading up?"

"No," he answered curiously. "If I did, I would have gone up them. And why the interest in the basement? I never thought of you four as being rule breakers... well, except for her."

"You and me both..." added Sigurd under his breath.

Kamara butted in, "We heard rumors about a beast living down there and wanted to know if it was true."

"We did?" asked Hickalik, sounding frightened. Kamara silenced him with a quick elbow.

"Well, I can tell you that rumor lived up to its reputation. Super not wick."

"That's interesting," said Kamara. "Well, enjoy your nefarious activities." She turned and walked away. Myles, Hickalik, and Sigurd followed.

After weeks of attempting to access the stairwell after their conversation with Gavin, it was decided that the best course of action would be a stealthy nighttime operation, at least according to Kamara. Hickalik seemed apprehensive about the idea but reluctantly accepted. Sigurd was the most obstinate and took the most convincing.

"It's not right," he would say. "It's not proper. Sneaking around like a nocturnal rodent. Breaking school rules." Eventually his desire to support Myles won him over. Kamara gave each of them a small ebenezer stone.

"What's this for?" Sigurd asked.

"You will need them to sneak out past Captain Paranoia," she stated, referring to Captain Nordic.

Hickalik stared at the ground in despair, "Between the dragons' wing slaps and Captain Nordic's shouting night terrors, I don't know how we will get any sleep."

"We could use these to silence his nightmarish screams," stated Sigurd, excited about the proposition.

"No..." corrected Kamara, "you would have to hold the stone by his mouth the whole time squeezing it. And they only last for a few moments until they are full."

"Plus, you would have to smell his breath the whole time..." added Myles. They all shuddered. "It's like tuna and eggs... but weeks old."

"Or sewage and caviar... and jalapenos," added Hickalik.

"What's wrong with the smell of caviar?" asked Sigurd.

"Oh, the proper folk..." Kamara belittled.

After discussing the plans further, they all went to their dorms for curfew. The mission was set, and the night came to commence their plan.

Chapter Twenty-One

The Resonating Room

Myles, Hickalik and Sigurd clambered out of bed in the middle of the night. They grabbed their dragons, coats and sound stones, provided by Kamara, and crept to the doorway.

"Okay, phase one. We have to sneak out past old sour breath," whispered Hickalik.

He held his sound stone to the door hinges and squeezed. Myles slowly opened the door, and to their amazement, the ever-creaking door was silent for the first time. The stone had absorbed the sound.

They peaked their heads out. The common area felt steamy with a pungent fishy odor. A loud whiny snore came from the sofa. They each held the sound stone to their feet as they walked, making their footsteps undetectable. They reached the common area door leading to the hallway. Hickalik held the stone to the doorknob, while Sigurd held his near the hinges.

Sigurd squeezed the stone, but instead of absorbing the squeaking hinges, he inadvertently played back the sound of his footsteps. He quickly tried to cover it up, but it was too late. Captain Nordic sat up on the sofa with a fierce snort. The boys didn't move. His head turned and looked toward them, but his eyes appeared to still be closed.

He spoke in his upright sleep, "Who trespassin?" grinding his teeth, "...vessel owned, ye vermin." Then with a loud whine, "Be departed... cretins." In his outburst, an object fell from his lap to the floor. He jolted his head back down on the pillow, moaning and grasping at his blanket.

"Thieves!" he yelled out, "Villains. My superbia, ye ferry users." His eyes searched underneath his eyelids. Myles quickly tiptoed over to the sofa.

Sigurd whispered anxiously, "What are you doing?"

Myles picked up the fallen object. It was a broken model ship. The masts were snapped in two with strings and fabric hanging about, disconnected and tattered. Myles glanced at the placard on the ship's haul, "Replica of the Celestial Dragon." He carefully slid the vessel under one of the captain's hands. Nordic clenched the ship, pulling it close to his chest. He let out a whimper followed by a long snore.

The captain turned away from Myles, cuddling his dilapidated ship. "Sweet lass," he mumbled softly. Myles stealthily returned to the others, and they were able to use the stones correctly to hide any sounds as they escaped through the door.

"We are past the point of no return," said Sigurd. They peered around each corner before proceeding. Eventually, they were able to get to their meeting spot.

Sigurd looked around, "She's not here."

Hickalik shrugged, "Maybe she got delayed."

"Or maybe she got caught," added Sigurd.

But Myles dismissed, "Come on, this is Kamara we're talking about. She is the sneakiest person I know."

"I hope she is sneakier than she is proper," added Sigurd. "Luckily she is really pretty and can use that to her advantage."

Hickalik shriveled, "Honestly, she scares me."

They could hear voices approaching from down the hall.

"Quick," Hickalik pushed Myles back to the opposite wall and pulled Sigurd with him, squatting down.

They could hear Provost Prudencia and a man talking as they walked down the hall towards them.

"Doesn't she ever sleep?" complained Hickalik, pulling Sigurd over and hunkering down. Myles followed their example. As he did, he noticed the shimmer of a bulrog next to him. Hickalik had cleverly hidden them behind the camouflage creatures lining the hall.

The voices were close enough for the boys to make out their words.

"As you can see Mr. Getz, we are taking every precautionary measure we can. And it still has not been determined that Ms. Blackwood was taken."

Sigurd whispered, "That must be the security advisor."

The clunking heels of the man's wooden soles grew closer, "Yes, I see the security measures you provided. But to say every precautionary measure has been taken would be quite over spoken. You do not possess the personnel for a facility of this vast complexity."

Provost glanced down the hallway, then she stopped and turned to the man. "Under no circumstances will I allow parliament watch dogs roaming these halls. You will see soon enough that these incidents will be terminated, and the culprits identified."

"Oh, is that what we should communicate to the Blackwood family? I know your little girl is missing, however the provost seems optimistic about her prospects, so I am sure it will turn out alright. Just like the Bunson child, who was released from your care, simply because your care was unsatisfactory. Listen closely, Provost. I will rule the facility soon enough, and by proxy, you as well."

Myles was listening intensely, so intensely he was holding his stone in his pocket and accidentally squeezed it, setting it off. The sound of a creaking door echoed through the hall. The boys stiffened.

"What was that?" Mr. Getz turned. Provost Prudencia didn't bother looking.

"It's just a squeaky hinge. The whole school is filled with them. Honestly, I think Haldor aged this place on purpose when he rebuilt, just to annoy everyone. Feels hundreds of years old again in a matter of decades."

Yes but..." the man gave a frustrated sigh, "...who opened the door?"

"Who knows," the provost shrugged. "We have faculty and staff members patrolling throughout the facility at all hours. Honestly, these attacks will be the death of the school if we must continue burning the candle at both ends like this."

The man continued staring down the hall. He took a step forward, investigating further.

"Did I tell you we have our first confirmed elden dragon here in the school? It was enseared with one of our first-years." The man halted, just before reaching the boy's position.

"I heard all about your elden dragon. Sharing a Nexus with the son of that traitor." He turned back toward the provost. "Had Chancellor Dragoon known who the boy was, he would have never let him register in the first place."

"Well, that seems unreasonable," countered the provost. "After all, I heard your father was quite the ruffian as well. Are you saying the apple always falls straight to the trunk of the tree?"

Mr. Getz was clearly displeased with this question, "I am turning in for the night. I will see you and your lollygagging staff in the morning." He walked past Provost Prudencia and down the hall from where they came.

"Yes," added the provost, still facing the direction of the boys, "We should *all* turn in for the night." Then she turned and followed the man slowly. They waited in silence for a moment.

Sigurd spoke first, "That was too close. Good thing you saw the bulrogs. I couldn't see them at all."

Then a soft thud was heard from behind Hickalik. A hand firmly covered his mouth. He let out a muffled scream, then realized it was Kamara.

"Where did you come from?" Sigurd demanded.

"Up there," she pointed to the rafters above. "You lot know what quiet and stealthy means, right?"

"Ha ha, very funny," said Sigurd, "What, were you up there the whole time?"

"Yep," she smiled, "and I heard every word." Sigurd's face turned a crimson red.

"Shall we get a move on?" asked Myles, tingling with excitement the closer they got to the hidden stairs.

Ducking around a few more corners, they made their way to the passage. Myles approached the mural and pressed in on the cave depiction once more. Just as before, the keyhole thudded into place.

Myles pulled his ring off and unfolded the hexagons. He placed it in the keyhole and turned. Just as before, the stones began to shift, revealing the spiral staircase leading down into the darkness. The key popped back out of the keyhole. Myles picked it up, folded it, and placed it back on his finger.

Hickalik had a look of immediate regret staring into the dark abyss.

Myles started descending down. "This is it." The stone steps were firm.

"Here," Kamara handed Myles a fire-stone from her bag as they followed.

"Do you have another stone, maybe?" inquired Hickalik, looking meek in the surrounding darkness. Kamara handed Hickalik another stone, which he took like a starving monkey who was offered a banana. The stairway was tight as it continued spiraling downward. Then the sound of grinding stones echoed again as the light above them closed.

"I guess we aren't going back that way," quivered Hickalik.

The walls were damp and cracked, with bulging roots following the curving path. The stairwell finally ended into a dark open room with one singular beam of light shining through a crack in the ceiling. As Myles stepped forward, stones lit aglow around the room's perimeter.

"Woah," gasped Sigurd. "I don't like to use slang, but this is totally wick."

Hickalik breathed easier, "I'm just glad your dad thought to add ebenezer stones for lighting."

The rounded room had seven closed doors leading out in all directions. In the center of the room, they gathered around a flat round stone covered in a white powder.

Hickalik surveyed the doors, "Where do they all lead to?"

"Look," Kamara pointed, "each door is engraved with a different pattern. And they all have symbols above them, except this bigger one," she gestured to the middle door.

Myles approached the stone tabletop in the center and grabbed a handful of the powder, letting it pour through his fingers. "It's sand... white sand."

Kamara joined Myles, "And there are crystal stones surrounding the table's edges. Eleven it looks like," she counted. She plucked one off the side, "These are ebenezer stones. And nice ones at that."

Sigurd spun around in awe, "What is this place?" Hickalik, lost in thought, muttered out loud, "It is definitely subterranean. Assuming the doors lead to other caves or halls, this room must be some sort of hub or centralized point. It's so well protected, the other tunnels must not lead outside, or if they do, are equally as hidden. But what's the purpose? Is it for moving around in secret? There are no signs of livable accommodations, so mostly for uses other than residency..."

"Hickalik, we get it," Kamara snapped him back to reality.

"Oh, sorry..." he apologized, embarrassed.

Sigurd chuckled to himself, "I think I liked it better when you were scared."

Kamara lifted an ebenezer stone up and squeezed it, but nothing happened.

"Maybe they are empty?" Myles questioned.

"No, that's not it, I think they were designed to operate differently, or under a direct application."

Sigurd laughed, "Careful Kamara, you are starting to sound like Hickalik."

"And what's wrong with being smart?" she asked. "Oh sorry, you wouldn't know."

Sigurd tried to steam up a response but was distracted by Myles' question, "What are these?" He pointed to one edge of the stone table, "There are three empty indents on this side."

Kamara walked over to inspect, then glanced back to the stone in her hand. She placed the stone in the indent. It locked in place like a magnet.

A humming sound began to resonate throughout the room as small bits of stone vibrated off the damaged ceiling.

"An earthquake?" asked Sigurd, "Is the floor moving?"

"Look," Myles pointed to the top of the wide stone pedestal in the center of the room. The white sands danced on the flat stone surface, forming a hashed pattern. Then the humming stopped. They inspected the pattern the sand created.

"It's a resonating plate," called out Hickalik. The others looked confused. "The sand just made a visible representation of the frequency we just heard." He picked up another of the crystals, "They are resonating stones. Each crystal must play a different frequency. The frequency vibrated the stone table. The sand follows the sound waves and shows the pattern of the frequency produced."

Myles picked up another crystal stone, "I get it." He placed another stone in an empty indent and the room hummed once more, this time with a higher frequency. Once more, the sand sputtered, changing the pattern. Once the lines were well-defined the humming ceased.

Myles looked around the room as an idea emerged, "Each door is covered in a pattern like the sand. Maybe if we can find the right frequencies, and make the sand match the pattern on each door, then the door will open."

Hickalik pondered, "That is way too complex."

"Why?" asked Sigurd, "You just have to put the right stones in to make a pattern, right?"

Hickalik rubbed his forehead, "There are three indents along the stone top, yes? And eleven stones to choose from. We don't know what combination or sequence of stones could open each door. If you need three stones to open a door, that is a one in nine hundred and ninety chance for each door."

"That can't be right," said Sigurd in disbelief.

"No, that's exactly right."

Myles held a stone and sighed, "Allen did say my dad liked puzzles."

"Puzzles? This is a prison," Hickalik grumbled. "It will take us weeks to try all the variations."

Myles scrutinized the new design made by the sand, "Maybe not. Look." He pulled the crystal stones and put back just one, the humming vibrations sounded again, and the sands shifted. "Each frequency has its own sand pattern. Once we know all eleven patterns, we can see which is close to the design of a door. Then we can add another frequency that looks like it may help get us the right pattern."

Sigurd shook his head, "You lost me."

"I hate to say it... hate to..." Kamara emphasized, "but I am with Sigurd on this one."

Myles took the time to try each stone by itself and had Hickalik draw each pattern in a notebook.

"You see?" Myles pointed to one of the patterns Hickalik scripted. "This one is close to this door's design." He pointed to the third door from the left.

Kamara compared the two, "Kind of... But the door has more curved lines. This stone's frequency looks more straight-lined and rigid."

"Now, look at this one," He said, pointing to a different sketch. "If we add this frequency, it might change the pattern to match."

Myles grabbed the first stone and placed it on the stone top. The same sand lines squirmed into place on the dark stone as was in the sketch book. Then he grabbed another stone and placed it in another empty slot. The two frequencies resonated in harmony as the sands bobbled once more. When the humming stopped, they all leaned over the table. The sand pattern was identical to the door.

"Now what?" asked Sigurd, expecting someone's explanation. Then the room vibrated again, not from a humming noise, but from a door sliding open. The door scratched its way along the stone floor until it stopped, wide open. There the group stood in the doorway looking down a dark hall.

"You did it," said Hickalik in amazement.

"Now, just six more times," Kamara added sarcastically.

Hickalik squinted at the symbol above the open door, "I think I've seen this symbol before. In an old text in the library. It's part of the first language. I think it's the symbol for earth, or ground... but I'm not a hundred percent."

"Kinda looks like a blaze after ensearing," added Sigurd.

"Do we go in?" asked Hickalik.

Without saying a word, Myles started walking in front with the fire-stone held out for light. "Where do you think it leads?" asked Hickalik, hiding between Sigurd and Kamara.

Myles lifted the stone's light to the walls, "Based on the roots growing in and the stonework, I think this is the basement that Gavin fell into."

"Earth," exclaimed Hickalik. "The earth symbol above the door. We are underground." His face turned from his normal meek, to concerned, "But didn't Gavin say he heard something down here?"

"Knowing Gavin, it was probably just a rat or something," Kamara belittled.

Myles held the light to the wall illuminating long deep scratch marks, "That's one big rat."

"I think we should go back now," recommended Hickalik.

Omni began to squirm and claw at Myles' shoulder, "What's up Omni?"

Then Hanish stood upright on Kamara's shoulder. She hissed towards the shadows in the corner. The shadows hissed back. From the darkness emerged a green snake with brown and black diamonds lining its spine. It hissed again.

"It's okay, it's just a snake," said Myles. Then a loud bleat from a goat rang out. This first scared the children half to death, then helped cut the tension in the room.

They let out a relieving sigh, half-filled with a laugh.

"We got a goat and a snake, huh?" said Sigurd, coming down from the adrenaline.

That's when Myles looked down. On the floor, he saw two large furry paws coming out from the shadows. The toes stretched out wide revealing large claws that scraped the stone floor. A yawning roar, like a lion, was heard from behind the snake. Two yellow eyes appeared, glistening from the glow of Myles' stone.

They stepped back slowly as Sigurd pointed, "That's no goat."

Myles turned to run, but realized the others already made that decision without him.

"Myles, come on!" Kamara called back. He glanced toward the beast once more as the eyes rose up from the ground. As it emerged from the darkness, Myles could make out two large fangs drooping down from its jaw. Its fur-spotted body was reminiscent of a sabretooth tiger, like the ones he saw in his history books back home.

Myles sprinted hard. He could hear the growling breaths behind him quicken with the sounds of claws scraping stone for traction. He pushed, not knowing when a large swooping paw would strike.

"Come on, run!" The others called out as they made it back to the room. Kamara quickly made it to the stone top and threw her arm across the sand, breaking the pattern. The doors started grinding closed.

Not knowing if he would make it, Myles held Omni in front of him. He tossed Omni through the gap to Hickalik on the other side. Then he leapt headfirst, turning his body. His head and chest barely fit through the door's opening. His feet hit the closing door but were dragged through from his momentum. He landed with a thud on the cold floor.

Just before the doors came to a close, out from the opening thrust the serpent's green head. It lashed out at Myles, just missing his leg. He gave it a swinging kick before it recoiled back through the gap. Then the door crashed shut.

Myles laid flat on his back, gripping his burning lungs.

Hickalik cried out, "Why is there a chimera loose in the basement?"

"That's what that was?" wheezed Myles.

"That was too close," said Sigurd, gasping for air.

Kamara was slumped over the stone table with sand in her hair.

"Kamara," Myles said between breaths, "Thank you."

She raised her head to look at Myles, "If I ever meet your dad, I will personally punch him in the face."

Myles let out a breathy laugh. Then the others followed suit. Even Hickalik seemed to have a little more life in him after surviving the encounter.

Myles eventually stood up and plucked another resonating-stone, "I guess we press on. I doubt they could all be that bad."

Myles used Hickalik's notes to figure out another door's pattern. The room shook as a second door cracked open. They stood on guard, not knowing what to expect this time. Kamara stood above the sand covered stone in case she had to strike the pattern away once more.

Once fully opened, Myles poked his head in the doorway, "The tunnel's caved-in."

Sigurd let out a sigh, "That was underwhelming."

"Two stones again?" questioned Hickalik, looking back at the resonating table. "I wonder why?"

"What do you mean?" asked Myles.

"If the doors only take two resonating-stones to open, why are there three indents?"

Myles looked up at the unlabeled door, "Maybe some of them, take three instead."

"It would make the doors more secure if they took three stones," replied Hickalik.

"Which door did we just open, Hickalik?" asked Kamara.

He looked up at the symbol above the open door. "I'm not sure. Sorry, I don't know this symbol." He took out his notebook and sketched the symbol. Kamara erased the sand pattern and the door to the collapsed tunnel slowly hinged shut.

"And what's behind door number three?" she asked, looking at Myles.

This time, Myles had more difficulty figuring out the right frequencies. While Myles and Hickalik poured over the patterns, Sigurd began placing and pulling stones at random, "It's like playing a very slow pipe organ," he bantered. But then a third door grinded open.

"Sigurd, you did it," Hickalik praised, but Sigurd was too shocked to celebrate. They all stood at the ready once more. The door thudded into the open position. A long curving tunnel led forward.

"Are we all going this time?" asked Hickalik, recalling the recent memories of the chimera.

"You can always stay here," said Kamara, "but there is no guarantee the doors will not shut behind us like the stairwell did. Then you would be all alone."

Hickalik quickly fell in line between Sigurd and Kamara again, "I think this tunnel is labeled fire," he whispered.

They entered the tunnel slowly this time, making sure to shine the glowing stone in every corner as they investigated. There was a warm breeze blowing toward them through the tunnel. As they followed the curved hallway a faint glow grew brighter. They could hear the echoes of a man's voice coming from up ahead, but the hot breeze made it hard to make out.

Myles was getting excited, "You think it could be Haldor?" he whispered, "Waiting down here for years?"

They came to the end of the tunnel and peeked around the corner. It was a warm large room with boxes, and medical equipment on shelves. Big metal pipes and ducting lined the edges of the room. A clunking sound caught their attention. A metal box, with small holes, jumped and jolted on a table. Then they saw her. Lying unconscious on the table was the missing girl, Maple Blackwood.

Chapter Twenty-Two

Bad Ideas

There, on a wood slab table, lay Maple Blackwood. There was a flat clear stone strapped to her arm. Small flames flickered between the stone and her skin. Next to her, the metal crate continued to bounce with whimpering sounds.

"It's Maple," Sigurd stood up but was quickly yanked down by Myles.

"Why are you hindering me? We need to help her."

Kamara held her finger to her lips and whispered, "Remember the man's voice we heard from down the hallway?"

Sigurd's eyes widened.

"The box," murmured Kamara. "It must be Maple's dragon."

A man's voice groaned out from the other side of the room, "Why does they all's takes so longs?"

A groaning voice answered, "For the last time, you blithering buffoon, he is not here to use his flame. We have to use these pathetic stones instead. But who cares, we get paid by the day. You got somewhere else to be?"

"No's. Not's particularly's."

"We don't know how long this one will take, or if it will even work. We've never done it to an enseared pest before."

The room was quite noisy, with the sounds of hissing pipes and humming machinery, but Myles, Hickalik, and Kamara recognized the voices immediately.

"It's Dax and Mordred," Myles informed. Sigurd was the only one who was surprised. "They were the ones that kidnapped Maple. We need to get her out of here."

Sigurd nodded. "Agreed."

Hickalik raised his hand, "Shouldn't we go get a pedagogue or warden?"

Kamara shook her head, "By then she could have her blaze taken like the rest. Plus, the staff will find out about Myles' ring, and the room."

Myles stopped her, "That's not important now. I won't have another person lose their future like Florky. We have to save her before they take her blaze. If we can get Maple without them noticing, then we can sneak back out the way we came."

Sigurd thought hard, "But then we will be stuck in the same room we were in before. And won't Dack and Mordril follow us once they notice the girl is missing?"

Kamara slumped her shoulders. "You have to be doing it on purpose now," she mocked.

Hickalik chimed in, "Chances are there is another way out of the room. We never checked the staircase again after it closed, and one of the other tunnels will most likely lead out at some point. Like how Gavin said the basement had a door that led him outside."

"We'll need a distraction," added Kamara.

Sigurd placed Gullynn on his back as she wrapped her tail around his neck. "I've got this," he said with heroism in his eyes. Sigurd pranced like a four-legged animal, darting from box to box, staying low.

Kamara watched Sigurd scurry, "You know... I can't say I don't like this side of him. Just look how undignified he looks."

Sigurd made his way toward Maple while Dax and Mordred were busy eating. Sigurd reached up and grabbed the pin holding the jumping cage closed. He pulled it out and the cage door slowly swung open. Out jumped Maple's dragon, Ubique, who immediately bit Sigurd's hand. He quickly retracted, holding pressure on the wound, biting his lip. Squirming in pain, he dropped the metal pin. A loud ding rang out in the room as the pin bounced on the floor between Sigurd's legs.

Mordred stood up, "What's was that's?"

"Probably just the dumb dragon trying to escape again."

Sigurd quickly clambered under a table. Mordred glanced over at Ubique. The freed lizard leapt over to Maple and hissed at the two men.

"Its outs agains," Mordred exclaimed.

"What?" Dax stood, knocking over his chair. "That stupid worm. This is why we don't take enseared brats — their dumb dragons."

"Quick, this way," directed Myles pulling Kamara with him. They stayed low, circling the room opposite Sigurd, but Hickalik didn't follow.

Before Dax and Mordred could charge the dragon, Ubique opened her mouth and blasted a fireball behind them, hitting the wall. In a blink, Ubique teleported to the wall where the flames impacted.

"Not again," howled Dax. "Grab that obnoxious lizard."

"I'm's tryin' to's," yelled Mordred as he tripped over the fallen chair, reaching for Ubique. Dax used his green flames to gather roots to bind the elusive dragon, but each time Ubique would teleport to a new location. The children ducked behind corners and maneuvered through the storage to keep from being noticed.

Mordred gathered a ball of fire in his hand, but Dax grabbed his arm, "No, you idiot. They said we need the dragon alive."

Myles, Kamara and Sigurd hid under tables, and behind crates, doing everything they could to stay out of sight. Once Mordred accidentally tripped on Myles' leg but was too distracted to notice what he stumbled on.

Sigurd tried to grab Maple, who was thankfully a petite girl, but never got the chance. Ubique was too quick, bouncing around the room, never giving Sigurd an opening. Then Ubique landed on a piece of scrap metal and grabbed on with his chameleon-like feet. He let out another flaming burst hitting the ceiling above Hickalik. In another flash, Ubique was hanging from the ceiling holding onto the scrap metal, but it proved too heavy. It fell down and hit with a clanging thud.

"Ouch," exclaimed Hickalik. The scrap metal had landed directly on his head.

"Who's was that's?"

Hickalik slowly stood up, peering over the crate he was hiding behind.

"It's that kid," Dax so astutely noted. "What's you doin's here's, kid?" asked Mordred. Both seemed shocked to see anyone else in the room with them. Hickalik panicked. He turned and ran down the tunnel from which they came.

"Where's he off too's?"

"It doesn't matter. It's a dead end that'a way," Dax slapped Mordred's back, "Go get the boy."

Myles spoke worriedly under his breath, "No...Hickalik." They had to do something, or Hickalik would be caught. But before he could think of a plan, he heard Sigurd's voice, "Stop you fiends." Sigurd popped up from his hiding spot holding an iron pot in one hand, as if wielding a weapon.

"What's this, now? Where'd you come from?" asked Dax angrily, not threatened in the slightest.

"We're here to rescue the girl," Sigurd shakily announced.

"Oh, are you now?" Dax sounded excited by the challenge, "Well, rescue away then."

Sigurd dropped his guard, "Really? You will let us take her?"

Dax grinned, "You fool..."

Sigurd glanced toward Mordred who was holding a ball of fire, "Nighties-nights, princes."

Mordred hurled the flames at Sigurd, who clutched the pot with two hands like a shield. The fireball went directly into the pot. The flames were contained, but the force of the blast flung Sigurd back. His body flew into the wall, dislodging more tools and scrap metal.

"That was easy," Dax held up a green flame and gnashed his teeth. He thrust his flame into the ground. Roots grew out from the floor around Sigurd, slithering towards his arms and legs.

"You golden fool," Kamara jumped into the open, brandishing her hilt. She whipped it forward. A Ruach strand could be seen connecting to a heavy chain hanging from the ceiling. She pulled and the chain came flying toward Dax, hitting him in the neck and pulling him to the ground. The roots stopped just short of Sigurd.

"Oi, there's more's in here's," called Mordred. He held out another fireball in his hand and wound up to throw. Myles stood up with a rounded piece of metal he found on the floor, making a shield.

"Watch out," he stepped in front of Kamara to block the incoming inferno. With Omni on his shoulder, they peered over the top of their shield. Then, just before throwing the flames, Mordred released his hand and the fireball vanished.

Mordred sounded confused, "It's the kid and's his pales dragons." Myles examined their attackers. They both appear injured, with bandages and bruises.

Dax finally lifted the thick chain off his neck, "Kill them all," he yelled in anger.

"But we's were tolds to nots hurts the boy and the pales ones."

Seizing the opportunity, Kamara attacked. She whipped her hilt to the side and a long Ruach cord wrapped around Dax as he stood, binding his arms to his body. Sigurd was on his feet and jumped into action. He dove onto Mordred's back and cleaved on like a newborn ape.

Mordred flailed, trying to throw Sigurd off by twisting and pulling at him, "Get offs me's."

Sigurd, with one arm around Mordred's neck, raised his pot and started banging it on Mordred's head. Being jostled around, his swings were small and the impacts were less than desirable. Gullynn had used her flames, igniting half of Mordred's coat into solid gold, making it near impossible for him to move around while Sigurd continued to bang his head unsuccessfully.

Ubique landed a flame on the table next to Maple and appeared next to her. He began chewing the bands that held the stone to her arm, but Mordred noticed and swatted his hand towards the dragon, "Aways with ya's." Ubique made another teleporting leap away.

Dax, still bound by Kamara's Ruach, grinned, "Do you know why most galliants don't use natural Ruach in fights, little girl?" With his arms still bound, he reached out his hand just enough to pick up a hollowed rod from the table next to him. "First, natural Ruach will exhaust you quickly, which will put you in a dangerous position."

Myles glanced at Kamara. She was breathing deeply and sweating more than before. Dax gripped the rod tightly. A green flame, shaped like a spear head, emerged from the end.

Myles saw the flame, "It's his hilt."

"Secondly," Dax continued, "It is weak against any type of flame. He waved his rod through the Ruach strand holding him captive. The green flames sliced through the strand like butter. The thread dissipated, freeing his arms. Mordred pulled Sigurd over the top of his head and threw him to the ground by Myles' feet. Dax and Mordred approached slowly. The children were backed into a corner.

Dax held his flaming spear and Mordred held out his ball of flames. "You foolish kids. You really thought you stood a chance against two flame wielders." Dax laughed, "Weaklings."

Sigurd was shaken up, still on the ground. Kamara looked too exhausted to move. The dragon pups were cowering in their bags and coats as the two men loomed.

Myles pulled out his hilt. "Don't touch us," he shouted, pointing his hilt at the two men.

Dax opened his hand, "Don't worry kid, you and your sickly pet are coming with us. But your friends weren't invited."

Myles thrust his hilt towards the man. Nothing happened. Myles looked down at his hilt, "Come on... please, help us."

Both men burst out in laughter, "You can't even wield threads yet?"

Myles yelled, "I will never know unless I keep trying." He thrust again, but this time a loud roar echoed into the room from the shadows of the tunnel. Out leapt the chimera. It hunkered lower with its snake-tail hissing upright. It snarled at Dax and Mordred. Sigurd scrambled to his feet, joining Myles and Kamara.

"A Chimera?" Dax questioned angrily, "What is happening? Where is everyone coming from?"

Mordred looked terrified. He threw his flames at the chimera. It battered the fireball away with ease, angering the beast. It lunged forward but was stopped midair and crashed to the floor. Dax was able to snare its hind leg with a root, halting the creature. The chimera quickly twisted around, breaking the root like a twig with one chomp of his powerful jaws. Dax and Mordred both ran in opposite directions, leaving Myles and the others exposed, but the Chimera paid no mind to the children.

"Now's our chance," instructed Kamara. She plunged her hand into her bag, "Here, take this." She handed Myles another ebenezer stone.

"What's this?" he asked.

"Sleep-stone. But it has to be close to work. We only get one shot, and there are three enemies in here now."

Myles looked at Maple, still lying on the table. Ubique had made his way back to her side, desperately gnawing at the bands on her arm. Myles and Kamara rushed over to help. Omni jumped out and assisted Ubique.

Myles attempted to wake the sleeping captive, "Maple." He shook her shoulders, "Maple." But she wouldn't wake.

Then a loud hiss tickled his ear. He flipped around and stared at the back side of the Chimera, and the coiled snake-tail directed at him. Omni jumped up on top of Maple and hissed back. The snake lashed out at Myles, just missing him as the chimera lurched its body, dodging a spear strike from Dax. The snake struck out once more, snapping right in front of his face as it was pulled away, just out of reach yet again.

As the snake coiled on the chimera's back, Myles heard a lazily drawn-out yawn from behind him. He turned and found Maple stretching, like she was waking from a long nap. Then her eyes opened. She observed the back of the chimera standing before them. A high-pitched scream filled the room. Even the chimera seemed impaired by the tone. Then, mid-scream, she was out once again, plopping limply back down.

Dax and Mordred were cornered by the fanged chimera. Kamara and Myles were between the snake tail and Maple, trying their best to protect her as Myles used his scrap metal to shield from several snake bites. The chimera lifted a paw to slash at Dax and Mordred, while the snake coiled for another strike. Then, the shock of one sound, immobilized the room.

The neigh of a goat rang out in the room. Dax and Mordred cowered in the corner while Myles was anticipating another strike. But the chimera didn't move. Again, a goat bleated from the tunnel where they came from.

Out from the shadows walked Hickalik, backward into the light. He was tearing off strips of his uniform and holding them out. Out came the goat, eating his offerings every few steps. The chimera remained poised. It motioned to strike, but the goat called out again for more of Hickalik's uniform, calming the chimera.

Hickalik continued walking backwards, leading the animal across the room. He shuffled between Myles and the snake head and over to steps on the other side of the room, leading up.

As Hickalik passed by, Myles stayed perfectly still, "Hickalik, what are you doing?"

Hickalik simply shushed Myles, keeping his unfettered attention on the goat. He led the hungry animal up the wooden steps. The goat sounded off once more. The chimera grimaced a last disapproving growl, lifting his paw back to strike, then turning instead to follow the goat, the tail still hissing discontentment.

There was a brief silence in the room, as everyone surveyed their bodies to confirm they were still in one piece. Then Dax hit Mordred on the shoulder, "Let's get the pipsqueak and the albino while we can."

They rushed towards Myles. Myles jumped up and grabbed onto a large air duct above. His weight pulled open the piping, spraying a large cloud of hot mist at the charging men. Myles grabbed Omni and leapt away, as the two men stumbled through the mist, colliding with the table. The shifting table frightened away Ubique, who once again began sending teleporting-flames around the room.

As Mordred fell bent over on top of the table, Myles saw it. Around Mordred's neck, hung his father's compass.

"That's *my* compass," he cried.

"Oh, this littles things?" Mordred held the compass up. "If's you comes, quiets likes, we'll's gives its back to ya's."

Myles picked up a rusty hatchet lying in a metal scrap pile next to him.

Dax stepped closer, "That's alright. I like the hard way." He twirled his spear and stabbed the flaming tip into the floor. Myles could hear the stones and wood crack around them. Omni hopped onto his back. Roots penetrated through the wall. Myles pivoted, swinging the dulled blade and cutting back the oncoming wave of branches. Dax grumbled. More sprang up from the floor. Myles stepped back and cut them down as well.

Distressed, Dax yelled at Mordred, "This confounded heat is dwindling my flame." Then Dax gripped his spear as hard as he could. His muscles shook as he let out a terrifying war cry. The whole room started to quiver. Myles stepped back, not knowing what to expect. He backed up to the tunnel leading to the resonating room.

Roots launched at him from every direction. Myles swung his rusty blade, but he could not cut fast enough. He was being backed into the tunnel. The number of branches kept growing. His foot was ensnared, immobilized. The roots covered the walls of the tunnel like snakes, growing inward.

Then a flash of light came from the wall next to him. It was Ubique, who had randomly teleported next to Myles. Myles glanced back toward Mordred and Dax, a will to fight boiling inside him. Dropping the hatchet, he snatched Ubique from the wall and held the dragon in front of him. He pointed the reptile at the shrinking hole left by the entangling roots.

"That's my compass," he yelled. He squeezed Ubique's ribs. The dragon let out a burst of silver flame, piercing through the condensing opening. The flame hit the ceiling above Dax and Mordred. They looked up, Ubique and Myles had teleported above them. As they fell, Myles had a crazed look of determination in his eyes. He turned his body midair to face the ground.

Dax and Mordred watched dumbfounded. Myles let out another cry while falling, "Give it back." He fell right between the two men. In his hand, was Kamara's sleep-stone. He slammed the stone into the ground, followed by his face. The stone shattered as a fiery blue cloud of haze engulfed the three of them. Inhaling the mist, Mordred dropped to his knees. With rolling eyes, he collapsed into a snoring coma.

Dax was swaying, but held on to his staff to keep him up right, "Infuriating little kids..." He was instantly asleep, then toppled over like a tree. Myles, Dax and Mordred lay on the floor together, still fighting with one another, but now, only in their dreams.

Chapter Twenty-Three

Flames Ignite

With a strong sense of deja vu, Myles found himself waking in the infirmary, this time at least feeling well rested. He quickly ran his fingers through his hair but found no healing-flames. Omni was curled into a ball on his lap, breathing deeply. Relieved, Myles stroked the dragon's scaly neck. He immediately regretted his decision as Omni woke up and pounced on his face with his wet sticky tongue.

"I'm glad to see you too," he said, pulling the overly excited lizard down.

When he looked up, there stood Provost Prudencia and Chief Gorthin, with Muddle to his side.

Worry clouded his mind, "Maple. Is she...?" but he was silenced by a hard smack to the back of the head.

"Maple?" cried Nurse Fletcher. "She was in and out of here in a day. You, however, slept for four days. Taking up my infirmary bed and wasting my time. And for what? An extra-long nap? What kind of idiotic delinquent doses themselves with enough sleeping-flame to knock out a behemoth." She smacked him again.

"Sorry... I'm sorry," Myles pleaded for his head's safety.

Prudencia lifted her hand, "That will be all, Ms. Fletcher."

Myles thought she was going to get one more slap in, but the narrow gaze of the chief seemed to make her wary. Prudencia then dismissed

Pedagogue Muddle as well, thanking him for waking Myles with his phantom-flames. He stumbled away.

She then addressed Myles, "We are glad to see you and Omni are well. I take it you are well-rested?"

"Yes. But how is Maple? And Kamara, Hickalik, and Sigurd?"

She gently shook her head, "Always worried about others. And putting yourself in danger to protect. Although I cannot condone your decisions of late, your heart is truly that of a future galliant, that is if you survive that long. You have a nose for trouble, or trouble has a nose for you. You are more like your father than you know."

The chief cleared his throat, "I am Chief Gorthin."

"Yes," Myles replied, "I saw you in the town before registration day. It's nice to meet you, sir."

"Yes... I'm sure," the chief spluttered. "We have been investigating these disappearances with the help of Pedagogue Muddle and the parliament. Both of the men in question have been arrested and are currently shackled in my penitentiary. The other students told us most of what we needed to know."

Myles was awake enough to figure Kamara wouldn't tell the whole truth, even if Sigurd protested, so he claimed ignorance.

"What happened to us?"

"You don't remember?"

"Not really, just bits and pieces."

"That's not surprising," the chief sighed. "With that potent of a stone, it's a miracle you were able to awaken at all."

Myles didn't realize how dangerous the sleep-stone was.

Provost Prudencia put on a stern face, "First and foremost, we are grateful you and the other children are alright. Maple Blackwood is well."

"What about her blaze?"

"Pedagogue Alistar was able to recover her blaze." Myles dropped his gaze with a comforted smile, "Oh, good."

"Amongst the storage down in the forge cellar, there were more clear stones found, some embellished with blaze markings. The A.R.A. is currently looking into whether these blaze markings were stolen from other children and if they can be re-branded, if you will."

"The A.R.A.?" asked Myles.

"The Authority of Ruach Affairs, a very tightly wound lot, I assure you. They are overseen by the parliament. For now, we will wait for their investigation to be concluded."

"Provost, you said 'down in the forge cellar.' Were we under the forge building where they made our hilts?"

"Your memory most truly is hazy. That is where Dax and Mordred had taken you children, and where you were found. I am assuming they wanted your markings as well."

The chief butted in, "We would normally have interrogated the two offenders for more information by this point. However, they have not awakened as of yet."

"Myles," Provost Prudencia sounded more stern, "you broke academy rules. You put yourself, and your friends in danger. You were reckless and quite nearly killed yourself." She paused and inhaled a deep calming breath, "But... Thank you. You helped save one of our students. You helped protect the reputation of this institution. We are indebted to you. It was imprudent, and consequences will be implemented, but do not let these overshadow our gratefulness."

Myles knew the story may not have been the whole truth and he understood why. He did not approve of the lying, but he felt proud. Proud to do something good for someone else, proud to protect and proud that he was able to push past his fear.

Myles smiled, "I am just glad Maple and my friends are safe."

Just then, a loud voice groaned its way into the room, "They took them!"

Miss Blumpkin stormed in through the door, "They're gone, my babies. Someone took them. Those vile fiends. Where are my babies?" she cried out in desperation. Omni covered his ears with his front paws, blocking out the piercing wails.

As Miss Blumpkin fell to her knees and wiped her eyes and nose on the chief's pristine coat, Prudencia stepped in front of the chief to ease his spiking adrenaline, "This is Ms. Blumpkin, the academy's beastmaster. She cares for the various animals and creatures that are housed on these grounds."

Prudencia looked down at the frantic woman, "Ms. Blumpkin, and to which creatures are you referring this time?"

"It's Henry," she blubbered, "and his calming goat, Giovanni."

"A goat?" Myles mumbled. His eyes enlarged as he realized what she was crying about. But Prudencia didn't seem worried. "And remind me again which animal this Henry is."

"My Chimera, of course," she spouted, "He is missing. The basement is empty. I went down to give him his weekly feast, and he was gone. Giovanni too. I don't know how they escaped. Giovanni would never just walk out, and Henry would never leave Giovanni." Her face turned to one of hysterical rage, "Someone must have taken Giovanni, knowing Henry would follow."

Prudencia held up her hand. "I'm sure they are safe on the grounds. Now, find Warden Managol and have her arrange a search party."

Miss Blumpkin continued to wallow, "First Blossom's legs and now this. It's too much. It's an ill omen… Evil is coming to the school. The animals are always the first to know."

"Blossom?" questioned the chief pulling his snotty coat tails away from her.

"One of her unicorns," the provost informed.

Myles stayed silent; his eyes still expanded. He feared if he spoke, Miss Blumpkin might harm him in a fit of rage, keeping him in the infirmary even longer.

Provost Prudencia called for Nurse Fletcher, who helped Ms. Blumpkin up to her feet, and instructed her to find Warden Managol and help translate the blubbering confusion.

Once the room calmed, Provost Prudencia went on to explain the house arrest rules for Myles and his accomplices. They were allowed to go to classes, eat meals in the great hall, and have study sessions in the open library areas, from after dinner until eight o'clock. Otherwise, they would be confined to their quarters. Myles didn't complain.

Now that the culprits behind the disappearance were captured, the school's safety measures were lifted. Curfews were extended to their original time frames. The night patrols were scaled back, and the outdoor deterrents were minimized.

Myles was released from the nurse's abrasive care and reunited with his friends who embraced him with open arms. Even the dragons seemed to wag their tails. The rumor about Myles taking down two flame users to rescue Maple had extended throughout the school. It was as if people forgot who his father was, or simply did not care anymore.

"Not bad, Briggs," some second years called out to him in the halls.

"Thanks for stopping those guys," called out another.

"Thanks for making me feel safe again," one girl even commented.

While walking between classes, Myles found the opportunity to talk with his friends, "What happened after I fell asleep?"

"Honestly, not much," Sigurd answered. "We tied up the two men the best we could with chains and ropes. Not that it made a difference, they were sound asleep. Then we carried you and Maple up the steps and outside. Turns out we were under the forge building the whole time."

"Yeah, that made sense," said Hickalik. Sigurd looked puzzled.

"Remember, the symbol above the door? It read 'fire.' The forge pipes are connected to an underground magma region."

"Oh..." Sigurd nodded.

Hickalik added his side of the story, "After I led the goat up the steps and opened the cellar doors, the eastern skies were already beginning to brighten. I could tell it was almost morning. The goat was fine, I threw the rest of the uniform coat to the side and the goat followed it. Then the Chimera came out from below. I slowly tried to back away, but I don't think it liked me interacting with its friend. Then a thunderous roar echoed above. It was Zalaph. The goat and the Chimera ran off together towards the woods. After that, I ran to the tower and found Pedagogue Zilberstein roaming the outer halls. She called for aid, and the rest is self-explanatory."

Kamara added, "But we were able to keep your father's room secret for a little while longer."

Sigurd pursed his lips, "I still don't like that we didn't tell them the truth. But I made Kamara promise when this is all over, that we would show the room to the school staff."

"Yes, yes... You are such a goody two-shoes," she remarked.

"It's called having integrity."

"Myles," Sigurd turned and held out in his hand a folded-up handkerchief, "I'm sorry." Inside was his father's compass, smashed into wooden shards and bent metal scraps. "When the heavier guy, Mordrag, fell, his coat was half gold thanks to Gullynn's flames. The weight crushed your compass when he hit the ground."

Myles looked over the pieces in Sigurd's hands. "Sigurd, it's okay... Really. I'd much rather have you all safe, than some silly compass. Besides, we already got the key from it. I think that's why my dad wanted me to have it.

"Well, at least something good did come from it," Sigurd tried to lift their mood.

"Maybe once we are off house arrest, we can go back down there and try again," suggested Kamara.

"Yeah, I'd like that. I want to know why my father did all this."

"Well, I hope you can be patient. It will be a while before we can sneak out again."

"Why's that?" Myles asked.

"We have a staff member sleeping inside our room every night, against the door."

"Who?"

"None other than the captain, himself," informed Hickalik.

Sigurd shuddered, "The room smells terrible."

That night as Myles lay in his bed, the room was filled with the spicy muster of the captain, as he snored on the floor against the door, ensuring the students could not escape again.

Myles rubbed Omni's head while the dragon slept. Omni had grown larger. Maybe not to the same percentage of growth as the other dragons, but still noticeable. His nubs were sprouting out and growing longer. His ribs seemed less pronounced as well. Omni was becoming healthy and showed progress.

The next day, Myles was pleased to find that Warden Managol's physical torture courses were absorbed by Ruach training, doubling their allotted time with Warden Petroff.

Petroff addressed the class with disapproval in his voice, "Despite my protests, this institution has seen fit to direct me in starting flame training." The students lit up with excitement.

"This will first be taught to you through your hilts. In future years, as you progress, you may learn to harness your flames by hand directly. For now, we will be using ebenezer stones as catalysts to ignite your flame for the first time."

He showed a display of stones laid out on the table before the class. "Your Ruach channels have now opened, due to our training with your body's natural Ruach. You will use the stones provided with the correct flame element. Meaning, if your dragon uses an ice attribute, you would select the water ebenezer stone, seeing as water is the base element for ice. We have supplied you with base element stones for fire, water, earth, verdure, air, and even arcane."

"You all know how to expel Ruach out of your body and into your hilt. The process has given you a good sense of what this energy feels like. Now you must learn to feel the Ruach around you. Pull it in, and harness it. Expel it through your hilt, then it can be ignited."

Warden Petroff held out his hilt. Nothing could be seen, but there was a sense of whooshing pressure.

Petroff nodded, "Warden Managol, if you would please." She picked up a stone from the table and held it to the end of the hilt.

The flame ignited a burst of blue fire, like a ball of flammable gases erupting. The flames died down to a thin pointed sword. There was no metal, no structure holding the flames in place, but the shape of the sword was clear as day, made of a perfect burning blue. His hilt was now a true sword, blade and all.

Petroff instructed the students to hold out their hilts, "Close your eyes. Feel the Ruach in the room around you. It's in the air you breathe. It's in the stone you stand on. Call it to yourself... trust it. Then when you are ready, release it through your hilt, just as before."

The room fell still, the concentrated silence was deafening, with the occasional grunt from Gavin trying to force out his flame. Then, they all felt it, a wave of pressure pushing passed. The source was Kamara. Her eyes were closed, as she had a tranquil demeanor, her hair fluttering from the pulsing waves.

"Very well, Miss Kinsley. You shall be first." Petroff picked up an air-stone off the table. He walked over and reached out to light her blade.

"Remember, envision the weapon you want to wield. Control its shape." With one touch of the stone's flame, a vigorous bolt of lightning exploded forth. The bolt clapped, curving upward. It struck a pillar, shattering pieces of debris that crashed to the floor.

Kamara opened her eyes and shrugged, "Meh."

Petroff lowered her hilt with his hand, "I think Miss Kinsley might benefit from a more... secluded lesson. Perhaps somewhere with no victims," he gestured for Managol to take her away.

After seeing this, the remaining students scooted away from each other now having a deeper respect for what they were trying to accomplish.

As they resumed, success was more attainable than expected. Next was Aberdeen, whose pressure felt less impactful than Kamara's, not that anyone dared tell her.

Warden Petroff grasped the verdure-stone and lit her blade ablaze with a vibrant green hue. She slowly whisked her dainty blade through the air. Unlike Kamara, her blade kept tight, like the warden's.

Petroff praised her in his monotonal way, "Very well done. I see this is an easy task for one so distinguished under the house of Gunther."

One by one, pressure whooshed from one hilt, then another. Hickalik soon joined the ranks of the victors as he lit a blue flame, similar to Petroff's.

But instead of a sword, the flames took the shape of a long-bladed double axe.

Hickalik waved it through the air. "It's so light," he commented.

Petroff scoffed in a dismal voice, "Two blades, for two heads, not surprising in the least... how impractical."

Some students wielded more flaming swords, but also, a club, maces, even a shield and a bow.

Xander was showing signs of frustration, then glanced at Myles, "You shouldn't be here." He turned, pointing his hilt directly toward Myles. Myles turned to Xander to return the favor, mirroring his stance. If they were wielding swords, their blades would be crossed, as they stared with animosity.

"You think accidently putting two men to sleep with a stone made you some kind of hero? It was a happy mistake, made by a powerless delinquent performing selfish acts. If you don't leave of your own accord, Briggs, I will end your career at this school, and with all future folds."

Myles could feel the anger boiling up inside, "You don't control my destiny, Xander. I will learn to control my flame."

"Learn to control? If you want something in the world, you have to take it."

Just then, waves of pressure, like no one had felt before, burst forth. The waves were so intense, it knocked the onlookers back. The pulsating force felt like a wild beast ramming you backwards, again and again.

"Who's is it?" yelled Sigurd over the whooshing noise.

Even Warden Petroff had to strain to approach with the fire-stone. Myles and Xander held firm, fixated on one another. Petroff outstretched his arm, reaching the stone between the hilts. A blast of flames erupted outward. All three were flung backwards. The bright flash temporarily blinded the room.

Myles sat up from the floor and looked around, finding his hilt on the ground beside him. No damage was seen, but no flames either. Then Myles glanced across at Xander. Xander stood up. In his hands he held his two-handed hilt, a large orange flamed blade burning in front of him.

Xander exhaled a sigh of disbelief. Then shook off his excitement, pretending he had no doubts.

"See Briggs? You take the power you desire. That is how to protect others. That is why I will become a galliant for this kingdom."

Petroff clapped his hand to his forearm, "Very nicely done, Mr. Xander."

The day ended with only a few students not yet wielding their flames. Kamara's training sounded extensive. The walls of the tower continued to rattle throughout the day as she attempted to hone her power in a secluded training room.

After getting ready to turn in for the night in the dormitory bathrooms, Hickalik and Sigurd joined Myles in their room.

"Myles," Sigurd asked, "can I talk to you about something?"

"Yeah, of course," Myles assumed it was about his lack of ability.

"It's..." Sigurd paused, "It's about Kamara."

"What about her?"

"I don't trust her. I mean, I trust her, but she concerns me, I guess."

"What do you mean?"

"Well, I've been thinking. She sneaks out at night all the time. She always has these dangerous ebenezer stones on hand. She is weirdly obsessed with getting you to your father's room. I mean, you weren't there, but after you knocked yourself to sleep that night, she was really pushy about keeping the tunnel a secret still."

"She just wants to help, I think," Myles dismissed. "I know she can be a little rough around the edges at times, but I think she has a kind heart and really wants me to find out more about my father."

Hickalik stayed quiet. The confrontation seemed to make him nervous. Sigurd nudged Hickalik, "It's okay Hickalik, it's not like she can hear us." Sigurd looked up at the rafters above, "...I think."

Then he looked back to Myles. "I'm not really sure what I am getting at. It just felt weird, I guess is all. You're probably right, though."

Then Captain Nordic flung open the door and yelled, "Dreams be controllin' vulnerable young whippers. Take heart or blazed be bled."

"Yes, thank you Captain, for that." Sigurd rolled his eyes as the captain slammed the door and flopped onto his pillow on the floor.

Once the captain was cuddled up with his model ship, both Hickalik and Sigurd stayed up playing quietly with their dragons. Myles noticed his roommates seemed more affectionate than normal with their dragons.

As days rolled by, Myles sensed a gloom hanging over the school despite the lifting of the curfews and the threat to the school being eliminated. Even at meals, other classmates and his friends spoke less than customary. They kept to themselves and just held their dragons or played with them when they could.

"Hey, can I ask you all something?" Myles inquired, "Why is everyone acting all sad and depressed?" I feel like things are actually going well, for once."

"You mean no one told you yet?" Hickalik asked.

"Told me what? Did something happen while I was asleep?"

"No, not really... " replied Hickalik, "It's just that..." but he went quiet. Sigurd's line of sight also fell.

"It's the dragons," Kamara forced out. "We have to release them back into the Caldera. We only have a few more days with them."

"What?" Myles questioned in disbelief. "But why?"

"Because," she picked up Hanish and held him close to her face, "they have to live in their world, not ours." Hanish tickled her nose with his tongue. "We took them out of their home, their world. They have other dragons waiting for them. The parliament believes it would be wrong for us to pull them out of their natural habitat. And... and I think I agree. They did not choose to come with us, we took them from their nests... from their homes."

Omni locked eyes with Myles, "I never thought about it like that. I thought I would have Omni with me forever." But the more he thought the more he remembered, "I guess Allen said Beira left him for a while as well, but he was able to find her again later in life."

Hickalik spoke, "Some galliants do go out to find their dragons again. That way, if the dragon wants to follow their Nexus partner, it will be a free choice, not the choice of a hatchling that doesn't know any better."

"That makes sense, I guess." Myles held Omni close, "I just... I don't want to give him up."

"None of us do," agreed Sigurd. "Sorry mate, I thought you knew. Sometimes, the hardest things are what's right for others, and not ourselves."

"Oh, now you're all wise and judicious," Kamara snapped, then realized it was not the time for her normal sass. "Sorry..."

"Kamara apologizing? This is serious," joked Myles, making them all smirk a little.

"When do we have to release them?" Myles asked.

"In two days," shared Hickalik. "It's called the Day of the Vale."

"I see. I guess we will make the best of the next couple days."

They did just that. Myles played fetch with Omni until the dragon couldn't run anymore. He got Omni one of Sigurd's old boots to chew.

They all played with their dragons, making last minute memories. Hickalik found some crickets for Galacia to hunt. Kamara would pull items on strings for Hanish to chase.

Sigurd would simply cuddle with Gullynn and rub her head, "There's a good girl, my Lady Gullynn."

All the students were doing the same. Classes were postponed the day before their farewells. Gavin was seen every once in a while running frantically through the halls.

"I forgot Draugr likes to play hide-and-seek," Myles said.

Hickalik chuckled, "It must be hard to chase something that can walk through walls."

Galacia was able to get in one more frozen boot on Sigurd, tripping him down to the floor. He looked at her annoyed, then softened, "Yeah, I'll even miss *you*, Galacia."

Myles held Omni close, rubbing his chin, "Our journey started with crazed pets and now is ending as old friends."

Sooner than any of them wanted, the Day of the Vale had begun as the pedagogues marched the students up to the foot of the Caldera's wall.

Farewells

The air was crisp and heavy, but their hearts felt heavier. The melted snow had made the trails muddy as they hiked to the foot of the Caldera. Xander almost slipped again, but Myles saw no joy from it on this occasion. Each dragon was carried in the arms of their partners, with the exception of Voldin, who was still carried by Bach in its metal cage, and Elowyn who rested on Aberdeen's shoulder.

Myles hadn't explored all the vast school grounds before and was astonished by the magnitude and the diverse topography. As the students clambered on, some would whisper to their dragons, others held back tears.

"Pfft," Xander scoffed, "Don't weep over these reptilian babies. They served their purpose. Now let them free."

"Easy for you to say, Xander," Sigurd interjected from behind, "You get to keep your dragon at the estate."

"Why are you even here?" asked Myles.

Xander glanced toward Warden Petroff, "I was told I must."

The cliffs grew exponentially taller as they approached. Eventually, they made it to the foot of the Caldera.

Wardens Petroff and Managol raised their hands, holding their rings up to two symbols etched into the rock face. The sound of grinding stones and rocks were heard as an enormous flat stone surface retracted revealing a large cave opening. The lump in the children's throats swiftly fell to a heavy pit in their stomach.

Warden Petroff faced the students. "It is time. If you would, Pedagogue Muddle." Pedagogue Muddle nodded and yawned as he approached Maple Blackwood who was closest in the line. "Say your goodbyes, Miss Blackwood."

Maple hugged Ubique tightly. Tears began rolling down her cheeks. She could barely speak, but was able to whisper, "Thank you. I will miss you so much. I promise... I will find you again."

Then Muddle carefully removed the dragon from her arms and cradled the lizard with one arm. He twirled two fingers materializing small dancing flames that twirled around Ubique's head. The dragon fell quickly asleep. Muddle handed the sleeping reptile to Pedagogue Alistair, who found himself also blubbering. Alistair walked the dragon into the cave opening and gently placed the sleeping dragon on the cave floor.

In sequence, Pedagogue Muddle continued down the line, giving just a brief moment for the students to say a heartfelt farewell. With each send-off, Myles held Omni tighter.

Then came Sigurd's turn. He held Gullynn out in front of him, so their eyes met. His chin quivered as he spoke, "Be good, my lady. Wait for me and be brave. I will find you again soon." Then Muddle took her in his arms, and it was done.

Hickalik was a mess. Snot cascaded out his nose as he tried to snort it back in, "I'll miss you, Gal... Galacia." He barely got the words out.

Kamara looked into the eyes of Hanish and smiled with one tear rolling down, "Thank you for everything. Now go show them what you're made of," she said proudly.

The tears muddied the ground further. All the dragons were now asleep in the cave, all but one. Myles felt sick. The reality of Muddle halting in front of him made his arms shake. Myles looked down at Omni. The dragon's neck was bent low with his tail between his legs.

Myles clutched his friend one last time, whispering, "I don't care if you have a flame. Thank you for believing in me, even when I didn't. You will always be in my heart. I love you, Omni."

"Xander called out, "Hah, he loves a dragon," but no one was in the mood, especially from him. Even Aberdeen glared at him fiercely for that one.

Muddle reached out and pried Omni from Myles' arms. Omni let out a whimpering screech as he tried to squirm back to Myles. Myles had to close his eyes and look away; the sounds were excruciating, until Pedagogue Muddle had him asleep.

Muddle passed Omni's slumbering body to Alistair, who was crying even harder now, "Such a waste, so much I could have learned from you."

Then Omni's eyes opened. The dragon turned its body and jumped toward Myles. Muddle somehow caught the dragon's leap. Omni cried out. Every shriek skewered deeper into Myles' chest.

"Silly dragon must have been faking," Muddle slurred as he pulled the scrambling dragon back. His iridescent flames floated about Omni's head once more, but the flames did nothing. Omni never fell asleep. He wiggled but couldn't break free. Muddle tried again, but still nothing happened.

"It's the strangest thing..." the pedagogue murmured. "Pedagogue Alistair, would you mind? Seems this one is immune to my effects."

He dumped the young dragon into Alistair's arms. Omni thrashed, pulled and pushed with his legs, but Alistair hugged Omni tight, like it was his own enseared dragon he was walking to the cave.

"Such a shame..." he repeated.

Omni howled and whimpered while being carried. Myles could not stop the well of tears.

Alistair tried to put Omni on the cave floor, but the dragon kept clawing at the ground, pulling toward Myles.

Alistair sighed, "Don't make this harder than it is."

He took off his scarf and used his bonding-flames to bond the end of the scarf to itself around Omni's neck. Then his flames bonded the other end of the scarf to the ground inside the tunnel, creating a makeshift tether. As he put Omni down, the dragon leapt forward, but was held back with a choking yelp. Myles covered his mouth, trying desperately to fight his trembling chin.

Alistair walked out and nodded to the wardens. They once again raised their black rings to the rock cliff walls. The stone began to close. Myles could hardly make out Omni's pale body through his blurry vision, as the desperate dragon pulled and gnawed at the scarf frantically. At last, the stone clunked into place, and the tunnel entry was sealed.

Alistair put his fingers together, then placed a hand on Myles' shoulder, "My flames are released, he is freed."

Muddle did the same but stumbled and almost fell asleep standing. "They are all waking up now, free to live the life they were intended."

But Omni's faint cries could still be heard from behind the stone.

Warden Petroff herded the group, "Let's head back everyone."

For the next couple of days, Omni's cries continued to haunt the students' minds and hearts. The children were given no time to mourn as they were thrust back into their studies. Kamara speculated this was to give the students something to focus on besides their loss.

As classes resumed and Ruach training intensified, rumors whirled through the halls.

"Did you guys hear?" asked Kamara after class.

"Hear what?" inquired Hickalik. "That you destroyed another room while trying to control your flame?" He didn't mean for this to sound like an insult.

Sigurd and Myles hid their inner laughter, but Kamara ignored them. "There have been reports of men sneaking into the Caldera. The parliament's patrols have arrested dozens entering the crater."

"Why were they arrested?" Myles asked. "Did they do something wrong?"

The other three looked at Myles bewildered. Hickalik took his usual role of informing Myles, "The Caldera is a protected land. It is for dragons only. Dragons are seen as sacred creatures. The Caldera is their nesting ground. Most people, including the parliament and the academy, believe dragons must have their own lives and habitat, uninhibited by others. That is why we had to give our dragons back to their natural environments and why entering the Caldera without consent is prohibited. If anyone could enter and steal dragon eggs for themselves, it could have terrible consequences."

Myles pondered this, "So that's why it is illegal for people to go there. Then why were we allowed to go and remove our eggs?"

"The laws allow for blazed individuals that are registered to enter and ensear, under the condition that the dragons be returned to keep the species protected for generations."

"So why are people sneaking in now?"

Kamara, who was waiting patiently, sighed, "Why do you think? What changed?" she asked, hoping the boys would catch up.

"The dragons," answered Hickalik with growing anxiety.

Kamara nodded, "But that happens every year, and this hasn't happened before, not like this."

The realization hit Myles, "Omni."

Kamara agreed, "Since the first elden dragon was published in the herpetology books, I'm sure the kingdom has been all abuzz about the mythical dragon's existence."

Now concerned about the danger Omni might be in, Myles asked, "What do we do? We have to help him."

"We can't go out of school grounds," Hickalik said, "We would be expelled for sure."

Sigurd added, "Plus, we wouldn't be able to sneak out with the captain curled up at our door every night. And even if we could, how would we get to the Caldera?"

"About that," Hickalik spoke up, "I have been doing some more research on the old symbols we found in the resonating room... above the doors. I was able to translate them. The first door to the basement area was labeled earth. I was right about that one. I found that the second door, which I wasn't able to read before, was the symbol for woodlands. That was the tunnel that was caved in. And the third tunnel we went into was labeled fire. And that makes sense with the magma river running below the forge building."

"What about the other doors?" Sigurd asked eagerly.

"I was able to translate the remaining doors. There was water, plains, and tempest, or storm. Myles, it looks like your father built tunnels to different places around the grounds, so what if the tempest door leads into the Caldera, to the top of the mountain?"

Excitement grew in Myles' voice, "That would make sense."

"Okay. I love where your heads are at..." Karama started.

But Sigurd interrupted, "Of course she does..."

"But..." she continued, "that leads me to the other rumor I heard. The bureau has almost finished with their investigation in the forge cellar. They will excavate the collapsed tunnel soon."

"What collapse?" asked Myles, now wondering if he did lose some of his memories.

"Oh, sorry Myles," Hickalik apologized. "I guess we didn't tell you."

Sigurd explained, "When you were in the tunnel and that Dexter guy had all those branches popping out around you, you were about to teleport out of there, but just after you three fell to sleep, the tunnel collapsed. Probably due to all the destruction his roots caused to the tunnel."

"It's Dax, Sigurd," Kamara corrected, "Daaaax. Anyways, yes. The tunnel collapsed and they are about to clear the tunnel again. Hopefully they don't have a stone-flame user, or else it could be cleared quickly."

"Okay, I get that," Myles confirmed, "but honestly, why do we care?"

"Because," Kamara emphasized, "once the tunnel is clear, they will investigate where the tunnel leads."

Myles widened his eyes, "The room."

Kamara looked around, then leaned in and whispered, "We have to go back tonight and open the last door."

"Tonight?" exclaimed Sigurd.

"Shhhh," Kamara shushed. "Yes, before they open the fire door from the other side and find the room."

"What do you mean by 'last door?'" asked Sigurd.

"Whichever door," she corrected. "Both the tempest door to find Omni, and the unlabeled door to see what Myles' dad may have left for him."

"There you go again with Myles finding something from his father," complained Sigurd. "We don't know what is down there and which door to use."

"Isn't it obvious?" she asked, "All the doors and tunnels lead around the grounds, but the unlabeled door is special. It has to be that door."

"She's right," agreed Myles. "In fact, the door labeled plains probably goes to the grass fields on the school grounds and the woodlands door to the forest region. The unlabeled door needs to be the priority... but after we get Omni."

Each one agreed, although Sigurd was reluctant as usual. They schemed with what little time they had left.

That night, Myles couldn't sleep, and not because of the smells or sounds in the room. Sigurd and the captain were competing in a duet of slumbering proportions.

Myles was too fixated on Omni, "I'll find you, Omni. No matter what." He closed his eyes, hoping to hear Omni's playful yelps once more. He could almost hear Omni's cries, then he thought he could, or at least he heard something. He sat up quickly in his bed. And looked around the room, but nothing had changed.

"I must have imagined it," he dismissed. He laid his head back down. Then he heard muffled voices, men yelling in the distance, outside.

What could be happening at this hour, he wondered. Could the Chimera be back? Did Dax and Mordred escape and return somehow? He sat up again. The commotion seemed louder. He leaned toward the window, squinting his eyes. Something was out there, outside his window. Then, a blur crashed a hole through the stained-glass window, painting the room with a rainbow of shattered glass. Myles was thrust back into his bed with great force as something struck his stomach, waking everyone in the room.

"Hairy death demons!" exclaimed the suddenly awakened captain in a frantic state, which scared Hickalik and Sigurd awake more vigorously than the crashing window. Myles had the wind knocked from his lungs. He took a big breath and coughed out the pain. Then the object that collided with him moved. He jumped, then froze in disbelief. In front of him, on his lap, was the skinny pale dragon he longed so dearly for.

"Omni!" Myles coughed out throwing his arms around the exhausted dragon. His body was much thinner. He was almost too weak to lift his head. Myles examined the injured lizard, cuts and bruises covered the reptile's scaled body.

"But how?" cried Sigurd, "How did he get here?"

"He must have flown down the mountain..." Hickalik answered in disbelief, "or at least glided."

Sigurd looked at the creature's meager state, "Looks like the poor thing has been through a lot."

But before the boys could tend to their injured friend, the window shattered again. A man landed on the windowsill looking in on the three boys and the captain. He remained crouched on the window frame, hanging into the room by one arm.

His eyes burned with intensity, like a predator homed in on his prey. He wore armor made of scales and a coat of leather with fur crowning his neck. But Myles was drawn to the man's face. He had two burnt scars dropping from his forehead down over his right eye and cheek. The burns weren't like a blazed marking, but scars from actual burns.

The man's eye fixated onto Omni, still lying on the bed amongst the shattered glass. He didn't say a word and pulled out a dark hilt. Myles swiftly shielded Omni with his body.

The crazed man swung his hilt and launched out a flaming green whip, swinging just above Myles and Omni. The whip coiled around Captain Nordic, capturing him in an instant, as it spun quickly around his body.

"Confounded creetins," the captain yelled as he toppled to the ground, bound tightly.

"Stay down old timer." The man commanded.

The man flicked his hilt, disconnecting the flame whip that still constricted the captain. He raised the hilt again and swung downward towards Myles. The familiar strands of natural Ruach formed and grabbed Myles by the waist.

"Get off, kid. You are not the prey I hunt tonight," he attempted to yank Myles off Omni, but Myles held the dragon tightly.

"I'm warning you, kid," the man urged.

Sigurd yelled out, "Leave my friend alone." He drew his hilt and pointed it at the man in the window. A burst of natural ruach fired out. Without hesitation, the man shifted his hilt creating a lucid shield and batted Sigurd's attack away, then whipped a line of natural ruach out again, this time finding Omni's battered body.

"No," cried out Myles trying to hold on, "I won't let you take him." But the man was too strong. Omni was pulled loose from Myles' grip. In a flash of blue flames, the Ruach strands were cut and the bed sheet frozen solid. Omni was freed from the threads and Myles quickly regained his embrace. On top of the now frozen bedding stood little Hickalik. His hilt drawn with his brilliant axe blades burning.

Hickalik paused to inhale his courage, "Omni is our friend. You can't take him. We... We won't let you."

The man grinned, "A beast as your friend, you say?" He found this amusing. "Beasts of this world are good for one thing... the hunt. I am with the Moon Stalkers. I have been hired to bring in your little pet. It's nothing personal, I assure you. But if you get in my way... well, I'll suggest you don't." The man waited for a moment, testing the boys' resolve.

The silence was interrupted by the moans and groans of an old man standing up. Captain Nordic pressed his hands together, "Thy feeble thwarted bristle the wind severs." A forceful burst of gray flames slashed outward through the man's green whip, freeing the captain.

"Tisk tock," the captain placed his hands behind him. "Bells sound the stalker." Just then, the warning bells could be heard chiming in the center tower. The intruder glanced to the tower, swiftly scanning the sky.

The captain murmured, "Impudent pup."

An explosion of gray flames detonated behind him, sending him flying forward like a missile. Everything in the room whirled in a tornado of wind. The captain propelled himself so rapidly, he was a blur of a gray ponytail.

The man in the window caught only a glimpse. He shifted his hilt once more, but was too slow to match the captain's speed. Captain Nordic thrust his body directly into the intruder, tackling the man back out the window from whence he came.

"Captain!" cried the boys with surprising concern as the two men fell out of sight into the dark cold night below.

The boys heard no sounds over the warning bells from outside. They raced out of the room. Most of the other boys in the dorm had been awakened by the bells and were gathering in the common area. They saw Hickalik, Sigurd, and Myles sprint out of their room toward the corridor.

"What's going on?" demanded Xander.

Gordon caught a glimpse of Myles running by, "Hey, is that Omni? It is. Omni's back. Omni came back."

But Myles and his friends continued out to the hallway. Myles could hear shouting and cheering behind them.

The boys crashed through the downstairs door into the night. Their misty breaths obscuring their vision.

"There," pointed Hickalik. Beneath the window above they found Captain Nordic, sitting on the man, who was both tied up and unconscious.

"A fool's years resign ye's astuteness, be presaged to not ensue."

Hickalik nodded his head at the captain, still breathing hard while Sigurd and Myles glanced at each other, baffled.

Footsteps approached behind them. "You three," Warden Petroff's irritated voice disparaged. The warden glanced down and saw the sickly white dragon.

He took in a deep breath to yell, "You...!" but he stopped and thought for a moment. Then a much calmer voice took over, "Get inside, take the dragon to the infirmary. We will meet you there shortly." Then he leaned in and held up his index finger, "Do not leave until permitted," he threatened.

The boys nodded their heads up and down as quickly as they could and did what they were told.

They entered the infirmary cautiously, so as not to ensue the wrath of Nurse Fletcher, with Omni wrapped in a blanket. Much to their surprise, there sat Kamara on a bed in the middle of the room. Her foot was ablaze with the nurse's healing-flames.

"What are you doing here?" questioned Sigurd.

"Well once I heard the warning bells, I assumed something went wrong and you three were most likely in the middle of it. Myles always ends up in the infirmary, and it turns out I was right."

"I do not," Myles protested but was quickly overruled.

Then Kamara explained, "Once the bells rang out, I knew our plan to sneak out tonight was not going to work, and if you three were involved, I would just wait for you here. So, I informed Ms. Blumpkin I twisted my ankle getting out of bed when the warning bell sounded."

"Ms. Blumpkin?" Questioned Hickalik, "Why was she there?"

"She's the staff person assigned to my house arrest... not that she does any good. She sleeps deeper than Sigurd and rolls away from the door the minute she falls to sleep. So, I can walk out whenever I want to, really." Kamara's attention was pulled in by the lumpy blanket Myles was holding.

"What's with the blanket?" she asked. Myles uncovered the battered dragon.

"It's Omni," shouted Kamara, but her excitement diminished quickly as she saw the state of the poor dragon. "How did you get him? Did you three go without me?"

"No," insisted Myles, "he crashed through our window while being chased by some hunter."

Hickalik explained, "He was a hunter from one of the illicit folds... Moon Stalkers, I think he said."

"Ooh, that's serious," stated Kamara.

"Sorry," Myles stopped the conversation, "What's an illicit fold? I thought the folds were all filled with galliants who protected people, not galliants who go around kidnapping dragons."

"They are," defended Hickalik, "but the illicit folds are groups of criminals. They are not sanctioned by the parliament and therefore, are illegal. They will do most anything for money: stealing, kidnapping, even murder, I hear. They are not the kind of people you want to cross paths with."

Kamara was deep in thought, "That means someone must have hired the man to hunt and capture Omni."

Then a demanding voice rang out, "What in blazing tarnation do you all think you are doing here?" Nurse Fletcher had walked in finding the four friends conversing. "Coming here at this hour and disturbing my patients!" she yelled threateningly.

As she clogged her way over to smack someone on the back of the head, she stopped suddenly. She noticed Omni curled up in Myles' arms.

Her demeanor changed instantly. She motioned to the bed next to Kamara's. "Lay him here," she instructed.

Myles explained, "He was being chased... hunted in the Caldera..." but the nurse waved Myles off with a "Zip bup bup," silencing him.

She examined Omni thoroughly, lifting his wings, listening to his chest, all the while setting small flickering flames on the wounds with two of her fingers.

Sigurd impatiently worried, "Is he going to be alright?" but Fletcher ignored the question and placed the dragon's head on a small pillow. Then she turned to smack Sigurd beside the head, "Never interrupt a medical professional you impetuous fool," she scolded.

She turned to Myles, "The patient just needs rest now. He is dangerously exhausted. Most of his grievances were superficial, but his breathing is strong and clear.

"So he'll be alright?"

"With rest and garnishment, yes," she answered, "And when his strength is back, he can be released to the wild again." Their excitement fell as quickly as it was given.

They could hear people arguing and approaching from the hallway. The click of a staff got louder until the wardens and Provost Prudencia barged in. Pedagogue Alistair was in tow, pleading his case, "Please, please, my Provost. It is the only rational way."

"Rational?" Warden Petroff barked back, "It will rationally ruin this academy."

"Well, I don't necessarily think it a bad idea," commented Warden Managol.

But the provost raised her hand and the three of them ceased their bickering. She looked at the resting dragon for a minute, then let out a soulful sigh, "The dragon will stay." The children were stunned. Alistair jumped up and down like a toddler on his birthday.

Warden Petroff protested, "But Provost, the safety of this institution must come first. The dangers this could inflict upon the students..."

But Prudencia halted his griping, "What good are our safety measures if we can't shelter one lonely dragon? It clearly has no other kin. And now, with the illicit folds after him, he will never have freedom of his own accord. This decision was already made by the actions of others, not by us."

Myles spoke up with a cracking voice, "He can stay? Omni can stay with us?"

Provost pondered, then leaned in toward Myles, resting on her staff for support, "This should not be taken lightly, young Briggs. This dragon, through no fault of his own, will bring you much strife and hardship if he is to remain at your side. This world has given you an unjust quandary. If you take this on, you and your dragon may be hunted for the rest of your days. This academy cannot provide you with protection outside our walls, but perhaps we can help prepare you for the grim future that may lie ahead."

Myles took her words in, but his emotions pushed them right back out, "I don't care. Omni chose me. Who would I be if I just turned away from him now. He gave me hope again... and he's my friend. I won't leave him to those men... I won't leave him alone... not again."

Provost Prudencia smiled, "Oh, the foolish bravery of youth. It will either make one great or clasp a fool in its grasp. I pray you and your colleagues are the former."

After a bit more discussion, much to Warden Petroff's dismay and Pedagogue Alistair's delight, the dragon's permanent boarding with Myles was finalized. Myles was permitted to stay with Omni in the infirmary that night, while the other students were deported back to their rooms. Omni slept for days. Myles was forced to leave his partner for classes but visited every opportunity he got.

The house arrest disciplinary measures had lapsed. The recent incident with the hunter had pulled the attention of the bureau away from their investigation in the tunnels for a short while, at least that was what Kamara informed them. Kamara had made Myles promise that once Omni was well enough, they would descend into the resonating room once more to finish what they had started.

Myles received quite mixed reviews about his dragon's return. Some students praised Omni's reappearance, excited to see the dragon again themselves and filled with glee for Myles. Others, however, were filled with envy, wishing their dragons had returned as well.

"It's not fair," mumbled Arica Eclat.

"That dragon will put us all in danger," others grumbled.

Not surprisingly, Xander was one of the most vocal of the naysayers, "It's a good thing for Briggs," he jested, "with a sick lizard to care for, he has an actual purpose here. I mean, without a flame of his own, the school would have had to send him home." Xander chuckled maniacally, amused by his daily roastings.

Later on, Kamara called an emergency meeting. Behind a closed door of a study room off the library, they congregated.

"Tonight is the night," she instructed. "We must go back tonight."

"Tonight?" questioned Sigurd. "But why?"

"Look," she explained in simple terms, "we got lucky with the hunter pulling the attention of the A.R.A away from the tunnels for a little bit. But with the man in custody and the case closed, they will be going back to the forge cellar soon to clear the cave in."

"If they aren't already down there..." added Hickalik.

"Exactly," she agreed.

Sigurd looked reluctant. "I knew we had to go back, but I just thought it would be later... like, the end of the school year, or something. Why go at all? Nothing good came from it. It's just a bunch of tunnels to places we can walk to outside."

"But what about the unmarked door?" Kamara inquired.

Hickalik spoke up, "Kamara's right. And I think we all want this for Myles, even if the chances of something being there from his father are slim."

The room turned to Myles, cradling Omni, "Then it's tonight. We go back down, tonight."

Chapter Twenty-Five

Cloaks and Daggers

Evening fell, but one would think Omni was now nocturnal. After sleeping for so long, Myles feared Omni might never sleep again. He bounced off the walls and pulled on everything in the room, as if the world was playing a game of tug-of-war against him.

Sigurd complained as Omni pulled the bedding off his body, "So much for getting some shuteye before we head down there."

Hickalik stayed quiet, pouring over his notes from his library research. At last, the time was upon them. The three boys, with Omni following curiously, tiptoed their way from room to room, carefully using the sound stones once again to hide any noise. Myles rather admired Omni's attempts at stealth, with his wings folded and tail pointed out straight, so as not to brush the floor.

To their surprise, the boys made it to the secret staircase without incident, not seeing another soul in the hallways.

"Phew," said Sigurd releasing all his tension, "I heard Pedagogue Greenwald was on patrol duties tonight. Glad we didn't run into her. I think she really hates me."

"I think she just hates everyone," Myles inserted.

Kamara then came around the other corner, quiet as a mouse. She seemed surprised, "You three are early."

Myles dropped his gaze to Omni, "Some of us couldn't sleep." The dragon glanced back proudly.

Kamara smiled and bent over to scratch Omni's chin. "Aww, did someone want to play with the boys?" Then she popped back up eagerly and rubbed her hands together, "Shall we begin?"

Myles pressed in on the cave depiction on the wall mural, and the keyhole appeared on the floor. He took the silver rings unfolded them. He placed the key inside the keyhole and turned. Once again, the stones opened below developing into a spiraling staircase. Myles scooped up the key, folded it back into a ring. The four of them started their descent with Omni nearly tripping Sigurd as the energized dragon bounced down the steps between their legs. Just as before, the room was illuminated, much to Hickalik's relief, followed by the sounds of the passageway closing up above them.

Hickalik gulped and started looking sweaty and anxious again.

"We're fine, Hick," Myles tried to comfort. "You got this."

"Okay..." Hickalik breathed out, never looking Myles in the eyes. He plopped down on the floor and got his notebook out of his pack, along with a very old-looking text. He poured through his notes as the others waited anxiously.

Then he finally spoke, "From what I can tell, the symbols from left to right are labeled earth, water, fire, then the middle unlabeled door, followed by woodlands, valley, and tempest, or storm if you will. I wrote down the resonating-stone combinations that open the earth, woodlands, and fire doors."

"Yes," added Kamara, placing her hand flat on the middle unlabeled door, "but what we really want to know is how to open this door." She drew in closer, "What secrets do you hold?" she asked softly. Omni sniffed the bottom of the door, then pulled away, raised his head up, and sneezed.

Sigurd cleared his throat to interrupt Kamara's deep thoughts, "Well, it wasn't that hard to get the first three open. Myles seems to have a knack for it. Give it another go, Myles."

Myles looked at the pattern on the door labeled plains. He took in a deep breath and exhaled. "Okay. Hickalik, can I see your notebook?" Myles studied the resonating patterns, but was not as quick to place the stones this time around.

"What's wrong?" asked Sigurd, who was becoming more excited about the potential of finishing early and heading back to bed.

"The patterns on the next three doors don't seem to match up as well as the first three. I guess I started with the easy ones. But I think..." he picked up a stone and placed it on the center pedestal. The room hummed as it did many nights ago and the white sand danced into a pattern atop the black stone pedestal. Then Myles chose another stone. But once the reverberations halted, the pattern did not match.

"Drats," said Myles discouraged.

"Hang on," called out Hickalik, "What about this one?"

Myles reset and led with the same stone, followed by the stone Hickalik suggested. The room vibrated briefly, then stopped.

"It matches," blubbered Sigurd.

"We know," commented Kamara. Then the door slowly began to open.

"Which door was this again?" asked Sigurd, already lost.

"The tempest door," informed Hickalik.

"And that's the weather one, right?"

"Yes," Hickalik simplified, "storms and stuff."

The door came to a thudding stop. Behind it was the beginnings of a large, long staircase leading upward as far as they could see by stone light.

"Do we go?" asked Hickalik nervously.

Myles answered confidently. "No. Our goal is the seventh door."

"Yes," agreed Kamara as Sigurd rolled his eyes.

Hickalik disheveled the sands and the door closed itself. Myles picked up the first stone they used and stared.

"This is the same stone I used second on the forest door. Are they just random?" he asked.

"Well, the ancient tribes who made these symbols do believe that everything in this world was made up of..." he paused. The room turned to Hickalik.

Hickalik's eyes widened as his body started to bounce, "That's it," he exclaimed.

"Now tell us," cried Kamara.

"Two elements. Two stones. The ancients believed each... thing... or each place or object was made of two primary elements, one element over another."

He pulled another timeworn book out of his pack, "You see," he pointed to two symbols on the page, "That was the tempest door. They believed the storms were simply the element of water over the element of air. That's why water falls down during a storm." He frantically flipped through the pages, "you said that stone was the second stone for the forest door, right?"

"Yeah," Myles answered, still confused.

"Woodlands," he excitedly explained, "they believed the woodland was verdure, or plants, over water. Because for a forest to grow and live, there has to be water underneath.

"I get it," said Kamara. Myles and Sigurd looked at each other puzzled.

"Can you explain it again for Myles?" Sigurd asked.

Kamara turned to Sigurd, "Two elements. Each stone represents an element, whether it be water, air, ground, fire, verdure... two elements make each item on the labels over the door."

"I knew that," Sigurd complained, "I said explain it to Myles."

Myles asked for himself this time, "So how do we know what they are?"

"Easy," said Hickalik. "Everything has a main element, and a secondary element. Myles, you opened the fire door last time. You must have used the fire-stone, then the verdure-stone. That is what the ancient saw fire as; fire that burns wood and plants. And that earth stone," Hickalik reached out and grabbed the stone, "This is what you used first on the basement door labeled ground or earth."

"But if the 'earth stone' was used on the 'earth door,' what was the second stone?" asked Sigurd, surprisingly tracking the concept.

Hickalik picked up another stone and then looked more puzzled than excited, "Air..." Then the others joined him in his bewilderment.

"Air?" Hickalik stated, losing his enthusiasm, "that can't be right. Air is not under the ground, it's above." He reached for his books and started flipping through once more.

"No," Myles rebutted. "It is right. The air is below the ground. The outer world. It is below us right now."

"That makes sense," Kamara supported the theory.

Hickalik found his page, "Here. You are right. That is how they translated earth. And the plains, or grasslands, is verdure above ground. And streams must be water over ground."

"So," Myles started dialoguing. "There are six doors and each door has a main element and a secondary element. Then why are there three indents on the table? Why not just two?"

This puzzled the group for a while. Omni continuously sniffed around each doorway as they pondered, stopping every so often to chase the white slithering tail that followed him. Then Omni sat like an obedient puppy in one spot in the room. A sliver of purple moon light showed through a very small crack, illuminating the happy dragon.

Myles stared at Omni, who looked as awake and content as ever. Then Myles started whispering to himself, "Hide in the light..." he reached toward a stone, then hesitated, "It couldn't be that simple." He grabbed a stone and placed it in the table inlet. The room hummed and a pattern was made.

"The storm is short..." Myles said out loud.

"Water..." Hickalik remarked in a shadowy whisper, "Water is the main element for a storm."

Then Myles picked up another stone and placed it, vibrating the room again as the sands shifted.

"The valley is wide..." Myles continued slowly.

"Verdure..." echoed Hickalik again, "Verdure is the main element for grasslands."

Then Myles picked out one more stone and recited, "The mountain is tall..." and placed the last stone, "destiny inside..."

"The earth stone," Hickalik said with anticipation.

The room hummed briefly, then fell silent.

"Was that it?" asked Sigurd.

"Sorry, Myles. It was a good try though," Hickalik said encouragingly. But the room began rumbling.

Sigurd pointed, "It's coming from the middle door."

A pattern arose on the door matching the sand pattern on the table. A flame lit above the door, burning a symbol in the stonework.

"Hickalik?" Myles questioned not looking away.

Hickalik was already scouring his texts, then he stood up.

"Blood," he read out loud. "The symbol is blood."

"Blood?" questioned Sigurd. "Creepy..." They all gawked at the large door, wishing it would open but it didn't.

Then Myles asked, "Do we try another sequence?"

"I don't know," answered Hickalik.

"Ouch," Kamara's voice sounded behind them. They boys turned to find Kamara sucking on her finger.

"Are you okay?" asked Myles.

No one but Kamara had noticed the large ornate needle that erected out of the center of the table, until now. There was a single drop of blood painting a few grains of the white sand red.

"It didn't work," she stated.

Hickalik inspected the needle, "No. Of course it didn't. It's not for you. This whole thing has been about Myles... It's for Myles. It's his blood. It has to be."

Myles reached out to touch the needle's point. With a downward pressure and a recoil of pain, they watched as a drop of blood fell from his finger staining a few more grains of sand.

Sigurd stumbled, "Hey guys... I don't do well with blood." Then his knees gave way. Myles and Hickalik barely caught him above the floor.

"Pathetic," Kamara commented. "Still finds a way to make it about himself."

Just then, the thick door became ajar. Dust flew out from the crack as it rumbled open, slowly creaking, until the doorway was wide open.

"It worked," said Kamara in disbelief, "This is it."

Myles and Hickalik helped Sigurd to his feet as the change in events was enough to distract him from the blood. The group huddled together as they stepped through the archway. Behind the door lay a large domed room with a pillar of moonlight focused down from the center. The light fell to a singular thin pedestal. Hickalik and Sigurd scanned the room, but found no notable threats lurking in the shadows, but Myles and Kamara were fixated on the center column.

"Is that...?" Myles asked, not believing what he was seeing.

"I think it is," confirmed Kamara, stepping closer.

"What is it?" asked Sigurd.

Hickalik gasped in disbelief, "It's the dagger.... The verdure dagger."

"It doesn't look like much of a dagger," complained Sigurd. "The blade looks too thick, like it's made of ivory."

Kamara stepped closer again, drawn to it.

"He hid it here?" Myles asked, "My father hid the dagger here, at the school? That means he did come here after he stole it."

"That means he left it for you," added Sigurd. "Your ring led you here. He gave you the key phrase for the clues. The key rings in your compass. And we needed your blood to get it."

Kamara stepped in closer again and began to reach out for the dagger, but Sigurd stepped between her and the pedestal, "This belongs to Myles," said Sigurd. "It's his to decide what to do with now." Sigurd grabbed the dagger's blade to present it to Myles.

"Don't touch the blade!" cried Hickalik, but it was too late. A giant green flame exploded out from the blade in every direction. Sigurd dropped the dagger as the flames pushed the children vigorously back against the walls. Hickalik dropped to the ground, the flames whooshed over his body as he lay flat.

The ground and walls rumbled and shook as the structure began to crumble. In every direction, roots began piercing through the walls, growing inward towards the dagger. The branches slithered in like snakes, absorbing the green flames.

"Is this Dax? Is he doing this somehow?" Myles shouted.

"No," yelled back Kamara. "The dagger, this is the power of the dagger."

"How do we stop it?" cried Sigurd. Larger bits of stones collapsed from the ceiling. Kamara, Myles, and Sigurd were slowly being encapsulated by the roots. Hickalik pulled his body forward across the floor, fighting the waves of forceful flames cascading over him.

"Hickalik," cried Myles, "you can do it!"

The roots had almost covered his friends. Hickalik gave a last push and reached out. His fingertips could barely brush the dagger's handle. "I... can't reach it," Hickalik exclaimed. Then Hickalik could feel a nudge on the bottom of his foot. It was Omni. The little dragon was pushing with all his strength, pushing Hickalik just enough, as Hickalik reached out one more time. He grabbed the dagger's hilt. The erupting flames were instantaneously condensed back into the blade, and the room settled.

Hickalik's head popped up. "Are you guys okay?" he shouted, looking at the cluster of wooden branches where his friends used to be. The branches started to rustle and crack.

"Yeah," answered Myles. "We're okay... I think." Myles started pushing through, breaking off branches to free himself and parts of Kamara.

"A little help," Sigurd's muffle voice came through.

"We'll get to you," promised Myles, "Just a minute."

"I don't know, Sigurd," Kamara started to emerge. "I think they're growing on you."

"Ha ha, very funny..." Sigurd murmured, "Get me out of here."

"Well, that's what you get for cutting me off and grabbing the blade. Who grabs a dagger by the blade?"

"It didn't look sharp or anything."

Myles and Kamara were half-freed when Myles looked up at Hickalik. He stood alone in the center holding the dagger, fixated on it. His face flushed to a pasty white.

"Hickalik, are you alright?" Myles asked while Omni helped by biting at the branches. Hickalik gazed up. His eyes were wet and glazed.

"I..." he couldn't get the words out. He stepped back and said, "I'm... I'm sorry." Then he turned and ran out the open door.

"Hickalik, wait!" Myles called out.

Sigurd couldn't see anything still. "What is he doing?" his muffled voice questioned.

Kamara spoke up in disbelief, "He's taking the dagger."

"What?" yelled Sigurd. "Hickalik, what are you doing? Come back here!"

Hickalik's voice trembled from the other room, "I'm sorry... I'm so sorry. I don't want to." Then the door began to move again, closing ever so slowly.

"No," gasped Myles. "Hickalik stop. Please."

But there was no reply.

Myles pulled most of his body free and lunged for the door. But a root was still tangled around his ankle and his body fell, smacking the floor. When he looked up, the door was almost closed. He shouted out in desperation one more time, "Hickalik!" just before the door thudded secure, sealing them inside.

Chapter Twenty-Six

Penance for a
Father's Sins

yles lay on the floor in the darkened chamber. The only audible noise was his deep frustrated breathing.

Sigurd, not knowing what just happened, broke the silence, "Why is it dark in here? Did I black out again?"

"Well, if you must know..." Kamara spoke plainly while breaking branches away from his face. "Hickalik stole the dagger and locked us in here."

"But I thought you were going to be the one to try and take the dagger," Sigurd confessed.

Kamara broke a branch very close to Sigurd's face, "Ouch," he protested, but his head was freed now. "Where did the light go?" he asked.

Kamara looked up, "The roots grew over the lightwell—they are blocking the moonlight."

Myles threw his clenched fist against the floor, "Hickalik!" he pushed out in a breathy outburst.

Kamara continued breaking Sigurd free, "It all makes sense."

"What?" asked Sigurd.

"The dagger being here. The dagger is said to have amazing botanical properties."

"What's that mean exactly?"

"It helps plants grow... Was that simple enough for your five-year-old vocabulary?" she belittled.

"Yes," Sigurd answered without the slightest hint of shame.

Kamara continued to explain, "It's because of the dagger that the forest training grounds are closed, and why the plants there were going so crazy. It also explains why the roots underground are everywhere. They were trying to reach the dagger. It must be a source of life and energy for all vegetation, just like roots searching out water. Even though the dagger was sitting here dormant, with the blade not touching anything, its presence alone was drawing in plants and trees for years, feeding them with Ruach from a distance. I can see how it could support the whole region of farmlands by itself."

Sigurd was finally freed and brushed off the dirt and dust, "And it packed a punch, too. That was crazy. I've never felt anything like that."

"And now Hickalik has it."

"Yeah," Sigurd punched his open hand. "We have to go get that traitor."

"No," Myles said. They couldn't see him, but Kamara and Sigurd could hear the determination in his voice. "We must save him."

"Save him?" questioned Sigurd. "That little weasel tricked us, lied to us, and took..."

"No," Myles said again. "You heard him. We all did. He said he didn't want to. Someone is making him do this. We need to find him and help him."

Kamara sighed, "It's the unicorn all over again."

"The what?" inquired Sigurd.

"Not now," dismissed Kamara. "The problem is, we are stuck in here. Hickalik is probably taking the dagger to someone right now. And we have no way of knowing who or where, even if we get out."

"Yeah..." Sigurd sighed, "It would take a miracle at this point."

Just then the room became a little brighter. They could make out the damaged walls and the frame of the doorway.

"Or..." Kamara contested, "maybe just a willing friend."

Sigurd and Myles turned. There was Omni. A faint glowing light was radiating from beneath his scales; his body was gleaming. The light became brighter. The three looked at the radiant dragon with awe.

"It's no flame," gawked Sigurd, "but it sure is pretty whatever it is."

Myles dropped to his knees, "Omni... you did it!" Omni leapt into Myles' lap. "Thank you... my little miracle. I am sorry I doubted you." He hugged his shimmering friend.

"Okay." Myles stood back up rubbing his eyes clear. "We need a way out of here."

"Well, that's an easy task, I think," Kamara searched around the walls. "No architect would build a room without an exit." She stopped next to the door, "Here."

As Omni and the others came closer they could see it. It was a keyhole, same as the one in the hallway floor. Myles took off his key rings and unfolded them again. He inserted it into the keyhole and turned. The entry door cracked loudly and began rumbling open.

"We're free," rejoiced Sigurd, as the door opened enough for Sigurd to slip past, he jumped with happiness in the other room as Kamara chuckled at the sight. Once the door finished opening, the key was ejected and Myles and Omni ran out as well. The door began to shut behind them.

"Hickalik," Myles cried out, "Hickalik!"

Sigurd stopped jumping, "Oh that's right," he called out too, "Hickalik?"

But there was no answer.

"Look," Kamara pointed to the earth doorway that led to the basement. It was left wide open. They inspected the resonating table.

"Hickalik must have used the stones to open the door and escape."

Sigurd scratched his head, "It's a good thing I didn't betray you guys. I would have been stuck in here for sure."

Kamara grabbed Sigurd's shoulder and looked at him with pity, "We know."

"Come on, we have to find him," directed Myles as they started running through the open door and into the basement.

"You don't think they put the chimera back in here, do you?" asked Sigurd following Omni's illumination.

"If they did, I call tails," demanded Kamara.

They found themselves at the basement's exterior door.

"How do we open it?" asked Myles.

Kamara caught up, "Gavin used his dragon's flame on it to pass through."

Myles glanced at Omni and the glowing dragon glanced back, twisting his head sideways. Myles shook the thought out of his head. "Yeah, you're right, sorry." Myles searched, but there was no keyhole, "Hickalik must have gotten through somehow," he said.

"It's an exit door. Everyone should be able to exit, right?" Sigurd questioned.

Myles inhaled, "Yes, you're right." He grabbed Sigurd's arm. He yanked Sigurd toward the door and slapped his hand against it.

"Hey, watch it," Sigurd protested. The door latch clanked and Myles was able to push the door open.

"How'd I do that?" asked Sigurd, examining his hand.

"Your ring," explained Myles, "Kamara and I don't have real school rings, but you do."

They stepped out into the purple moon-lit night, "Okay, now what?" asked Sigurd again.

Kamara slapped the back of his head, "You are becoming quite the pessimist, aren't you?"

"Ow... I was just askin'."

They scanned the fields. There was no sign of Hickalik in any direction. Kamara searched for footprints while Myles continued to watch the dark horizon, listening. Then, for no apparent reason, Omni jumped up on Sigurds back, climbed to his head, and jumped off, pushing him back.

"Ahh..." Sigurd complained, "Myles, your dragon's gone loony."

Off Omni sprinted. "Omni, come back," Myles called out, but the eager reptile pushed on.

"Let's go," instructed Myles as he too darted off. Sigurd and Kamara pursued. Omni continued using a combination of running and gliding to navigate the rolling terrain.

"What are we doing?" questioned Sigurd from behind.

Myles turned his head and answered, "Following Omni of course."

"You have a better idea?" challenged Kamara.

"Nope. Just asking."

Omni was determined. He snorted the ground every chance he got, dragging his snout through the grass.

Myles slowed to let the others catch up, "I think Omni can smell him."

"He can do that?" huffed Sigurd.

"I have no idea, but I trust him."

Through the grass field and round the forest region they trailed the hunting dragon, their pathway littered with blooming flowers.

Then Kamara spoke, "Don't tell me."

"Tell you what?" asked Sigurd. Omni had stopped but stood with his back scales standing upward. The three stopped as well, catching their breaths. In front of them stood the forge building once again. Lights illuminating the surroundings from within.

Sigurd pointed, "You think Hickalik is in there?"

"It would make sense," added Kamara.

"In what possible way does that make sense?" demanded Sigurd.

"Dax and Mordred. Remember? The cellar is where they were operating."

"Yes I remember, but why would that matter now?"

Myles' face lit up, "Because they had help."

Kamara concurred, "We know they were working with someone else. And that someone must have set them up here, in the cellar. That must be the same person who Hickalik is here for."

Sigurd sneered, "It's got to be that Pixie... I don't trust her one bit."

Kamara shook her head. "Somehow, I doubt that."

With their breathing back under control, they snuck up the porch. Sigurd pressed his ear to the door and listened. Myles and Kamara peeked through a window while Omni sniffed the area.

"There's Hickalik," whispered Myles.

Kamara adjusted, "Who's he with?"

"I can't tell. But look, Hickalik is pulling out the dagger."

Sigurd stood up and grabbed the door handle. Both Kamara and Myles whispered sternly, "No, don't...." but it was to no avail.

Sigurd burst in through the door, "Hickalik and the dagger come with us," he declared. Omni jumped in behind, head low and sprawled out.

Kamara and Myles scrambled through the doorway as well, "So much for stealth." All three had hilts drawn and at the ready. In front of them stood Hickalik, who appeared both shocked and scared, or, in Sigurd's words, normal. A woman with a cloaked hood stood adjacent. Startled by their entry, Hickalik had shoved the dagger back in the pack he was holding. At the woman's feet lay a large man's body.

"That's Pedagogue Muddle," exclaimed Sigurd. "You killed him!"

Then the stout pedagogue snorted loudly and twitched his nose.

"He's asleep..." Kamara observed. Then the woman unveiled her hood to confront the intruding children. It was Pedagogue Greenwald. Both Myles and Sigurd tensed at her gaze.

"And what in the great dragon's breath are you three doing here as well?" she demanded.

Kamara answered quickly, "We were chasing after our friend, Hickalik. He ran off and we were worried about him. We thought he might get hurt or do something..." she paused and locking eyes with Hickalik, "he might regret."

Hickalik tried to speak "I..." but the words were lost to him.

Pedagogue Greenwald looked at Muddle's slumbering figure, "Seems I caught him just in time."

"Caught him?" asked Kamara.

"Of course, you daft children. I have been tracking his movements for months now. Seems he was the pedagogue that helped abduct the children and steal their blazes. That is why there were never any signs of a struggle or break-in. He would use his phantom-flames and control students while they slept. The students would walk out at night and meet with those dastardly villains who would then take the students' marks. He even went so far as to plant a pufkin with his victims as a clever misdirection."

Myles lit up with a realization. "That's right," he exclaimed. "Xander had a pufkin in his sack when we found him walking away that night. He didn't seem delusional, but like he was in some kind of trance or sleep state. And I saw Muddle's flames float through Xander in class before that night. That must be when Muddle's control entered Xander's mind."

"There's a disturbing thought," remarked Kamara. "That's one mind I would never want to enter."

Greenwald kneeled down and examined Muddle's clothing. "Seems we can finally rest well knowing we found the culprit who arranged these disappearances and helped those two men sneak onto the grounds."

"But, how did you take him out?" asked Kamara curiously. "I mean, I thought you didn't have a flame of your own?"

Pedagogue Greenwald sighed, "You are correct. I have no flame, just my knowledge of botany. However, I was able to synthesize a powerful sleeping potion with some herbaceous plant pollen. Seemed to do the trick quite nicely."

"Now," she turned to Hickalik. "You were saying you had something to give to Pedagogue Muddle before I interrupted this encounter?"

Hickalik looked terrified. Pedagogue Greenwald held out her hand, expecting him to hand over whatever it was. Hickalik looked at the snoozing teacher, then at Myles, then back to Greenwald. He grasped his satchel tightly and stepped back.

"Hickalik, don't run," encouraged Myles. "It's okay. It's over. Let us help you."

Greenwald pressed in toward Hickalik. "Give it to me, Mr. Milbred. I need to know what Muddle was after."

Just as Hickalik looked like he was going to run for the hills, Kamara cut the tension with another inquiry, "Pedagogue Greenwald?"

The pedagogue's hand recoiled as she turned. "Yes, child? What could you possibly need that cannot wait?"

"Well, I was just thinking... Why did Pedagogue Muddle give Myles' compass to Mordred? And why did he want it?"

"I hardly think those things are relevant at this time," she stated irritated. "Who knows why he did what he did?" She adjusted her gaze to Myles. "In your report about the incident in the cellar, you stated that those other two men had your stolen compass, yes?"

"Yes, that's correct."

Greenwald pondered, "I suppose he gave the compass to them after portalling it from your room. And who knows why he did any of this."

Myles tensed up, "I never told anyone it was taken by a portal."

Greenwald whipped her focus to Kamara, who had a pleased smirk on her face. "You clever girl." Then Greenwald turned to Hickalik, snatched the bag from him, and pushed him to the ground.

"A bit too clever for your own good." She rolled her eyes. "All you had to do was listen and go back to the dorms, then this all would have been over. But no. You had to work your little curious brains and have all the pieces fall into place. But alas," her eyes dropped to Hickalik. "I don't need the help of your miserable companion anymore." She stepped closer to Hickalik, who was immobilized at her feet.

Myles yelled out, "Don't touch my friend!"

She froze, "Friend?" The word seemed to incite her curiosity more than her wrath. "This friend?" She indicated Hickalik with her hand. "The friend that betrayed you? The friend that spied on you, for me? The friend that befriended you simply to do my bidding? You are trying to protect this... friend?"

"Yes," argued Myles, "and I would do it again. I don't care what he did, or why he did it. Hickalik is my friend. I know who he truly is, and he would never betray us if you hadn't made him. I don't care if he wants my friendship or not, he will have it whenever he needs it." Myles glanced at Hickalik still on the floor, tears of regret were now filling his eyes.

These ideals seemed to strike a chord with Greenwald as she started laughing, "Oh dear boy, I didn't make him do anything. This was all of his own choosing. I merely gave him a choice; one he and his family would benefit from if he chose to assist me. You see, I own the land that his grandfather still calls a farm—a woeful one at that. They cannot grow much of anything anymore and cannot pay me. At this point, any sane person would have no choice but to evict them. But I was merciful and offered Hickalik a choice. Enroll in the academy this year, find me the son of the traitor, and I will deed that desolate farm to his dear grandpapa."

"Myles?" questioned Kamara, "You wanted Myles?"

"Of course I did. That's why I sent Dax and Mordred to find him. That's also why I fastened the looking stones to your ebenezer crafting textbooks to spy on the dorms. That is, until this brat smashed the stones. But it was too late, I had already found you."

Needing to know the answer for all the chaos he had been through, Myles asked, "What do you want with me?"

She glared at Myles with disdain, "Not a thing now." She lifted the bag in her hand. "I have what I came for. This dagger belongs to me. Your filthy, wicked father took this and everything from me." Her voice now trembled with anger, "Greenwald is not my maiden name; it is Landsbury."

"Landsbury?" questioned Sigurd, "That sounds familiar."

Kamara explained, "The Landsburys were the owners of almost all the kingdom's farmlands back before the wars."

"Yes, we were," the crazed pedagogue acknowledged. "We were as wealthy as kings. The lands were ours. The workers were ours. No one in this kingdom ate food that wasn't produced by our people from our lands. We were nobles, exalted into great social status. I even married into a wealthy retired galliant's family."

She stopped. Her hand was trembling. "Then... your father came and took everything from me. He stole the dagger, knowing full well the devastation it would bring. The dagger had been in that shrine for generations. It protected this kingdom by providing every resource needed imaginable. Your father came to our villa, pleading for my father to give him the dagger. He lied about evil people coming to take it for themselves, but in the end, the only wicked person who came was him."

"After he stole the dagger from us, our farmlands shriveled and died. Our fortune turned to dust before our eyes. The nobles turned their fattened backs to us. We were the kingdom's only resource, an oversight that was not our mistake, yet the blame was only ours to bear. Then the wars started. My father and my husband went to war to help redeem our family titles and honor. I never saw them again."

Myles' heart broke for her—the pains she endured and the sorrow she still carried because of his father's choices. But Myles swallowed his pity, "The dagger will not be safe with you. If you use it to restore your lands, people will come to take it again. It will be just a matter of time until someone strong enough will succeed."

"You... you are just like your father. You think you know what is best for others. Your arrogance and naivety destroys everything around you." She pulled out an ebenezer stone from the inside of her coat. "You will not be taking this dagger from me." She held up the stone. "This is a blast-stone. If it goes off, we all would be paying the piper an equal toll." She backed away slowly. "I am ready to die for my family's honor. Are you willing to sacrifice your friend's lives for yours?"

"Hickalik," Kamara directed, "come to us, now."

Greenwald shook her finger, "Ah, ah ah... You see, he is a useful brat at times. And well, I can't let you all go free now. My plans may be impeded if word were to get out that I had some involvement with the disappearances and the blaze thefts. Foolish Briggs, your father ended my life, it is only poetic for me to end his line, in return."

As she raised her hand to throw the stone, Hickalik leapt up and grabbed her arm. "You traitorous rat," the pedagogue sneered as she twisted around to detach the boy.

"Run," Hickalik yelled. "Get out of here. Please. I am sorry for everything."

But before Hickalik finished his words Sigurd was already charging forward, hilt extended outward, pointing at Greenwald. Sigurd plunged his hilt into her coat, completely missing her and forgetting to awaken his flame before striking. His momentum carried him through her coat, like a bull through a red muleta. As he stumbled forward, his hilt activated with a golden flamed blade. He fell on his face, but the blade pierced a large anvil on the other side of the room, turning it to solid gold.

Even with their impending doom, Kamara watched Sigurd's spectacle, "I can die happy now."

Greenwald grunted, "That is now inevitable," as she hurled Hickalik towards Myles and Kamara's feet. She raised the stone once again.

"Wait," begged Hickalik with his hand held out.

"It's too late for you now, boy. You sealed your fate."

Then Hickalik reached into his shirt and pulled out a small satchel. Inside, he revealed the dagger was with him.

Pedagogue Greenwald gasped, "No..." She lowered the stone and searched inside the pack she was holding, but she found nothing but sticks. In outrage, she threw the bag on the ground.

"Give me that dagger," to which Hickalik shook his head. Myles and Kamara stepped in front of Hickalik to face the enraged pedagogue.

"You think you've won?" she asked, still holding the blast-stone in her right hand. She raised her left arm and swirled a circular motion in the air. A familiar purple flame burned an oval shape next to her while another appeared next to Hickalik.

"A portal," warned Myles.

Sigurd pointed at the enlarging circle from across the room, "She does have a flame."

Greenwald plunged her hand through the portal and out it came from the other, reaching Hickalik. Hickalik dropped the dagger, letting it fall out of her reach. Seeing this, Greenwald reached in further to catch the falling dagger, as her fingers clasped the handle of the dagger and pulled it back through the portal. She held the relic in front of her eyes, mesmerized by the return of her wealth and power.

She pointed the blade at the three remaining children, "That was foolish, farmboy."

"No," Hickalik corrected, "That was a distraction." He held up the blast-stone. Greenwald looked at her right hand, the blast-stone was gone. "I reached into the portal and grabbed it while you were busy catching the falling dagger."

The pedagogue seemed impressed by Hickalik's sleight of hand, "This changes nothing. I have the dagger."

Kamara raised her hilt and pointed it at the pedagogue.

"The girl who can't control her flames," Greenwald belittled, "or even hit a target. Point that hilt at me and I am in the safest place in this room, little girl."

"You know," Kamara started speaking in her usual sarcastic confidence, "he may be dense, dull, naive, thick headed, and clumsy, but Sigurd has one great quality I very much appreciate."

Pedagogue Greenwald turned to look at the boy on the floor, whose face read nothing but confusion.

The room filled with a buzzing static as everyone's hair stood on end. Kamara enlightened, "Sigurd..." she said confidently, "is a great conductor."

A booming bolt of lightning connected from Kamara's hilt to the now golden anvil of the other side, passing straight through Pedagogue Greenwald. A shrill scream of intense pain rang out after the echoing explosion. Greenwald fell to the floor with her clothes smoldering.

"She's down," called out Hickalik over their ringing eardrums.

Then they heard muffled sounds of a man coughing in the room. A dark blurry figure sat up. "What in blazing breaths is going on here?"

"Pedagogue Muddle, you're okay," stated Hickalik.

He continued coughing and waving around to clear the smoke, "Why on Escalia am I in the forge building? And what is..." He stopped abruptly. "Greenwald!" He saw his colleague on the ground. "What happened here? Students, explain yourselves."

Hickalik spoke up, "She was the one behind the disappearances. And she was using you, or at least your flame, to perform the abductions as well," explained Hickalik, hoping this would help calm the frantic pedagogue.

Myles stood up and ran over to Greenwald's body lying on the floor, "She is still breathing, but pretty burned on her side. Sigurd, fetch some water quickly to cool the burn."

"This is preposterous," stated Muddle as he stood up tall. We need assistance from the tower and real medical treatments."

Just then, little transparent flames floated around his head. Muddle watched in disbelief, "But these are my flames?" Then his body began to sway, "I feel...."

Then he fell to his knees with his eyes rolling back and collapsed to the floor once more. His snoring began almost instantaneously.

"Did he just put himself to sleep?" asked Sigurd.

"I think we are just as confused as you for once," stated Kamara.

Then, from the next room over, a slow clapping started. They were not alone. The sound of clunking wooden heels approached from the doorway. The students gathered in the middle of the two pedagogues' bodies, all eyes fixed upon the doorway, hilts at the ready.

Then a chill crept up Myles' spine as an unseen shadow loomed behind him. A warm whisper ghosted across the nape of his neck, "Impressive, indeed," the voice exhaled.

Chapter Twenty-Seven

Greed Incarnate

A sinister aura suffocated the room. Myles jumped away, almost tripping over the sleeping pedagogue, their hearts nearly leapt from their chests.

"Careful," the man instructed, holding his hands out toward the snoozing body on the floor. "Don't damage my property. That teacher of yours has a very special gifting. I wouldn't want to lose his flame."

Before them, stood a slender man, who exposed his crooked tooth as he smiled mischievously. His eyes were like a hawk's, homing in on his desired prey as he straightened his high collar. The man observed Pedagogue Greenwald on the floor, "Defeating your enemy and then tending to their wounds. You are an enigma, Mr. Briggs."

Sigurd had a worried expression, "Hickalik, who is this guy?"

"It's Mr. Getz, the security advisor from the parliament."

"Bravo," the man praised. "Impressive, very impressive. A couple of first years outwitting a pedagogue." He fluttered his finger in the direction of Myles and Sigurd. "I say a couple because you two didn't seem to do much."

"Hey, I helped," Sigurd protested, pointing to the golden anvil.

"And you are telling me that was a purposeful ploy?" asked the man.

Sigurd narrowed his eyes, not having a response, "I don't trust this guy."

Myles interjected, "We need to help the pedagogues and get..."

But the man raised his voice, "I'm sorry," he erupted. "*I* am here now. It's about me, now. You can let lay those more insignificant!" He drew in a deep breath.

"Sorry," he quelled his emotions as quickly as they arose, "but I am much too important for you to ignore," he said with a crooked smile.

After searching his mind, Myles blurted out, "Your voice, I recognize it. You were the person talking to the provost in the hallway. And Hickalik and I saw you in the town center with the chief."

"So...." Kamara spoke up, "you are here to clean up this mess for the parliament?"

He softly chuckled, "Oh no, my dear. I am here to get whatever I want. That is what I do. I take that which has value to me. It's a great cover though, security advisor. One of my favorites. It gets me into all sorts of places."

"So, you don't work for the parliament?"

"But of course I do. I play many roles for them and boast many titles. I am the advisor, an investigator, judge and jury at times, if necessary."

"You are a thief, then?" clarified Sigurd.

"Like the provost mentioned about your father in the hallway," added Myles.

"No..." the man didn't seem to like that comparison. "My father was a pathetic low-life criminal; he thwarted as much as he stole, and he only ever stole money. So... boring. So... pedestrian. Who wants money... pfft." He waved his arms dismissively. "It comes, it goes, it's easy to take money. No... I am no thief; I am an owner. My name is Tiberius Getz." The man bowed down low, as if he offered some great pleasure in meeting him.

Kamara started circling the room slowly, "What do you mean by owner?"

"Oh, you know. I take what I want... not money of course. I want power, influence, people and titles. I want their loyalty, their secrets... their flames. Like this one, here," he kicked Pedagogue Muddle who moaned in his sleep. Mr. Getz held up his hand as colorfully translucent flames orbited his fingers.

"Those are... Muddle's flames," announced Hickalik, "But how? How do you control his flames?"

"But I told you," a sense of wildness enveloped him. "I own whatever I want. If I want it, I will own it. People are easy, of course. Find their pressure point, their crux, and you control them. You own them."

"Let's examine dear Pedagogue Greenwald here, shall we? She agreed to help steal the blazes from children. She thought it harsh at first, but when I told her I knew where Haldor's son was, she practically held the children down for me, just for a glimmer of hope to see her precious *dagger* again. I don't know where she picked up those other two, but they were useful for a time. She did all this just to find you, Mr. Briggs. And now she is in too deep... thus I own her. Not to mention she controls Mr. Milbred here, so by proxy, I own him as well."

His focus redirected to Pedagogue Muddle, "But, I got lucky with this one. The school assigned him to assist Chief Gorthin and the townsfolk to investigate the disappearances. He was good, too. He found us out, caught us in the act of taking a child's burn. Dax and Mordred charged him without thinking, but with one flick of his flames, they were both out cold. A powerful ability indeed. And oh.... I wanted it, so it became mine."

"I used his own flames against him. He couldn't remember if he found me out or simply dreamed me up. Since then, I have been controlling him whenever he sleeps. He hardly ever rests, the poor thing. Works for me when he sleeps, works for others during the day, enslaving children's dreams on my behalf. Hard to survive without two jobs these days. A true testament to our failing economy, I suppose," he laughed at his own joke.

"But how did you make his flame yours?" asked Hickalik again, trying to gain understanding.

"Yes... yes. That is the right question, Milbred. How indeed. I was gifted a flame of my own, you see. It's called the copy-flame," he snapped his fingers and held up an ordinary flame, like one you would find on a candle. "Once my flames touch another's, I can copy their flames, and control their attribute. I have stored up quite the collection. Only the truly unique ones that catch my eye, if I'm honest."

"But now..." his eyes widened with a glint of selfish greed, "I see two objects in this room I will call my own. Now that the dagger has reappeared after so long, I will claim ownership." He slowly turned to Myles, "and of course, the pale dragon comes with me."

"Never!" Myles stepped in front of Omni. "Omni is not a thing to own. He is my friend, a free dragon, to live how he wants. I won't let you near him."

"My dear boy, I was not asking you for permission. I was merely telling you what I now own."

While Mr. Getz boasted, Kamara skillfully maneuvered, strategically placing Getz directly between herself and the golden anvil. She raised her hilt once more, "You don't own us," her tone laced with confidence.

The room filled with the same static tingling as felt before. Myles and Hickalik covered their ears, but the booming strike never came. A silver flash of flame puffed from Kamara's hands. Kamara jumped. She examined her hands, then glanced around the floor, confused, "My hilt?" Kamara scanned, "It's gone."

Getz held her hilt in his hand, raising it to his nose and inhaling deeply, "Electricity, a rare and formidable gift, but too unpredictable and difficult to control," he remarked, before discarding it over his shoulder.

"How did you do that?" Myles asked, still on guard.

The man raised his voice, "I already told you that. Listen when people explain," he reiterated. The man's abrupt anger made them all raise their hilts. Sigurd was even able to successfully call forth his flaming blade. Then, Mr. Getz exhaled, his frustration evident. "You should pay more attention when people speak, Mr. Briggs."

Annoyed by their lack of understanding, Getz flicked out his copy-flame. As the small flame sat poised on his thumb, he strutted around to give them all a better look. He touched it to the tip of Sigurd's burning blade. His flame changed colors, matching the golden sword's hue perfectly. He held the flame up to his cufflinks, which engulfed and transformed from silver metal into pure gold.

"You see now," boasted Getz as he turned back to face the room, "his flame is now my flame." Getz turned his back to Sigurd. Sigurd raised his sword above his head and thrust down, aiming for the man's shoulder. There was a sparking collision as the golden blade struck the air, floating above Getz. Purple flames held Sigurd's strike back, never connecting with his intended target.

Getz smiled maliciously, "A strike in the back? How unchivalrous, Mr. Lemont." With a swift motion, Getz flattened his palm, conjuring a flurry of gray flames. The flames propelled Sigurd backward against the wall with a torrent of wind. The impact sent Sigurd crashing to the ground behind Getz, moaning in pain.

"Sigurd!" cried out Kamara.

Realizing Mr. Getz had no peaceful intentions, Hickalik scanned for a solution. His eyes fell to the verdure dagger lying on the floor next to Greenwald. He hoped he could somehow use it to their advantage. He darted forward, lunging for the dagger. But before he could reach the forgotten weapon, a purple flaming hole materialized next to it, and a hand emerged, swiftly seizing the dagger and pulling it in. Hickalik stumbled to the ground where it had lain just moments before.

"Fair attempt, Milbred," Getz taunted, "but you will have to be quicker than that," he said, flaunting the dagger in his hand.

"That was the same flame as Greenwald," Myles accused.

Getz applauded, "Exactly right. Who do you think gave her the portal-flame? I knew she would need some help collecting children for me, so I gave her a blaze of her own."

Hickalik retreated toward Myles and Kamara, "You gave her a blaze?"

Getz raised his finger, "If a blaze can be taken away," his face softened with a hint of delight, "it can be given, as well. Grant a person power, and they will feel compelled with a sense of gratitude. Another effective method to claim ownership."

"And now sadly, I fear our time is almost up. I will be taking that dragon now," he stated, pointing the tip of the dagger towards Omni, who cowered behind Myles' legs.

Myles gripped his hilt firmly, "There is no way we will let that happen."

The man slowly raised his hands to eye level, a black flame ignited in his palm, darker than even the provost's. "Now...Ensnare."

The same eerie flames arose in a perfect circle around Hickalik, Myles, Kamara, and Omni. The flames flashed inward over their bodies. A crashing weight thrust them to the floor. They lay prone, ensnared by an unseen force, rendered immobile. Each breath became a struggle against the crushing weight.

Myles gritted his teeth, his voice strained, "What is this?"

"Do you like it?" Getz cackled. "This is my gravity-flame. It is a very useful attribute... one of my favorites to be sure."

But Getz was so enthralled with himself, he failed to notice Sigurd from behind, still sprawled on the floor. Sigurd held out his flaming blade and sliced toward the man's ankles.

In an instant, the dark oppressive flames extinguished, and Getz vanished in a dazzling display of bursting yellow flame. He reappeared in a distant corner of the room.

"You are a persistent nuisance," Getz sneered at Sigurd.

"That's right, he is," agreed Kamara, pushing her body off the floor, "but he's *our* nuisance."

Getz held out his hand again, as the black flame reignited in his palm. An idea sparked in Hickalik's mind. He lifted the blast-stone he still held from Greenwald and hurled the stone toward Getz.

"Hickalik, what are you doing?" questioned Sigurd nervously as the explosive object left his hand.

Getz quickly released the black flames and called forth his purple flamed portal. The stone travel straight through the portal's inky blackness and vanished. Outside, a faint explosion was heard in the distant night.

"Brazen move, Milbred." Getz seemed almost impressed.

"I figured it out," Hickalik blurted. "He can only use one flame at a time. That's why he released us from the black flames. He had to use a teleporting-flame away from Sigurd's blade."

Getz seemed more impressed than angered, "Smart boy. Very few have figured that part out, and none so young. You would have quite the bright future, if I allowed you to leave."

As Sigurd propped himself back up, wincing in pain, the other three spread out around the room.

Mr. Getz let out a demeaning laugh, "You could have twenty students here, it matters not. I have conquered soldiers and galliants alike. You haven't even gotten to your second-year combat training. By the end of the night, that dragon will belong to me, one way or another."

With a unified battle cry, the students surged forward. First to fall was Hickalik when a whipping of green flames entangled his legs. Sigurd leapt to the forefront, his golden blade raised high, but Getz swiftly countered with a lash of gray swirling flames, sending Sigurd crashing to the ground again, his hilt sliding across the room.

Omni lunged at the man's ankles, jaws open, only to be repelled with a swift kick. Myles held his hilt up high to strike. Mr. Getz countered, raising his palms to conjure a purple flaming barrier; however, Myles never activated any type of blade and swung his hilt straight down to the floor. Getz snickered, realizing he countered for no reason.

While he was distracted, Kamara retrieved her hilt once more and jumped back to position.

Sensing the tingling surge of energy in the air, Myles swiftly dove out of harm's way, "Do it," he yelled.

Before the explosive energy could be unleashed, Getz extended his hand, and in a flash of yellow flames, the golden anvil materialized above Sigurd. He rolled to the side, narrowly escaping being crushed as the anvil landed, shattering the floorboards.

Kamara unleashed her devastating bolt. But the blast's trajectory diverged from Getz and veered towards the anvil. Sigurd had a look of terror as he was nearly crushed, then barbecued, and could now hear nothing but his own drumming heartbeat.

Hickalik, still grounded, ignited his blue flames from his hilt, freezing the floor beneath in a desperate attempt to impede their crazed attacker. But Getz was quicker. He unleashed a downward torrent of scorching hot flames. The icy floor hissed and crackled as the intense heat melted the ice into a swirling mist, obscuring everyone's vision. Through the haze, Getz emerged above Myles, holding the verdure dagger downward between his clasped hands.

"Your dragon now belongs to me," he lifted the dagger and thrust downward with lethal intent. Myles braced for the inevitable. A choking thud struck his neck, then released. Myles felt only a warm drip of liquid on his cheek as a blood curdling screech echoed through the room. He opened his eyes to see Getz standing above him, the dagger embedded in the thicker region of Omni's tail. Myles touched his cheek with his fingers, finding them smeared with drops of crimson blood.

Getz gnashed his teeth, "You imprudent worm." He pulled out the dagger, making Omni squeal once more. Then Getz clutched his leg in pain and hobbled to the side.

Hickalik had frozen the man's leg. Getz seized the end of Omni's tail and hobbled away. Despite Omni's rebellious scratching at the floorboards, Getz dragged the squirming lizard with him.

"This isn't over!" the frustrated man yelled through the clearing fog. Kamara had made her way to Sigurd's side to check on his injuries. Getz waved his dagger-wielding hand in the air, conjuring a large purple rimmed portal. "I got what I came for," he snarled, stepping into the void, dragging the desperate dragon with him.

Myles forced himself to his feet and lunged forward, but Omni's head disappeared into the dark void. Myles collapsed with his hand outstretched, "Omni!" he cried.

The flaming portal was shrinking rapidly. As it reduced to the size of a pumpkin, out popped Omni, flying through the air like a cannonball, landing directly on Myles' face. Myles wrapped his arms around the balled-up lizard as the purple portal shriveled to nothing. Kamara assisted Sigurd over to the others, while Myles and Omni held their embrace.

"His tail," pointed Sigurd.

"It's okay," Myles said with a teary-eyed face. "It got stabbed when he saved me."

"No," emphasized Sigurd, "it's gone." Myles lifted his head. Omni's tail was completely detached, disconnected from the base.

Myles petted down Omni's spine to where Omni's tail used to be. "So that's how you got away. You poor thing... but you did it Omni, you made it back to me," Myles praised.

But their time to process their victory was short lived. The fiery circle re-emerged and the air thickened with purple desolation. The dooming glow sunk their hearts back to their depths, as Mr. Getz stepped back through the portal once more. The dagger was secured to his belt. He closed the portal and summoned a glowing orange flame to defrost his leg, while the other held forth a wiggling scaled white tail.

"That was a dirty trick my pet." He discarded the wagging tail to the side, and limped closer. "I see the only way for me to truly own that dragon, is to be rid of its Nexus partner."

Myles shouted back, "You will not have him, I told you, not ever."

He stopped, and grinned greedily, "Have you all forgotten already, I am Mr. Getz." His tone dropped, "And I get what I want."

The warming flames on his leg were released as he raised both his open hands igniting black flames once more.

"Get away," Myles directed to everyone, but there was not enough time. Getz propelled his hands downward. The crushing dark flames engulfed the students yet again, pushing them down onto the floorboards. The wood timber creaked and cried out as if the very building was in pain. They grimaced in agony under the pressure; their lungs were squeezed of oxygen. But Omni stood tall, chin out in defiance and growling amongst the darkened fire.

Getz reached out, "Come to me," he commanded. He reached into the dark flames to grab Omni's neck, but Omni bit the man on the wrist. He recoiled, then grabbed again, clutching the nape of the dragon's neck and lifting him out of the flames. Omni squirmed and wiggled as Getz held the dragon up at a safe distance, displaying the pale dragon as his prize.

Myles could barely catch a glimpse from the corner of his eye, his head immobilized. For the third time, he witnessed his companion being forcibly taken from him. A surge of righteous anger ignited within him.

"You... can't... have him," he forced out with grit. Getz's attention rolled downward to Myles, then he stepped back. Tiny flashes of white sparks sporadically danced across Myles body as he heaved. He pushed upward and roared with every ounce of strength he had. Bolts of energy were shooting across the dark flames.

The downward gravity squeezing them minimized. Kamara, Sigurd and Hickalik were able to inhale a life saving gasp of air. Myles resumed his relentless upward drive with a wailing cry. The white energy now sparked more vigorously. Myles was able to push his body just high enough to swing his foot out in a kneeled position.

He raised his chin to Getz, "You will not take Omni from us," he gnashed through his teeth, lifting what felt like the entire building on his back.

Getz took another step back, his confusion morphed into fear. Myles pried his way up through the oppressive flames.

Retreating further, Getz shouted angrily, "If you won't lay down to be crushed, then you will all burn."

He released the frantic dragon and ceased the dark flames as the foursome gasped for air, struggling to move as their bodies reacclimated. Getz pulled his hands close to his chest as a circle of spiraling flames whirled in front of him.

Myles could feel the terrible heat radiating from the growing inferno. He glanced back at his friends, but they were immobilized, barely conscious. Omni ran behind Myles, and hid between his legs. Myles searched for his hilt, but had lost it while they were being crushed.

Then, with a thrusting push, Getz threw his tornadoing flames toward them. There Myles knelt. He had nothing; no plan, nor power... no device, or ebenezer stone to help, but his hands seemed to move on their own. They stretched outward, reaching in front of him, as if to catch the flames before they could hurt his friends. Myles let out a courageous cry and shut his eyes, waiting to be engulfed.

His hands burned. The heat was so intense, but somehow familiar, like the day he enseared with Omni. He squinted his eyes open. A cascading dome of pure white flames surrounded the area around them. The burning onslaught from Getz was being diverted to either side. The bright flames emanated outward from Myles' outstretched hands.

Omni looked up from below Myles, the reptile seemed to almost smile, as if the dragon was proud to finally gift Myles what he was waiting so patiently for. Getz yelled out louder as he pushed into his assault, making his fiery torrent even more intense. But Myles held his ground, as the brilliant flames cascaded around them, protecting them all.

"No," yelled Getz as he ceased his flaming tornado.

The white flames stopped. Myles inspected his tingling hands with wonder. There were no burns, no injuries at all.

"How?" questioned Getz. "You had no flame. And with your hands, no less?"

"I don't know," Myles muttered. "I'm not sure if it was even me."

"I don't care," Getz shouted. "I will have that dragon!" He lifted his arms over his head and formed a swelling ball of dark flames between his hands. The light in the room darkened. The heavy timber bowed and cracked while being pulled inward.

"This is your doing, Briggs."

Getz arched his back to heave the dark burning sphere toward them. Omni scurried up Myles' back with his talons.

"Enjoy being crushed by a black hole," Getz bellowed victorious.

Then Omni clambered onto Myles' shoulder, his head back and wings fanned out. The pale dragon thrust his head forward releasing the same brilliant white flames that protected them. The flames coned out from his open jaw, encapsulating the dark fireball, melting it away.

Myles gawked in awe, "Omni... your flames." But the feeling of safety was a fleeting moment. As Myles looked to Getz, who was directly below Omni's fiery burst. He displayed a crooked grin on his face.

He snapped his fingers, igniting his copy-flame, "Now, I own your flame, little elden." He lifted his flame up to touch it to Omni's.

Myles shouted, "Omni stop," but it was too late. Getz was holding a small flickering flame of pure whitened light.

"It's too late, my boy. I have the power of an elden dragon now," he said in awe with himself.

He outstretched his fingers and flexed his palm. The singular flame deflagrated into a brilliant fireball in his hand. "I wonder what I can do with this?" he pondered, mesmerized by its beauty. He lifted the glowing ball up, to cast it towards Myles. The flames grew larger but then engulfed the man's arm.

"Ahhh, hot... it's hot," Getz shrieked. He flailed his arm around trying to put out the flames. He patted his arm with his other hand causing both hands to burn with pain, but no physical scorching could be seen.

Getz screamed out in pain, "It burns!" He collapsed to his knees and looked up. His eyes lit ablaze with white flames burning outward.

"It burns," he repeated. Then all at once, the white flames extinguished, leaving no trace of injury. His body swayed back and forth. He stared off into the distance, then spoke softly, "My greed... was my folly," before collapsing, face first on the floor.

Chapter Twenty-Eight

Trial by Flame

"Hickalik Milbred," the panel speaker's voice echoed around the room, "You are present today to be judged for conspiring in kidnapping, blaze unbranding, and concealment of a powerful artifact. You are being represented by Rhetta Prudencia, the current interim provost at the Feylux Academy. How do you plead?"

Hickalik sat in the middle of the courtroom with his hands facing down on the table. The back of his hands were lit with flickering flames. He leaned forward to speak into the amplification-stone in front of him, "Guil…" but Prudencia quickly snatched the stone away and held it to her lips, "Not guilty, your honors."

The courtroom buzzed with chatter. Myles, sitting with Sigurd and Kamara in the observation deck above, leaned over, "What are those eleven flames on top of the pillars for?" he asked.

Kamara whispered, "Each flame represents a parliament member. They all start as innocent, which is represented by the flame still burning, but if a flame goes out, then that judge believes him to be guilty."

"And if they find him guilty, then what? Does he go to jail?"

"Yeah," Sigurd added, "what does happen then?"

Kamara slapped her forehead, "This is not a criminal trial, Hickalik is too young. If he is found guilty, he will be expelled from the academy and forbidden to ever use his flames again."

Sigurd counted the flames, "But I thought there were twelve members of the parliament."

"Yes, but the chancellor does not partake in voting. Now, hush."

"Order," the panel speaker demanded into his stone. "Order."

Once the crowds quelled, he continued, "Mr. Milbred, were you, or were you not, in the employment of Pedagogue Greenwald throughout your time at the academy?"

Provost Prudencia placed the stone back on the holder in front of Hickalik, "Yes, but only because she was threatening..." but the speaker held his hand up, silencing Hickalik.

"A simple yes, or no, if you would please. And do remember, the truth-flames on your hands will know when you lie."

Hickalik's body shriveled, "Yes."

"During that time, were you aware she was colluding to abduct children to unbrand."

"I suspec..."

"A yes, or no, please."

Hickalik swallowed, "Yes." The gathered onlookers mumbled again. Three of the eleven flaming pillars instantly burnt out.

"Were you aware of Mr. Tiberius Getz's involvement with the disappearances?

Hickalik answered quickly, "No."

The man scowled, "What were you instructed to do for Pedagogue Greenwald?"

Confusion fell on Hickalik, "Yes?" he questioned.

The man sighed and rubbed his temple, "You can answer the question fully; the yes and no does not apply to this type of question."

Kamara couldn't help but smirk at Hickalik's awkwardness.

"Sorry," Hickalik apologized. "I was told to find the son of Haldor Bridger."

"And did you? Did you find him?"

"Yes," answered Hickalik. The room buzzed again with a range of babbling rumors.

"Order, order," the speaker demanded. Then his attention homed back to Hickalik.

"Did you tell Greenwald you found the son of Bridger?"

"No."

The man leaned back in his chair and pondered for a moment before slinging another question, "Why did Greenwald want to find the son of Haldor Bridger?"

"She wanted the verdure dagger. She thought Haldor's son could have it... or at least know where it was."

"And did he have the dagger, or know its whereabouts?"

"No."

"Then how was the dagger found?"

Hickalik glanced his eyes up towards Myles, but Prudencia stepped between their gaze, catching Hickalik's eyes. She gave him a trusting nod.

"We found the dagger after following clues left behind by Haldor for his son."

"Then, pray tell, how did Greenwald obtain the dagger?"

Hickalik dropped his head, "I gave it to her... after we found it."

"So, you admit you knew of her involvement with the kidnappings, you befriended the son of Haldor, helped him find the dagger, then took this powerful artifact and gave it to her?"

Defeated, Hickalik slumped over. "Yes, sir."

Just then, three more flames disappeared from the eleven pillars.

"There are only five flames left," commented Myles worryingly.

"If it doesn't change soon, he will be found guilty," Kamara explained. "He needs six flames so there will be no majority against him."

Prudencia approached the floor below the panel, addressing them all, "Speaker, you ask about all the 'what's' but seemed to be leaving out the very important 'why's.' Mr. Milbred, what did Pedagogue Greenwald tell you would happen if you didn't assist her?"

Hickalik raised his head, "She would evict me and my grandparents from our home and the farm."

"Do you think your grandparents would survive finding new employment or skills to work?"

"No, Provost. Not at their age," he answered.

"Objection," called out a panel member, "she is leading the witness and bringing emotional irrelevance to the trial."

"Overruled," a booming voice rang out from above.

Sigurd looked up, "Who's that?"

Myles recognized the elderly man, "It's Chancellor Dragoon."

"But I thought he wasn't a part of the trial," stated Sigurd.

"He doesn't vote," informed Kamara, "but he does oversee the proceedings."

"Thank you, Chancellor," Prudencia gave a slight bow. "Mr. Milbred, at the time of your agreement with Pedagogue Greenwald, did you know of her involvement with the abductions?"

"No," Hickalik answered with a bit more hope in his voice.

"So, to your recollection, when you agreed to help her, she was a respected institutionalized professional, whom you were willing to help to save your grandparents and their farm? At the beginning there was no knowledge of wrongdoing or ill intent. Seems quite a logical choice for any person."

"Correct," Hickalik agreed.

"And as you gathered information for Pedagogue Greenwald and befriended Haldor's son, did you continue to help her, or did you withhold information?"

"I withheld who he was from her," but the flames on his hands burned red as he gasped, "I mean, yes, I did tell her the names of a few people I thought it could be. But after that I told her I didn't know." The flames died down back to their original orange glow.

Prudencia waved her hand through the now docile orange flames. "That's quite the conscience you have there," she smiled. "And did you do anything to fight back once you realized Greenwald's intentions were not noble?"

"Yes," Hickalik explained, "I seared the name off of Myles' headboard so she would not discover him."

Shock fell on Myles, "That was Hickalik?"

"I also told Pedagogue Greenwald I thought it could be Bach Lobtail to try and throw her off the scent," said Hickalik.

Kamara whispered, "That's probably why Bach was yelling in the halls at the beginning of school. It wasn't the pufkins at all, it was Greenwald."

Hickalik continued, "And when she stole Haldor's compass, I smashed all the stones on the ebenezer textbooks so she couldn't see inside the room anymore."

Sigurd recalled the incident, "I totally forgot about that."

"But in the end, you did give Greenwald the dagger. Why, Mr. Milbred?"

Hickalik extended his neck toward the stone, "To save my grandparents and to protect my friends from her."

Prudencia spun to face the panel, "If you were being robbed while someone else's life hung in the balance, would you not give the money freely to save that hostage? Mr. Milbred intelligently weighed the value of life and safety versus an old relic."

"And let us not forget, these events were put into motion by this very parliament. If it were not for oversight of Mr. Getz's employment, and lack of supervision, these events would have never transpired, and poor Mr. Milbred would have never been put in this predicament."

"Voting guilty for Mr. Milbred is voting yourselves guilty for your own negligence."

The five flames burned alone. Seven empty pillars remained dark.

"It is time to declare the verdict," the chancellor's voice announced. Hickalik dropped his head in terror. Myles was too distraught to watch, his hands covering his face to cope with the stress.

"The verdict... is not guilty."

Myles and Hickalik both sprang up, six flames danced on top of the pillars. Sigurd jumped out of his seat with excitement, almost falling over the banister, as the three friends cheered for Hickalik.

Back at the academy Myles, Kamara, and Sigurd were summoned to the provost's office where they found the provost accompanied by their friend.

"Hickalik!" Myles raced over and hugged him. But Hickalik was hesitant, shocked at the outburst of affection. Sigurd squeezed the poor boy next, then Kamara followed up with a punch to the shoulder, "Welcome back, champ."

Prudencia gestured for them to sit adjacent to her and Hickalik. "We have some items to discuss, I believe. After all, you four haven't seen each other since that night in the forge... the second one, that is."

Hickalik's manner appeared as meek as ever, "I'm sorry," he apologized, keeping his gaze low. "I should have told you. I know I can't ever make up for what I did, but I hope you all can forgive me, and it's okay if you don't, I don't deserve your forgiveness. I just..." but Kamara stood up midsentence.

She walked over and slapped him on the back of the head, "Just tell us next time you goof."

Prudencia didn't seem shocked by this. "I can't say I condone the action, but I do agree with the sentiment."

"Seriously, Hickalik," Myles confronted. "You are our friend, of course we forgive you. You were forgiven the moment you took the dagger."

"Literally," laughed Sigurd. "You should have heard him, he was all 'we must save Hickalik' like the minute you left."

But Hickalik argued back, "But I betrayed you, I lied to you all."

"Did you though?" Kamara questioned. "It's not like we asked you, 'hey, are you being blackmailed into spying on one of us?'"

Myles met Hickalik's eyes, "You were forced to do it, and you even fought back for us. You did better than any of us could have done in that situation." Kamara nudged Myles, "...perhaps save for maybe Kamara."

Kamara flicked her hair back proudly, "Thank you."

Sigurd addressed the provost, "So what will happen to all of them now? Like Greenwald and Getz, I mean?"

Provost Prudencia sighed, "They have both been found guilty by both the courts of the kingdom and parliament and have been incarcerated. Mr. Getz is still in a mentally unstable state since the altercation. The kingdom courts have repossessed all of Greenwald's assets.

Hickalik got excited to share, "Oh, our farm was entitled to my grandparents after it was repossessed."

"That's great Hick," Myles exclaimed.

The provost continued, "Greenwald has taught at this academy for many years, and was a trusted staff member. I believe Mr. Getz targeted her because of her status. Mr. Getz's greed wanted access to the best crop of blazed children he could find. Once he found Greenwald's history, he found information he knew would entice her employment."

But Kamara was pondering, "What about Pedagogue Muddle?"

"A bit of good news in that regard," Prudencia announced, "He had no recollection of his deeds and use of his flame in the disappearances. Greenwald's testimony helped collaborate his story, thankfully, and he was found not guilty in both courts. Hopefully he can now get the rest he deserves."

"And the dagger?" Hickalik questioned.

"The dagger is to be kept in the vaults of the parliament for security and study. Not much is known about its flames and origins yet, but with time, more uses may be developed from its discovery. When it was in the farmlands, it was just a fabled talisman that was thought to bring good luck to the crops and harvests, but now we know, it was much more. And in the wrong hands, it could be very dangerous."

Myles petted Omni, who was curled up in his lap, as a question arose in his mind. "Provost, what is Omni's flame? One minute he is glowing, then I think I used his power to overcome Mr. Getz's flames. And he let out this brilliant fire that caused Mr. Getz to burn and go insane."

The provost bent over and petted the lollygagging lizard's head, "Time will tell. Not all flames are what they first appear to be. Watch over him and he will share it with you in time."

"Oh, that reminds me," Prudencia walked over to her desk. She grabbed a stack of envelopes and handed them to Myles, "These are for you."

Myles scanned the pile, "These are all from Allen."

"Yes," she confirmed, "they were found in Greenwald's office. She must have been intercepting them in the hope that Allen would divulge something about the dagger or your father in the letters. Unfortunately, the envelopes are all we could recover." Prudencia pinched some dust in a dish on her desk, "Looks like she burned the letters after reading them. I am sorry we do not have more for you."

As the school year came to an end at the academy, the first-years were summoned to the great hall for one last assembly. Provost Prudencia addressed the student body with a pleased undertone.

"Well done all of you for enduring a rather difficult... and different year. Although we will not be together during the summer months, focus on your studies and continue to hone your skills with your flames. Next year you will be judged according to your individual performances. You may even be selected by a sponsoring fold. But remember, under no circumstance are you to use your flames against another person or for your own nefarious reasons. You do have your flame, but you do not have your provisional licenses as of yet."

The children packed their belongings and waited out by the front gates for their guardians to collect them. Omni found a pinecone to entertain himself while they waited.

Sigurd waved to his parents in the distance, approaching through the gate. "Well, I'm off. I will see you all next year," he said, shaking their hands. Kamara begrudgingly accepted.

Kamara was next to leave. "Thank you for making this a worthwhile endeavor you two," she said with a smirk to Myles and Hickalik while backing away.

Then Hickalik turned to Myles, "Who is coming to pick you up?"

Myles looked out of the gathered people traveling in and out of the gate, "I'm hoping Allen comes to bring me back to the orphanage."

"You should come stay with me and my grandparents at the farm," Hickalik invited.

"Really? You'd do that? And they wouldn't mind me staying there?"

"Absolutely not, I mean, you would have to help out around the farm probably..."

"That wouldn't be a problem at all. To be honest, it would be nice to have a simple and normal couple of months after what we all went through," Myles said as they both laughed. "And we could help train each other."

Just then a shout came from behind them, "Look out!"

A ginormous rolling ball of swirling black and blue flames cascaded down the hill behind them. The flames fanned out around them as a large glistening form propelled outward tackling Myles to the ground. He was pinned down by large claws.

Looking up, Myles saw Beira, head lowered and baring her teeth threateningly to the others around them. She growled at the onlookers.

"Beira," Myles said in shock, with the wind knocked out of him. But she did not reply. She spun around, keeping Myles pinned. As the last of the flames burnt off, there stood Zalaph, wings fanned out, snarling back at the ice drake. Omni leapt toward Beira and bit her ankle to defend Myles. Beira's eyes shifted down as she flicked the pesky lizard aside, like she was flicking an ant.

Zalaph puffed out his chest and walked forward, raising his wings. Beira opened her mouth as blue flames escaped her jaws, ready to blast.

"Wait!" a man's voice rang out, "Wait. Stop!"

Everyone's attention turned to a man navigating the slope's terrain from where the dragons came, desperately waving his arms at the dragons.

"Wait, Zalaph! Stop Beira!" the man yelled. It was Allen, trying desperately to catch up. Finally reaching the area between the two dragons, he held out his hands in protest. "Just wait…" he slumped over catching his breath. Resting his hands on his knees, he tilted his head in Beira's direction. "I knew bringing you was a bad idea," he huffed for breath.

"Mr. Allen?" questioned Myles looking up from the ground.

"Hey Myles," he breathed, "good to see you again."

Hickalik's mouth fell wide open, "You're Algernon Binford?"

Allen held up his hand, "Just Allen, thank you."

Then a shrill voice called out, "Algernon Binford."

Allen straightened up and looked up at the sky with an exacerbated exhaust, "Ahh, yes. Prudencia the prude." He then looked to the enraged approaching provost. She clutched her hand into a fist and pulled. Allen's shadow lit a black blaze and was pulled out from under him, pulling his feet with it and slapping his back onto the ground.

Beira snarled in his defense, but Allen rolled over with a groan and raised his hand to the defensive drake, "It's okay girl, I probably deserve that."

"You deserve far more than that," the provost stood above him with her staff on his collar, "Why would you bring your dragon here?"

Allen stood back to his feet, "She was going to come either way, you know how she gets when her mind is made up. But after she caught a whiff of Zalaph… well, just like old times." Allen snickered.

The provost repressed her disapproval, "I assume you are here for Myles?"

"Yes." He turned to Beira, "It's okay girl, Myles is safe."

Beira slowly released Myles, and Allen helped him to his feet. "I think she thought you were in trouble," he explained.

Omni raced to Myles, "Mr. Allen, this is Omni, my dragon." Myles presented.

Allen bent down, "Hello there, Omni. I have heard a lot about you already. He's a bit smaller than I was imagining," Allen stated. Beira reached her snout closer and sniffed, then apathetically snorted, unimpressed by the sickly pale dragon. But Allen and Beira were interrupted by a low growl from Zalaph.

"I think it best you and Myles head out now, Allen," stated the provost.

"Perhaps you're right." After getting Myles' belongings loaded on Beira, they both climbed onto their scaly ride, and began trotting towards the gates with Omni sniffing the ground in tow.

Myles turned and waved, "Bye Hickalik, I will see you soon," he called back. Hickalik waved farewell to his friend with a smiling face.

"Allen," Myles questioned, "I thought Beira was not allowed in the city."

"Don't worry. We'll be gone in a jiffy."

"Did you find my parents?" asked Myles.

Allen sighed, "We have a lot to talk about, kid."

~THE BEGINNING~

Glossary

- **Attribute** – One's attribute tends to reflect the heart. It is the elemental group a flame ability belongs to. For example, an ice flame is a water attribute.

- **Banana Slugs** – Long snail-like mollusk with no shell and slimy yellow-green colored bodies. Banana slugs can be found in both the inner and outer worlds in dense forest areas.

- **Blaze** – A special marking blessed upon few individuals that allows them to bond with a dragon egg. Also known as a burn marking.

- **Bulrog** – A large toad-like creature that can camouflage itself in nearly any environment. Its stomach acids can dissolve most anything within minutes.

- **Caldera (Kal-dare-uh)** – A vast crater where dragons of all types nest once a year and leave their eggs for years at a time.

- **Chancellor** – The lead chair of the Parliament of Dragons who is elected by parliament vote. The chancellor acts as the liaison to the King on the behalf of the parliament.

- **Chief Officer** – The highest ranking official of the local law enforcement.

- **Chiliagon (kil-ee-uh-gon)** – A one thousand-sided wall that surrounds the city of Calderian.

- **Chimera (Ki-meer-uh)** – A mythical creature of the outer world that is very real in Escalia. A beast with the head of a saber tooth tiger, the body of a spotted lion and a viper snake for a tail. Most often found with a calming companion of another species.

- **Dirigible (Dir-i-juh-bul)** – An airship with a giant balloon-like structure elevating it to travel throughout the skies. One of the fastest modes of transportation in Escalia, with the exception of using a portal.

- **Ebenezer (Eh-buh-nee-zer) Stone** – A crystalized stone used to store a person's flame ability for later use or sale.

- **Egg Harvest** – The event when students from the Feylux Academy are permitted by the parliament to enter the Caldera to search for a dragon egg to ensear with.

- **Ensear (En-seer)** – When a blazed person makes a connection with a dragon egg, linking the two beings in a Nexus.

- **Escalia (Es-kay-lee-uh)** – The inner world located on the inner side of the earth crust.

- **Feylux (Fay-luks) Academy** – A special academy for the blessed and blazed where students come to find their nexus partners and learn to control their newfound flame abilities.

- **Fold** – A group sanctioned by the parliament with the authority to use their flames to provide protection over the land and accept pleas posted by the people of the land.

- **Gaffer** – The highest position within a Fold. The leader of a Fold who reports to the parliament.

- **Galliant (Gal-ee-ant)** – A member of a Fold who has completed their probationary time and is now able to accept pleas on their own without supervision.

- **Gatekeeper** – Ancient creatures that guard the gateways between worlds. Usually considered to be mythical by those in the outer-world.

- **Gateway** – A passageway between the outer-world and Escalia. Usually found where the topography of both sides is low, making the two worlds touch as a singular point.

- **Guzzle** – A plated wolf creature that preys on the nests of larger animals and can disguise itself as a large egg when it curls into a ball.

- **Hilt** – A handle that is imbued with a dragon's flame by placing a part of a dragon hatchling into the smelted materials.

- **Nexus** – The connection shared between a dragon and a blazed person after they have enseared.

- **Noghogs** – A creature reminiscent of a wild boar with bull-like horns matching its long tusks.

- **Parliament** – A council of twelve that rules over all Ruach related affairs.

- **Pedagogue (Ped-uh-gog)** – Teachers at the academy and gurus of their trades. Many are retried galliants.

- **Pixie** – A little old lady who has dedicated her life to legal documentation and clerical work, usually has a smell of dust around her.

- **Provost** – The head of the Feylux Academy who is appointed by the parliament.

- **Pufkin** – A fish-frog like creature that secretes a toxic slime, known to cause hallucinations.

- **Ruach (Roo-akh)** – An energy that flows through all things and connects all creatures and creation.

- **Snuffle** – A large slug (much bigger than banana slugs) that burrow underground and spray pheromones to attract other snuffles and ward off predators.

- **Unicorn** – A black horse-like creature with large, feathered wings and a single jagged horn. Known for their aggressive behavior and ability to snort flames from their nostrils.

- **Verdure (Ver-joor)** – Meaning plant or life giving.

- **Warden** – An academy pedagogue who is charged with watching over a specific year of students.

- **Wibbly Ball** – A loved game made up by the first Fold that is now played competitively throughout Escalia.

- **Wubbalub (Wub-ba-lub)** – A creature from children's stories who can use Ruach flames and guard the dragon eggs of the Caldera.

Join the movement. Visit our website at www.ensearedbooks.com. Make sure to follow us on our social media platforms for the most up-to-date information.

Love what we are doing? Leave a review on Amazon to help support our mission to reach more young readers with encouraging stories.